D0805472

a good family

a good family

peter j. smith

doubleday

new york • london • toronto

sydney • auckland

PUBLISHED BY DOUBLEDAY
a division of Bantam Doubleday Dell Publishing Group, Inc.
1540 Broadway, New York, New York 10036

DOUBLEDAY and the portrayal of an anchor with a dolphin
are trademarks of Doubleday, a division of
Bantam Doubleday Dell Publishing Group, Inc.

Book design by Maria Carella

This novel is a work of fiction. Names, characters, places, and
incidents are either the product of the author's imagination or are
used fictitiously. Any resemblance to actual persons, living or dead,
events, or locales is entirely coincidental.

Library of Congress Cataloging-in-Publication Data
Smith, Peter J., 1959–
A good family / Peter J. Smith.
p.　　cm.
1. Family—New England—Fiction.　I. Title.
PS3569.M537912G66　　　1996
813'.54—dc20　　　　96-13997
CIP

ISBN 0-385-47787-2

Copyright © 1996 by Peter J. Smith

All Rights Reserved

Printed in the United States of America

September 1996

First Edition

1　3　5　7　9　10　8　6　4　2

acknowledgments

The author wishes to thank the following for their sustaining guidance and patience during the writing of this book: Deborah Futter, Anne Freedgood, Amanda Urban, William Zinsser, Alice Quinn, Jennie Guilfoyle, Charlie Conrad and, for their extraordinary generosity, Maggie, Sam, Lily and Susannah.

a good family

$$1.$$

there are five of us children, four boys and a girl, and—with the possible exception of my sister, Sarah—we've chosen to align ourselves, in spirit and other places where it counts, with our father's side of the family: his ancestry, East Coast origins and, certainly, with the idea of his money. Knowleses, in one form or another, have been around New England forever, our father often implied. We have their good looks—square chin, arrowhead nose, and heart-shaped mouth—and woody bits and patches of their original land, as well as their various susceptibilities: heart disease, alcoholism and drowning. (Our Knowles ancestors, for all their love of sailing and water, were crude, confused sailors; you can't sail a boat all that well when you're stoned.) One time my younger brother Sam went rolling in the pasty leaves of an early fall, staggering back inside the house, his hair disheveled, his arms suspended limply in front of him, pretending he'd risen up, mummylike, from underground. "I'm a descendant of da Knowles," he intoned. "Will somebody pliz fix me a Bloody Mary wid a slivah of lime in it?"

Everybody in the room laughed, I remember, except for our father. Hunched over a mess of books and papers, he glanced up sharply. "Be glad you come from something," he commented. "Most people have to make it up as they go along."

One of our myths was that we—the Knowleses—didn't have to make anything up, that we stood for something lasting, something stubborn and exemplary, though what that thing was, was never made entirely clear. I know for a fact we're not alone in this—a lot of families have a sense of rogue uniqueness; it may be necessary to live, to want to go on—and perhaps it derives from the idea that people's lives, and the way they're conducted, can make much of a difference to anybody.

For the past few years, since my father's death, my brothers and sister and I have contributed to the upkeep of the house off the southeastern coast of New England where we spent our summers growing up. We've paid out property taxes; replaced a portion of roof; paid for a set of floodlights to be installed in the trees following a night of vandalism during which two clay pots were shattered; and ultimately ended up hiring a strong-shouldered local man, a moonlighting fisherman and, in my wife Caroline's opinion, a walking time bomb, to scrub down the windows and vacuum the floors every month. Last summer, though, my older brother Jay began a campaign to convince me that this arrangement was pointless. None of us visits the house anymore—most of us live too far away, and as for those who don't, well, the excuses are weak and various: not enough time, too many ghosts, too cold, too gloomy—and my mother, who lived there alone for a time after our father died, now makes her home in Florida with her second husband.

Once, last year, when I was visiting the house, I was mowing the front lawn when one of the tractor wheels became lodged behind a pine stump concealed in the declivity that runs between our father's old vegetable garden and the gnarled border of the marsh. To my surprise, I found myself on the verge of tears, filled with rage and frustration and what I realized only later on was grief. It was late afternoon, the bay was rough with whitecaps; and as I stood there on the lawn, with the abdominal groaning of the buoys rising up over the soft slapping of the tide, and the bridge to the mainland disappearing under a cover of fog, something inside me seemed to unloosen and fall away. Later that afternoon, I called up my brother. "Fine," I said.

"Fine what?"

"Fine," I said. "Just sell it."

Two or three weeks later, after very little discussion, we put the house on the market. And for a long time after we divided up and carted away the furniture, there were no offers on the house; then, several months ago, the broker called our family lawyer to report that she'd been approached by a buyer. Sarah, my older sister, who despite her reluctance in recent years to have much to do with the rest of us, had decided she wanted to keep the house "in the family," and who frankly was the only one among us who could afford to buy it.

Did I have reservations about selling the house? Yes, but the plain fact of the matter was that we needed the money. Jay flew in from Boston, and he and I met with our lawyer in New York, and we signed the purchase and sale agreement. No money changed hands: it was a cash deal, involving the liquidation of some twenty thousand shares of a Southwestern utility company, with no conditions attached other than a house inspection, not even a paint job or the repair of the back porch, torn through, accidentally, by Sam one day on the tractor ten years ago and never repaired.

"Well, Jam, at least we know the place is in good hands," Jay remarked as we were leaving the lawyer's office, and when I didn't answer, his eyes narrowed slightly. "You know?"

My given name is John. I'm known, though, mostly by the members of my family and by my friends, as Jam. It's a name whose every variation—Jam, Jambo, Jammer—I find wearisome and cloying, and like most people who are saddled early in their lives with nicknames, I often wish that mine, with its robust, middling, good-guy associations, had never stuck. Though Caroline used to tell me that if I have to have a nickname, then Jam is better than, say, Porky or Mr. Personality, the latter uttered with great derision by some witty, impatient woman.

The origins of the name aren't certain, and they're probably not all that riveting, either. Sarah says the name derives from a filthy pair of red pajamas that I insisted on wearing night after night as a kid. Sam insists that I was always getting into trouble of some kind—jams, ha ha—though frankly I don't remember myself as being much of a rabble-rouser. My mother claims it has to do with my young love of the beach plums and blackberries that looped in broken tangles along the fences lining our road and that she occasionally pulverized into strange-tasting spreads; and my father, who never called me anything other than my given name, had no opinion. It doesn't matter. I bring it up only to suggest that those people who know me as John, or Mr. Knowles, are like those guests who come to the front entrance of your house, not knowing that the side door off the kitchen, the one with the leaf-trampled pathway and the screen door slightly off-kilter, is the one used by family and friends.

Only a few weeks following the sale, Sarah underwent an—to me— unbelievable about-face. She engaged a second broker, an aggressive red-headed woman, new to the island, who not only managed to resell my sister's house in the space of a month, but at a substantial profit. The new owners, a software king and his French-born wife, had read about the island during a recent, highly publicized presidential visit and were anxious to see the same, say, rosebushes that more illustrious eyes had passed over. That Sarah had decided against keeping the house made me furious, but there was nothing I could do. I heard about this whole thing, in fact, thirdhand: from my mother, who'd heard it from Jay, who in turn had been awoken late one night by a phone call from Sam. In our family, at least, this has long been the way interesting news transforms itself, bob-bingly, from gossip to hearsay to rumor to fact.

· · ·

*I*t was during the fourth week of November that I decided, on the spur of the moment, to drive east and board the ferry for the hour-and-a-half-long crossing to St. James Island. I wanted to see the house one last time before the new owners moved in, or at least this was how I phrased things to myself. It was a couple of days before Thanksgiving and, as all the local newspapers and television stations were beginning to point out, only twenty-eight more shopping days before Christmas. I hadn't given that much thought as to where I'd spend the holidays, though a couple of invitations had come in from the well-meaning wives of teaching colleagues, and I had a standing invitation, as ever, to visit my mother and stepfather down South.

But I hadn't decided what I'd do. It was hardly the time of year for traveling. The roads were dark by four o'clock in the afternoon, and the air was cold and dry and practically odorless. That's one of the stranger things about the Midwest: there are no smells. Walking along the sidewalks and bike paths of town, dodging the remains of smashed pumpkins and the chalk declarations of teenage desire and resentment ("I love Lois"; "Kill the Cops"), I sometimes had the feeling that I was being followed. Yet when I'd whirl around, all I ever saw were leaves. Orange, yellow, cranberry red. Whole and in pieces. Crisp and flat, or soaked, pinned under panels of frozen water. Skipping and skittering, they'd sounded to me like footsteps, as though someone exceptionally agile were following me.

But since I've never liked being the odd man at anybody's table, it seemed to me that the best way of getting around the Thanksgiving dilemma was to be in transit; no one could take pity on me that way. Yet by the time I'd nosed my car onto the lower deck of the ferry, and proceeded up a set of worn white stairs to the third-floor balcony, my equanimity had darkened, somewhat confusingly, into an inexplicable moodiness.

It had to do with the snow, I think. The first flakes began without any fanfare, as though an old library throw rug had been emptied of a season-long accumulation of dust. As the ferry cruised past the adjoining peninsula that forms an elbow to the harbor, the flakes were sped along by the wind, and by the time we were halfway across the ocean, my shirt collar was soaked, my face raw and stinging. As we'd pulled away from the mainland, I'd had company on the balcony—a few stragglers in sweaters and brightly citric slickers pressed against the railing, and a group of kids around my son Ike's age, gesturing and yelling and kidding around; but looking around me now, I saw that I was by myself, that everybody else had gone downstairs in search of cover.

The weather report on my car radio, I remembered, kept talking about a "lake effect." This is meteorological jargon having something to do with northern winds picking up moisture from over the Atlantic Ocean, and changing whatever precipitation there is in the air from rain to snow, but there was only a slight chance that this would come to pass, and rain, rather than snow, was anticipated for the islands. (I tend not to take weathermen seriously, given the fact that they all get their information from the same home office. Barometric pressure? Dew point? Jet stream? What's a jet stream? Plus, they've all been wrong so often in the past that I didn't give the forecast much thought.) So I was surprised when an hour later the snow was still coming down, and more surprised that the flakes appeared to be sticking.

Despite the fact that a commuter airline service connects the mainland to St. James, I prefer the ferry, and not only because I have a paralyzing fear of flying, particularly on those planes where the pilot demands to know how much you weigh before you board and, based on your answer, determines on which side you'll sit. ("Why not just invest in a pair of wax wings?" I said to Caroline once. "The outcome'll be the same.") I enjoy the ferry for other reasons, not the least of which is that when I'm on the water my life seems to possess a coherence that it lacks when I'm onshore. I was standing alone on the upper platform, benign as an astronaut, getting snowed on, and when I caught a glimpse of myself in the reflection of a window, I looked (I thought) sober and capable and even imposing, the kind of man who could scheme the overthrow of a country, or lead the third-graders out of the burning school bus, though the dull truth of the matter is that I was merely squinting to keep the flakes out of my eyes.

I take a kid's delight in snow. Though I'm nearly forty years old, it still has the power to evoke sleds and the crumpled tinfoil of coasters, steep hills, the prospect of no school, Christmas morning, presents under the tree, *yaahh!*—but by then the flakes were coming down so thickly that I ended up seeking refuge on the second floor, inside the snack bar. The scene there resembled a diner in a hard-luck rural town—cigarette smoke gathering under the ceiling like an eerie tide, old men slumped over in booths designed to seat whole families, mothers with shadowy-looking children—and this sad-sack atmosphere had a worsening effect on my mood. It occurred to me, an hour or so later, as the ferry began its gradual movement into St. James harbor, past slender, pipelike stretches of sand where a few cottages sat in line, shuttered for the winter, that my destination was not the island where I'd spent my summers at all, but a condition of disappointment and disillusion.

As I started down the stairs toward the landing where my car was parked, I felt, for the first time that afternoon, embarrassed, even furtive. Taking a trip such as this alone, and in communion with a memory as faulty, jangling and reproachful as mine, seemed wrong, a bad idea. If I'd had a hat and dark glasses with me, I would have put them on, skulked ashore, or else thrown a paper bag over my head; and it was then that I considered not exactly turning back—I couldn't; my car was positioned in a solid row of others, and I wasn't about to leap over the railing and swim back to the mainland—but staying on the ferry until it was time to turn around and go home.

A few fishing boats came into view, huddling coldly offshore; the flurrying, razored hum of the engine grew soft; the boat commenced its slow backing-up into its berth, and I realized that, for better or for worse, I was home.

*b*y that point the flakes were coming down in wavy, erratic sheets, and the temperature had plummeted to twenty-six degrees. Snow carpeted the tidy little army of blue mailboxes in front of the post office, as well as the canopies of the few commercial stores clustered around the terminal. People were waiting around to board the ferry for its return trip—the line snaked twice around the square—and it was only when I spied a couple of taxis that I began to suspect that the airport had been shut down.

There was a feeling of exhilaration in the air. A young couple staggered around the parking lot with their mouths open to catch the falling flakes; a group of teenaged boys clawed at the snow packing the hood of a parked car, and though the flakes weren't the right consistency for snowballs, they flung what there was at one another. My first impression, though, as I drove through the square, was that people were overreacting. In the Midwest, we tear off our shirts with the abandon of nudists whenever the temperature snakes up into the mid-twenties, and there's a patch of mud visible on the front lawn, or a flower shows its stem under the ice. It's brave, and hopeful, in a way, this easing of restraint—it's still twenty degrees out; it's just not minus thirty anymore—but given what I knew about the weather patterns on the island, I predicted it would snow for maybe an hour, an hour and a half longer before it all turned to rain.

On an impulse—a good one, it turns out—I detoured into the parking lot of the local Key Food, parked and made a dash for the entrance. Inside, it was pandemonium, and I could barely maneuver my basket down the aisles. People here prepare for disasters as they might for wartime, and already whole sections of the store had been cleaned out; there was a panicked absence of milk and bread, but I loaded up on cold cuts and cheese and peanut butter and crackers, as well as a couple of six-packs of beer, before climbing back inside the car and getting on with my journey.

There was practically no traffic. The visibility on the road was poor, and the snow was falling so densely by then that I felt I was navigating by memory. Like a fine, blond, ghostly sand, the snow spun and twisted beneath my headlights, and the few cars and pickup trucks on either side of me were steaming like tea kettles on a burner. Making my way past the public high school and the fire department, I turned onto Route 7, which winds along Crane's Bay. Before long, the telephone poles and the houses grew farther apart, and only the broad chimneys and the widow's walks, blunt rectangles resembling fighting rings, were visible through the snow.

Yet in the sight of the water and the marsh stretched out now in front of me lay a richness that I'd always imagined and envied Southerners having, a sense of being possessed by a place; as a child, I saw none of this and might have told you, if you'd asked me, that I'd been raised in rooms devoid of light, color, scenery and distinction. But the Eastern coast was where I'd grown up, and its salty, ragged heart pulsed inside me. I'd swum off a strip of sand beyond a narrowing, honeysuckle-scented beach path; I'd sailed, rowed, drifted on my back in the warm water with my brothers and sister; we'd dunked one another under and then, springing back up, water swelling our cheeks, ejected it in fountainous spurts, the way we imagined dolphins did. In the summer, all five of us had escaped our parents' parties and come down into the marsh, jazz horns serenading us from the house, a slick, dazzling coast of white light radiating from the windows of the gazebo, where my mother had hung strings of pale Christmas bulbs, and we'd gotten drunk on wine we'd stolen from our father's cellar, and laid low inside the dinghy, and gotten splinters in our hands and on the bottoms of our feet.

It's a truth generally accepted that people prefer the first water they know, and I'm no exception. I was brought up to stand in awe of the Atlantic Coast, with its fierce, uprooting power, and, in some indirect fashion, to emulate its lack of ostentation. My father raised us to thrive on simplicity and even discomfort. By my mid-teens, I was able to glean a modest moral superiority from cold showers, thin towels, scarcely heated rooms and painful soles, the latter the result of pecking my way along the sharp-sided stones and crushed seashells of New England driveways. I was prejudiced against other waters. The air coming in off the Pacific, for example, was mild, irresistibly scented; it was hard to believe it could ever tip a boat, or pull a person down, or break the back of a house. In the West there was scarcely any smell of salt, of fish, or industry, only a sense of stretch, and entrepreneurial possibility. Walking along the beaches of

Southern California, or South Padre Island, I was still able to dream of the infinite variety of people that it wasn't too late for me to impersonate.

But six months later, I spent the better half of a morning strolling along the far-western bight of St. James, where I was reminded not of the assortment of people I could still turn into, but of the wordless, unfamiliar one that Caroline told me I'd become. The wind was violent, almost clubbing, the blown salt smelling of rot and starfish and the outboard gas of passing boats. The waves unraveled onto the sand with such recriminatory force that they seemed to have been bowled ashore by giants, and despite my best efforts to maintain an even course, I kept tripping over cast-off, washed-in, sun-dried things—dead rays, bits of buoy, mainsail rope, stays, wood, stones, crab claws and lobster pots that the tides had torn in two. No colors stood out; the satisfaction of the Atlantic Ocean has always seemed to me to lie precisely in its lack of fanfare. The water was not a backdrop to a photograph, a come-hither invitation on a postcard, a view from a bay window or the latter-day reward to a successful career in business. It was not a guest but an indifferent host, and in its insatiable neutrality, I was reminded not of the future, but of my own unclear place in the past.

The terms of occupancy allowed the new owners to take residence of the house at the beginning of the new year, which is another way of saying that I was confident there would be no one in the house. If there had been, I had an excuse ready, one that happened to be the truth—that a seizure of nostalgia had brought me to the island, and I wouldn't be staying. A rickety, red-lettered SOLD sign stood a few feet outside the postern, and I pulled my car into our driveway before turning sharply left, where visitors usually parked. But the ground was pure slush, and the two front wheels skidded, kicking up a spray of snow and mud and scattering it in drops across the windshield as the front of the car swung, as if it had an ambition of its own, toward the postern. Though to my relief, it came to a stop an inch away from the stone.

When I put the car into reverse, the wheels spun, whining, and I was frustrated to find that the same thing happened when I put it back into drive. After going back and forth like this for a few minutes without any results, I unlocked the door and got out, and stood there in the thickly falling snow, staring at the chassis as though I could force the wheels to move through sheer concentration of will. Presently, I reached back inside, put the stick in neutral and, with one leg on the driver's seat floor and the other on the ground, grasped the door rim and began rocking the car back and forth, delicately at first, and when that didn't work, more forcefully. But the wheels were entrenched, and though they loosened slightly, it wasn't enough to make a difference.

I pushed then. From the rear and from the front. I closed my eyes and concentrated, pretending there was an emergency, that a child or a woman was trapped underneath the wheels, in the tabloid hope that a preternatural strength would come into my arms and I'd be able to push the car twenty or so feet backward. But it hardly moved at all.

It occurred to me that a tool of some kind might be useful, and I made my way over to the garage and, with some strain and yanking, slid the door up. It was hard to make out much of anything at first—the room has no overhead light—but the late-afternoon sky made it possible for me to begin to discern the contours of familiar things: the crisscross of rotting beams along the ceiling; the knot of an old rope swing, fist-fat and ginger colored; a Sunfish's mainsail; a hammock stuffed in one corner, as well as a few pieces of pine haphazardly stacked beneath the stairwell. As a child, I used to be drawn to the confusion of cellars and attics—in the stalled anarchy of boxes and old furniture there always lurked the possibility of illicit discovery—but the garage had been cleaned out in preparation for the sale, and there was nothing in front of me now that I didn't recognize, disappointingly: the unconstructed Ping-Pong table, an old black kettle grill, cartons of old records and books, an antiquated stereo system, irregular pieces of china, wedding presents that hadn't quite made the cut. Sarah's things, mostly.

I'd already spotted the shovel leaning up against a side wall, one of those old heavy-headed monsters so rusted and sorry-looking it was impossible to know what it might originally have been used for. Still, a few minutes later, I was digging out grassy slush and mud from under all four car wheels and hurtling it over the hedge in the direction of the road. Two or three inches of snow had already fallen, and after shoveling for another fifteen minutes, I climbed back inside the driver's seat and restarted the engine, but the same thing happened—an insistent whining, a high-pitched complaint as the wheels spun in place, whether I was in reverse or drive or neutral, whether I was gunning the accelerator or merely touching it with my foot.

I gave up then, and started across the lawn toward the house, avoiding the softly snow-packed front entrance and going around to the rear of the house instead, up the back stairs and onto the porch. The floorboards, I saw, had begun to erode in places. Standing still, I heard something—termites?—ticking in the snowy dirt, and when I leaned my shoulder against the porch railing, it threatened to give way. But despite the cold and the snow, the view, as usual, made me stop. Tree branches formed dark, wiry cracks against the sky, and from every angle of the porch, over the tops of pines, I could make out not only the dimly finite parameters of the bay—east toward the narrows, west toward Arden's Pond and the meandering, salt-sweet creeks and, farther on, the salmon orange cliffs of Carey's Landing—but also the foggy, broken islands scattered across the horizon like knots in a shoelace.

But distinctions, and divisions of property, tend to lose relevance under a cover of snow, or darkness, and the whole of the island, based on what I could see from the porch, seemed to have been overtaken by a white, sleeping body whose fatty edges molded themselves around even the minutest, hard-to-get-at places—fence posts, flowerbeds, chimneys, gutters, bushes. The snowflakes were regular and soundless. The stillness of the gray bay water and the snow felt to me like a paralysis—as though time and the world had ceased to go forward—and when a sudden gust of wind sent the pine needles scattering down onto the snow in a fitful drubbing, I realized that my mind was drifting unproductively, that it was later than I thought, and that I should hurry up and do what I had to do.

I was still carrying the shovel, using it as a kind of impromptu walking stick, and I traipsed around the porch until I reached the front door.

Kicking aside a soggy tennis ball, I inserted my key into the lock. It didn't fit, I discovered a moment later; I'd brought along the wrong one. I searched for a spare in all the obvious spots—behind the drainpipe, under the floormat—but I found nothing, and all the windows on the ground floor appeared to be well secured. Attempting to hoist upward one of the solid, dull-featured storm windows facing the porch, I had trouble maintaining my grip, and, temporarily defeated, I took a step backward to consider my options.

I did something then without thinking; for that, perversely enough, I was pleased. I'm not a violent man or much of a fighter. I remember once in my teens, being at a dance in high school, and informing the most popular boy in my class, whom I claimed as my best friend (almost everybody did), that I'd danced with *eight different girls* so far that night; how many girls had he danced with? This boy, wiry, long-lashed and smug, who streaked away from the fast-footed girls on school fields and who, by graduation, would stand no taller than he stood on that night, replied, somewhat accusingly, "You're not supposed to *count*," the point being that those who dance, and, in this case, those who're well-acquainted with violence, don't keep score—they just do it. Where violence is concerned, I can say that I've been involved in two fights in my life, that while it doesn't matter who won, the impulse toward destruction isn't often in me.

But a moment later I picked up the shovel, which had been resting on the porch, raised it over my head and, after hesitating only slightly, swung the rusted head against the window that was nearest me. Expecting the glass to reach out and hit me, and not the other way around, I was surprised to hear nothing more than the dull pop of a plasticene sheet coming off its frame, toppling toward me, and, still intact, wobbling there on the porch floor like a heavy coin.

I felt foolish—that goes without saying. When you experience a rare, dark inclination and risk following up on it and it backfires, you feel ridiculous, no better than some two-bit actor at the onset of his monologue, who's glanced up to see a tinfoil moon falling toward his head. I swung the shovel again, harder, this time shattering the interior glass. As the fragments flew backward into the kitchen, the sound I'd expected materialized: ringing, troubled, adversarial.

Clubbing halfheartedly at the cruciform window brace, I attempted to dislodge the leftover pieces. The marsh amplifies and heightens the faintest sound, though when I stood still, I could hear nothing but the wind, which had picked up slightly, and the sound of snow coming down and, gathering inside the budless bushes that flanked the broad porch, a faint hissing, like a pot slowly cooking.

I ducked through the broken glass, and a moment later, after some angling, I was inside the kitchen. It smelled, familiarly, of cedar and damp cardboard and the stale odor that baking soda left too long in the fridge imparts to a room. The faucet, frozen in place, hovered over the spotless and dully gleaming sink, a chunk of dried soap and a withered Brillo pad the only evidence that someone had once stood there, washing dishes. In an attempt to warm the kitchen, I flicked on the switch that activated the ceiling light, but the bulb had gone out. The lamp on the kitchen table worked, though, and illuminated the room with a dim, servile glow.

Still gripping the shovel, I made my way into the hallway, past the closet that had once held piles of shoes, boots, sneakers, tennis racquets, balls, cross-country skis, badminton and volleyball stakes. Now it held nothing but a few strangely shaped pieces of driftwood, a couple of dried-out sand dollars and a battered, ancient Yellow Pages. The furniture in the house was sparse, mostly stuff that no one among us had wanted—the overstuffed green couch and matching love seat, a juice-stained wicker chair, a side table missing its knobs. In the living room I opened a window, and the screen—there are no storm windows on the bay side—fell backward, as if in slow motion, toward the bare floor before I caught it with my free hand. On the marsh, a group of cormorants were studying their reflections in the creek, and thirty yards offshore, quahoggers, undeterred by the snow, were moving painstakingly across the shoal waters, their strides sturdy, almost penitential. The water rose up to their thighs, and as I watched, the wind gathered in tense buds on its surface, then skittered out in the direction of the outer islands.

I took a fast tour through the rest of the house. The living room with its glassed-in shelves and few remaining books—captains' diaries, ship manuals, yellowing paperbacks. Underneath them a stack of dusty board games. A frayed kilim in the hallway and, above it, the banister with its elegant, petrified resting paw. Upstairs was clean, shockingly, antiseptically, the closets empty except for a few clumps of dry-cleaner plastic. A painting I'd never seen before, ghostly doves shocked upward into a black night, hung in one corner of Sarah's old bedroom.

Downstairs, the snow had come into the kitchen through the broken window, creating a trim, powdery trench across the linoleum. A dustpan and broom sat propped up by the side of the stove, and I bent over to collect the broken glass from the porch window, digging under the cabinets and the old white appliances for stray pieces. Noticing a few scattered red beads on the linoleum, I realized that I'd cut one, if not both, of my arms, though I continued collecting glass fragments, which I discarded outside into some bushes.

My watch said that it was five-thirty, nearly two hours since I'd arrived on the island, and though the snow hadn't abated, it had lost its formal, methodical quality and was now falling without any discernible pattern. I made my way across the lawn, until I was standing in front of the gazebo. It's a simple, elegant octagonal construction, fifteen feet high with plywood floors, designed by my parents shortly after they were married, and even when it was being used, it was decorated sparsely. The wind was whipping by then, and I was rounding the corner of the house, heading back in the general direction of the porch, when I glimpsed the cruiser parked halfway through the postern and the driveway, silent and oddly majestic, except for its top lights, which were blinking madly, reflexively, like skin prickling on your leg when you've just woken up from a long, agitated sleep.

I let the shovel drop; instantly, clownishly, it duplicated its outline in the snow. I didn't see anybody—not then, at any rate—though I was fairly certain I was being watched.

And I've thought back a few times since then about what it was they saw, although my imagination probably underestimates its oddness. The man in front of them must have struck them as strange, all right. He wasn't dressed right, at least for a snowstorm: a shetland wool coat, a dark red necktie decorated with the scales of his birth sign, and jeans whose misted wornness suggested (he hoped) a certain youthful carnality. He was six feet tall if he stood on his tiptoes. He weighed in at a hundred and seventy-five pounds. No gut, not a lot of muscle either. He wore size 9 New Balance running shoes, scuffed and thickly cushioned in the heels. He wasn't a man's man, or a lady's man, or much of a fantasist anymore, and the concerns of adolescence had given way in his late thirties to a pained, spotty indifference—a marveling that certain things had ever bothered him the way they once did. He no longer believed in fate, or in the permanence of anything. He was attractive, women and men might have said, with a full head of hair on the verge of turning gray, and given the lack of any baldness in his family, it was unlikely he'd lose any of it anytime soon.

And yet he must not have looked at all promising. He hadn't shaved in two or three weeks. There were circles under his eyes. He was maybe too thin. He was standing on the darkened, snow-blown lawn of a drafty summer house, and his face wore an unflattering expression of confusion. There was blood on his hands as well as along the angle of his right elbow, and some of it had gotten onto the pocket of his shirt, too. And when a cop appeared, finally, from behind the house and told him not to move, he, the man, that is, did what he was told.

"What can I do for you?" I could hear a second voice in my own, a calmer, bolder man's, doubtlessly an echo of my father's. "I'm not a burglar. As you can see—" I gestured loosely behind me "—there's not all that much to take."

I'd begun reaching for my wallet, but the cop told me to keep my hands by my sides, please, where he could see them. He was older, fleshy-featured and patient-eyed, and his flashlight blinded me momentarily—it gave me, I'm sure, a look of indignant, animal surprise—before it settled, bobbling, on the soaked laces of my sneakers. He asked me if I was acquainted with the owners of the house.

"You might say that," I said, explaining that the house belonged to my family, and that I was visiting for the night.

"Visiting." He seemed to find this very funny, and I suppose maybe it was. "What's your name?" When I told him, he added that his department had received several calls inquiring about the noise. At which point a second car pulled into the driveway behind the first; it seemed they'd sent for the posse.

"What's going on, sir?" he went on. "Domestic problem? Wife? Ex-wife? Who's in the house right now?"

"No one," I said. "It's closed for the winter."

"Then what's going on?" he repeated.

My mind was improbably vacant; I had no good answer for him. "What law have I broken?" I said finally.

He didn't answer. With policemen, it seems, you're always waiting for something, yet a formality had come into his manner. I think he recognized my name, or my family's name, not through any achievement but through provincialism; the island was small, only twenty-eight square miles, and for better or for worse, people tended to know one another's business. "May I see some ID, sir, please?"

The beam of his flashlight touched the wallet I handed over. He took out each one of my credit cards, as well as the loose sheath of plastic identifying my membership at two video stores, the public library, Triple A, the university health plan, as well as cards signifying my blood type O-positive and my preferred-customer status at the local kitchenware store. The cards gleamed in the dark as the snow landed on them, sparkling and then melting. "Sir, have you had anything to drink this evening? Any alcoholic beverages?"

"I had a cup of coffee on the ferry."

He ignored this. "Then what's going on here?"

I had enough knowledge of civil law to know that I'd done nothing wrong, at least in a criminal sense. Private property is, for better or worse, considered the holiest commodity in this country, and until the end of the year, the house behind me, and the land I was standing on, still belonged to my sister. "Nothing," I replied, the remnants of an old entitlement in my voice. "I just broke a window, that's all," and I shrugged. "Had to get in somehow, right?"

I'd spoken without thinking, and when his beam skimmed my face I had to look away, feeling as though my eyes might shatter if they met that light. But whatever he was going to say, he didn't, and by then he'd found my university ID. "What are you a student of, Mr. Knowles?"

"I'm not a student of anything," I said very softly. "I'm a professor. College."

By then another policeman had joined us, a soft-cheeked younger man who stood staring at the frame of the house, his radio blaring solemnly at his belt. He looked too young to be a policeman; as a matter of fact he resembled a trick-or-treater dressed up as one. He had a child's snub nose and a restless, insincere gaze, and obviously he'd determined I was more or less harmless since he felt free to stretch his arms and do a few experimental shoulder rolls. "This is *his* house?" he said to the first cop, and also to me.

"What law have I broken?" I repeated.

*f*or a long time after the police had left, I remained on the top stair of the back porch, listening to the buoys clanking, and the dense, skittering quiet of the falling snow, and the occasional car distantly swishing past. Before leaving, the second cop, the one who looked like a child in disguise, shook his head at me disgustedly. "There's blood on your shirt. You should get yourself cleaned up."

He was right, unfortunately; and after I was sure they'd left, I plunged my arms into the snow outside the kitchen door, binding them with a strip of towel I found in one of the upstairs bathrooms. I felt weak—physically weak—and faint-headed, a condition due mainly to the fact that I hadn't had anything to eat since breakfast. Fetching the grocery bags from the trunk of the car, I retreated into the living room, and using the side table as a tray, improvised for myself a Boy Scout's meal of crackers, peanut butter and cheese. Afterward, feeling cooped-up and uncertain, though with no real destination in mind—where was there to go?—I buttoned my coat, retrieved my hat and my gloves from the kitchen and made my way back outdoors.

The snow was coming down hard, the flakes needling, closer now to sleet than to snow, an almost certain sign that the storm would end sooner rather than later. Despite the tripping unease in my stomach, the world that night seemed beautiful and unmarked. The sky was a delicate dark orange. The air was musky with the smell of burning cedar. My ears picked up the cornetlike squawk of geese from somewhere across the water, a sound so gorgeous and lonely that it took me a moment to realize how odd it was that they'd be flying at night, and in a snowstorm, no less. The flakes slanted across the streetlights, and objects on the street—were they mailboxes? stalled cars? pay phones? fire hydrants? by then it was hard to tell—were milk white and featureless. And the more it snowed, the more their edges grew rounder, lost their contours, drifted into one another.

I walked directionlessly along the side of the road. The visibility had improved slightly, though most cars—and there weren't many of them—were traveling no faster than ten miles an hour. At the entrance to Lily Valley Road, two police cars surrounded a red Mustang that had spun into a pole divider, and I craned my neck as I passed, a nod to childhood curiosity that hadn't improved in time. The road had been partially, clumsily cleared, and snow, discolored by chips of uncovered earth, sat on both sides of the road in rusted, heaped-up banks. But my memory was able to supply what the snow and the fog obscured. Clumping past a small graveyard and a cranberry bog and the continuation of the bike path, I reached the Fort District, a pompous and misleading name for what consists only of a car lot and a single, broken battlement from the American Revolution, walls and tunnels buried under years of graffiti. It was there that I caught sight of the anorexic girl, dressed as if for a summer morning in white shorts and a T-shirt, quite alone, spectacular in her aloneness and her thinness, jogging around and around the ancient yellow-striped parking lot, headphones gripping her head, her legs barely holding her up anymore, her lope tortured and intent, panicked to get in her miles before the day ended.

I stopped; and though I raised my hand in a mild wave it took her a few moments to realize that there was another person standing there in the parking lot. She didn't return the greeting; the stare she gave me, in fact, was so full of hatred and resentment, as well as anxiety that she'd been seen, that I could only look back at her helplessly, and when she loped out of the parking lot, disappearing down the road into a hail of flakes, I was more shaken than I wanted to admit, and I turned back to the house.

Certainly the look in her eyes—the terribly untender privacy of it—had unnerved me, but I retraced my steps for other reasons. The first and most obvious one was that I had nowhere to go. My socks and sneakers were cold and soaking, and I was having trouble feeling the tips of my fingers. I'd already decided that given the blizzard, and my stuck car, and the probable lack of any motel rooms this time of year, I'd spend the night at the house; it was either that or curl up in the car. Another reason was clumsily, dopily metaphorical: the house was a familiar haven, though heading back there signaled a retreat not only backward but inward. I struggled uphill against a vicious wind and, reaching the driveway, hesitated there for a long time, imagining the house as it once was.

It was the end of summer; I was sixteen. That week the weather had been cool and sunny; in the thick, inclining grass and the newspaperlike crackle of the overhead leaves, there was an intimation of fall, and of time and imminence. The locals, when I glimpsed them on the sidewalks of town, seemed dreary, infuriatingly slow-moving. And the light was confusing, conflicting, draining. It reminded me (not that I needed reminding) that school was impending, and with that also came the fear of leaving behind what I knew. This awareness of how little time there was left made me greedy, as though in the next two weeks I'd be obliged to grab ahold of the essence of the summer, a task I knew to be only slightly more difficult than trying to suck a star out of the sky. But later that afternoon, as the breeze picked up and the clouds were blown out toward the ocean, I forgot about leaving. The bay was a perfect mirror. Eelgrass braided in salt-and-pepper clumps covered most of the beach. Birds scattered formlessly over the orange cliffs of Ames Point. The distant islands were bathed in a mustard light, and the air was so clear you could make out the smallest bristle on the farthest tree. It was a sight that practically stopped my heart, in part because I knew that even if I weren't looking at it, it would be beautiful still, that it could survive neither happily nor sadly without me.

My father, anticipating his own return to school, was in a proprietary mood that night; as we were getting ready for dinner he clasped my shoulder fondly. "Good to have you around here, boy," he said; then he let me go. During dinner, the music of the Second World War filled the room, and even when I went for a brief, solitary stroll after dessert, I could hear it from the road and, if I cocked my head, through the high, black tangled trees. I'd had my share of wine with dinner, and wine, of course, can put anyone in an amorous and hyperbolic frame of mind. But as I stood still on the top of the driveway, the strands of white, winking light that hugged the roof and the sides of the gazebo seemed as magnificent as the lights of a private coastline; overcome by a surge of magnificence, I ran down the hill and into the living room, just as Jay was suggesting to Tom that a bunch of us—the boys, that is—go down to the beach for a last swim.

Ten minutes later, we were clomping across the marsh with the gusto of painted warriors, and once we reached the water's edge, Tom stripped off his clothes. Most of us looked at him in vague surprise, though I pretended not to look; he'd turned toward the bushes when removing his underwear, and a few moments later, he was wading into the shallow water before he abruptly thrust himself forward and under. In time, the rest of us followed his example, all except for Sam, who'd taken a seat on the stern of an overturned dinghy. "I'd go in," he called out, "but I'm getting a cold. I don't want to end up in some hospital room."

He was shy, that was all it was, and embarrassed of his body, but no one paid him much attention. Jay was busy draping his clothes and boxer shorts on the front seat of another boat; I'd already chucked my jeans, my sandals and my T-shirt into the marsh grass as if onto the outstretched fingers of a mannequin. And while Sam repeated his excuse a few times over the next few minutes, the rest of us were occupied and even exhilarated by our sudden emancipation. Jay, following Tom's example, threw himself forward, thrashingly, before rolling over onto his back and thrumming a monotonous beat with his feet, while I hung twenty feet out from shore, feet and elbows chopping pockets of air to the surface. In the cold, dark water my body contracted, freed up and shrunk at the same time. Standing, my nipples so icily pointed they must have looked almost accusing, I clamored as if through a liquid snow toward the shore, aware as I was toweling off of Sam's sweeping, bemused gaze.

A few minutes later, we were all back on the sand. I was surprised that none of us appeared even remotely self-conscious, though perhaps the dimming light had something to do with this. I'd brought down the only towel, and as I was drying my legs, Jay snatched it from me, and when I grabbed it back we had a brief tug-of-war, which accelerated when he seized me in a gentle headlock, his ankle reaching around to trip me backward. Then he toppled onto the sand after me and against me; a second later I felt his damp penis squashing up against the skin of my knee. I froze at first, and then, surrendering, relaxed my muscles, aware of his teeth and his breath, as though a harmless lion had upended me; when Tom pulled him off me, both of us stood there on the sand for a few moments, grinning and panting.

On the way back to the house, along the path, with the sound of gulls crying and echoing from somewhere beyond the cliffs, I felt elated. The mellow air seemed like a benison, and it worked on my optimism, transforming it from a fear of the future into something more protected and assured, something worthy of anticipation rather than white knuckles. Our lives seemed marked, blessed, golden. All of us would get what we wanted—that went without saying; fate, that longtime ally of our family, wouldn't have it any other way.

Reaching the lawn, we trooped, as if by whimsical consensus, into the gazebo, damp-chested and exultant, our shorts and T-shirts smocked with water (all of us except for Sam, who'd detoured into the back of the house for another shirt), where we found Sarah lounging on one of the couches. "Hey, everybody," she called out.

I never tired of looking at her. She had my mother's thin bones and high cheeks, a fair, freckled complexion and an expression of slightly gummy, white-toothed amusement. Her hair was shoulder-bone length and flecked with strands of blond—it caught between her teeth, a vision of enticement mitigated only by the fact it was my sister's hair, and not a stranger's. Sometimes her good looks practically pinned me to my seat; and like many beautiful girls, who were accustomed to being regarded endlessly by boys and men, she'd developed a restless, seemingly indifferent manner, one that indicated that she knew full well that if the man in question had his way, he'd spend all day gazing at her dumb-eyed, and it was thus incumbent on her to keep things moving.

"You guys are all fags," she remarked a moment later. "Really. That's all so-called male bonding is anyway."

"You're just jealous," Jay said.

"Oh, right, so jealous."

"Just because you can't take off your shirt," I said slyly.

She could take off her shirt, she replied, anytime she wanted to. A moment later, she reached down to light two of the curling candles on the coffee table, and it must have been a few minutes later that Sam reappeared in the doorway, freshly changed into jeans and a T-shirt, holding a beer. "God, it looks like a slumber party in here," he remarked.

The candles on the coffee table fluttered and spat; one of them began to drip; a breeze swung one of the light strands on the roof and sent it clacking, and the fan resting on the edge of the coffee table flushed the room back and forth, like successive waves of shame.

We were a good family—they said that about us. It was an antiquated expression, but people used it seriously, even reverently. And I remember us that way, that night, frozen in the act of becoming: Tom, quiet, hunched forward, bare feet crossed; Jay sprawled on one of the side chairs, his hair still wet from swimming; Sam slackly crooked in the doorway; Sarah twisting the ends of her hair in a concentrated way, as if mining for gold. The music had stopped and I kept waiting for it to reverse itself, or go on; a few moments later, I could hear the distant blurting tidal lapping of the needle against the end band. Later, someone—I can't remember who—would comment on the look of ferocious nostalgia in my face that night, as though my eyes weren't seeing but were already trying to remember.

Our house was always filled with teachers. It's late at night, and they're standing in the open doorway, with one arm half-up a sleeve. They're squatting on the outside stoop, under a bug-speckled porch light, curling their car keys over and under the length of their hands, like a magic trick. Or wondering, with a faintly apologetic shift of their eyebrows, if one or the other of us, licensed or not, would mind giving them a lift back to the dorm. They've all had too much to drink. The political science teacher has said something cruel, or clumsy; his wife has a headache; the elderly classics teacher in his gleaming red bow tie has library duty in the morning; others have papers to correct, reading to do, drives ahead of them. And there's no more liquor in the house; somebody's broken a vase, a plate, the stem of a wineglass, some object that my mother contends was ugly anyway. In fact, breaking that thing was actually doing us all a favor.

One teacher helps his wife on with her coat and begins fumbling with her buttons, like a gorilla and a little girl. Blankly, gravely, she pushes away his fingers; she can do it herself, thank you. These long good-byes are a ritual stretched out to conceal the obvious: we'll see the gravel-voiced American history teacher in class the next day; the reverend with the cauliflower ears is Tom's lacrosse coach: the Castilian who taught us how to flamenco dance is Jay's academic advisor; my math teacher is passed out in the living room. The old teachers, who, like my father, fell into teaching jobs after the war that lasted for a lifetime, call us "old man" or, with laborious formality, "sir," as in "yousir!" their handshakes swiftly sincere, or else they bow at us with a sly stillness, their eyes humorous, decorous. The wives—they're not teachers themselves, though mock jobs have sometimes been created for them around school, teaching typing or helping out in admissions—kiss us on the mouth and tell us that they love us.

Tom, my older brother, was annoyed to find out that Miss Hand was coming to stay with us over Memorial Day weekend. "She's my teacher," he kept saying to my mother. "How would you like it if I invited one of *your* teachers to come and torture you?"

"She's lonely." She poked the hose around a heating grate as the Electrolux trampled tiredly behind her, making rude, sudden squeals as it rounded corners, its elephant gray cord snuffling and spasming. "She has nowhere to go. She doesn't know anybody. Besides, it'll be your father's birthday, and it's fun having people—"

"She's my teacher," he repeated carefully.

"*Was* your teacher, yes. The year's practically over. You're a senior."

"A *real guy*," Sarah intoned into her clasped hands. She was eighteen and home regrouping before she left in two weeks for Thailand, where she planned to spend the summer doing volunteer work for a refugee organization. After only a year away from us she seemed to me as mysterious as a member of your own family could be. "Maybe you could go out with her, Tommy. That happens a lot these days. Older women, younger men—"

"Oh please, Sarah, stop. You've been reading too many magazines," my mother said. Her voice rose over the sound of the vacuum. "Your father's a teacher. And so sometimes we have friends who are teachers. The two aren't mutually exclusive."

"Why doesn't she have other friends?" Tom was pretending to plead now.

"Yeah, does she have rabies or something?" Sam piped in. "Doesn't anybody else like her?"

Susan Hand, Tom's photography teacher, was due to arrive that Friday afternoon on the four-thirteen ferry. It was the end of her first year teaching, and since she wasn't going to be returning to Emery in the fall (in September, she planned to move back to California, where she was from, to devote the year to her own photography), my parents had invited her to spend the long holiday weekend with us on the island. I'd seen some of her work at a campus group show—snow-iced phone poles in winter, bike wheels and their shadows, close-ups of buds and flower petals—and while it wasn't exactly to my taste, she'd won prizes and fellowships here and there. According to my mother, she'd come East following the failure of a love affair. "Poor thing," my mother said now. "She's had a rough time of it. Whoever the man was, he really did a number on her."

"Whose fault was it?" Sam wanted to know. He was fifteen, a slender boy with long, floppy, schoolboy arms, whose habit of chopping off his own hair when it got too long over the ears made him look erratic and out of sorts, and even slightly crazy.

"Whose fault was what?" She'd killed the vacuum and had proceeded over to the windows that overlooked the water, which she was now busy polishing with a dish towel.

"Who caused her love affair to go bad?" I said. "Who was it with, anyway?"

"Sometimes it's not anybody's fault. Sometimes people grow apart. Or they weren't good for each other in the first place. Their timing was off." Her arm movements varied suddenly, widening, as though she were embracing all the possibilities of love and disloyalty, before she turned to tap Tom's nose with the towel. "Anyhow, even if I knew, I wouldn't tell you all, you'd spread it all over the place."

"I'll bet you it was *her* fault," Sam said, with inexplicable contempt.

Along with Miss Hand, the other guests expected that weekend were Mr. and Mrs. Noerdlinger, the headmaster and his wife, who were old friends of our parents, and a French teacher named Olivier—I didn't know his last name and never found it out—who was teaching in the U.S. for a year on an exchange while his American counterpart toiled at a lycée outside Paris.

Mr. Noerdlinger and my father had known each other for almost

forty years, since the time they were roommates together in college; my
father had managed the tennis team the year Mr. Noerdlinger almost won
the Heisman Trophy for the best college football player in the nation, a
distinction practically unheard of for an Ivy Leaguer. He was not only
headmaster of the Emery School, where my father taught, but also a part-
time teacher. He led a senior-class seminar known as Ethics. Students sat
around in groups of four, discussing whether or not Harry Truman should
have dropped the bomb on Hiroshima, whether marijuana should be
legalized or, if you could get a million dollars just by pushing a button
that would electrocute a randomly selected Asian migrant worker—with
no criminal consequences for yourself—would you do it? His hair was a
rusty red color, and he was a large man, with a chest whose obstinacy
reminded me of a beer barrel. At six-four, he dwarfed my father. He was
hale and hearty, accustomed to greeting and reassuring trustees, parents,
alumni and donors, and his smile was frequent and, I felt, insincere. His
given name was Montgomery, though practically everyone knew him by
his nickname, which was Bump.

His wife, Hope, was a fastidious, literal-minded woman whose
weight was different every time you saw her; that weekend she looked
too thin. She came from an illustrious East Coast family whose name
people associated with government and scandal, and because of her
money, and because she'd been married twice before and her only child, a
son, had died in an accident fifteen years earlier, people seemed frightened of her. Now and then I'd catch her glancing off to one side or
looking down, and the tentative, shattered expression on her face at those
times made me think that the interest she showed in the world was a
pretense. "She's a sad woman," my mother told us once.

"Sad?" I said. "If I had all that money, I'd wake up every morning
clapping my hands."

"Money brings its own set of problems."

"Yeah, like, what shall I *buy*—"

"No, more like . . ." and although I'd hoped she'd explain herself,
she said only, "Everybody has problems, John, and Hope has more than
most."

"Getting ready for Mr. Noerdlinger?" Sarah had inquired slyly that morning over breakfast. My mother was bustling around the kitchen in one of my father's old formal shirts, knotted at the waist like a white, oversized bone, though instead of answering, she began scrubbing the edges of the sink. "You *are*," Sarah said, staring at her with mock disbelief. "Jesus, will you look at this? She won't even look at me!"

"I've decided not to dignify that question," my mother replied, adding, "You guys don't seem to get that adults can be old, good friends."

"Sure we do," Tom said innocently.

"Sure we do," I echoed. That summer I idolized him, and tried to incorporate his serious, graceful manner into the clumsy stitch of my own.

Sam, who was sprawled out on the couch, lifted his eyebrows up and down. "*Special* friends, if you know what I mean."

My father looked up from his desk in the corner of the living room. "You guys are perfectly awful," he commented, bemused.

"I know," Sarah said airily. "We practice. At night. In front of the mirror."

There was a joke in our family that Mr. Noerdlinger was a little in love with my mother, and that she, if not a little in love with him in return, certainly did not refuse his attentions. It followed, in our way of thinking, that our father and Mrs. Noerdlinger should be a little in love, too, though this match seemed fairly improbable; Mrs. Noerdlinger wasn't what you'd call seductive. The subject of the Noerdlingers and our parents, and their friendship, had become, like most of our running jokes, a comfort, part of our humor, which we took to be unique, and the suspicion that somebody had a crush on our mother, even if he was married, and she was, too, flattered us.

*b*y the time I turned sixteen, my father had been teaching at Emery for twenty-five years or so, and over the years I'd pretty much gotten accustomed to his presence on campus. Before leaving for college, Jay had counseled me that I could avoid the places where I was liable to run into him, but during the day I invariably managed to cross his path anyway. There he was tearing open his mail in front of the faculty mailboxes, crunching up flyers; he was on the sidelines with the other teachers during the morning assembly, tissue tacked up against his shaving cuts; he was in the cafeteria at lunch, murmuring his standard grace—*For these and all Thy mercies may God's holy name be praised*—for a tableful of boys. Sometimes I passed by the faculty smoking room, a space as dark and terrible as a dungeon, where now and again I spotted him standing against a wall, taking furtive, businesslike puffs on his cigarette. Whenever we bumped into each other during the day, he seemed surprised. "What are *you* doing here?" he'd demand. "Shouldn't you be someplace else?"

I'd developed a habit: two or three times a week, usually at the end of the day, I made my way across the campus and stood outside the door of his classroom. Week after week, I found myself drawn there, and though I'd managed to convince myself that I was motivated by simple curiosity, it wasn't until much later that I realized I was jealous, jealous of the boys who came over to our house at all hours, whom he advised, who knew things about him I'd never know.

I could find my way there without even thinking or looking. Across the street, over the speed bump, a yellow welt swollen on the road, and into the administration building. The school buildings resembled the blue-brick ruins of an ancient city. Past the hockey rink, plywood-floored and tarp-covered, and farther back, a wing of changing rooms and squash and handball courts. In the winter, you heard pucks booming and banging, the boys swooningly, laboriously elegant under the bulge of their padding. Down a sloping, grassy incline were the varsity and junior baseball fields, a black-cindered track, the goalpost's white arms raised high in triumph.

Inside, I nodded once at the secretary, with her gum-pink lips. No matter what time of year it was, the heat in the building was smothering. Mud and dirty water covered the stairwell steps, where the mailboxes gave way to a gray-carpeted jetty. Twenty feet farther along were the deans' offices, tucked behind a bulletin board tacked with random announcements. Framed photographs of teachers who'd been at the school for a long time stared down from the blue walls, continuing past an interruption of heavy doors, the heads rounding the corner, too.

Science was first, men and beakers and faucets and sinks. Then languages—French and Spanish and Italian and Latin—began after the double doors and pulled you farther along the hall, where the stairway led into the pipe-warm asbestos maze of the cellar. Humanities came next. Sinks, faucets and language labs gave way to bookshelves, amiably ransacked–looking desks. Above the water fountain, like a moon in the sky over a castle, loomed my father's photograph. He was holding his glasses by the temple, and though the picture had been taken at least ten years earlier, he hadn't changed in the slightest. His hair was the same—short-cropped, faintly yellowish, like ash—and the frames of his glasses gave off a sour metal glint.

His classroom was on the second floor, the last one on the left, across from a bank of empty cubicles. A few secretaries, silently, privately efficient, glided up the stairs, heels clicking, mouths and fingers signaling mute greetings. I posted myself in front of the double pane of glass, clamped in tightly and clouded with smudges. Inside the room there was a chalkboard with a bright gutter, a tall, military-green can for trash, a desk stapler, a mug filled not with coffee but with pens and pencils. Then there were the old chairs, bourbon brown and organized haphazardly; folding arms like beaver tails flopped up and over, entrapping you; initials were imprinted in the wood, the exquisitely precise markings of men who were now middle-aged, or old, or dead.

There they were. The seniors. All the boys I admired the most. The quarterback of the varsity football squad, with his shoulder-length blond hair and sneering, angelic mouth—"like a corrupt angel," I'd heard my father describe him—and two chairs away from him was the foreign student, whose parents owned sugarcane plantations in Argentina, and who went around school with a look of glazed, pearly toothed boredom. I could never be friends with these boys—they wouldn't give me the time of day—and yet they seemed to worship my father. They sought out his company, left him presents on his birthday, showed up on our front doorstep at all hours, and long after graduation, they wrote him letters or drove long distances out of their way to see him.

One time he caught me. I'd come up to his classroom during the final period of the day and taken my place outside the door, which I pushed open a crack. I came in in the middle of what was no doubt an everyday occurrence: my father was picking on someone.

"*Strike one*," he boomed, his voice laboriously pleasant, in response to an answer given by a plump, red-haired boy in the back row, and he spun toward the blackboard before directing another question at the same boy. The arms of the other students shot up. Little gasps escaped from mouths, and my father gazed imperiously over the room. But ignoring the upstretched arms, his eyes again found the same boy in the back row, who said something in a voice so helplessly low I couldn't make out what he was saying.

"*Strike two*." My father's voice was less amiable this time. Another question, a third, a last chance. Again, other arms thrust upward, pumping, and once again he called on the same boy, the only one in the room with his hand not raised, the boy who hadn't been able to answer the first two questions. "I don't know, sir," I heard him say, but my father had already given up waiting for an answer—none, clearly, was forthcoming— and it was then that I saw his fingers grope for the blackboard eraser and tuck it inside his palm. Without warning, he whirled around and shot the eraser across the room at the boy's head. But it missed, landing on the boy's blue blazer instead, leaving a prim, steaming, even smudge, like dry ice, on the lapel.

"*Strike three!*" My father hooked his thumb toward the doorway. "*You're out!*"

The room fell silent. The few brief, starting-up laughs were replaced by throats clearing and mildly thoughtful, philosophical looks. The boy rose up from his chair and, gathering his books and his tablets, left the room, not looking back as he made his way out the door, past me, though I could see from his expression he was close to crying.

As the door opened, I froze, and when I did, my father noticed me. "Well, well—" he began. His mouth closed, then opened again, though nothing came out.

I was prepared in case this happened, in case he ever caught me. I rehearsed it every time I stood outside his doorway. The boys who filled the seats in his room may have been his students, but I was his son. I saw him at night and in the morning. I knew his habits, the good ones and the bad ones. I knew that he drank his coffee with milk and two sugars; he liked corned beef hash; he fed our dog scraps from the kitchen table when my mother wasn't watching. I knew what his bedroom looked like, the old neckties like flowers amid their petals of tin, the two or three good jackets, the loafers. I knew he didn't like to spend money or say very much.

My presentation would be vague but pointed. It would be not only a model of brevity, but it would consist of something only a member of our family would know. For example—did he know what we were having for dinner that night? Had he seen my shoes anywhere?

He stood there staring at me. "Is there an emergency?"

"No," I said, "but I wanted—" though by then he'd already turned back to his class.

There was no spring that year—winter and summer seemed to have collapsed into each other—and when we drove to the ferry landing to meet Miss Hand, the sun was blazing overhead, and the roads were empty and exposed. The street tar was a rich, glittering, doughy black. Ragweed flew over the sidewalks, creating a frenzied, delicate mock snow that rose in feathery tangles above the parking lots and left its molt on parked windshields and in two-inch-high banks, like the clippings on a barber's floor, around the roots of the bushes lining the town common. The view from there—the Catholic and Unitarian churches, a white-columned summer-stock theater, the pilgrim's graveyard, sparsely populated with the headstones of old whaling captains and babies who'd died in infancy—had always reminded me of the freshly fork-split insides of a baked potato. Beyond the harbor, the land straightened into a flow of beach and marsh, succeeded by a narrow colony of identical beach shacks, before ending at the slender, phallic monument that commemorated lost and dead sailors.

"Maybe Miss Hand won't like it here and she'll turn around and go home. Wouldn't that be too bad," Tom remarked from the front seat. "Maybe she fell over the side and drowned."

Knowing how he felt about Miss Hand spending the weekend, I was surprised he'd even bothered to come along with us. He'd claimed he needed to pick something up at the hardware store, though it was a plan that now seemed to have slipped his mind. At seventeen, he was a year older than I, a handsome boy with a dark complexion and a sloping, roughened aspect to his face that reminded me of the profile on a nickel. His features, which seemed patched onto his skin, in fact resembled my mother's. He had her blue, light, piercing eyes, and like hers, the track that led down into his top lip was pronounced, and made his mouth appear querulous and pouting, as though he were concentrating intently on a project six inches away from him.

"So've you decided what you want for your birthday?" I said to the back of my father's head as we pulled into the ferry landing.

He would be turning fifty-three on Saturday. His reply was ancient and succinct. "A smile from my children."

"No, come on, really."

Every year he said the same thing, or something like it: "A smile from my children." "A-pluses, not A-minuses." "Silence around the house."

"For real," Tom said now.

"A little Christian charity." He was varying it, a little, this year.

"No! *Real* things," I said impatiently.

"As opposed to what? Fraudulent things? Bogus things?"

"What if you *had* to be given something?" I persisted. "What if somebody were forcing you—"

"Nobody's forcing me to do anything."

Tom said, "What if they had a gun?"

"And a blindfold," I added. "And water torture. They were poisoning you by sticking things under your fingernails." I was beginning to enjoy this. "Knives and pliers and tarantulas and scorpions and rattlesnakes and thumbtacks . . ."

With a gentle widening of his eyes, my father lifted his hands in anticipation of the peculiar, and slightly sinister, finger-curling motion he sometimes performed at the wheels of cars, at the conclusion of a trip, to test the dexterity of his joints. "I don't," he resumed, "want any more *things.*"

"What about a sailboat?" Tom said innocently, and I elbowed him in his side, though my father seemed not to have heard the question. As Tom let out a slow, temperate breath, I glanced up to see Miss Hand confidently descending the ferry planks. "Oh," Tom said. "She didn't drown."

My father kissed Miss Hand politely on the cheek. "Kid, you're a sight for sore eyes," he said as Tom gave up his seat, climbing into the back and shoving me aside. Miss Hand climbed in next to my father and, with mock gravity, reached across the backseat to shake hands first with my brother and then me.

"I brought along my bathing suit," she said to Tom. "What's the water like?"

"Oh, it's not bad," he replied, shy, suddenly.

Everything about Miss Hand was a revelation to me: her jeans, her dirty Saucony running shoes, her cigarette, her blue-and-white-striped rugby shirt, as well as the casual, confident way she tossed her duffel bag into the back trunk. The few times I'd seen her around the halls of school and we'd said hello—she knew I was Tom's brother, as well as a senior colleague's son—she seemed friendly, and her sense of humor, in a precinct where a sober local legendariness seemed to be the rule, and where she was one of the few female teachers, was obvious and self-deprecating. She was pretty, I decided, once you got her outside of school. Her hair was cut short and shapelessly, and at the time I attributed the concentration of lines around her mouth to age, or unhappiness. It wasn't until years later in my life that I'd come to realize that on that long May weekend, she was no more than ten years older than I was.

"God, you must be relieved the year's over," she said to Tom as we were leaving the bumpy, cobblestoned streets of town, and when he grinned and looked down, embarrassed, she added, to my father, "I've been hard on this guy."

"The harder the better," my father said. "Give 'em an inch, they'll take a you-know-what." He was only partially kidding.

She added that since she'd never taught before that year, she probably made a lot of mistakes. "Don't you dare agree with me, Tom," she went on with a laugh, "or I'll have to take you behind the barn and beat you up."

"No." His reply was diffident. "You were fine." Maybe that wasn't believable-sounding enough. "You were good, I mean."

"Miss Hand Job?" Tom, seemingly amused, met and held her amused stare, while his mouth, despite himself, fell open in casual protest. "I've heard—"

"*I* didn't make that up."

"—all the names you guys have for me. I suppose it would be different if I were Susan *Jones*—"

"It was—" and he named the boy who'd coined it, but Miss Hand had already turned her attention back to my father, who either was ignoring this conversation or didn't know what a hand job was. "This is such a treat, sir, I've heard so many things about your house."

"Don't believe them," I interrupted eagerly, suspecting what was coming, and amused by the "sir." "It's a piece of junk," and I glanced over at Tom, but he'd fallen into a puzzled, turbulent silence. "I thought we were supposed to be going to the hardware store," I whispered, but he didn't answer.

Ten minutes later, we had stopped. My father had killed the motor and was sitting back, the keys barely chiming in the ignition, appraising the property. "Here we all be." There was pride and a note of forlorn, wandering grandeur in his voice. "It may not be much to look at, but we call it home." He motioned for me to collect Miss Hand's duffel bag. "We thought we'd put you out on the porch," he went on, delicately. "There's a hammock there. And you don't mind using an outhouse . . ."

It wasn't a question. It was the way things were, and if she didn't like it, well, that was too bad. Miss Hand, who was halfway up the walkway now, shook her head no. No, she wouldn't mind.

I was surprised, and a little annoyed, that the cars habitually parked in the driveway—an aged truck, a Falcon with its convertible top sheared off, a woods-green VW bug—were nowhere to be seen, but otherwise the house looked the same: a boxcar-shaped split-level on a quarter acre of frumpy-looking top marsh. In the twilight, the overgrown grass looked almost black; a madras car seat that someone had dragged out onto the lawn served as a sun mat; blue and pink toys lay scattered on the stoop, and beside the hedge, under a clothesline, was a grouping of old, split cobblestones, the foundations of something imagined but never built.

I remembered something suddenly, and I tried to make my face look especially downcast. "We don't have food here either. There's nothing to eat. Nothing to drink. Except for the moisture in the floorboards when it rains. We get down on our hands and knees and we suck on the wood. Like harmonicas."

Tom, who hadn't bothered to get out of the car, looked bored and impatient. "Could we please get going?" he said to nobody in particular.

My father persisted. "You don't mind roughing it?" he called across the lawn. "You California girls aren't afraid of Indians and boa constrictors, are you?"

Miss Hand stared back at him. "No." She was making her way across the lawn now, and she must have sensed, at some point, that we weren't following her, because just before she reached the front steps, she turned around with a hesitant, questioning look on her face.

I couldn't stand it. "We're just kidding!" I howled. "We don't live here!"

It wasn't our house. It belonged to some neighbors we didn't know, who were never at home, and it was considered the eyesore of the road.

My father was laughing. "Had you going, didn't we?"

It was a trick he liked to play on his guests, the ones who'd never visited us before. He'd been playing it for as long as I could remember. It was a test that seemed designed to evaluate a guest's ability to conceal his disappointment, and when it was over, when the guest found himself relieved that the house wasn't ours, and he was back inside the car and resuming the trip, it made the actual house, which was only a mile farther down the road, seem palatial in comparison. Young women were the best game, and my father knew it.

The ruse was, at heart, not very nice, and we knew it, too, though in time we all had become enthusiastic co-conspirators. And afterward, usually, the guests laughed nearly as hard as my father did. Though this time, I had a feeling that we'd just revealed something cruel about ourselves.

The Noerdlingers had already arrived when we pulled into the driveway; their navy blue Mercedes station wagon was nosed up rudely into a bush, denting it, and assorted pieces of luggage were still stacked in the backseat. On the lawn, Mr. Noerdlinger, jacketless, though still wearing his school uniform—formal shirt, striped tie—was pounding a lean, rusted stake into the ground, while my mother stood beside him, with one hand on her hip. "What are you guys doing?" Tom called out the car window.

"What does it look like we're doing? We're putting up the badminton." Sometime in the next few days she planned to mount a doubles tournament; she'd been talking about it for the past week. "At midnight. Under the full moon. We have enough people—you, Olivier, Susan, John, Sarah, if she's around." She turned to Mr. Noerdlinger. "D'you think Hope would ever play?"

The question was phrased with apparent innocence, but Tom, making his way across the lawn, looked suddenly exasperated. Whistling something light through his teeth, Mr. Noerdlinger replied, "You never know," and wiping his hand on his trousers, he extended it to me. In a small school, people gained notoriety for characteristics that went unnoticed on the outside, and Mr. Noerdlinger was known for his crushing handshakes, or, as he put it, "pressing the flesh."

"Come on, *squeeze*. I can't feel that. That's not a handshake, that's a fish," and when it was Tom's turn, Mr. Noerdlinger pretended to be in real pain.

The inside of the house was cool and cedary; the arrival of guests—even the anticipation of them—had transformed its mood, and the rooms seemed filled, almost rearranged, with the sharp, ravenous textures of strangers. The sight of unfamiliar objects—the dainty, powder blue lining of an open suitcase on the couch, sneakers with yellowing Teflon straps instead of laces, a handbag that wasn't my mother's or Sarah's—made me excited and apprehensive. "Who wants a drink?" I heard my father call out.

Olivier, the French teacher, who'd hitched a ride with the Noerdlingers, was stretched out on a lawn chair on the porch, wearing nothing but flimsy red bathing trunks and sandals, and when we came out, he rose up lazily from his seat. "As you can see," he said, "I have made myself at home. Sarah found me all my needs. An ashtray, a drink and a murder mystery. She is, by the way, charming as she is beautiful." His English, for all its eccentricities, was very precise, almost without accent.

My father seemed to notice me for the first time. "John, you're standing around fiddling while the world's at low tide, forgive the mixed metaphor." He turned to Olivier. "*Vous connaissez* the expression 'low tide'?"

"I think it may be your own private expression, Father," I said kindly.

"*Drink*," Sam explained to Olivier. "As in *cocktail*. As in *The Lost Weekend* and so on."

"Oh, Sam," my mother said. "Honestly. What are we going to do about this one?" she added to Miss Hand, as though referring to an incorrigible scoundrel, tolerated with affection and good humor by both of them. "You guys always have to wreck it," she went on, her voice hurt and small, her glance encompassing me. "My little ironists here. I've decided I *hate* irony," she said to Mr. Noerdlinger, who'd come up behind her. "It's cold-hearted and it's *mean*. I'm going to start an anti-irony league. Who'll join me?" She glanced around her for support.

"The most civilized attribute known to mankind," my father crowed softly.

"I don't agree. Give me some old-fashioned *feeling*. People who tell the truth. Who say what they *mean*."

"You tell 'em, Blondie," Mr. Noerdlinger said to her. That was his nickname for my mother, and despite its connotations of brassiness, I could tell that it charmed her.

I was expert at making drinks, so long as the adults stuck to the clear liquids. Scotches and bourbons and whiskies baffled me; I couldn't tell them apart. Fortunately, everybody wanted white wine. "Make mine with a little fizzy water," Mrs. Noerdlinger whispered to me as I was passing by, as though it were our private secret.

The last time I'd seen the Noerdlingers, they'd shown up at our house for a costume party in April, in honor of my mother's fiftieth birthday. Mr. Noerdlinger had come as an Arab, or an Egyptian, I wasn't certain which. He wore reflecting sunglasses and a headdress, and a string of colored, twinkling lights was draped twice around his waist. At one point, late in the evening, he had toppled into the dry sink in the gazebo, knocking a stack of old summer records, and himself, onto the floor. Bleeding from a cut behind one ear, sweeping himself off, he rose to his feet and extended a hand toward my mother. "Let's dance, baby!" he had shouted.

In spite of the invitations specifying that you had to come in costume, that night Mrs. Noerdlinger was wearing a simple black dress and a choker of pearls. She stood by herself most of the night, holding her drink in front of her with both hands, eavesdropping on other people's conversations, occasionally taking a step forward, her face lit with the tepid radiance of someone who'd been waiting, for most of the night, for something interesting to happen. She wasn't a beautiful woman—age had stripped away the delicacy her features might have once had, leaving a cragginess that seemed neither male nor female—and when I came up to her at one point and asked who she'd come as, she hesitated for only a second. "Just myself, dear. An older woman."

*M*iss Hand was given the room in the back of the house, the one with the unobstructed view of the marsh and the water—it happened to be my room—and I moved for the weekend into Tom's makeshift bedroom, off the laundry room in the basement, where he'd insisted on moving that winter after he'd caught me nosing through his file cabinets. "There's no privacy in this house," he'd complained to my mother. "I can't make a move without somebody watching me."

My mother, assuming, I think, that Hope had been accustomed all her life to luxury, gave the Noerdlingers the third floor, which consisted of a separate apartment, a kitchen, and a balcony from which you could see, on a clear night, all the way to the end of the island. After dinner that first evening, my mother suggested that Tom give Miss Hand a tour of our property, and when they came back into view an hour later in the fragrant, darkening light, both of them had wet hair, and Tom was holding his balled-up shirt in his hands.

Miss Hand was giggling. "I think they're horrible. *Ugh.*"

"No, they're not," Tom said, although he spoke without conviction. He swiped at a tangle of gnats that hung delicately suspended above the porch steps. "Plus, they're using horseshoe-crab blood now to cure cancer or something."

"Oh, come on, you can't love them. It's impossible."

"Well, I do, too," and then he was laughing, too. It seemed to me that during their walk, or their swim, they'd found a joke, or a secret, in common, or else they'd managed to invent one. It was strange to hear Miss Hand utter his name so familiarly, as if she felt obliged to reclaim him as someone other than just another boy from one of her classes, and Tom, for his part, seemed pleased to be showing his teacher the place where he spent his summers. I imagined that with Miss Hand at his side, his occasional restlessness with the slow rhythm of island life had been transformed into an offhanded proprietorialness. Houseguests, like children, made old things seem fresh. From a distance, as they scrambled barefooted across the marsh, Miss Hand sidestepping puddles, her white gym shorts secured loosely over a one-piece bathing suit, and Tom gallantly holding back branches for her, they might have been two adolescents in love.

"You go in in your clothes?" Olivier said to Miss Hand, suspiciously. He was crouched on the back stoop, smoking his stinky Gitane cigarettes, while from inside the house, my father's favorite music, 1930s big band jazz, floated out the windows and onto the lawn.

The salt water had rimmed Miss Hand's eyes red, and she rubbed at them pleasantly, like a child just waking up. "I had my suit on underneath."

"I would have liked to go too," Olivier said. Miss Hand shrugged, unkindly, I thought.

"The tide's still high," Tom drawled. For some reason, he seemed to find this terribly funny, as did Miss Hand, though I didn't. Was I missing something? What was so hilarious about the tide being high?

"Too late," Olivier said. "It's not at all fun to swim alone. Maybe Sarah will take me at another point." Before they reached the door, Tom and Miss Hand burst out laughing again. "What?" Olivier said unhappily. "What is it? What's so funny here?" and when neither of them answered him, I felt suddenly sorry for him.

The relationship between Miss Hand and Olivier wasn't clear to me, and I was puzzled why my mother had invited them both that weekend. The faculty was comprised mostly of married couples—single people were known to have a hard time of it—but if it was her informal attempt at matchmaking, it became obvious to me fairly early on that Miss Hand wasn't going to have anything to do with it. She treated Olivier politely but distantly. She wouldn't let him help her bring her bag into the back room, and when she'd set out for a walk along the road only minutes after her arrival, she turned down the offer of his company. Later, when my mother suggested that Olivier and she go to the movies or out dancing— "just to get away from us old fogies"—she wasn't interested. Olivier, who'd never been to a drive-in before, seemed disappointed, until finally Miss Hand said, "Olivier, will you please stop pestering me, I'm here to *relax.*"

He was a pale man with a cherubic, unclean face and shapely lips, built compactly, in trim miniature, like a doll soldier. He seemed to have memorized at least three American idioms and expressions, which he used over and over again. "Very *cool,*" and "Tell it to the Marines" and "In your wildest dreams, baby." At dinner, he pronounced himself a lover, an aficionado of food and drink and good conversation, and he vowed to us all that before the weekend was over, he would make his famous pasta *ragu.* "The problem with you people in your country," he said, "is you have no idea of your death. You go through your lives carefully, carefully, like people on tiptoes. You don't smoke cigarettes, you don't drink, your dining room table is a prison. But you have not accepted that your lives will be someday over and done with, and so you have no passion for living. To have passion you have to *not care.*"

"*Right,*" my mother said.

"Teach us to care and not to care," my father pronounced. He was sitting at the head of the table, his eyebrows knit, as though a thread there had been delicately pulled in tight. "Teach us to keep still. *Sit* still," he corrected himself.

Olivier was staring at Sarah, as I'd caught him doing a few times. "But people who sit still are rather boring, right, Sarah?" *Sah-rah*—he pronounced her name with a tender, obstinate slap, and that night she seemed to have riveted his attention. Earlier, he'd reached across the table to feed her a spoonful of vichyssoise—a soup she didn't like and had refused a helping of—and when she shook her head violently, he gazed at her with an amused, familiar frankness, as if he knew more about her than she did herself. Over dinner, I found out that in Neuilly, the Paris suburb where he'd grown up, his family had owned a funeral parlor. This was news to everybody. "You mean you grew up with dead bodies in the house?" Miss Hand said, crinkling her nose.

"No wonder he has death on the brain," Sarah remarked coolly.

Olivier shrugged. "You get used to it. It's not a very large deal."

"I don't know if I could get used to it," Miss Hand said.

"Doesn't that—" Sarah looked both superior and embarrassed "—I mean, wouldn't it *smell*? The house? The dead bodies were in the house while you were in the house too?"

"Where else are we going to put them, baby?" Olivier said gaily. "Outside, in the garden? Tell it to the Marines, why don't you!"

"You'd smell too if you were dead," my father said to Sarah, conversationally, and everybody but Olivier laughed.

"Have you seen a dead body?" Olivier said to me, and when I admitted that I hadn't, he advised me, in a supercilious voice, that I should, I must, the implication being that once I'd seen one, I wouldn't be the same. "I would not have missed the sight of my parents dying—the actual moment it happened, I mean—for all the money in the world," he added.

In the silence, my mother aimed a short glance at the Noerdlingers. "Let's talk about *live* bodies," she said suddenly.

"To life and to beautiful women," Olivier said, lifting his wineglass. "To our host and our hostess."

In the middle of dinner, Mr. Noerdlinger posed a question to the table: If an intruder broke into your house in the middle of the night, and you happened to have a pistol underneath your pillow, would you feel entitled to take his life?

"It depends on whether he looks like Clark Gable," my mother replied instantly. "Does he?"

Everybody laughed. "That *would* enter into one's thinking," Hope interjected as the laughter was settling down. She came in just late enough to sound ridiculous.

"For you, Blondie—" Mr. Noerdlinger said, putting his arm around my mother's bare shoulder "—he looks like Gable. He looks like whoever you want him to look like. He looks like *me*—"

"Well, in that case, then, it's no decision whatsoever." My mother looked stunning that night, with her shoulder-length blond hair tucked behind her ears, and her cerulean wraparound dress low on her shoulders. Next to her—they were seated knee to knee—Mrs. Noerdlinger was no contest. The idea of her money, which ordinarily insulated her and lent her the suggestion of uninhibited choice and freedom, seemed to weigh against her that evening. She seemed coarse, finicky, cloistered.

"Is this one of your Ethics questions?" Tom asked politely. When Mr. Noerdlinger said it was, he put his head in his hands and pretended to think. "I'd kill him," he said finally, though this time no one laughed. "No, actually," he went on after a small silence, "I wouldn't kill him."

"Even if they were going to kill you?" Miss Hand said. "I certainly would."

"I'd trade with him," my mother said. She'd come forward slightly in her seat, her face cocked, her fingers splayed under her chin, an enraptured student. She was partially deaf in her left ear, although she refused to wear a hearing aid, and most people didn't know that on some nights, she could barely follow the conversation. "I'll tell him he could have whatever he wanted. Gold, silver, jewelry. Not that I have any jewelry to speak of—"

"You can't do that," Sam broke in crossly. "You have to follow the rules."

"Oh, following the rules is *boring,*" and the glance she gave him was swift and pitying. How had she ended up with such stodgy children? "If a girl follows the rules, she might as well be in an old folks' home," and she gazed at Hope for a few seconds before adding, "Right, Hope?" and then she let out a low, dark, thrilling laugh.

That laugh shocked me—I don't think I'd ever heard it before. It was the laugh of the most popular girl at a dance, and it filled the room with all the power and nastiness of exclusion. It was the laugh of someone who, impatient with the company, with her children, with her husband, with the roof over her head, had found recourse in private jokes. Unlike my mother's usual laugh, it lacked any qualities of contagion, and it asked everyone at the table to consider the proposition that Mrs. Noerdlinger was a wallflower, or a child, stubborn and shy, who had to be prodded into speech.

Yet rather than come to the defense of his wife—and maybe it wasn't clear that she had to be defended against anything—Mr. Noerdlinger turned to Tom and me and my father and, indicating my mother, said, "Blondie here can do anything she wants. She's the eighth wonder of the world, this girl is."

He was saying: none of you here appreciate her. There are things about your mother, your wife, I know, things you'll never know. Later, over dessert, he reached his arm across the table, palm up, his wrist rearing a little, and my mother didn't hesitate to take his hand in hers.

Across the table, Mrs. Noerdlinger was staring up at the ceiling. If she'd noticed her husband and my mother holding hands, she wasn't letting on or she didn't care. How could she not care? I did. "That sound seems like it's coming from inside the house," she remarked.

"It is," Sarah said.

"How does a cricket manage to get inside a house?"

"The same way you did," I said, slightly rudely. Her vagueness had begun to irritate me. "The front door."

"I love that sound," my mother said. "Crickets are good luck."

After dinner, Mrs. Noerdlinger stood up and began to help clear the table, but a minute later, we heard the sound of breaking glass coming from the kitchen, and when we went in to see what had happened, Mrs. Noerdlinger was standing in the middle of the room, with one hand clasping the dry sink and the other hand touching her chest. She looked almost hysterical. A cricket had sprung across the floor in front of the refrigerator, she said. "I think I managed to kill it. Did I? Kill it?"

My mother knelt down and picked up the squashed cricket and held it in her palm, but it didn't move.

"If it's alive," Sam remarked, "that means we have to feed it with an eyedropper for the next fifty years. Which somebody *else* other than me can do, by the way."

"It's dead," Sarah said. "Get rid of it. Throw it away."

"They're so magical and beautiful," my mother said, still on her knees. "How do you think they make that wonderful, liquid sound?"

"Mother, stop acting so strange," Sarah ordered. She practically snapped her fingers. "Get up." My mother didn't move. "Up. Come on, up. *Up.*"

I remembered suddenly a joke that I'd once seen George Carlin tell on a late-night TV show, and now, to break the silence, I repeated it. "Does everybody know that God isn't perfect?"

Nobody answered, or even ventured an answer. Finally, Sarah said, with patient sarcasm, "No, Jam, we didn't know that. Would you care to elaborate?"

"He can't be perfect," I quipped, wide-eyed. "He lets things die."

When George Carlin had told the joke, everybody had laughed; some audience members had even applauded. But now everybody was quiet, and I noticed that Mr. Noerdlinger was eyeing me critically. "Most people would consider that part of His perfection, John," he said at last.

there were no rules for houseguests. They could do whatever they wanted: go for a swim, play tennis at the country club down the road, play miniature or actual golf, drive to the big brown rock jetties at Conquit, stay in the house and raid the refrigerator, sleep, read, do nothing. "There's no pressure," my mother liked to say. "Put school and books and students behind you." On Saturday morning, I woke up early, and despite the low tide and the mirrored calmness of the bay water, I decided to go for a swim. Retrieving a beach towel from the hall closet, I started down the path to the beach, and as I rounded the corner to the shore, I glimpsed another swimmer in the water who, upon closer inspection, turned out to be Mr. Noerdlinger.

He was standing fifty feet out in the water, and although there was nothing significant or remotely attention-grabbing on the horizon, he appeared to be gazing, as if transfixed, at something—a seagull, a boat, a small plane; maybe just the phenomenon of distance. As I got closer, I saw that he was naked. The morning light gave the shallow tide a sultry, faintly reddish cast, and it reached up only to his shins, which were as blank and hairless as two pipes. He dipped both hands into the water and began rubbing his body distractedly: first his chest and then his abdomen, then the hair bearding his crotch, then back up under his armpits, before swishing his hands in the water and rinsing them. His elbows and fingers dripped salt and oil, and his slackly muscled bull's thighs seemed to tighten and expand as he moved out slowly toward the channel. As I looked on, he froze, and a second later, with both hands on his hips, he urinated a stream six feet onto the water. Then, as if half-heartedly remembering a teenaged diving maneuver, he wishboned both arms over his head, plowing red hair first underwater, and then resurfacing for breath thirty yards later beside the tiller of a boat.

My mother was in the kitchen making coffee when I came back into the house. "That wasn't a very long swim," she said.

"I didn't go in," I said. "Mr. Noerdlinger's swimming."

She didn't turn around. "Well, so? Can't two people go in at the same time? Or is that against the rules?"

"He's not wearing any clothes," I said. "I think he may be taking a bath or something."

She began laying out forks and spoons and knives. "How refreshing." Her smile was slight. "Will you see who wants coffee?"

The sight of Mr. Noerdlinger in the water upset me. When he returned from the beach, his virility seemed to threaten the house. It wasn't that he knocked anything over, it was his presence—his forthrightness, his big head, his linebacker's hands. He strode in the dining room with a white towel clenched around his thick waist, his lips a light blue from the water, his nipples shaking slightly as he walked, just as he'd strode into our view, the bay water, and peed into it, thus appropriating it for himself. He snapped at the sleeping cat with his damp shirt, and laughed when it took flight. He was too big for our house. His aggression made the decorations in the room—the portraits of old aunts and uncles, the leaning plates, the little wood and glass knickknacks that my mother liked to collect—look sentimental and fussy and phony, and the unsettled feeling I had in my stomach wasn't helped by the morning, which had dawned hot and white and sticky. While my mother and Sarah made final preparations at the beach, Miss Hand suited up and went running. When she got back, her skin was pinkly flushed, and as she sat on the couch her entire upper body seemed to click silently, like seconds passing.

Following lunch, the adults had discussed what made a good teacher. "He's a disciplinarian," Mr. Noerdlinger said. He rapped his pipe on the edge of his armchair, and with his other hand snaked a smoked almond, quick as electricity, into his mouth. "A limits-setter. He's consistent as hell, and he doesn't take any guff from anybody." He glanced around him. "Not that any of that matters anymore, with the quality of some of the students we're letting in these days."

"Those black kids," my father said in a disgusted voice. He was standing at the mantel, framed by curling candles. "Jesus." He gazed at Miss Hand. "We don't want those funny black kids in our school, do we?"

"Absolutely not," my mother replied gaily. "Or any of those spics, either."

Both of them gazed over at Miss Hand. Mrs. Noerdlinger was staring straight ahead, not wanting to be taken by surprise if my father had actually meant what he said, although having known him for as long as she had, she probably knew he hadn't. A peculiar smile had formed on her husband's lips. He was not as bright as my father—as a headmaster, I'd heard him described, both admiringly and scornfully, as a money man, as opposed to a scholar—nor as facile with language, and like many men who suspect that they're more often than not being fooled, or put on, he tended to behave, instinctively, as though he were.

Still staring at Miss Hand, my father pointed his finger at her skull, and let the first two knuckles drop. "Got you again, kiddo," and he laughed, as everybody else did.

"You know, I can never tell if you're being serious or not," Miss Hand said, though she didn't sound angry. "I think it has a lot to do with the class. *Our* class, Tom," she added, directing her conversation to the doorway, where he was standing unsurely, not knowing what his role was. Host? Son? Student? "It wasn't a bad class, it just didn't work for whatever reason."

"Could be because you're new this year," Mr. Noerdlinger said. He turned his pipe over in his hand. "Could be because you're female."

"Tom would know," my mother said, as he ambled over and took a seat finally, interested.

Miss Hand turned to Tom. "Well, OK, so why do *you* think it wasn't all that great?"

She seemed vulnerable to me suddenly. She wanted an answer, though at the same time she didn't, and I hoped nobody would say anything hurtful. "I thought it went OK," my brother said innocently. His eyes showed no indication that he thought, or had ever felt, otherwise, though I knew in fact he didn't think much of Miss Hand as a teacher: she was too scattered, too easily taken advantage of. Brushing his hand through his hair, he tipped back lazily in his chair, the dark straw squeaking, the toes of his sneakers filthy and tensed.

"What about the fact she's a woman?" Mr. Noerdlinger said.

"No. Well, of *course* it had something to do with that. She *is* one." Tom's voice was irritable. "You *are* one," he said to Miss Hand. "A woman."

Miss Hand gazed back at him humorously. "Right, and you're a man. So?"

"Boy," Tom corrected. "Whatever." Now he was the one getting red.

Miss Hand, squinting, pretended to appraise him. Ankles, knees, calves, thighs, shirt, arms, shoulders, face, hair, then back to his face. "I'd say you were a man, Tom," she said finally, with an odd delicacy.

They were embarrassing him; there was no end in sight. "So, as a representative of your *gender*," Miss Hand went on, "what's it like for you to have a teacher who's a woman? Do you treat her any differently than you would a man? *I* certainly know what it's like having fifteen boys in a class."

"A madhouse," my mother said faintly, "hormonally speaking."

"I just don't think boys at a certain age respect women," Miss Hand went on. "Or understand them." She must have realized how prissy this sounded, because she added, "Well, why in the world should they, they're teenagers."

"I respect women," Tom said. "Sort of." He added, "Just kidding. No, I do," he went on, more strongly, "actually."

Miss Hand said, "Well, you certainly go out with enough of them." As Tom stared at her uncomprehendingly, she said, "This boy is a major-league heartbreaker." Her voice was lightly teasing. "I've seen him fix girls with those eyes of his and they *melt*."

Tom, glancing down, pleased, shook his head, not in denial but, suspect, in confusion. Was a teacher supposed to notice a student's eyes? Or know details about his personal life? Although any gesture at that moment would have been seen as characteristic, even defining, he chose to sweep the hair out of his eyes, a gesture of unintended nervousness that came across as vanity. Everybody laughed at him.

"I think a good teacher is someone the students like," Mrs. Noerd-linger interjected, and Tom glanced at her gratefully. Her lips seemed sticky, for some reason, and she stumbled on her words. "The teachers I liked most in college were the ones I wanted to do the best work for."

"Nobody teaches you how to be a good teacher," my father said. "Or a good anything." There was something sad about the way he said it, and I was reminded, again, that teaching hadn't been his first choice of profession. That he'd wanted to be a writer once, and he still kept a manuscript in the attic, in a plastic bag. "The book was a little bit before its time," he'd informed me once, chastely.

• • •

at three o'clock that afternoon, we gathered on the front lawn. Sam and I had both changed into our Jams—thigh-long bathing suits with yellow and mint dope-leaf graphics that floated down past the bones of our knees and flooded out, bubbling, like skirts, in waist-deep water. Despite the humidity, my mother was wearing a lime-colored slicker, and holding a couple of blue boat cushions. "Where's Daddy-O?" she said to my sister. "Where's your father?"

Nobody knew. She hollered his name several times, but there was no answer inside the house, just the old jazz drifting from the turntable, a wounded clarinet that sounded, already, like a formal elegy for the summer that hadn't begun yet. The smell of honeysuckle filled the lawn with a close, intricate staleness. Everything—the marsh, the unmoving water, the baked grass on the lawn, the distant halyards making their *tink-tink-tink* sound—seemed inert, slowed down, and the bagpipe-shaped clutch of weeds offshore that I used to calculate the depth of tides had vanished from sight. "The water doesn't come up to the house, does it?" Mrs. Noerdlinger said, sounding worried.

Sarah was standing stiff-shouldered in front of the hammock with her arms crossed, her chin ducked into the neck of her blouse. "What if people had a birthday and nobody came," she drawled.

"For some reason, I don't think Father's totally *into* his birthday," Sam said.

"Oh, really?" I said. "What makes you think that?" That year, I'd made an art out of facetiousness, instinctively recasting most of what I said.

"Put some shoes on before you go down to the beach, Jam," my mother ordered. "It's soaking down there."

I was sent into the house to find my father, and did, finally, in his room. He was lying on the bed, in an undershirt and boxer shorts, his watch and glasses gleaming on the bedside, and as I was standing over him his lids snapped open. "Uncle Sam wants *you*," I said.

When he appeared outside, finally, he was frowning. There were dark sacks under his eyes that the silver frames of his glasses barely managed to obscure, and his lips were faintly set. "What is this?" he murmured, annoyed. He was carrying his book with him, as though during whatever we had planned he'd be able to finish his chapter. He stared at my mother, though I could tell that he was holding his tongue because we were there, and there were guests, too.

"OK, everybody," my mother said. "One, two, three . . ."

"Happy birthday!" we all yelled, and then sang it, off-key, and when it was over, we all applauded politely.

My mother handed my father the spool of string. "Come on." She was all business now. "You get to do it, too. You know the drill."

On our birthdays, she woke up early to make a labyrinth of kite string, tying it in loops and angles that led one pitching, swerving high and low through the house. It twined tautly under cabinets, desks, the greasy cones of formal chairs, curling around the hallway sconces and the TV antenna before ending up in the attic, or the back of the garage, where it lay knotted around: your big present. Sam was downplaying its importance. "The whole thing's kind of inane," he explained to Miss Hand. "We kind of humor our mother, though . . ."

There was a fineness to the warm mist on the marsh. Fog was starting to come in, transparently light. As we made our way down into the marsh, the low, ugly bristles snapped and bent under my feet, and brambles caught the sleeves of my shirt, thorns the color of pistachios, but with points like stingers.

"Follow the string," my mother kept saying. "You know the drill." She was in the lead, on the path now, my father fifteen feet behind her. We followed, Tom, Sarah, then me, with the guests, evidently shy about getting in the way of an unfamiliar ritual, coming up in the rear.

My father seemed to want to get this over with as soon as possible. Tangles of string laced across and under the marsh bushes, snagging the roots, yet rather than carefully unraveling the string, he tugged at it, and the branches snapped off; several, freed, dragged along behind him, unsmoothly, like tin cans trailing an old car; at one point, he turned to shake the string angrily from the raised oarlock of the dinghy waterlashed to the marsh, and when it wouldn't give, he went ahead without it.

"This is like the Von Trapp family," Sam said softly to Tom. "Aren't we all like this one big happy singing family? Maybe Dad'll sing 'Edelweiss' later on.''

"Sam, sshh," Sarah said. Then, "Why do you always have to make everything so—" she didn't know what "—cynical," she said finally, though it was not the right word. *"Self-conscious. Glib."*

"It's because it already *is* self-conscious," Sam replied hotly. "I'm just reflecting it. I'm like a reflection of life. I'm like art."

"Art the plumber, maybe," she replied.

Our birthday present to our father was a sixteen-foot sailboat. My mother had bought it at a marina in town, but all of us had chipped in to pay for it, and the night before, we'd signed our names with a flourish to a card that Sarah had Scotch-taped to the bottom of the mast. At that time, we had no boats. The Boston whaler had been sold the summer before; another boat, a Chris-Craft that my father had bought twenty years earlier, was now a flower and herb garden, an eyesore, its gargoyle motor stripped and sold. The last rowboat we'd owned had provided a season's worth of kindling for weekend fires the winter before last.

Up ahead of us, small things now attracted my father's eyes: a white property marker tipped to one side, loose in the soaking grass; a portion of unmown marsh; the shell of a horseshoe crab, broken into two crisp, nearly perfect pieces. My mother was still in the lead, tanned feet in blue sneakers, her blond hair flying, bangs damp. The approach to the beach is straw, mixed with high grass and broken shells, and Tom and I caught up with our father and then overtook him: wouldn't he please hurry?

Then we were on the beach; Miss Hand and Olivier and the Noerdlingers behind us, though at the point where the marsh grass gave way to sand, they stalled in place, glancing around them confused, as if they'd all managed to misplace something at the same time. Ahead of us, the blue boat stood aloofly in the high black water, rocking slightly, though its anchor lay moored in the weedy, upright bushes upbeach, and there was the end of the string, too, knotted tightly around the base of the mainsail.

Everything seemed to distract my father: boats anchored offshore, the hot snarl of a power saw from somewhere across the water, the fog on his glasses. At the edge of the beach, he stooped over to pick up a green beer bottle, its flaked label hanging wet off it.

"Happy birthday!" we all shouted.

"Happy birthday!" my mother said, a little helplessly, and began to explain. "The kids helped pick it out." This wasn't altogether true, though it just might help her case.

My father said, "For Christ's sakes." His arms hung by his sides, the tips of his fingers twitching. Only the row of ragweed-trimmed bushes he was staring at might have witnessed the initial look on his face, but as it was, all we saw, when he turned to us a moment later, was his expression of disgust and unhappiness.

"So do you like it?" Sarah said. Tom glared at her.

Mrs. Noerdlinger had taken a seat on the stern of an overtipped boat, though Mr. Noerdlinger remained standing, expectantly. Suddenly, despite the presence of Miss Hand on the other side of me, and Olivier, with his arms crossed over his jersey, and Tom staring down into the sand, and Sarah gazing stiffly at my father, there was nobody on the beach but my mother and father. This was between them. They faced each other without speaking, and my mother was the first to break, if biting down on her lip and looking down could be considered breaking. Ragweed made its way down my collar, and I shifted my feet in place, to shake it off, as well as to remind them of our presence. Tom, glumly attentive to something apparently at knee level, ducked to pick up a straw stone and squinting, hurled it softly between the two sharp-tipped channel markers, where it gave a dull plunk before falling silently to the bottom. Sarah gazed out at the water, her eyes now as cold as I'd seen them, as though she were contemplating a voyage around the horns of the world.

We'd disappeared. And when my father stared at my mother and said, in a foul, precise voice, *"I don't want any more things,"* I couldn't stand to look at either one of them.

My mother wouldn't be beaten. Not in front of all of us, not in front of her guests. "This isn't a *thing*. It's a *boat*. And it's not just for you either, it's for all of us."

This time his words were spaced, shunning, absolute. He repeated what he'd said: *"I don't want any more things."*

He turned his back to us and proceeded wordlessly past the Noerdlingers, back toward the start of the path, and my mother called out suddenly, "Bump! Tell him he'll love it!"

Mr. Noerdlinger, cornered, stayed silent. He'd known my father for nearly forty years, though it was unlikely that their relationship had ever involved a moment such as this one. He was a guest, gifted with the freedom to leave anytime, yet inhibited, at least during his visit, by formality and good manners. As my father trudged past him, Mr. Noerdlinger's mouth was pleasantly ambiguous, though his eyes appeared to miss nothing: the almost imperceptible rocking of the boat, the pleading look in my mother's eyes, the dumbness on our faces, not yet anger, as we were left on the beach by ourselves.

My mother smoothed her hair and began doing something with the rope, and I thought I could see her wince. "I can't believe he did that," she said to the Noerdlingers, who'd edged closer. "In front of everybody. All of you. I can't believe that."

"Oh, no. Really." Miss Hand shook her head and pursed her lips. But she couldn't think of anything to say—no one could—and then everybody began talking at once. It was a time for simple, monotonous remarks, the same ones, I guessed, that my mother might have made if they had found themselves in her position; now, touchingly, they were repaying her, yet she didn't appear to register anything anybody was saying. "I should have said it was from *all* of us," she said, coiling the string. A moment later she seemed to be picking invisible fuzz off it. I realized, finally, she was making a game. "Who remembers Cat's Cradle?" she asked shyly.

"I think the boat's neat," Sarah said. She moved her bare feet in place, befuddled. "The tiller's long enough so you can stand while you're in it."

"Great," Sam said. He seemed disgusted by all of us. "Neat-o, keen-o."

Sarah whirled around, her eyes as low and vicious as a snake's. "Fuck you, Sam. I'm sick of you—"

"Oh, come on, you guys," my mother said.

Sam didn't reply, and then Miss Hand moved. She strode softly across the sand and kissed Tom once, hard, on the mouth. She kissed Sarah on both sides of her cheeks, and then did the same with my mother. Finally, she kissed me on the mouth, too, and then took a step backward. "It's great," she said firmly. "It's a great present. Your father's lucky."

"Well, *I'm* glad we have this boat," my mother interrupted, "even if nobody else is," and in a rush, her social manners returned, a drowned body revived. "Hey, Noerdlingers," she cracked, her voice a moll's, "ya wanna buy a boat cheap?"

Everybody chimed in at once then, words intersecting like six pairs of scissors furious on a sheet of paper. "Do you like to sail?" "Where would you take a boat this size to?" "Could you sleep on it? I don't mean 'Would you want to sleep on it,' but could you, conceivably, ever?"

*b*y dusk, the house had emptied out. The tide was low again, and the marsh exuded a worn, salty smell. The only sound in the house was the laboring hum of the dishwasher, playing to a sponged and deserted kitchen. There was no sign of the Noerdlingers, of my father, or Tom, or Miss Hand, though Olivier, I could see, had fallen asleep reading in the hammock, with one arm hanging down, grazing the dirt. After we'd come back up from the beach, he'd squatted down beside me on the porch steps and lit a cigarette. "I imagine it is quite difficult for you to go to a school where your father is a teacher," he said to me politely.

"Oh," I said after a moment, "no. It's not all that bad."

"Maybe I should not smoke or drink alcohol in front of you? Since I am a teacher? And I am supposed to be providing a good example? Maybe I should behave myself?"

He offered me a cigarette, which I declined, and then lit a new one off his old one. In the distance I could make out Miss Hand strolling along the edge of the water. "Aren't women beautiful?" Olivier inquired, and when I didn't answer him at once—I wasn't really sure he expected me to—he started peppering me with questions about Sarah. Did she have a boyfriend? Boyfriends plural? How old was she? When would she be coming back from Thailand? Did she know what she was getting herself into? She'd better watch her back. "Literally," he said with a faint smile. "A beautiful woman," he went on gravely, and then he squinted at me. "How many men do you think she's been in bed with? My guess is three men. Four, maybe. Four *boys*, on and off. Boys are in a rush." His eyes, serious and wounded, seemed to be awaiting a response, but when I stared back at him stupidly, he cleared his throat. "Are there more you know about, maybe? She doesn't tell you, though, right? She keeps all the details to herself?"

His questions shocked and embarrassed me. I knew nothing about my sister's sex life—I didn't think about it—though I presumed she had one. And since she'd come home for the summer, she seemed changed. Sometimes I caught her staring at Tom as though he were not her brother, but instead a burgeoning artwork, and I was aware sometimes of a strange, passive tension between them, and for that matter, between her and me. "You shouldn't part your hair on that side," she'd told me a couple of weeks earlier. "It looks better the other way." Another time, she'd asked me to show her how my new jeans looked from the back. "They're not tight enough," she said after a moment, in her placid voice. "You have a nice butt. You should show it off." It was as though she were both fearful and proud of her own descent into the world of men and sex, and was anxious for one of us at least to remain innocent and constant.

"I don't really know anything about that," I told Olivier, slightly curtly, but he'd moved on to another subject.

"Have you ever noticed how the best—really the best—things in life have the smell of sex to them? Like caviar? Like good cheese? And what else? The chlorine that you smell in swimming pools. Porcini mushrooms." He laughed. "These are also some of the most expensive things. There's a connection there, maybe; a scientist should investigate, probably."

"Yeah," I said uncertainly. I had no idea what sex smelled like.

"Have you been with a woman, ever?"

"Sure," I said, "tons of times," and I fell silent, not because I wasn't telling the truth—I wasn't—but because I'd heard that the gentlemanly way to act when this topic came up was to say nothing.

He took a hasty drag of his cigarette. "So what were their names? Quick—tell me. What were all their names?" and when I didn't come up with an answer fast enough, he looked terribly amused. "You don't remember. Now—is that possible you don't remember their names?"

At that moment, I wanted to get away from Olivier as quickly as I could. I was blushing in shame, and in anger. He'd known all along I was a virgin, a pretender, and he was just playing with me. "I don't have a good memory," I said, standing up. That was my third lie.

After the birthday fiasco, a group of us had gone out in the new boat. With the exception of Tom, none of us were good sailors, though once we'd managed to get the sails up, it was fairly easy handling. Tom pushed us out a few feet, his shorts up high, and then, pushing off with his sneaker, he took a flying leap over the seat and into the hold. With five people aboard a boat that was designed to accommodate half that many, the bow bent down, nearly grazing the surface of the water. Our course took us past the town landing and into the boatyard. "Sailing is boring," Sam complained presently, "and it takes too long. I hate sailing. You never get anywhere."

"Who knows what a spirit is?" my mother asked suddenly. She was sitting between Tom and Sarah, her slicker sleeves rolled up past her elbows.

"A spirit," Sam said. He swished the word around in his mouth, as though it were a new taste. "OK, I give up, Mother, what is a spirit, tell us."

"Who knows what happens when somebody's spirit is crushed."

There was a silence as the Widgeon furled forward on the rolls of a motorboat's wake. A scalloping boat passed us on the left, a crew-cutted boy at the wheel, erect as an arrow. "So," Sam said in an impatient voice, "what. What happens."

"Maybe you should go off on a trip somewhere," I suggested to my mother. "Alone."

"He's not very nice to you," Sarah said.

"Oh, come on, now," my mother said. "He's your father."

Sarah stared at her. "He's a jerk."

"He's boring," I added. "God."

"No," my mother said. "He's quiet. He's a quiet man. And he's fair."

"What does that have to do with anything?" Sarah interrupted.

"He likes to stay at home. He doesn't like to go out. He likes people coming to him." Her laugh was sudden and acrimonious. "I invite people over to the house. People invite *us* out. Do you know what he says? 'I'd rather stay at home. Why don't they come to us?' Just once, I'd like to put on some nice clothes and a necklace and some good earrings and go *do* something."

Nobody knew what to say. "You should have an affair," Sarah said sharply. I glanced over at her. She was not, I could see, joking. Her glance was passionless, and she was picking at the plastic cushion strap with her fingers. I did not know whether my mother and she were close, whether this comment was, in fact, part of a long-standing conversation between them, or whether my sister, being younger, and perhaps more experienced, was simply suggesting an alternative to my mother's life as it was. But I was frightened by what she'd said, as well as amazed that two women could, without emotion, discuss a topic I'd imagined only as a humorous fancy. I no longer felt flattered by Mr. Noerdlinger's interest in our mother. Instead, I found the idea of him menacing, and suddenly I wanted more than anything to return to shore, and to be near my father, and to conduct my life the way he did.

"Maybe you should marry Mr. Noerdlinger," Sarah suggested.

"Nope. He's already married," my mother said. "To that cold, dull, spoiled, unimaginative *witch.*"

We all pretended to be shocked, and, in fact, it did come as a shock to hear what my mother really thought about her. "Mother!" I said, stroking my index finger. "Shame! Shame!" Sam laughed nervously, but then he looked pleased.

"Imagine," my mother said. "Imagine bringing a *sound machine* to the *ocean.* She came pounding on my door last night, stoned on whatever pills it is she pops, because the socket in her room didn't fit her *sound* machine. She has this portable sound machine that goes along with her wherever she goes. She can't sleep without it. She says. But what," she paused, "will you tell me *what* the point is of having a machine that makes *wave* sounds when the real thing is only a few hundred feet out your window? It goes to show you that money can buy a person a lot of things, but it can't buy you an imagination, or talent, or interesting—" she paused again "—*ness.*"

"Maybe he snores," Sarah suggested with a yawn. "Maybe that's what she needs a sound machine for."

"I wouldn't know," my mother replied a moment later, "if he snores, dearie."

"Heh, heh, heh," Sarah said, and my mother said it right back: "Heh, heh, heh."

*t*he next day, Tom and Miss Hand, both wearing tennis whites, disappeared to the country club to play tennis. The Noerdlingers had gone off sightseeing, and wouldn't be back until later that evening. It was as if the gift of isolation that the house provided had become a burden. After lunch, my father took a nap that stretched past two, and then three o'clock, but then, suddenly, he materialized in the kitchen, barefooted. He looked squashed, weightless and intent. He sat down on the stoop and began opening quahogs. With a hectoring motion, he scraped the small, black-handled knife under the watery pink, thumb rigid in the air, his palms and fingers juice-slick, then, rather brutally, he slipped the blade under, scooping the salty inside up and over onto itself. One after another. He laid the torn, hectic-looking shells on a tray, and when I addressed him he only grunted.

My brother and Miss Hand didn't return until nine o'clock or so, just as my parents and Mr. Noerdlinger—Mrs. Noerdlinger had gone to bed early, claiming the salt air had wiped her out—were finishing dinner. They joined us in the gazebo for dessert and coffee. Miss Hand seemed flushed, and I could tell that they had stopped for a drink on the way home. "Tom gave me a tour of the island—"

"—and then we went to see the sunset at Conquit," Tom finished.

"Was it the most beautiful thing you've ever seen?" my mother said to Miss Hand, though clearly, she did not expect an answer. My mother seemed to be in a vague, defiant mood that evening. There was an exquisiteness to her manner, a slowing down of motion mixed with what seemed to be a heightened self-regard. Whenever she gestured, which she did more than usual, her fingers seemed to hang in the air a moment longer than they did ordinarily, and she gazed down at them philosophically, as though they were vague notions she was contemplating. The woman from that morning, making coffee and toast and eggs, her voice a clutch of brightly colored flowers, had been taken over by another woman, one dissatisfied with the boundaries of her life, and after coffee, her voice, ardent and injured, rose. "I think that we should all put on some music and *dance*," she said. "Who will dance?"

My father begged off—he rarely stayed up later than ten o'clock, a habit from the school week—and she said to him, "Fine. Go sleep. Go do what you have to do. Pleasant dreams." She waved him, a pesky servant, away. For a moment, he stood there, blinking, looking confused in the doorway, all eyes on him, and then slowly, he brought his hand up to his forehead in a salute, and told Tom and me, as always, to lock up, turn off all the lights, rules we knew by heart.

"Well, I'm staying up late and having fun," my mother said when he'd gone, as if there were any doubt that she wouldn't. From out the window, a faint fusillade of thunder could be heard, and she went around the polished room, reeling in the windows. The gazebo, which stood a hundred yards from the house, was protected by a phalanx of pines, and as the wind gathered strength, I could hear an occasional, abrasive scratching against the roof. "Let's all *dance*," my mother exclaimed. "Who'll be the deejay? Olivier? Will you? What's the word for deejay in French?"

"Dee-Jay," Olivier replied with a slack grin.

"No. *En Français, Monsieur. S'il vous plait.*"

"It's deejay. Just like in English."

"I don't believe him," she said to Mr. Noerdlinger, who'd taken a seat on one of the green couches, "though if it's true, what a bore." Olivier, kneeling, began to rifle through a pile of old record albums while my mother stood at the door, gazing out at the floodlit lawn, and the black, wavering, storm-broken branches, and the sound of the wind collecting around the house. "It's going to rain," she said, as he placed a record on the turntable, and jazz began to crackle, overloudly, through the room. "We need the rain." She turned suddenly toward him. "Since my husband has gone to bed, I'm afraid this girl has no one to dance with." She added, in a syrup-heavy Southern accent, "And does that sound like I'm a po' l'il pickaninny? 'Cuz I *is*."

"Maybe you should go to bed, too," Tom said. Ordinarily, he disguised his annoyance toward my mother under a veneer of sweet-tempered indifference, but the volume of the music on the record player dulled his inflections, and she took him literally.

"Not on your life!" she replied. "This l'il ol' girl wants to have some *fun*."

"Will you let me have this dance?" Mr. Noerdlinger said to her politely. "Since *my* wife has gone to bed?"

We—Tom, Sarah and I—took seats on the couch, and watched as Mr. Noerdlinger took my mother by her hands and led her out into the middle of the room. They began dancing a modified jitterbug, but soon he established a slight distance from her, and began pumping his arms up and down in an awkward imitation of how he must have thought teenagers danced, and then my mother followed suit. Everyone seemed to want to join in then. Olivier pulled my sister up and led her, faintly protesting, out onto the floor, just as a slower song began. A moment later Miss Hand extended her hand to Tom, who'd been watching my mother and Mr. Noerdlinger with an expression of sad amusement.

He shook his head, his lips flat. "Come on," I heard Miss Hand said. "Please?"

Without waiting for an answer, she pulled him up onto his feet and towed him onto the floor. Standing opposite her, he looked embarrassed and uncertain, and then, questioningly, he positioned his right hand against her lower back.

"No, no, that's not right," I heard her say. "That's not the way you dance with a woman. Let me see if I remember. From a man's point of view." She took a step backward, appraising him thoroughly, and a moment later she pushed toward him again. "Put your hand *here*. Farther down."

"Here?"

Her voice, soft and evasive, was a conspirator's. "If you put it there, I can get out from under you. You want to enclose me, sort of. Don't worry about hurting me, you won't hurt me." Slightly dreamily, she took a small sip from her wineglass. "Now take my other hand. My fingers. There. That's it."

As they began to dance, my attention was riveted back to Mr. Noerdlinger, who was holding my mother closely to his chest and executing, it seemed, an aggressive and humorous boxstep that seemed designed to lead my mother away from the other dancers, into the corners of the room. They were a glamorous, sophisticated couple, and I felt a tug at my heart. They were like somebody's fabulous parents, mine but not mine. I imagined them picking me up in a long black car at the end of the school year, and the other students gazing at all three of us with stupefaction and envy. My mother's chin was on Mr. Noerdlinger's shoulder, not resting there but effortfully held an inch above the corduroy of his jacket, as if for air, or buoyancy, and at one point she opened one eye, found me, and winked. Then she directed my glance toward Tom and Miss Hand, who were rocking, very gently, with their arms around each other. My mother seemed pleased by the sight of them, encouraging, even faintly exonerated. It was as though now that Miss Hand had shown what seemed like a weakness for my brother, for dancing, for wine, she was no longer a threat, if she'd ever been one. She was just another teenager.

When the song ended, everybody applauded. *"That's* how you dance with a woman," Miss Hand said to Tom. She had a gentle, bemused expression in her eyes.

As Mr. Noerdlinger flopped down heavily on the couch and started fanning his face with one of the cushions, Olivier bolted from the room suddenly, trailed a few moments later by my mother, who said she was going to check on the coffee, though when she returned to the gazebo, she beckoned me to the doorway. "Sweetheart, could you and Sarah go help with Olivier? He's had too much to drink, and now it's all coming up." She looked at me pleadingly. "He's on the other side of the house. Jam, you're so good when these things happen."

In an instant, there was heat lightning over the tops of the pine trees, bright, sudden flashes that revealed, like a memory, the day that had ended a few hours before. I made my way around the side of the house, past the porch and the hammock and the standing grill, and a few yards beyond the garden there was Olivier. He was slumped on his knees, and as his stomach emptied out onto the lawn, I kept repeating, lamely, "You'll be fine, Olivier. You'll be OK. You'll be just fine." In time the heaving ended, and Sarah, who'd appeared a moment earlier on the porch, holding a roll of paper towels, handed them gingerly to Olivier, who'd risen up unsteadily onto his feet. Then his balance, for what it was, seemed to leave him all of a sudden, and he grabbed me by the elbows, almost knocking me over. Righting himself, he stared down distrustfully at the grass under his feet as I gradually let go of his upper arms. "I'm sorry," he kept saying in a mournful voice, over and over again.

We led him upstairs to his bedroom, and I sat him down on the end of his bed while Sarah pulled down another blanket from the closet and set it down gently on the dresser. "There's aspirin in the medicine closet," I said, trying unsuccessfully to conceal my excitement, "and there's also vitamin B, which is supposed to work just as well."

Fumbling at the buttons of his shirt, Olivier gazed at Sarah, thick-eyed, thick-fingered, and as I stood up to go, he glanced first at me, warily, and then back at my sister. But his eyes remained on her.

"I want to fuck you," he said heavily.

Sarah's face, as I gazed at it wonderingly, didn't change. "I don't think so."

He said it again. "You," he added, his eyes abruptly meeting mine, "can get out of here."

"He's not going anywhere," Sarah said. Her expression still hadn't changed. "Plus, I don't think you could fuck me even if you wanted to." More generously, she added, "Get some sleep." And she left the room.

In the living room, I ran into Tom, who was wearing not only his usual jeans and T-shirt, but who had a cranberry beach towel wrapped, togalike, around his lower torso. "In case anybody wants to know where we are," he said calmly, "Susan and I are going swimming."

"Susan?" I knew, of course, who Susan was. I was just surprised he was calling her that, and that they were going swimming so late at night. "Olivier got sick," I added, and I paused dramatically to let this sink in. "He threw up all over the sprinkler," and then I told him what Olivier had said to Sarah in the bedroom, and what she'd said back. I waited for his reaction: I wanted him to like me, though I was never sure that he did. This time, Tom shrugged. "It's getting late, everybody's tired," was all he said.

I watched as he slid the screen door open and crossed the lawn, and joined Miss Hand at the edge of the marsh. Although it was dark, I caught sight of a sudden spurt of yellow-orange that seemed to vanish, partially, inside a pair of cupped hands. Something was being lit, and presumably inhaled, and then someone, probably Tom, passed the orange-tipped object to Miss Hand, and seconds later she passed it back to him, and I knew then that they were smoking a joint. I had the direct impression that they'd done this before, and feeling a weakness in my stomach, I could suddenly comprehend their shared, confused laughter when they'd come back from their walk the day before, why the words "high tide" had left them in such odd hysterics. I felt jealous, and for some reason, betrayed, and I decided, after only a moment's hesitation, to follow them down to the beach. I was trying to cut down on my spying, yet the relationships between teachers and us seemed particularly complex, and daring, that night—the borders of authority were more than usually blurred—and leaving the house and the lawn behind me, I traced their steps down the incline and into the marsh. It was then I felt the first rain—clipped, luke-warm and sticky. And as I arrived at the start of the shore and knelt to fashion a cave for myself in the high grass, I could make out the dark, absent silhouette of the new sailboat, and scattered along the beach, facedown in the sand, the gloomy farm-animal shapes of rowboats.

Fifty yards ahead of me, Tom banged his knee on something and swore.

I heard Miss Hand's voice; she had the joint in her hand, and it must have been burning her, because she shook out her fingers, and it fell onto the sand. "Where's the water? I can't see *anything.*"

"Here." In the darkness—there was no moon, no stars, only clouds—I could make out their figures, though I couldn't tell my brother from Miss Hand; all I could do was trace voices back to their sources: a higher, older voice combined with a lower, younger one. Then I heard shells crunching underfoot, and the light tongue-click of the rain against the fiberglass boat sides, followed by a limp, splashing sound, and I knew Tom was going into the water.

Miss Hand giggled. "We should go skinny-dipping."

A moment later, Tom said, "I already am." And then, softly, "It's nice."

Vaguely, I could make out Miss Hand's clothes sitting in a heap atop the upset hull of a rowboat, but otherwise I heard only the light, turbu-lent flush of water as Miss Hand waded into the bay, and Tom's low, slightly uncontrolled laugh, and then Miss Hand's voice, stern all of a sudden. "No," I heard her say.

"What? No what?"

My eyes, by now adjusting to the darkness, made out Miss Hand, now making her way back to the beach. "Oh, God," I heard her say.

"Come on back in, what's the matter?"

Miss Hand was reaching for her clothes now. "This is all wrong."

"*What's* wrong? *What's* all wrong?" Tom repeated when she didn't answer. "Where are you going?"

"Back to the house. I've had too much to drink. This is . . . I shouldn't have come down here." Her voice was cold, and for what seemed like whole minutes, there was silence, and I could imagine Tom, standing there grimly naked in the water, staring at her like a statue. Then, there was the splashing of bone and skin against water, and I heard him making his way back to shore, and then his shape moved in front of her, momentarily blocking what I could see.

Then I heard Miss Hand's voice, sudden and furious. "*Stop* it, Tom. *Quit* it."

"Oh, come on," he said.

"*Don't touch me.*"

Tom laughed, but his laughter had no friendliness in it. "God-damnit," he said, wearily.

"*Don't touch me,*" she repeated, backing away.

He imitated her. "*Don't touch me.*" Then he said, "D'you know what you are? D'you know there's a word for women like you?"

Her voice was quietly impatient. "You don't have to *prove* yourself to me, Tom."

His reply was cruel. "Get out of here," he said, but by then I was already on the marsh path and racing back toward the house, with my head down. Behind me, I could hear my brother shouting: "You're a *terrible* teacher. You're the worst teacher I ever had. You couldn't teach your way out of a bag. We *hated* you. All of us *hated* you."

There are two ways to get back to the house. One is under a bower of trees, past the rowboat, through the marsh, up a small incline and across the lawn. But that's the long way, and the darkness and the rain and the unpredictability of the earth, as well as the idea of running into Tom or Miss Hand, neither of whom I could stand facing just then, made me hesitate. Instead, I sprinted through a clearing in the old driveway, until I arrived at the road, and walked the hundred or so yards up a hill until I came to the white gates at the top of our driveway. The distant strip of white lights festooning the gazebo glittered through the damp black pines, and I kept those lights in my sight until I'd reached the warmth of the parked cars. By now, the rain was silent, and constant, and the faint wind off the water felt like a warning.

Then two figures emerged from behind the gazebo.

My mother was kissing Mr. Noerdlinger's mouth in a manner I can only describe as frantic. And he was kissing her back, though for that moment, at least, he was the one being kissed, and obviously liking it, and in their sad and jumbled ardor, neither of them noticed me at first. My mother looked unkempt. There was mud on the sleeves of her dress and on her collar. The blue sash of her dress had come untied, and it hung slackly between her knees, practically touching the ground. It was Mr. Noerdlinger who saw me first, and startled, he pivoted away from my mother's arms, bending down suddenly as if to tie one of his laces, and then, just as abruptly, straightening back up. He stood there, breathing shallowly and irregularly. My mother gazed at me without recognition, and then, finally, her eyes lit up. It was as though I were the most inter-esting, original person she'd met in a long time, but she could not, for the life of her, remember my name. "Hello . . ." she began tentatively.

"John," Mr. Noerdlinger said, nodding formally. "How's tricks with the boy?"

"Jam, what are you doing skulking around here?" my mother said.

"Maybe I should ask you the same thing," I said, my voice far braver than I was feeling. I remembered, suddenly, that I was still holding a glass of wine, and I lowered it to my side, casually, as though I were a gun-slinger, the wine an essential cog of my equipment, a spur or a holster.

"You scared us, darling," my mother said. "We thought you were a thief."

"An interloper," Mr. Noerdlinger added, and he gave me his best administrator's smile.

"What are *you* two doing?" I said.

"Blondie and I are out walking in the rain," he replied. "Very pleasant, indeed," he added.

"I love the smell of the lawn after it rains," my mother commented
pointlessly. "We thought you were a thief," she repeated, in a shy voice.

There was a silence. Then Mr. Noerdlinger pointed to a tree and
said to my mother, "Is that one of the ones with the gypsy moths?"
though when I glanced over to where he was looking, I could feel his gaze
on my face like a hot light. My eyes swept the ground; from his loafers—
narrow, purplish, tasseled, rain-covered—to the old vines growing at the
base of the tree, to my mother's bare ankles, back to Mr. Noerdlinger's
socks and their thready, fatuous Christmas red.

"Yes," my mother said in a dignified voice, "it is."

For the first time, Mr. Noerdlinger noticed the wineglass in my
hand. He pretended to splutter. "What's this? What's this?"

"Oh," my mother said casually, "we let them."

"School year's in session for thirteen more days."

"We let them drink here at home. Better than in some parking lot
somewhere. With police—"

"Well—" Mr. Noerdlinger was quiet for a moment"—we won't say
anything about it then. I can keep a secret, John, and I know you can."
He thought of something else, and when he spoke, he was making an
effort to sound offhanded. "Hey—y'ever decided what you'd do about
the intruder?"

But I'd already turned back toward the house. "Jam," my mother
called after me, helplessly. "How about it?"

She came looking for me later on that night, or by then was it the
early morning? I wasn't certain what time it was, but I could hear her
going from room to room. Upstairs, through the living room, where Tom
had fallen asleep in front of the TV, leaving a large stain on the pillow
from his wet towel, his baby-blue thongs exposing feet whose hard curves
and nails resembled a mythological animal's; past the big room where my
father and she slept; the door behind which Sarah was sleeping; then
softly down the stairs and into the basement. I heard her tentative knock,

and when I didn't answer immediately, the door opened, and she came into the room anyway, bright-haired and fragrant, her jewelry like stars against her dark skin, and with a fierce and tender animation in her eyes. She moved aside a quilt and took a seat at the end of my bed. "So," she said finally, "what are you doing here sitting alone in the dark?"

I didn't answer her. She seemed gaudy to me, suddenly, and irrelevant.

"John?" she persisted.

"Nothing," I said.

"No, what? Tell me."

"Nothing." Then, hotly, "You think I'm really dumb, don't you? You were *kissing* him. Admit it. You probably *slept* with him, too."

My mother stared at me, perplexed. "I was what? Kissing him? Sleeping with who? Or should I say 'whom'? What are you talking about?"

"Mr. Noerdlinger. You were *kissing* him," I repeated. "For all I know, you *slept* with the guy."

She laughed. "He and I were *talking*."

"You were *kissing*," I said. "You were *making out* with him."

Again, she laughed. It was that thrilling, scornful laugh, the same one she'd given Mrs. Noerdlinger at the dinner table, though now it was shaded for me, the greenhorn, the acolyte, someone who'd known neither urgency nor compassion in his life. "Don't be naive," she said, rising suddenly and glancing at herself in the mirror over the dresser. "I don't even know what that expression means, except to know it's probably vulgar. Besides, I don't kiss anybody but your father."

"I *saw* you."

"I can't hear you, John. You'll have to talk louder," but she didn't wait for me to repeat myself. "You're making things up again," she said abruptly. "I don't know *why*, but you are. And I don't want to hear another word about it."

I was incredulous. "I *saw* you!"

She waved me away. "You're a romantic. Just like I am. Do you know what a romantic does? He *improves* on nature. Nature's ugly. It's neutral. That's where a romantic comes in. He converts it to something better. It's terrible, being a romantic. They set themselves up for disappointment. Maybe it's just better to accept the reality of things. Old, stupid, ugly, cruel life.'' She heaved a dramatic sigh. "Like this basement. Something's got to be done about this basement, it's a disaster area. Tom—'' And she stopped, and then was silent for a moment before resuming, eagerly, *"No. No.* It's much, much better to be a romantic. Listen to the rain. Smell. Can you smell it? What a nice smell, when it rains.''

She came over to the bed and placed her hand against my cheek; her fingers were as cold as her eyes were warm. "You saw what you *wanted* to see, which is different from what actually *happened."* She hesitated. "It must mean something's wrong. Don't cry,'' she pleaded suddenly. "Please don't cry, because if you cry, then *I'll* cry.''

How could she have known then that I wasn't crying about Mr. Noerdlinger? He was of no consequence. Or about her not telling the truth? That was of no consequence either. There were tears falling down my face for one reason: I would miss her. The experience I'd had with people and events that day came together in one keen, shocking realization that someday—I didn't know when—my mother would die. And as she sat at the end of the bed, staring at me with concern, and with love, her eyes illuminated with a version of the truth of that night, she was a picture of vivacity, of blood and complication. I loved her! I crossed my arms in defense. She would die someday; how could I have told her then that I was only crying about that?

3.

the cold in the Northeast is damper than the Midwestern cold, which
sears your lungs and leaves you swearing at the wind that whips in from
off the lakes, though that night the air coming in off the bay in front of
the house was crisp, sharp, almost shocking. I stood in the driveway for a
few minutes longer, taking in deep, lung-cutting breaths with the de-
prived ferocity of a starving man. A weather vane whirred brusquely and
frantically atop a neighbor's roof, and somewhere down the road I could
hear the coarse, metallic repetition of a shovel against concrete. The fire
hydrant that sits outside the left postern had swollen to nearly half its
size, and resembled a kneeling child about to race foolishly into traffic;
and as I made my way past my stalled car, up the front steps and into the
house, my thoughts turned back again to the fallout from that night.

Tom had apologized to Miss Hand, much later on. He was on the

West Coast several years afterward and looked her up. She was married by then, and a mother, living in a simple house in a coastal town. She no longer took photographs except for her own enjoyment, and Tom, after staying for a cup of coffee, told her he was sorry for that night, that he'd been young back then. I was too, she told him with a laugh.

Tom told me once that there were perhaps half a dozen people in the world who saw things the way they actually were—if there were that many—and it was after that night on the island, I think, that I'd vowed to myself to become a member of their ranks, to see things from then on as clearly as possible. And yet the cover of snow on the ground made that night—that time—seem frustratingly out of reach. Snow resembled time, the past the ground underneath it, and the more it snowed, the more the past was buried.

It's easy to be reductive about the members of a large family. The normal complexities and contradictions of people are reduced to a kind of fairy-tale shorthand. Sam: impulsive, troublemaking, over the top. Sarah: headstrong, stubborn, mysterious. Jay: successful, conventional. Me: effortlessly normal, apt to believe what people say about me, an amiable and poker-faced judge. Tom? Spiritual, some people had called him, though I never liked that word. I'd grown to detest all words as lame and insufficient, though Caroline, who's a clinical psychologist, and who's made a career as a listener-for-hire, told me that was all most people had. "Well, it's not enough," I said. "Talk, talk, talk. The American cure. The American remedy. Talk your guts out on a TV show. Spill the beans. Sell your indiscretions."

"I was just asking you to tell me about him, John."

"What do you want me to say?" I asked. "That Tom was a good guy? That he was virtuous and wise? That he threw little baby fish back into the sea? What good does that do?"

"What's the problem you have with remembering your brother?"

"The problem is that then he becomes just *words*, Caroline. He has to rely on our memories. *Our* memories, Caroline. Our spotty, hole-filled, imperfect, imprecise, compromised memories. How would you like to die and be reduced to being remembered by the people around you? People who can't even agree on what you were like?''

"John, why does this matter so much to you?''

"Because everything in this culture is hurry, hurry, hurry. Read the obituaries in the paper. So-and-so died. Noted. Another person dies. Noted. Noted. Noted. Noted. Noted. *Noted.* Nothing about them, what they were like, who they were, what they liked. It all just goes down in the column marked *noted. Next.''*

"Well, *tell* me then. *Talk.''*

I couldn't. From the beginning—it had been a year—I couldn't, not to Caroline, not to anyone. And recently she'd announced to me that she could no longer live with a stranger. "You've changed,'' she kept telling me.

"I thought people were supposed to change.''

"They are. Not the way you have.'' Caroline's back was to me. "This is all about Tom, isn't it?''

"It has nothing to do with him.''

"Do you really expect me to believe that?''

"You can believe whatever you want.''

"Thank you, I'm pretty intelligent, I will. John, you have to face certain things—''

"Is that code for going to a shrink? I live with a shrink twenty-four hours a day.''

"I'm not your shrink. I'm your wife, remember? And I *thought* I was your friend. But you don't talk to me anymore. You don't talk to your kids anymore. You don't talk to anybody anymore, everybody gets shut out, equal opportunity, very democratic.''

"If there's something to say to someone I'll say it.''

"How about 'good morning'? How about 'good night'? How about, 'How was your day today?' ''

"That's implicit.''

"Oh, where have I heard that word before? John, I'm getting com-passion fatigue, if you must know the truth. You're not interested in doing anything anymore. Or going anywhere. You snap at the kids, that is, if you even bother. It's not like they're not old enough to notice." Caroline stood and went over to the sink, and when she turned back to look at me, her eyes seemed robbed of a familiar light. "It's like I'm competing with your past. With people who aren't even alive anymore. So it's not like I can fight them, or do anything about it. *You* have to. It's your decision."

It was then she told me that she thought I needed some time. Apart from her. Apart from the kids. "So you can think what it is we mean to you. That is, if we mean anything to you anymore. Which I'm not sure about." Caroline was silent. "I'm willing to wait. I'm willing to be alone with the kids for a while. But I'm not waiting forever."

A day later, I moved out and rented a house within walking distance of town, 50 percent of a house, that is, the top part. And alone I think I'd counted on regaining a certain clarity. A kind of early midlife tabula rasa. A retreat to a remembered bachelorhood, with its inconsequence, its dash, its vanities, its occasional lack of honor. But this wasn't possible anymore. My family had wrecked it for me. I thought about them, I dreamed about them, I worried about them. Though they weren't there, I heard the sounds they made, or thought I did. In the squeak of a car door closing. In a footstep. In the retreating intersection of voices on the front sidewalk. After a week of this, I called Caroline and told her I was coming home.

"What's changed?" I'd never heard her voice sound so cold.

"Nothing's changed yet," I said a minute later.

"Well, when it does, you're going to let me know, right?" and she hung up the phone.

In the days following that conversation, I found myself yearning for the coast. For some combination of marsh and water and salt air. For sails and sand and tacking winds. For crabs and cormorants and terns, those miracles of agile flight, fork-tailed and clear-eyed, graceful beyond belief, effortlessly diving from twenty-foot heights. I remembered the night of a new spring moon when Tom led a group of us down to the beach, stopping at the intersection of path and sand. "Watch," he said softly, and we must have stood there for close to an hour, awed and unmoving as the female crabs, skillet-black and heavy with tucked eggs, rose up onto the scalloped, falsely lit sand, a dark, populous armada of martial curves and dragging tails, the males, sometimes two of them at a time, clasping the shells of the females from behind. Those crabs hadn't changed in over two million years, and neither had the miraculous rote drudgery of their egg-laying. By the next morning they were gone.

The lives of most people are ordered in a way that implies a lack of faith in their impulses. It's as though without some system of honor in place—schools, colleges, marriages, churches—they'll unravel. Tom had found an answer on the water; he'd spoken mysteriously of fishing as the best teacher he'd ever had. Recently Sam seemed to have found it in A.A. Jay and Sarah seemed to have found it in other people. And I knew it wasn't the coast I yearned for. It wasn't the water, or the salt, or the shoreline, but something else, some exhilaration, some bursting out (but into what? into where?), and presumably I must have known it at the time.

When Emery opened for my junior year, several members of my class had been assigned to my father's classroom, a situation that made me want to keep my distance from them and also from him. I feared, suddenly, that the only reason my friends liked me—if they did—was because I could put in a good word on their behalf at night, change B's to A's, or in some other way alter their academic histories.

And so I boycotted him. I waved good-bye to him in the morning, slipping out the side door, and once on the street, I walked along hurriedly, with my head down, fearing that any moment his car might go by, that he'd offer me a ride, and I'd have to say no. I continued this camouflage during the day. If I happened to run into him in the halls, I'd turn the other way, or glance down, pretending to be thinking abstractedly.

Once I passed him while he was talking to a group of other teachers in front of the library, and when he attempted to reel me in, I pushed my way past him. "Can't," I called over my shoulder, "I'm in an unbelievable rush," and to demonstrate, I broke into a jog that didn't let up until I was safe inside the library. Another time, in the cafeteria, I heard him calling out my name, and when I glanced furiously across the room, our eyes met. I pretended they hadn't. He kept it up, and finally, I felt a gentle, familiar, adamant hand on my shoulder. "Didn't you hear me?"

"No," I replied. I'd cocked my chair into a superior, tensile angle to him, so that the other boys would know he didn't intimidate me. "It's noisy in here," I replied carelessly. "I can't even hear myself think."

He seemed hurt and bewildered by my behavior, and I suppose he had every right to be. When we were much younger, my brothers and I had come to his classroom at lunchtime, flocking around his desk, climbing into his lap, playing with the things on his desk. Just two years earlier, we'd met up in front of the library at the end of the day and driven home together, but when my junior year began, I no longer showed up, though it might have been a kind of revenge, since at a certain point he'd stopped talking to us.

I can't remember when, really, or how, or why. It might have been the summer he took us out sailing with him, and Sam stubbed out one of his pastel-colored Sobranies on the fiberglass, leaving a burn that wouldn't come out. Or once during a picnic on the outer beach when I stepped backward onto his pipe—it was an accident—snapping the stem. Or the time our dog was knocked off the bow of the Whaler, and Tom went overboard after her, though he wasn't being brave, just practical. The blades of the motor had torn her stomach, and afterward, back in the boat, shivering, Tom bound her up in his towel. Behind the wheel, my father's hand were mitted in front of him like an old, fiendish woman's. "Don't get the blood on—" he kept saying, though he didn't have to finish; all of us knew he meant the dog's blood on the towel, it wouldn't wash out.

Or maybe it was simply the sum total of all the mistakes that we made growing up; I don't really know. And I don't mean to imply that he stopped talking in a literal sense, or that he wasn't always polite to us. In other respects, he acted like a traditional parent. In high school, he read our report cards; in college, he wrote us newsy letters on the backs of old exams, signing them "Dad," though in quotation marks, as if to mock its hackneyed suburban Americanism. He'd call us up regularly to find out if we needed any money, before handing the telephone over to our mother. He was in charge of finances; she was in charge of everything else. And he never shut out the girls, though in general, he tended not to take women all that seriously.

I always felt the war must have had something to do with his silence. He'd been a navigator, though he didn't like to talk about those days very much. Occasionally, words, expressions were flung out as if under pressure, through the crackle of temporal static. *Roger*, he'd say before he hung up the phone, and three o'clock in the afternoon would turn without warning into fifteen hundred hours. He'd lost friends and classmates there; every year they received the same brief notation in the alumni notes of his college report, while around them the living prattled on about grandchildren, retirement, vacations. Back then, I assumed confidently that death was selective and largely accidental, the result of bad luck (mortars) or naivete (a lit cigarette tip in the bunker seen by the enemy), that he'd simply been unfortunate in his choice of friends, unfortunate in the choice of college he'd attended. I never saw him, for example, as lucky.

My mother was always trying to get him to talk about those days with us. "Just ask him," she'd whisper, urging my brothers and me forward as if onto a stage. "Ask him. It's so interesting. And you see, if he *knows* you're interested . . ."

We came forward then, dour and uncoordinated, taking seats on the couch in the living room like mourners who'd never met and who weren't altogether sure of their roles in the life of the man being eulogized. My father, standing as ever in front of the mantel, wore an expression of tactful distaste.

"Did you know he was in charge of bombing missions?" my mother went on. "Did you know he was a hero?"

My father shot her a migrant, warning look—*don't*, the look said. His shoulders seemed to twitch slightly, as though he were trying to rear her lightly off him and onto the ground. Not to hurt her, just to teach her a lesson.

"That's great, Father," I said at last.

"That must have been intense," one of my brothers added.

"Indeed." He was holding the stem of his wineglass tight, like a child strangling a flower. "Intense it was."

"We *need* heroes," my mother broke in. "Right, everybody? Was I the only one who read the article in the paper that said there aren't enough heroes today? That there's a shortage? I saved it, by the way, the article, if anyone's interested," she added, when no one said anything.

She stood in the doorway for a few moments longer. Brushing her bangs away from her face, she gazed sidelong at Sam, who'd begun nodding shyly, obediently and without conviction. Across the room, Jay was staring down at the bloated green mat beneath the rug that kept it from sliding when you walked across it. I was aware of her eyes searching out our averted ones. She needed help. She couldn't do this alone. Here was our chance—where were we? Her eyes traveled back and forth, to my father, then back to us, and seeing nothing, finally, no hope or compromise, she surrendered, slightly ostentatiously, like the enemy she'd become. "You guys—" her voice was exasperated "—are all hopeless."

Things didn't improve all that much with time. In college, I'd come home for the weekends sometimes, arriving late Friday night and leaving early Sunday afternoon. I would have preferred to fly home—there was a plane that left on the hour—and yet I was anxious to put forth an image of myself as prudent and consistent and sensible. For a long time, my father had made it clear how frivolous, and even spoiled, he considered flying, that for half as much money you could take the train. Granted, four more hours of travel were involved, but you could use that time to read or study. And since he didn't like driving into the city to the airport, and the train station happened to be closer to the house, it made sense all around. "Why don't I *walk* home," I asked him once. "That would *really* save us all some money." But he didn't laugh.

The train would make its approach into the station, the bell clanging flirtatiously, and I'd get off and cross over the platform, the three red-eyed radio towers behind me in the distance, and walk cautiously, experimentally, down the stairs to where my father would be waiting.

From him, I seemed to have inherited a strong dislike of hellos and good-byes; not on principle, but because they took the measure of a person, and both he and I invariably came up short. Our pleasure in seeing each other was at odds with our handshake, which was light, always faintly botched, though this was infinitely preferable to a tight, drawn-out grip, which would signify something was wrong, that I'd been summoned back home as opposed to returning voluntarily. Sometimes, glimpsing him waiting on the other side of the platform, I'd grip the fat leather handle of my duffel with two hands, as though its contents had suddenly gotten unmanageably heavy; that way I could avoid having to greet him at all, and thus face my own shortcomings. Later, as we both got older, and I grew impatient with myself, I'd take to kissing him roughly on his cheek; the first time I did it was like dashing up to a door, ringing the bell and dashing back out onto the sidewalk. He looked surprised; he may have blushed, I think, though in time he grew to expect it, and even to initiate it. But in my early twenties, at the train station, I shook hands weakly and stiffly, as though it were my first attempt at greeting someone after a long rehabilitation.

Inside the car, his breath was like the stale air of a continent I'd visited as a child. "Well," he'd say, and I'd repeat the same thing— "Well"—and that might be all until we got home. "How was the trip?" he'd ask sometimes, and I'd wave my arm dismissively, the smallness and the old leather of the front seat an insult to my new worldliness. "Oh, you know. The usual."

"What does the usual consist of?"

"Nothing," I said. "It was, you know, your basic train ride."

Two miles from the house, my father's lips parted. "What's it like for you, being back?"

In the dark, I shook my head softly, and probably with more vehemence than was called for. "I don't know yet," I answered truthfully. "I just got here. I mean, the train pulled in just a second ago."

"Your first impression, then. *A, B, B*-minus, *C, C*-plus . . ." He liked to grade things—foods, wines, movies, books, people.

"Oh, *A*. Definitely *A*," I'd say, and he gave a docile grunt of satisfaction. As a matter of fact, I was always glad to come home, glad that he and I were reuniting in mutually familiar territory. One time, recently, we'd met up in New York City for Sam's birthday, and I took the train in from New Jersey for the day to have lunch with them at a Chinese restaurant on the Upper West Side. The check came to forty dollars, and when my father peeled off two dollars for the tip, Sam raised his eyebrows. "Dad, these poor Chinese people make minimum wage. They spend all day sitting at a table chopping up snow peas."

"A gratuity rewards service."

"Yes, and the service was *great*, actually. I counted *three* waitresses. We got *free* plum wine."

My father replied that he had no interest in subsidizing the management, and we left the restaurant, though not before Sam had managed to slip an additional three dollars onto the table while my father was putting on his coat. Afterward, in the middle of Broadway, he looked confused; the city roared and honked behind him. "Will one of you fellows point me to a decent transportation system?" he inquired politely.

"Penn Station," Sam replied immediately. He'd moved to New York a year earlier, to attend college, and was anxious to show off his expertise.

"And where might Penn Station be found?"

"Oh, it's easy. You just take the Number Two down to Thirty-fourth Street."

"Two to Thirty-fourth Street," my father repeated. "And then go on to Penn Station."

"No, Thirty-fourth Street *is* Penn Station."

"What exactly does the Number Two represent?"

"D'you want one of us to come with you?" I said. A flicker of relief passed over my father's face, and I understood suddenly: he was frightened. New York scared him. Its impatience. Its strangeness. The smells that wafted above the sidewalks. Its bad air, its mysterious pipe steams, its sweatiness. The construction work that obliged you to have to cross the street and walk down narrow, blond rickety tunnels, where around the corner you could just as easily meet your doom as you could bump into someone who would change your life.

All the seats were occupied on the local train, and my father clutched the black hanging strap as though it had been offered down from heaven to a sick or despairing man. When we emerged onto the platform, his walk was bowed and unsteady. "I fear this is a young man's city," he said as we stood among the milling, preboarding crowd of students and commuters.

"You have to watch that big black board up there for your train number," I said. "I think it's the *Yankee Clipper* you want."

My father was staring past my finger. "I'm not altogether sure exactly what you're referring to, John, you'll have to help me out here."

"Actually," I went on, "I can wait here till it comes. I'm not in any rush." I was, actually, but it didn't matter.

"Whatever suits you," my father replied softly. "I don't want to hold you guys up any."

At one point, Sam left to get a couple of hot dogs, and I joined him at the kiosk counter. From where we were standing, we could see my father where we'd left him, his shoulders slumped, his worn leather bag trapped in between his ankles. He was gazing up at the pearl numerals twisting across the black board like a child searching for stars in the night sky. Neither of us said it, though I felt it, and Sam must have, too: he looked small. Undefended. Vulnerable. And the thought made my stomach ache, as though I'd been caught in a lie.

So I preferred being on turf familiar to both of us, though as my brothers and sister and I moved away from home, and our lives became less connected to his, my father's strategy of reacquaintance took the form of an interrogation. "Describe college," he began, when we were a few miles from the house. "Compare it with high school. Better, worse or the same."

"Better," I'd say automatically, annoyed. Even if this weren't the truth—though it happened to be—it was a matter of pride that the world I was in now was better than the one I'd left behind me. This interrogation lasted until we got home, and while I kept dropping the name of the girl I was seeing, hoping we'd be able to discuss *her*, he concentrated on the quotidian. How would I rate my teachers? How was the food? Was I set for money? I'd recoil from these questions, replying to them with the sullen succinctness of a prisoner of war; no more and no less than what was necessary. As we pulled into the driveway, invariably he'd conclude with "Your mother will be glad to see you." One Friday night, more frustrated by these questions than usual, I turned on him. "What about you?"

Releasing one hand from the wheel, he cupped one ear, as though he hadn't understood the question. But I refused to set him an example— I couldn't, even if I'd had the confidence to; he was supposed to be setting *me* the example—and when I spoke, my response was even more stilted and detached than his. "I meant, what about you in the glad-to-see-you department?"

For a moment, my father didn't answer. He turned off the car and pulled out the keys. "Well, that's a donnée," he said at last, adding, in a low hoot, "Look, look," and he pointed at the side of the house. "What's that?"

I didn't see anything.

"Peeling paint!" he exclaimed.

"Oh," I said. I didn't get it. And he turned to me then with such odd vehemence, the expression on his face a mixture of so many things— joy, weariness, delicacy, relief, even enchantment—that I was left completely bewildered.

• • •

*J*azz was our common ground. He was a fan of big bands from the twenties and thirties and forties, the sort of music that plays over newsreel footage of couples kissing good-bye at train stations before the men go off to war. In the evenings, I used to hear music coming out from under his office door. Benny Goodman. Artie Shaw. Duke Ellington. The Dorseys. Sometimes when I'd get home from school, he'd be standing in front of the mantelpiece, gazing at nothing, a glass of wine resting beside his elbow. He'd look up at me. And point toward whatever was playing. Charlie Christian, he'd say. Or someone else—Gene Krupa, Teddy Wilson, Lester Young. "You can't get much better than that," he'd say.

I'd started piano lessons at age twelve, rushing through elemental chords and sight-reading, and on the side, learning everything I could about the history of jazz, from New Orleans up to the present. Alone, I made recordings of myself on a tape recorder, playing each piece over and over again at night until I considered it as perfect as it was ever going to be. I made a solemn pact with myself—that I wouldn't play any song in public that I hadn't played at least fifty times in private. When there was nobody in the house, I used to slip into my father's office and turn on his tapes and records and play along with them. (At one point, in my mid-twenties, I made a little list and figured that I knew exactly 217 songs. Ranging from Duke Ellington to the Gershwins to Irving Berlin to Fats Waller to Ivor Novello.) But even that didn't bring us all that much closer. I'd reached an age where I didn't want to be associated with him. The hardest part was trying to escape him during the day. I was sick of my friends telling me what he'd done in class that day, telling me he'd ejected this boy or that boy, or tossed a surprise quiz, or made a remark that caused everybody in the class to laugh uproariously. But then something took place during my junior year that caused a rift between us.

It happened one day in the middle of April, a month and a half before the term ended. I walked into the fourth-floor classroom one afternoon, in preparation for Mr. Carmody's English class. He was among my favorite teachers at Emery, a worn-looking Englishman who, rumor had it, was carrying on an affair with an older woman who worked in the development office; unlike the majority of the faculty, who lived in dormitories or close enough to campus that they could commute by foot in the mornings, Mr. Carmody wore the patina of the city fifty miles away, a faint, pleasing aura of romantic experience and dissolution. I took my usual seat by the window and waited for the bell to ring, and when Mr. Carmody hadn't shown up after ten minutes, the room grew bothered and restless.

And then the door opened. But it wasn't Mr. Carmody, it was my father, and immediately I slunk down into my chair in the vague but unrealistic hope he wouldn't notice me. Taking a seat behind the desk, he announced that a relative of Mr. Carmody's, some great-aunt, had died, that Mr. Carmody had gone back to England, probably not to return to school for another couple of weeks. Across the room, a boy started to his feet, clumsily collecting his books, but when my father asked him where he was going, he hastily retook his seat.

I was aware of a sickly, apprehensive sensation in my stomach, particularly when my father took out a sheath of cards and proceeded to conduct a roll call.

"Carpenter."

"Here."

"Dolan."

"Here."

"Here, *sir.*"

Dolan, a freckled boy with a rabbity overbite, grinned. "Here, *sir.*"

"Garrison."

"Here."

"Jackson." Jackson wasn't there. "Has anyone seen Jackson around the premises?" Again, no answer.

"Jenkins."

"Here, sir."

Then he called my name. "Hi, here I am," I answered, waving gaily. While I wanted to blend in with everybody else, pride and familiarity wouldn't allow me to answer in the same way the other boys did.

His voice was unamused. "Here, *sir.*"

"Here, sir," I replied, taken aback.

It's hard for me to recall that first class, though I remember my father did most of the talking. We were given a syllabus of the poems we'd be reading over the next few weeks, and then with twenty minutes left before the bell, he went around the room, saying a few words to each student. I made it a point to try and catch his eye, hoping that he might find my presence in the class as hilarious as I did, but for the most part, he ignored me. Just as I felt secure he was going to pass over me altogether, his gaze met mine. "Mr. Knowles, is that gum in your mouth, or are you mimicking a farm animal?"

"It's gum, actually."

"Gum, *sir.*"

If he wanted me to act like a private in the military, I would. "Trident sugarless gum, *sir,*" I repeated. "Spearmint flavor, *sir.*"

"Spit it out." I gazed up at him, startled, as he brought his hand up under my chin. Embarrassed, I plucked the gum out of my mouth instead and proceeded to wrap it up tightly inside a piece of theme tablet paper. "You'll dispose of it properly, I'm assuming," he went on.

"Yes, sir."

"Right now, I mean."

Thirty eyes were on me as I stood up and carried the paper-covered gum across the room and deposited it delicately in the trash can, my face warming with shame.

"By tomorrow," my father announced a few minutes before class ended, "there'll be a new seating assignment on the front door."

The boy in front of me raised his hand. "Mr. Carmody doesn't have seating assignments."

He was not Mr. Carmody, my father replied. And this was no longer Mr. Carmody's classroom. "In general, those boys who've chosen to conceal themselves in the rear of this room will now be taking their places in the first two rows on the theory that intelligence should not hide itself under a bushel. And, too, on the not entirely illogical theory that those who have gravitated to the back have done so for a particular reason, that they are shy, laconic, hostile or otherwise have something to conceal."

A few days later, I made an appointment with the dean of students. "There's been a mistake," I blurted out in his office. "In fact, there's been a crisis of major proportions." I explained that I found myself in a basically untenable situation, that my father had taken over Mr. Carmody's course and was there any possible way that I could transfer into another teacher's classroom? At least until the term was over?

The dean seemed to find my presence in his office more amusing than anything else. There wasn't much he could do, he said.

"Isn't there a school rule of some kind? You know, conflict of interest and nepotism and so forth?"

The dean told me that he'd look into it, and in the meantime, to sit tight, and that was the last I heard from him.

It was the reaction of the other boys that troubled me the most. A few days later, when I walked into class and took a seat, I was aware of a vague stirring behind me. "Hey, can you get us a copy of all the tests?" one boy asked.

"Gee, I wonder how *Knowles*'ll do in this class," someone said.

"Knowing him, he'll probably give me an *F*," I replied cheerfully.

But our relationship in the classroom turned out to be formal, almost comically so. He didn't call on me any more than he called on the other boys. Most days, in fact—and the class met four times a week, at the same time—he bypassed me completely. I was a little bit mixed up about this—relieved, and at the same time vaguely insulted. Only once did he allow our personal life to intrude, the day I showed up to class wearing blue jeans. "Mr. Knowles," he said, as I slid into my chair, "surely you're familiar with the rule about denim."

I stared back at him. "They're allowed if they're pressed. And if they're clean."

"Precisely. And that particular pair I seem to remember you wore last night during dinner. They are neither pressed, nor are they clean. Please go home and change them."

"Please go home?" I repeated.

"You know the way."

There was another rule—that any boy who wanted to go to the bathroom had to raise his hand first, and excuse himself. "Yes," he said one day in response to my urgently flapping arm.

"Can I please go to the bathroom?"

"I don't know, Mr. Knowles. *Can* you go to the bathroom?"

The rest of the boys laughed, but I didn't understand. "Can I?" I repeated, slightly helplessly. "Go, I mean?"

"You mean, can you, are you able to, have you ever learned how, have you mastered the ability?"

I understood finally. "*May* I go to the bathroom then?"

"No."

"No?"

"There are five minutes left in this class. I think you can wait."

Before class ended, he gave us an assignment: to memorize a long poem by Tennyson by next Monday. "I want it word perfect," he said. "I want you to be able to recite that poem in your sleep."

I forgot about the assignment for a couple of days, and I didn't get to it until the end of the weekend, and by then I'd accumulated a mountain of other homework. Late Sunday afternoon, I knocked on the door of his office, and when he told me to enter, I hovered in the doorway.

"Can I ask you a question about the poem we're supposed to memorize?"

The room was rancid with pipe smoke. "Shoot."

"Are we supposed to learn the whole thing? Or just the first part? Or the last part?"

"What's wrong with memorizing the whole poem?"

"What's wrong with it? It's three pages long and single-spaced, that's what's wrong with it."

He didn't look up. "The whole thing."

"Oh, come on," I said after a moment. "How about a little favoritism here? I won't tell anybody. Give me a break."

"The whole thing."

"Please?" I said. "Pretty please?"

At last, he glanced up, a tired look crossing his face. "I'm liable to concentrate on the first fifteen lines," he said.

*a*t two-fifteen the next afternoon, I filed into Mr. Carmody's classroom, took a seat in the front row, crossed my legs and waited for class to begin. This was going to be a breeze, as far as I was concerned. Such a breeze that I hadn't even bothered to begin memorizing the poem until that morning before breakfast: by the time I'd left the house, the lines were practically spilling out of my mouth.

My father began his lecture with a few words about Tennyson. Among other things, he said, Tennyson was a poet who adored beauty, and who painted scenes of almost overwhelming luxuriance, despite the strength of his narratives. To my shock, his eyes found me in the front row. "I'll start you off, Mr. Knowles. 'It little profits that an idle king . . .' "

It was so unusual for him to call on me that at first my mind froze up. " 'By this hearth, among these crags,' " I managed to blurt out.

" 'By this *still* hearth, among these *barren* crags,' " he corrected.

" 'Matches with an ancient wife—' "

"*Matched*—past tense—with an *aged*—not ancient—wife."

"Whatever, Father. I mean, Mr. Knowles."

"No—not *whatever*." His voice was without humor.

" 'By this still hearth, among these barren crags,' " I went on. " 'To whom I leave the scepter and the isle—' "

"That occurs quite a few lines into the poem."

"What occurs a few lines?"

"That line you just recited."

My mind was blank; I tried to picture the poem laid out in my anthology, but all I could come up with was the page number.

"Have you done the reading?"

"Yes, sir."

"Please give me the last fifteen lines of the poem."

This was worse than I could have imagined. "I thought we were just going to concentrate on the first part."

"Whatever gave you that idea?"

"Nothing, sir. I just thought—"

"The assignment was to commit to heart the entire poem. You've had more than a week to do so. I might have said I was liable to concentrate on the first fifteen lines, not that I intended to. I'll start you off: 'Come my friends. T'is not too late to—' "

" 'T'is not too late to—' " but my mind was an empty web in which nothing but trivia had managed to stick.

" '—seek a newer world. Push off, and sitting well in order smite the sounding furrows; for my purpose holds—' " He was standing directly in front of me now, his belt, the one Sarah had made him last Christmas, staring back at me. "Mr. Knowles," he boomed, "I'm beginning to suspect that you fudged the assignment."

"I did not fudge the assignment."

"Then please do as I asked."

" 'To sail beyond the sunset—' " I resumed haltingly " '—and the western stars—' " but he cut me off again.

" 'To sail beyond the sunset, and the baths of all the western stars until I die. It may be—' "

" 'It may be—' " but I didn't have the slightest idea what came next. "It may be absolutely terrific—" I went on, hoping for a laugh that never materialized.

" 'It may be that the gulfs will wash us down; It may be that we shall touch—' "

He waited. Time passed like a very old man with a cane trying to reach a far curb; it wouldn't ever pass so slowly again. "I don't know," I said at last.

"You don't know." My father's eyes scanned the room and found Dolan.

" 'It may be that we shall touch the Happy Isles,' " Dolan chirped.

My father had turned away from me now, as he he read off the last few lines. " 'One equal temper of heroic hearts, Made weak by time and fate, but strong in will. To strive, to seek, to find and not to yield.' "

It snowed all night and into the next morning. At various times, the weight of it thundered down off the roof, and as I lay there, not quite awake and not quite asleep either, surrounded by so many old blankets that at first I thought I must be enveloped in a nest of hospital bandages, I convinced myself that the bed I was sleeping in pressed against a bare wall to the right of a second-floor door, that a lamp with an old wine bottle base stood next to me, above a TV set and a VCR that the kids had fractured by inserting pennies and crayons into its mouth: that in fact I was back at home, with Caroline asleep next to me, and Ike and Isabel in their rooms down the hall. Though when I opened my eyes in an attempt to find some logic in the darkness, I found myself curled up on the old soft couch in the living room of the St. James house.

It's rare that I've ever felt trapped on the island. Not during the famous hurricane of my thirteenth year—famous to me, that is—a storm so virulent it pitched three houses into the ocean and caused a three-day-long electrical blackout. Or during the annual period in late spring when shocks of pollen streak through the air, compelling half the island to stay indoors. Not during weekends in college when I'd visit St. James with a girl and, carless, we'd hail a taxi to take us to the house, hiking or biking the three miles into town whenever we needed anything. Or even during July and August, when the population almost quadruples, and it can take up to thirty minutes to make a right turn onto Water Street. The island then is too distracting, and so are its easeful sights. The wavy-haired girl sitting in the open back of the pickup truck like a sporting accessory. The little boys straining up over the seats of their bikes as their big wheels tick to a stop. The old men taking their morning walks. The flocks of tourists, shy and tentative in the sunlight, touching each other's arms as though they've fallen through a trap door and can't get their bearings; and everywhere the day-trippers from the mainland, blade-shouldered, fearlessly tanned, the girls in sleeveless jerseys or snow-white tank tops, the boys ardently joking and showing off, navigating shambling, lacy, guileful half-circles around the girls.

But when I awoke, I found myself possessed by a strange frenzy, a kind of low-level claustrophobia akin to the awareness that passes through the mind of a driver now and again when he gazes down at the steering wheel in his hands, the brake under his foot, and realizes that he is hurtling along a highway in a metal cradle at sixty-five miles an hour, and that he can't extract himself even if he wants to. Familiarity takes leave. Old bland things take on illegible meanings. For the first time in memory, I felt the pinch of entrapment, of optionlessness, and it panicked me. The bay, shrouded by fog the night before, appeared out the window like a moat. I remembered what Tom had told me once, that in less than a thousand years there wouldn't even be an island, that the tides were painstakingly subtracting inches, then feet, then yards of sand every year, that we lived on nothing more than a temporary spit of raised, fertile land, inhabited by people misguided enough to have built houses there, that in fewer than a dozen lifetimes, it would all be gone.

Eventually I got up, crossed the room and lifted one of the shades. I'd been wrong about the snow turning to sleet or rain: the flakes were falling at the same pace as they had been twelve hours earlier, and judging from their drab, rhythmic evenness, there was no wind, nothing to push them off-course or send them back out onto the water. During the night someone had plowed the rotary, but snow had already filled up the tire ruts, leaving fat, ribbonlike indentations. There must have been a foot and a half of snow on the ground. At least. I sat on the living room radiator for a long time, gazing out at the lawn and the driveway, until my forehead began to sweat from a combination of heat and sleeplessness, a moisture that stung my eyes and which refused to wash out even in the shower.

Much later that morning I was passing through the dining room when my eyes landed, not for the first time, over the Steinway.

Though it was my mother's most fervent desire that her children become artists, any so-called "creative" abilities I might have been born with started and stopped with a fairly decent flair for playing jazz piano, which I used to supplement my income during college. It was a method, a good one, too, of concealing my shyness, a way to participate and not participate at the same time. Back then, I had a pretty good singing voice too, one that many women said reminded them of a poor man's Nat King Cole, and that made them want—so they said—to take care of me. Not that I was aware that I wore my heart anywhere near my sleeve.

The baby grand was parked in one corner of the room, its forlornly curvaceous form covered over by an old king-sized bedsheet. A moment later I'd lifted up one flap of the sheet and was picking out a few bars. Finger exercises. The blues scale. The first few notes of "Mountain Greenery," followed by a little bit of "Just You, Just Me." The keys, which time had turned an odd pink-yellow hue, were covered with dust and bits of wood, and the notes had a corny, music-hall sound to them, though a tuning would take care of that. But it was still a staggeringly beautiful instrument, and I responded to the keys as I would to the embrace of an old friend I hadn't seen in years. In quick succession, I played a few choruses of the first song I'd ever learned—"Who Cares?" by the Gershwins—followed by "Silent Night," before covering the keys back up.

Caroline and I didn't keep a piano in our house; music seemed to have gone out of our lives, despite the drawerfuls of tapes, records and CDs that each of us had accumulated over time, and that had come together in their own private union when we were married. Once, when my car was in the shop, I borrowed hers. Caroline was inside the house when I turned on the engine, and the burst of music hit my ears—a blast of loud, thumping seventies dance music coming from way far over on the dial. The song, whatever it was, hit me with the force of a betrayal, as though I'd discovered the existence of a lover I knew nothing about, though when I mentioned it to Caroline later, she told me that she liked listening to music, loud, when she was by herself. "I can act like I'm seventeen again," she said. "Why in the world would you want to be seventeen again?" I joked, though when she didn't answer, I didn't pursue it.

I hadn't played the piano for years, though there was a time in my life when I'd wanted more than anything to turn professional, and to make my living—or so I imagined—playing around the country in bars and restaurants. What could I have been thinking, I wonder? Was I planning to support myself and a family on the proceeds from my tip jar? But back then my fantasies were detailed, and extravagant. I saw myself surrounded by beautiful women and men, the talented person other people called on to enliven a dull party. Shyly, but with total confidence, I'd make my way over to the bench. Do you know this one? I'd call out. Or this one? My musical role model was George Shearing, the urbane English pianist, though my plans on attaining his level of unflamboyant artistry were typically, youthfully vague. I'd applied to various conservatories, figuring that a solid background in composition and technique would benefit someone whose ultimate interest was in jazz. I got into one, too, though maybe not the best. But after college, I quit playing altogether.

despite its bold and cheerful name, Princeton was a ferociously competitive place, and as I settled into a routine of classes my freshman year, and joined an eating club, I experienced its premature social pressures as both fearsome and vaguely ridiculous. Why were people in such a hurry to act like their parents when they'd turn into them eventually anyway? At first I felt as wobbly as a calf, or a table with three legs—chipped and partial. I ventured out shyly at first, gradually gaining confidence and even a certain breeziness, and by the end of my second year, I'd become an eager-jawed, back-slapping son of the East, someone entitled by the luck of his birth to those chaotic prizes and possibilities that for many people appear too distant to contemplate. I was also spending as little time on campus as I could manage, having discovered the pleasures of New York City to the north, an hour away by commuter train. I'd established something of a ritual in fact: one weekend every month, I'd drive my little blue Subaru to New York, alone, or better, with a girl I liked and wanted to impress, and we'd spend the better part of three days eating Chinese and Indian food and going out to hear music in the clubs of Greenwich Village.

Girls were my new joy, my new discovery, and I found myself suddenly, confoundingly popular with them. "I'm juggling three women at the same time," I bragged to Sarah one night on the phone, and I was surprised when she replied, sadly, "Be nice, Jam. Don't be like most men are." Her comment blurred in my mind immediately as irrelevant—what did she know about anything? When I brought a girl home for the weekend, as I worked up the courage to do now and again, my mother would invariably take me aside sometime before dinner the first night. "You'll be in *your* bedroom, of course, Jam," she'd say, "and I've made up the guest room bed for—" and she filled in the girl's name. "Or she can sleep in Sarah's room. Whichever she prefers. There's towels and washcloths in both. And she can use whatever bathroom she wants, just maybe not your father's and mine."

She'd gaze up at me, pleased at her own industry and enthusiasm, her bright gaze intended to conceal the point of all this, that my father and she had no intention of allowing the girl and me to sleep in the same room. I don't know if he cared at all, or had definite feelings about the matter. She'd always been the face of morality, of limits, of the night and where people slept, an ensign sent by my father to translate his frowns and silences into words and rules. One time I leaned studiously against the wall, a single sneaker trained at her like a machete through brush. "Look, Mother," I said with a harsh laugh. "She and I've been sleeping together a couple of months now. I don't really think it makes a helluva lot of difference *where* we sleep. For chrissakes,'' I added.

I stood back then, proudly, suavely, a sexual athlete as well as a prince against hypocrisy, a truth-teller, someone dangerous yet essential to society, and if my mother found my new persona shocking or comical, she didn't let on. "Of *course* it doesn't matter, Jam,'' she said at last, her hand as light as a breeze on my arm. "Frankly *I* couldn't care *less* where people sleep. But there are rules in this house.'' I could practically recite the words along with her. "It doesn't have to do with me. But your father—''

"—has standards, quote unquote,'' I'd repeat wearily, feeling a familiar surge of annoyance, my mind already racing ahead, plotting how to get around this arbitrary and preposterous rule. Usually I found ways; all of us had over the years. Having less at stake, the girls were usually much more adventurous than I was, and invariably beforehand we would've worked out a signal—a clock's chime; a match struck outside a back window; midnight. Trying to keep from bursting out laughing, we'd dash down to the beach and use the sand and seagrass as a mattress. Or venture out onto the lawn under the cover of lilac-scented darkness. Or else we'd repair to the front seat of my car, whose seats, I'd recently been elated to discover, reclined flatly backward. One time, a girl and I carried half a dozen candles down to the wine cellar and placed them along the dusty, warped shelves, amid the cans of Ajax and olives and artichoke hearts, and made love amid the warped, flighty, ritualistic light. Another time, after one of these nighttime excursions, I contracted a case of poison ivy that made my face swell up like a catcher's mitt, and for the next couple of weeks, I was convinced that everybody I ran into was aware of how I'd contracted it, that my pink, flushed, itching swelling was a florid advertisement of the battle scars of licentiousness. I wasn't ever caught.

At home on weekends, though, I rarely informed my parents of the contents of my life. That I was frequently lonely, and homesick. That it was difficult to make friends. That I hadn't made the orchestra or my first two choices of eating club. That a dark-faced, prodigiously flirtatious girl, all tanned skin and flashing pearls whom I admired from afar, had pronounced me to a mutual acquaintance as "stuffy." That I'd discovered a taste for Old Grand-Dad bourbon, and the occasional Marlboro. That time had sped up; did this happen to everybody? Only a summer ago, it seemed loping and long-winded. But now the days and weeks slid past, greased and faceless and in no particular order. Oh, and I'd experienced my first two deaths—a friend, leukemia, and a classmate who attended a New Year's Eve party in New York, went out for a walk to clear his head and then disappeared, seemingly, off the face of the earth.

It was at home that I found solace, and comfort from these deaths; home, in fact, was the only place where these deaths were secondary to the idea that by putting me through an experience like this so early on in my life, these so-called friends hadn't acted like friends at all.

I was just as reticent about my brothers and sisters. Sarah was attending school out in Oregon, apprenticing at an architecture firm; Sam was in college in New York, and when fall had come around, Tom had stayed behind on St. James, where he was working odd jobs. "He's taking a year off," my mother said slightly dismissively, to anybody who would listen and then she'd change the subject. "He'll be reapplying to colleges later on. When he feels like it."

The truth was another matter. I knew, for example, that Sarah had had her second abortion by the same man, and that she found Oregon sallow and rainy, but would never admit it out of pride; that on the same theme, Jay had gotten yet another woman pregnant, his third; I knew that Tom had applied to seminary school, though he wasn't really hopeful about his chances of getting accepted. But the pinch of my own dishonesty was most acute when the subject of Sam came up. "He's doing fantastically," I said to my mother whenever she asked. "He's really taken to New York in a big way."

There was a reason for my equivocation, and it had to do with a simple fact: I didn't wish to oblige Sam to have to undergo more scrutiny than he received ordinarily. Because his uncertainties were bolder than the rest of ours, he seemed to have been selected as the representative of everything dark and ragged and extreme about our family. And so despite my increasing worries about his state of mind, I did everything in my power to help him avoid the hot, hushed glare of familial publicity.

At eighteen, he was a tall, slender, slightly fatigued looking boy. *Boy* was how he referred to himself, too, in a bemused and slightly wistful way, as though he hoped he might be mistaken for a kind of playful, casual American youth he'd never been. What I'd always found most curious about him was his peculiar combination of self-consciousness and vanity. When he was very young, maybe nine or ten years old, he was discovered with his hand laced cautiously inside the fingers of another boy, a scared stranger seated beside him at the movies, and this incident made our mother worry that he might be homosexual. While most of us found nothing wrong or fearful in this prospect, the summer before, our mother had begun encouraging all her friends to send their nieces Sam's way. At one point, it seemed to me, Sam was on the receiving end of two or three nieces a month; nothing came of any of these introductions, except that these girls, occasionally overlapping, got to meet one another.

For as long as I could remember, he'd set his sights on someday becoming an actor. He'd been in a few amateur productions at Emery, and the summer before last, he'd apprenticed at the local St. James summer repertory theater. In September, though, he'd announced he was giving up acting, and instead concentrating on writing. "Acting's too sad," he informed me. "It's boring and narcissistic. Writing's easier." He'd taken to his new vocation with a broad and somewhat ostentatious passion, toting a yellow legal pad around with him on which he jotted things down, with particular relish, it seemed, when there were other people around. "I'm writing down something Sarah just said," he'd reply self-importantly when I'd ask him what he was doing. Or, vaguely, "Jam, you just said something mildly interesting that might work somewhere."

He'd moved into a narrow one-bedroom apartment on the fifth floor of an ancient bricklike building on the Upper West Side; and if one's first apartment is supposed to reflect independence, the first thrusting expression of individual taste, then Sam was playing it safe, allowing our parents' rugs and paintings and knickknacks to guide his friends' perceptions of who he was. He'd taken—or borrowed—a series of Currier and Ives prints, which he'd hung over his fireplace; my father's old shaving mirror stood in a corner of his bedroom; porringers gleamed pointlessly from tables; and yet elsewhere there were traces of an idiosyncratic style tending toward kitsch. A plastic green Gumby on the windowsill of his bathroom. An inflatable Tennessee Tuxedo. A line of green rubber palm trees lining the mantel above his shower and puncturing the dry dirt of his ficus tree, selected because Sam had heard it needed no care (its eventual deterioration cause for humorous alarm), a family of assorted miniature plastic pink flamingoes.

"It's weird living by myself," Sam announced during one of my visits.

"What's so weird about it?"

"Well, the problem is that if you need, say, a sponge, then you have to go out to the store and buy one." Noting my bewilderment, he elaborated. "See, there always used to be a sponge there if I ever needed one. At home. Under the sink. Next to the Windex or whatever. But now if I need a sponge, or a can of, say, Lemon Pledge, I have to go out and get it."

"God, Sam," I breathed, "you poor baby."

He seemed to be enjoying New York. More so, in fact, than he liked attending college. "I have a terrible thing to admit," he told me once in a tone of guarded confidence, a few months after classes were underway. "I'm smarter than all of my professors."

In fact, he'd taken to not showing up at his classes, an attitude of disdain that almost resulted in disaster; at the end of his first year, he nearly flunked out of school, and after being summarily called before one of the deans, who told him to "shape up or ship out"—Sam liked to imitate the dean's no-nonsense delivery, punctuating it with a salute— he'd begun attending classes and spending less time traipsing around what he'd come to call, with a brusque, flippant and oddly irritating nonchalance, "the city." He'd turned into what Jay referred to as a "call-waiting kind of person." Our phone conversations were hurried and unsatisfying and punctuated by dim silences signaling incoming calls. Once, when he'd kept me waiting for a full minute, I hung up, and a minute later, Sam called me back. "Did I disconnect you?"

"No, I just got tired of waiting."

"Why?"

"Because your pecking order is so insulting. I called first, remember? Not the other guy?"

"Oh, give me a break, Jam," though from then on he made it into a habit to say, "Oops, gotta go. Let's see if this other person calling is more interesting than you are."

On one of my visits to New York, Sam took me on a tour of his neighborhood. We strolled along Riverside Park, dodging runners and rollerskaters, and at one point I asked him whether he'd heard from any of the magazines to which he'd sent his short stories. Sam yawned, or pretended to. "Yeah. Well, form letters. From-The-Editor, Thank-You-Very-Much types of things. I don't think they really understood my themes, or my characters. My stuff's kind of complicated." He paused dramatically. "But it doesn't matter anyway. I've decided to give up writing. Nobody reads anymore these days. This country's a bunch of illiterates. People's attention spans are too short. Baseball used to be the national pastime. Now it's basketball. Basketball is quicker. There's an anology there. And writers are a dime a dozen. Plus, I never know whether I should be timeless or not."

"Timeless?"

"Yeah, you know, whether or not I should write that such-and-such character went into a Dunkin' Donuts, or whether he went into a quote unquote 'doughnut shop'—i.e., if I should reflect the time I'm living in, or whether I should aim for generations to come, posterity and so forth." Readers three hundred years from then, Sam went on, would probably never have heard of Dunkin' Donuts.

"You'll be dead anyway," I said, "so it hardly matters what people think."

"Speak for yourself, Jam. Anyway, I didn't want to have to decide whether or not to be timeless, so I ended up bagging the whole thing."

His new plan was to write screenplays, though when I asked him what he knew about it, he looked at me with sympathetic pity. "Oh, come on, Jam, give me a break. It's easy. When you look at most of the junk that's being made out there, somebody like me would be heads and tails over most of that stuff." Kicking aside a stick, he seemed to grow melancholy. "The problem is, being who I am and all, I'm not sure I have the common touch. The whole unwashed-masses common-denominator thing. But—" and he brightened suddenly "—I'll just hang out with some lowlifes and write about them. See, not to be egotistical or full of hubris or anything, but I've always *known*. I don't know if I ever told you this, Jam, I doubt I have because I haven't told it to practically anybody, but I have this *thing*. This *thing* that goes on with me."

"What thing?"

Sam was hanging back on the path almost apologetically. "Just . . . this *thing*." He chose not to elaborate, and we continued walking, though when we reached the transverse that fronted the boat basin, he paused. "*It*, I call it *It*."

"It?" I said. "What are you talking about?"

"It. That thing I was talking about just a second ago. *It*."

"What's 'it'?"

"It's just this thing. This private thing. This private part of myself. I call it *it*. It's this—" Sam didn't seem to know how to explain, and then he tried again. "It is like this *thing*; I mean, not to be full of hubris or anything, but it's this feeling of knowing you have—" and defeated, he stopped again. "It's this *different*ness. This feeling that I'm going to amount to something whatever—"

"Something whatever what?" I said when he didn't finish.

"I don't know. Something *amazing*. Something *notable*. I always had this feeling growing up that I was going to be famous. Didn't you?"

"Know that about myself?"

"About me. Not to always bring it back to me, but let's."

I never thought about it, I told him. "I had enough things on my mind growing up."

"Well, I didn't. I always knew it about myself. I'd be surprised if something doesn't happen to me during my life. Something famous-oriented. Otherwise I'm misreading the zeitgeist." Something occurred to him then, and he looked confused. "Wouldn't it be depressing if I *didn't* turn out to be famous? If I turned out to be a broken, dissatisfied man? A hollowed-out failure living in an SRO somewhere? Shit, I hadn't thought of that." He resumed walking, and I followed. "Not much of a chance of that," he added quietly. "I think I'm sort of doomed, actually."

As a kid, Sam wasn't remotely snobby or class-conscious (I remembered him instead as heavy, quiet, secretive, concerned, mostly, intently, with being liked), and it was at first with amusement, and then dismay, that I'd noticed how closed-minded he'd become over the past few years. More and more I noticed that his perceptions about people were limned in the context of money and social class and even religion, though when I pointed this out to him once, he answered, somewhat sneeringly, "Don't tell me it's something you never think about, Jam."

At the start of his freshman year, in fact, he'd undergone a transformation. He took up squash, running, smoking and drinking. The earring went into storage, as did most of his old friends. He started shunning things he loved: bumper stickers, T-shirts with writing on them, brand-name liquors. "People who have nothing to prove can afford to serve cheap, no-name vodka," he told me once, piously. "Only frightened, insecure people feel like they have to serve Tanqueray." I could tell this presented a dilemma; he'd always loved Tanqueray, after all, though he seemed willing to give it up for the sake of appearances.

This transformation continued through the next year. He joined the stuffiest fraternity on campus, started spending weekends at the second and third houses of his new fratmates and casually declared an interest in the music of Cole Porter, sailboat racing and the fluctuations of the bond market, these last two especially endearing him to Father. The slim, brown, scrubbed and rather similar-looking girls he began bringing home on weekends (according to my mother) all had money, good background—right schools or both—girls who kept brightly colored Rabbits or Hondas in the city, front seats strewn with cassettes and Velamints wrappers. ("Her mother's a ——" Sam would hot-whisper to me. "Her father's the head of ——; he also owns ——; gave me keys to his place in ——; and he told me—us, whatever—I can use it anytime.")

Nothing ever came of any of these women. They lasted for about a month, then Sam invariably found something the matter with them. Too uptight, he said about one. Neurotic, was his assessment of another. A third made puns. "I don't like women who are witty and wisecracking," he told me. "It's not sexy. Besides, there isn't room for two witty, wisecracking people, and I was here first." A fourth committed the sin of liking him too much. "I hate people who're in love with me," he told me. "They're pathetic. They should get a hobby." At the same time, he seemed to have cultivated an androgyny, as though he fancied himself neither male nor female but something in-between, a third sex that combined the best characteristics of the first two. He'd always listened to music none of the rest of us did—female singers, usually at the ends of their careers, whose huge voices sailed out from the stereo like a call to revenge—and when he made tapes of these records for me, he seemed disappointed and angry that I didn't respond to them the same way he did. He was all bone, style, rolling shoulders; he seemed to subsist almost entirely on coffee and Russian cigarettes—it was rare I ever saw him eat— and increasingly, white wine and gin and tonics.

Late one September, he came out to New Jersey for a visit, and when he hopped off the train in Princeton Junction just past noontime, I thought I could smell liquor on his breath. This struck me as strange; the train had no club car that I knew of, which seemed to suggest that Sam had packed his own supply. At the entrance to my dormitory, I finally said something. "I see you've already gotten a head start."

"What do you mean?" though when I told him, Sam looked offended.

"I haven't had anything to drink, Jam."

"Well," I said slowly, "it's a mystery then. Because I can smell it coming from somewhere. Maybe it's the wind or something."

"It's not me." And yet he must have realized that this explanation didn't make much sense, and when we reached my dorm room, he amended it. "Okay, *Herr Doktor*, I admit it, I had *one*."

"One what?"

"One glass of wine. I told you before I had none because one *is* like none. Could we possibly go someplace *off* campus?" he pleaded when I suggested we have dinner at a local diner popular among students. "Someplace a tad more *up*scale, maybe?"

We wound up at a dark, low-ceilinged, practically empty Indian restaurant several blocks from the campus; it occurred to me afterward that by *upscale*, Sam meant a place that had a liquor license. "Two glasses of wine?" I inquired after he'd ordered.

"It saves time, Jam. See, I know I'm going to have a second glass after I finish the first glass, and so I might just as well order it now. Seeing that there's only one waiter, and he's old and slow. You know what your problem is, Jam? One of your problems, rather? You don't have any gusto. You don't have élan. You don't have brio. What's the point of having just one glass of wine?"

"What about the taste?"

Nobody drinks wine because of the taste, Sam replied happily. By the way, did I have any money on me, because he didn't. "Could you maybe cash a check for me later on? Or are you planning on being a charming, effervescent host and paying for everything?"

Sam was always complaining about money: he never had enough, and over dinner he told me that there were times near the end of the month when he was forced to get down on his hands and knees and parse through the shag rug in his living room in search of fallen dimes, nickels and quarters, in the hope that together they could form enough money to buy a sandwich or a six-pack of beer. It was close to the end of our meal. I was drinking tea and Sam was having a last glass of wine—I'd lost count— when he blurted out, "Jam, if I ask you something, will you be absolutely truthful, on the level, et cetera, with me?"

I wasn't sure what to expect. "Sure."

"Absolutely, no fooling, honest injun, Boy Scouts, Brownie Scouts, Girl Scouts, Mother Teresa save-the-whales-and-the-baby-seals-and-the-spotted-owls-Paul Winter-Consort-Free-Tibet-You're-on-Candid-Camera?"

"Just tell me."

"Just tell me," Sam mimicked, though not unkindly. "Jam, the thing with you is you're so bloody literal all the time." He gulped down the rest of his wine. "I wanted to know if you could lend me some money. Now wait a sec, hold your horses—" and he held up his hand "—I know, *know* what you're going to say, and I don't want to hear it. First of all is, you're going to ask me why—"

"I wasn't going to ask—"

"You were. And the answer to *that* is that I've had a bunch of car repairs recently. I had to have a tune-up. My muffler got jerked around when I went over a pothole. And keeping a car in the city is expensive."

There it was again, *the city*, as though there were only one. "Why do you even need to keep a car in New York?"

"Why? To *get* places, obviously. Why the hell do *you* need a car?"

In the country, without a reliable bus or subway system, you needed a car to get around, I told him. "It's actually kind of essential for me. Otherwise I'd have to depend on other people."

"And you don't want to. Right? Well, I don't want to depend on other people either. How the hell did we get started talking about this subject anyway?"

"You said you'd been spending a lot of money on your car."

"*Right*. And I'm short a lot. I don't even spend much money. It's not like I'm this high-flying high-liver who jets off to Rio de Janeiro every other second. I'm actually a very level-headed fellow."

"Have you asked Father?"

"I don't want to ask him. He'll just think I'm being irresponsible or something. It's part of his whole puritan thing. This whole American problem that people have about money. As though they'll get a reward in heaven if they've been misers all their lives." He mimicked our father's voice. " 'You kids don't understand the value of money. I grew up during the Depression. Why, back when I was a lad—' "

Father had never said anything remotely resembling that. "I think you've been watching too many late night movies," I said, but Sam wasn't listening.

"I grew up during the Depression, too," he went on. "My *own.*"

"You should ask Father," I said again. "And if he says no, then you could always get a part-time job."

"Oh, please, Jam. Honestly—"

"What's wrong with getting a job?"

"I don't *need* a job. I don't *have* to have a job."

"Well, if you're short of money—"

"I'm not *that* short of money."

"I know tons of people with part-time jobs."

His tone was condescending. "I'm sure you do. But I don't happen to be one of them. I'm not the sort of guy who flips hamburgers for the minimum wage, okay?"

"I'm not talking about flipping burgers. There are other jobs in the world."

"Okay, the french-fry person. The onion rings person. Mr. Clamroll. The Slurpee guy. Will that be a medium size, sir? Coming right up, you fat piece of shit. I'm not the type."

"What type is that?"

"Nine-to-five. I'd be like a spy amidst them. I'd be like Benedict Arnold. Besides, I want to leave enough time to do my writing. Otherwise I wouldn't be able to finish my screenplay. Since I'm going to become this famous, Oscar-winning screenplay writer." He leaned back in his seat, looking pleased. "Aren't you going to ask me what it's about?"

"What's it about?"

"None of your business. Writers hate it when you ask them that question. It's about *you.* No, just kidding. I told Mother I was writing a screenplay, and she said, I hope it's not about me. She *wishes.* They all wish. They say they don't want to see themselves in print but then their vanity gets the better of them. Then she said, Sam, I hope it's a *happy* movie. There's too many sad movies around. *I* know, she says, you should write a movie called *The Happy Movie*. About all the good, *happy* things that people do." Sam paused. "I don't think so. So Jam, can you?" he went on a moment later. "Couldja, wouldja?"

"Could-I-would-I what?"

Money is sap, he explained. Besides, he knew that I had some sitting in the bank that I wasn't touching "because you're such a cheapskate. I mean that in the best way. I mean that in a joshing, affectionate, fraternal sense. What's the point of having money that sits there when there's somebody in need who can use it, i.e., somebody like me?"

If his argument was constructed on the idea he'd be turned down, he was wasting his breath. "Sam," I said, "I won't lend you the money."

"Oh," he said, his face falling. "Oh. Well, then—"

"I'll *give* you the money."

"Oh, no. Jam, I want to do this *right*. Strictly a business proposition. Neither a borrower or a lender be, et cetera, and I know people aren't supposed to lend money to family members, and so on—"

"Let me finish," I said. "I'll give you the money on one condition. That someday you come across some other person who's in the same situation you are, and you give him the same amount. As a gift. That's the only string attached. Okay?"

Sam listened to all this, his face unchanging. The lashes of his eyes appeared unusually long, and it occurred to me, before I quietly banished the idea, that he was wearing mascara. "That's really nice of you, Jam," he said at last, adding earnestly, "See, I happen to be writing this big bucks screenplay right now. Possible auction, and so forth. The master plan is this: sell the thing for a million or two smackers, plus the agent's fee—"

"I thought it was minus the agent's fee."

"No, it's plus. The agent kicks in a little of his own money, as a bonus."

"Well, how do they make a living themselves?"

Sam shrugged, impatient; that wasn't the point. "As I was saying,

I'll get an agent, and sell it to one of the studios for a million bucks, plus the agent's fee. Then I'll move out to L.A. to one of those weird canyons they have out there. You know, with Joni Mitchell as my immediate neighbor. And that's just on one side of the canyon." Sam paused. "I'll let you meet all my new pals, if you're still my friend. Rather, if I haven't blown you off. Joni and Marlon, and Warren and Jack—Nicholson—and all those types of people. You can be my Boswell, Jam, if you want. You can sit around the side of my swimming pool drinking mineral water and transcribing all my pious ejaculations."

"Keep your ejaculations to yourself," I replied tiredly.

In retrospect I wish I hadn't given him any money, and not only because of the awkward position that it forced upon me. The loan wasn't the problem—he was right, in a sense, that I had money I wasn't using—but it had the effect of narrowing my vision. Now, the next few times I saw my brother, all I could see were the new things—the English suede walking shoes, the cashmere overcoat, the two new pairs of glasses—that I assumed my money had paid for. Tom, though, was more tolerant. "He's just trying to make a noise in the world," he said. "He'll be all right."

Tom's decision to attend divinity school had been greeted by an assortment of reactions. My father had said nothing; my mother, on the other hand, seemed both enthusiastic and ambivalent; religion and fanaticism went together, she must have assumed, and so did religion and madness. When I heard the news, I was surprised, in large part because the rest of us were, if not agnostics, then bored, indifferent, hair-fingering churchgoers. These days, when we were home on the holidays, we maybe attended Christmas Eve services—that is, if we were awake; a few of us trickled in on Easter Sunday; my mother, I knew, went to church whenever something bad happened, once when a friend's child had died, once when she'd learned another friend wasn't expected to recover from an illness.

Among us, only Tom had ever attended church regularly; he thought nothing of excusing himself on Sunday mornings. By nature he was contemplative; all of us had always been wary of his stillness, his silences, his concentration. He felt most at home on St. James—cities made him un-comfortable—and when he'd discovered a local college on the mainland, he'd enrolled, going back and forth on the ferry, and graduating within two years. By then, until deciding to attend divinity school, he was living full-time on the island, in a suite of rooms off the kitchen of the main house.

After twenty-three years, the island still enraptured him. He knew the water better than any of us, including my father, not just the water, but the channels, the winds, the buoys, the locations of rocks and lobster pots and tidal pools and tern and osprey nests. Growing up there were times when I'd catch him gazing out at the ocean, bare arms flat against his chest. "We live in the most beautiful place in the world," he'd say. "I can't believe anybody would ever want to live anyplace else."

He lasted at divinity school two months. "He quit," my mother told me on the phone one night, sounding mystified. "I don't know what happened, he won't talk to me about it." She had no idea what his plans were. "Maybe you can convince him—"

"Convince him what?" I asked when she didn't finish.

"Convince him that maybe the island isn't the best place for some-one his age to live. It's lonely. He should enter the real world. Like the rest of you. I mean, it's lovely and familiar there, but it's not the world," though when I repeated parts of this conversation to Tom, he laughed.

"I wonder why she thinks I'm at all interested in the world," he said. "I would've thought she knew me a little better than that."

"How do you mean you're not interested in the world?" I said.

"You don't have to sound so alarmed about it."

We were walking along the beach in St. James on a pale, chilly morning early in the winter, collecting dried skate cases. It was the after-math of a storm, and dried brown branches lay lazily twisted on the sand, along with pale rocks and a few calcified human remnants—drinking straws, cigarette butts, a few caps and twist tops. "So what's the matter with the world anyway?" I asked him.

We'd reached the end of the beach, and now we turned around. Tom didn't say anything for a long time. "I just—" he started to say, and then he stopped and tried again. "It's just that the world prides itself on things that I—this is just me speaking—that I don't find important. That I don't find essential."

"Like what?"

"Like what? Like a lot of things. Success. Security. Money. Ego. Vanity. The desire for things. Earthly things, I guess. I don't know how else to put it." He stepped carefully over a skein of fishing tackle. "I feel as though I've left the world behind."

"How do you mean you left the world?"

But he couldn't describe it any more simply than he just had. "I've just left it, that's all. I didn't want to—who would want to leave the world while they're still here?—but I have. Like a kid who leaves a room. A warm, close room that's filled with lots of colors. Lots of *stuff*. I feel as though I stepped outside that room, and I can't get back in now. I look back and I can see the room, see all the things in it, the people. But I can't get back in." He smiled ruefully. "But now that I'm outside of that room, I finally see how little it has to do with me. So—it's over. *Requiescat en pace.*"

"What does that mean?"

"It's Latin for 'rest in peace.' It's the only Latin I know."

By the room, he went on, he meant his life. And most people's lives. Recently, he said, he'd been aware of how vain he was. "I don't mean when I look at myself in the mirror. I mean it's my *will* that I want to annihilate."

"Why would you want to do that?"

The wind propelled us without struggle down the beach, as though we were being blown home. "Because I can't see things clearly otherwise. Because otherwise all I can see is me. All I can see is some reflection of myself. Because it's impossible to see things the way they really are unless you've quit clutching them and hugging them to yourself." He chucked a rock sharply into a slow wave. "I thought going to divinity school would help, but it's just more of the same thing."

He'd shown up to find only theoreticism and academics, a mixture of students hoping to get a degree in religious studies and those hoping to become ordained ministers; for the latter, which Tom had once had a thought of becoming (though he hadn't quite decided), the courses were geared toward eventually choosing your denomination. And if you were planning on ordination, you had to play your cards right. You had to campaign. To make friends with the right people. "I don't really know what I expected. Silence maybe? Solitude? Isolation? Do you know what I find keeps growing on me the most? The desire to be alone. Totally alone. And to keep still. Look out there," he added, and I did, past his finger, at the dark blue water, the few loafing boats. "Don't you find that beautiful?" I nodded shyly. "Do you know why it's so beautiful? It's beautiful because it has no value."

Expressions of exultation from other men had always made me uncomfortable, for the simple reason that I wasn't used to them. And I still didn't quite understand what Tom was talking about. "But you just said it was beautiful," I said.

"Don't you think it is? It's beautiful because it's nothing. Because it's totally neutral."

"It is *not* nothing," I said a moment later. "There's boats, there's the sailing camp, there's buoys, there's a bunch of channel markers—"

"John, it's nothing. Which is the reason why it's beautiful. Separate from what I think about it, from what you think about it, or bring to it, or what you associate with it, it's nothing."

"I still don't think it's nothing," I heard myself responding. "Anyway, so what are you planning to do here then? With your life? Mother says you won't be happy."

"Well, I don't think people are here to be happy, necessarily."

We'd reached the house, and as we crossed the lawn to the back door, I remarked that someday maybe I'd start believing in something, too. "Maybe I'll start going to church one of these days. Maybe suddenly I'll be seized by a rush of faith. Maybe I'll be walking along one day and I'll see a teardrop coming out of the eye of a Virgin Mary on somebody's lawn."

"It doesn't work that way. You know why? Because in the meantime, you're probably doing everything in your power to prevent that from ever happening. You have to make the leap for yourself. Having faith in something, you have to *want* it.'' He was silent. ''Do you know how I want to live?''

''How?''

''I want to live—and I don't know if this is possible—I want to live according to life's rules. According to life's sense of time. I want to let life alone. I want to go along as *it* goes along. And I want humility. True humility. I want to love my own nothingness. My own insignificance.''

''Tom, I don't really understand what you're talking about,'' I said miserably.

He placed his hand against my chest, and very softly, he pushed me over onto the grass. ''Hey,'' I started to say, rising, ''just because—''

''Look, you fell just the way you should have fallen.''

I was back on my feet again. ''Why'd you push me?''

''You said you didn't understand.''

''That's no reason to push me. Do it again. Do it one more time.''

''Why?''

I wanted to show him that I wasn't weak or susceptible. ''Do it again.''

''Okay.'' He did what he'd done before, one hand on my chest, and then he pushed. This time, tensed up, prepared, I didn't go down but simply wobbled there in place.

''Ha ha—'' I said.

''Relax your arms.''

''No. Because then you'll push me over.''

''Right. You're scared. And if you're scared, you won't be able to do this right.''

I gazed back at him, perplexed. ''The only reason I'm scared is because I don't want to be knocked over again.''

''You told me you wanted to do it again.''

''Yeah, but this time without *falling.*''

He started walking away. ''Wait—'' I called out, and at the top of the stairs, he turned.

''If you tighten the muscles in your arm like that, and you fall, you'll

hurt yourself," he said. "You'll break something. Now why do you keep
your arms as tight as all that? It's because you're worried about falling and
embarrassing yourself. You're scared. But see, if you keep your arms relaxed and extended, then you won't get hurt. When I push you down,
you'll go down with the push. It all has to do with the grip that you use. I
don't mean just in your arms, I mean in everything you do. Your grip is
too tight. You want a loose grip."

How had he ended up on one path, Jay another, Sarah a third, Sam
a fourth, me a fifth? The more Tom explained it to me, the less I understood, though I'd made it a habit to pretend I did. He'd "died," as he put
it with a wryness I found bleak, in order to enter into a second, richer life,
in which he was no longer interested in things or, for that matter, in
himself. It was as though he'd begun looking down on the life the rest of
us inhabited from a sudden cutting distance, and he was able now to see
patterns and intersections that the rest of us were too involved to discern.

Politely rejecting my parents' offer to live in the Menemsha house
rent-free for as long as he liked, he proceeded to buy seven acres of land
along a desolate and largely undeveloped stretch of oceanfront, with the
nearest store more than two miles away. For the past year, he'd been
working as a crewman for a local day-boat fisherman, and recently he'd
begun construction on his own house; while it was being worked on, he
lived in a trailer on the outskirts of the property, and in the spring, when
I'd come to the island for a long weekend, he gave me a tour. The house
was at the end of a long dirt road, surrounded by scrub oaks; a narrow
path through the woods led to its front door, and a hundred yards in front
of it, a clearing led onto the beach. The house was simple, uncomfortable,
a wooden A-frame. "I know it's not a lot to look at . . ." Tom said,
shrugging.

He'd furnished the rooms with the bare minimum. There was a
mattress on the floor, and next to it, a primitive lamp; there was no
television and no telephone; the porch girding the ocean was the largest
area in the house. When I remarked on the bareness of the room, Tom
replied that he'd given away a lot of things. "When I moved in, I began

dividing up clothes and books," he said. "Putting the ones I wanted in
one pile, and the ones I wanted to keep in another pile. Then I realized
how easy it would be to do without either pile." He grinned. "So I got rid
of everything."

I was fingering an old trophy he'd won in his teens from an island
tennis tournament. "What about this?"

"You can have that if you want."

"Don't you want it?"

"Why would I want it?"

"I don't know," I said. "So people'll know you were the mixed
doubles champ of the island?"

"Why would I want people to know that?"

I didn't have a good answer. "I don't know," I said a moment later,
before replacing the figurine down on the table, though I felt a wave of
confused nostalgia for the brother I'd known growing up.

Our father, to my surprise, supported Tom's decision. He seemed
pleased that one of his children had responded to St. James enough to
want to make a living there, and perhaps Tom's asceticism mimicked his
own quest for plainness, for paring down and traveling light. His own
accent changed when he came onto the island. It quieted, lost its curl and
relish, took on a simple, earnest, unornamented timbre, particularly
around working men, whose ranks his son now intended to join. A large
part of every day he spent outside. He took pleasure in tasks I found
monotonous—stripping vines from a Dutch elm, sawing fallen branches,
planting carrots and chard, scratching for quahogs in the shallows of the
bay. It appeared to be a stand against some phantom accusation of effete-
ness or sophistication. Leaning on his rake, or bent down over his saw, he
was able to convince himself that he was a simpler man than he was, and
that the tasks and responsibilities before him were clear, and ancient, and
necessary. The earth was quiet, and quietly demanding, and he was too,
and they worked in unison.

Our relationship in those years was marked still by a certain indirection and implicitness. We spoke without words. We traded whole sen-

tences through our eyes or mouths, he the teacher, me the student, and although this wordless communion originated in shyness and formality, over time for me it had become synonymous with manhood; this was how men spoke, it was pitiful, and since I was one of them, I was pitiful, too. I wanted more from him, though I couldn't signal this without feeling weak or needy. And perhaps he wanted the same, but it was too effortful. In the future I knew women would have to help me along, and I'd be obliged to resist their efforts, as my father always had. It saddened me sometimes, watching him struggle with what he wanted to say and not being able to say it, and one day I even brought it bitterly to my mother's attention, never thinking it might someday come back to me. But it had, in the summer of my senior year at college.

There were four of us that night in the house—I can't remember where my mother was; shopping, probably. In the summers, she got bored easily, and took every occasion to drive into town to pick up something she'd forgotten on an earlier trip—a tomato, a head of lettuce, a quart of milk—though I'd grown to suspect that she forgot things on purpose in order to give herself permission to go on another errand and kill another hour: the car represented mobility, sprinting; the shops, company.

Jay glanced up briefly when I came into the living room that night. He was crouched over his old teenaged guitar, fingers finding and discarding chords, strumming forced to compete with my father's tape machine, which was broadcasting low, crackling 1930s swing music, the high-pitched male vocalist sounding like a girl out of breath.

"Too loud?" my father called out at one point. He was sitting at his desk, his head bowed over the usual chaotic mess of books and loose papers, and when I told him it wasn't, he rose to turn the volume up. Eventually Sarah wandered into the room, raising one limp hand in greeting before flopping down on the couch next to Jay. But my attention wasn't focused on her, for once, but on my father, who'd taken a few tentative steps in our direction, hesitating to brace both hands against the top of the couch in a moody hunch. Then he resumed his approach, positioning himself in front of the mantelpiece, with one elbow resting along a trail of dried candle wax. He waited there for a minute or two, and then his lips parted. "So . . ."

Jay had a look of confusion in his eyes, something feline and embarrassed. "So. Weird weather out."

"Weird weather," my father repeated. "Dank." He hoped for rain. It had been threatening to pour all day, and the garden could sure use it; the ground was scorched, with patches of white visible beneath the green. Sarah began complaining about the hot weather; the single avocado with salad dressing that she'd been craving all day had turned to mush in the sun, which led to a brief discussion of dinner; what did people want? Nothing: it was too hot to eat. In the silence, a lone boat buzzed distantly across the water, like a fly.

"Your mother . . ." my father began, then stopped.

"Your mother what?" I said when he didn't finish.

"Your mother—" these were words difficult for him to say "—has on certain occasions remarked that I do not tell you guys things, quote unquote. That I do not, as it were, share with you, I believe is the expression making the rounds these days—"

"Wait, *who* said that?" I asked stupidly; he'd just told me, after all, and when he said her name again, I sank back into my seat, guilty and confused. "What do you mean, tell us things?"

"Tell you things. That I do not communicate things to you efficiently. *Feelings*, as it were. That's all." He turned toward me with a kind of stern, springing motion. "Although if you ask me, there is far too much talk of feelings in this world nowadays, and not enough thought."

His face was flushed, his ears bright purple, though whether it was because of the topic or because of the wine he'd been drinking, I wasn't sure. "I questioned her on what exactly I'm supposed to be withholding," he continued, "but she was unable to come up with any specific examples. And so." He paused. "And so I'm merely throwing this out to you," he began again, with a kind of weak politeness.

What right did she have to tell him something like that? Even if it was true, it didn't concern her; it wasn't her business. Forgetting I was the cause, I hated her suddenly; she didn't understand men, the conversations they had with one another that most women couldn't hear. They were jealous, that was all, jealous of a club they couldn't join.

"Twenty questions," my father called out suddenly.

I didn't understand. "Twenty questions what?"

"Twenty questions is what you may ask."

"Wait—we're supposed to ask *you* twenty questions?"

Confused, I was repeating the same things over and over again. That's exactly what he'd said. Twenty questions. A game none of us had played in years. If we'd ever played it at all. "Anything," my father said. "Anything at all. I will try to answer your questions to the best of my ability." With that, he took a seat on the edge of the coffee table, his legs slightly apart, his thin arms hanging past his rapt knees and madras shorts.

"Wait," I said slowly, "anything at *all?*"

My father eyed me. "You're wasting time here, John, no?" he asked.

Sarah's eyes widened, and then a moment later, she stood up. "I don't think I want to play this," she said calmly and left the room, her feet picking over the rug as lightly as a bird's. "No, hey, wait a minute, you can't leave," Jay called after her in mock entreaty, but she was gone, leaving the three of us alone.

Twenty questions. Was this for real? Was he serious? And if he was, who would start? Me? Then again, who else? Then again, the conditions were perfect. The heat helped things. Its languor unknotted my throat, and so did the wine I was drinking. I glanced over at Jay, but he was bent down, busy doing something with his sock, a piece of stage business intended to communicate that this game didn't really interest him much. I was the one who'd always complained about our father's silences, not him. This was for me, and so I knelt forward in my seat.

"How old are you?" was my first shy entry. I was just testing the waters.

Sixty-three, my father replied, after a hesitation of silent math.

"So that makes it what year were you born?"

He told us; it was a year I associated with war and heedlessness and people drinking champagne out of municipal fountains. Jay sat back on the couch, his eyes dully drifting, but I could tell he was listening, hard. I asked a few more questions such as: so when did you meet our mother? Where? How old was she? All of these he answered quickly and acutely— New York; thirty-five years earlier; age twenty-four. "You're wasting this particular opportunity," my father pointed out. "Surely you can ask better questions than that. If I were you—"

"If I were you what?"

But he crumpled up the thought like paper. "If I were you, nothing. Go ahead."

Even if he hadn't said anything about the everydayness of my questions, I was ashamed of what I'd been asking, though I knew that those first few queries functioned only as a warm-up, a foundation. Jay broke in just then, eagerly. "OK, then what are your hobbies?"

Perhaps he'd hoped to discover some private obsession, but he came up empty. Reading, gardening, listening to music was my father's swift answer, but these three we already knew, and I was starting to get impatient. Though before I had a chance to get a question in, Jay added, hastily, "So how long have we had this place?"

"Which place? This place? This property?" My brother nodded. "Good question." I sank back in my chair; it wasn't a good question, it was public record. Anybody could look up the answer in the town hall. "Quite a while," my father said finally, quoting a long-ago date.

"You know something?" I interrupted. "I don't really know anything about this place, actually. This house and all."

"Is that a question? Is that question number . . . what are we up to? Fourteen? What don't you know?"

"Just . . ." And despite myself, I waved my arms, foolishly, like a windmill. "Just . . . everything."

"Ask me sometime."

"I'm asking right now," I said boldly. "Actually, right this second I'm asking."

"And what is it that you'd like to know, exactly? Sip your wine, John, don't gulp," he added. "Savor it. Savoring is like sailing. The destination isn't nearly as important as the ride."

I glanced over at Jay for help and unanimity. "Jay, what else is it that we'd like to know?" but he shrugged.

"I'm fine," he said, "over here," and then he yawned.

Taking a deep breath, I turned to my father. "So what was the war like? And why don't you ever talk about it?"

"Which would you like me to address first?"

"What was it like?"

"Question number fifteen. What was the war like. What was the war like. It was—" my father hesitated "—it was extraordinary. Extraordinarily difficult, and extraordinarily rewarding."

"And?"

"That's question number sixteen."

" 'And' isn't question sixteen. It's just 'and.' It's just a connector." I felt a sudden groggy wave of defeat. "And the answers you're giving us aren't really answers. You asked us to ask you stuff, and all we're getting back are these monosyllabic—" I stopped, unable to form sentences anymore.

"It is indeed an experience," my father said suddenly, "to hold the body of a good friend in your arms."

There was a long silence. "Who?" I asked finally, rough-voiced, the voice of war, I must have hoped.

"No one you'd know."

"What was his name?"

He paused. "Why, I can't even remember now."

"When was that?"

"I don't recall really. Forty-three, forty-four, somewhere in there. One of those years." He glanced down suddenly at his watch, as though this game, or experiment, or whatever it was had more to do with time than with questions. "One more," he went on. "You haven't asked me anything at all." There was a plaintive quality to his voice. Was I imagining it, or did he seem hurt? "If I were you, I would have gone into much different territory."

There was so much I didn't know. I knew nothing. I didn't know about him as a boy, as an adolescent, as a young man, as a man, as a father. I didn't know what his ambitions had been once, and how he felt about losing them. Was he happy? Was he satisfied? Had it been a good enough life? Who, what person, had the twenty questions revealed? Anybody I knew? By then the wine had gone to my head; my body felt no less languid than the air in the room. And it was probably that wine, and that air languor, that gave me the courage to ask what I did next, though when the seven simple words flew out of my mouth—"Here's one: Dad—do you like us?" he looked pained, I remember. He looked me up and down, his gaze wanly impatient, and he struggled to find the words. Behind him a clarinet solo tumbled from within its orchestral clench, and all of a sudden I realized, or thought I did, why he liked jazz as much as he did. But rather than answering, he cupped his ear, his gaze shiny, boyish, beatific. "Listen to that!" he cried.

The subject of his life really never came up again. Not until a conversation that took place late in the summer about me, and the piano, which occurred the first time I brought Caroline to the island.

Following our introduction at a Manhattan party—we'd had a short, animated conversation about dogs—I assumed I'd never see Caroline again, that she'd become one of those fragile, vanished women whom you caught sight of walking through the revolving door of a department store, or striding past you in a park on another man's arm, women whose presence seemed to confirm the notion of a destiny, though one based almost exclusively on proximity. Since New York parties were the exception rather than the rule for me, and I came into the city only occasionally, it appeared our friendship had nowhere to go.

But a couple of days after I'd returned to campus, I worked up the courage to call her, suggesting we meet for a picnic lunch in the park the following weekend. When we met, the trees were in the bloom of early spring, and we spread a blanket out under the garish, aromatic blossoms and ate and drank wine for close to three hours. Caroline was from Rhode Island originally, I learned, and was getting her master's degree in psychology before embarking on her doctorate, with eventual plans to become a therapist.

"I'm kind of on the outdoorsy side," she warned me, and so when she came to New Jersey a week later, we spent a morning walking along the high brown hills of the Palisades, with the city directly ahead of us, gleaming and despondent in the morning fog. "I think I really detest hiking," I said to her afterward. "Can we not ever hike again?" By then we'd seen each other three weekends in a row, though we hadn't discussed what, if anything, this meant, an omission that had mostly to do with my shyness. But a couple of Sundays later, after I'd put her on the train at Princeton Junction and I was heading back to campus, I heard my name being called, and when I turned around, Caroline was standing there, out of breath. "I can't stand this anymore. *One* of us has to say something. It can either be me or you. And if it's not going to be you, then it'll be me." She stared at me. "I really like you a lot. I haven't liked somebody as much as this for a long time. It's scary. I think I may even be in love with you. And I didn't want to leave without one of us saying something." Then she dashed back to the train.

After that, we saw each other a great deal. I'd halfheartedly planned to get a job in New York for the summer, but the presence of a girl I liked who was living there clinched my decision, and I was able to decline my parents' offer to spend the summer on the island. As luck would have it, two months before the end of the semester, the father of one of my college classmates found me a job at a small computer magazine, copy-editing text.

I moved into a narrow third-floor studio in the West Village, and a few weeks later, I saw an ad for a Steinway baby grand for sale, which I bought on the condition that the previous owners help me lug it up the stairs. Once it was in place, I had everything I needed. My job turned out to be uninteresting and undemanding, and so I was left with a lot of free time, most of which I spent with Caroline, who was taking off the summer before beginning graduate school in the fall, and practicing on my new piano. As a newcomer to the city, I'd been occasionally over-whelmed by the racket of aspirants: sopranos and horn players, tenors, classical pianists, the gamut of artistic apprenticeships that poured out of half-opened windows, noises I found both disrupting and moving. Mostly, I was thrilled to be a part of a city where you could open your door, or your window a crack, and hear a soprano parading through her scales, though there were times, too, particularly when I was trying to read or sleep, when the sounds of saxophonists or bassoonists practicing any piece until they got it right seemed sadistic and bullying.

There was something about summer that made the city seem ineffa-bly erotic. It might have been the fungal moisture in the air, the rot of sweat and garbage creating an extra layer of intimacy among people. Once a balding, well-dressed man came up to me on the subway, with his hand out. Without thinking, I took it; did he want to shake, for some reason? But I felt only paper, and then he fled, having left me, I realized a few moments later, with a twenty-dollar bill. Who was he? I'd never know. Another time, as I was hailing a taxi to attend a mid-summer formal wedding, an attractive middle-aged woman approached me. "Dar-ling, you look very dashing," she said, "but your necktie is wrong. Didn't your daddy ever teach you how to do a bow tie knot right?"

"No," I replied, blushing, and a moment later, she'd come up be-hind me and was pressing herself against my back, at the same time fiddling with my collar. "I do my husband," she murmured. "But I can't do it from the front. I have to do it from behind." Despite the half-inch of tuxedo fabric separating us, I could clearly feel her breasts mashing up against my shoulder bones, and when she was done, she turned me around and looked me up and down. "Go wow them, sweetheart," she ordered softly, and that was the last I saw of her.

But New York in the summer could also be oppressive, and like many of its denizens, Caroline and I had begun spending our weekends out of town, usually at her parents' house in Rhode Island, where we'd bring a picnic lunch to the shore and swim in the black, rock-filled water, though one day late in the summer we took a ferry over to St. James.

If I'd felt nervous presenting Caroline to my family for the first time, it turned out I shouldn't have. From the start, she seemed to be enjoying her visit, and my mother, obviously comfortable with her, kept assigning her tasks to do. "She can wash the dishes," she said on the first or the second night, "and Jam, you can dry them." When I reminded her that the dishwasher not only worked perfectly well, but that in my experience guests weren't supposed to lift a finger when they were on vacation, my mother frowned. "She's a member of the family. Aren't you, Caroline? At least I hope you will be soon."

"Gee, Mom, hint, hint," Sam said sarcastically.

Of all of us he seemed the most entranced by Caroline's field of study. To throw a lasso of familiarity and possession around her, almost immediately he'd given her the nickname "Liner," a derivative of the last syllable of her name. "Liner, do you think I'm neurotic or psychotic? Impulsive or compulsive?" he badgered.

We were sitting on the porch on a hot twilight evening. Sarah was over on the far side of the lawn, filling up the bird feeders with corn and cracked seed, and then replacing the sugar water in the hummingbird feeder. Across the expanse of cold, blithe water, the sweep of the marsh, a few sailboats twisted and feinted on their moorings, and some thirty yards offshore, at the edge of the sandbar, a lone clammer, olive-suited from foot to waist, was bent over scratching cold-packed underwater sand. Crows sounded. They appeared now and again on the lawn, singly, like omens.

"Ugh, crows," Sam remarked. "Agents of death."

Sarah glanced up from the bird feeder. "Did you know crows can count?"

"Oh, bullshit."

"They can. They're the only animal in existence who can count."

"What about man? I mean, men?"

"Except for man."

Sam stood, stubbing out his cigarette on the porch, and, picking up his coffee cup, faced the trees. "OK, guys," he yelled, "OK, you crows. What's a hundred times seven, minus four, plus eight?" When the crows declined to answer, he turned back to Sarah. "See? They're morons."

We'd spent most of the afternoon playing tennis at one of the courts in back of the "country club," as they called it, a simple, gray-shingled building on the far western end of the island, overlooking the harbor. Sarah was on one side of the court, Jay another, the orange and green ball whizzing over the net like a volley of hot accusations. Sarah won the first set, but they'd decided to play a second, since it was still light out, and neither of them was tired. Sarah was serving. Her form was good but not interesting, and though it was only the half point of summer, she was all brown, especially her knees, though the old scabs there made the skin look in places lighter, glassed over.

"About that weird girl," my mother called over to her at one point. "If there are two people in the world who look exactly alike, same finger-prints and same handwriting and so forth, it's probably a law somewhere that they have to live on opposite sides of the country. And one or the other of you shouldn't be on this island, probably her. Your ancestors were here before practically anybody's. Anyway, she's lucky to look like you."

She was referring to a girl that my sister claimed to have spotted that morning in the center of town. Sarah was at a fruit stand, and while she was stuffing grapes into a Baggie, she noticed a girl standing in line at the salad bar who looked exactly like her, and when she returned to the house, she claimed to be undone. There were so many people in the world these days, she said, there were bound to be duplicates, and she'd just seen hers, a girl at a salad bar, and what was even worse, almost everything about the girl had annoyed her.

Sarah won the next two points. "Bravo," my mother called over. "That's a Martina-Chrissie shot."

She was damp still from sailing and swimming. Earlier, from court-side, I'd been able to make out the sailboat, a slender sliver of red and white, as the wind had picked up and suctioned it toward the shore, as well as the two of them, Sarah prim-kneed in the stern and Jay crouched, trying to maintain his balance as he strained to lift the centerboard. A few minutes later, the sailboat had swerved into the marsh grass, and Sarah had slipped into the wet, shallow salt, commencing a delicate, high-stepping wade toward the shore, the hem of her white T-shirt twisted up over her navel, and then Jay joined her, pulling the boat behind him, and when it was on the beach, he had begun dismantling the mast and the sails.

Afterward, everybody had gone in for a dip, though when Sarah kicked her flip-flops onto the sand and unzipped her jacket to show a dark red single-piece bathing suit underneath, Sam gazed at her in disgust. "Jesus, doesn't she even bother to shave under her arms anymore? Where does she think she is? Italy?"

All of us had stared rapt at those two plugs of dark hair as my sister strode into the water, foam spilling over her ankles. She swam out with a humorless stroke, past the float and the protruding, blue-tinted rocks, past the first flushed buoy, until she vanished from sight, though eventually I caught sight of her head bobbing and ducking in the middle of the bay. She didn't come back in for another forty-five minutes, rising blithely up out of the water, squeezing the drops from her hair, seemingly impervious to the fact the rest of us had been waiting for her.

Now my mother shifted in her courtside seat. "You know what I really love watching? The men on TV. Borg—"

"Borg doesn't play anymore," Sarah called over. "He took the money and ran."

"Can you blame the guy?" Jay replied.

"He does too still play."

"Mother, he does not. Borg retired about a million years ago."

My mother seemed not to have heard her. "I love Borg's concentration. The way he stands absolutely still when he's waiting for the ball to be hit to him. He doesn't let anything on."

"Mother, he quit. He got married. Though I don't know if he's married anymore."

"Well, then, he's eligible again, Sarah."

"So?"

"So—consider it. I think it would be sensational having Borg around here. He could give us all lessons. Be a good example to us."

"Oh, right. I really want to marry a man whose neck and facial muscles never move. What fun for me. A man who never reacts to anything. Meaning me. Great marriage, Mother, very promising. I can't wait." Sarah began bouncing the ball hard with the heel of her racket.

"You could name your baby Bjorn, Junior," Sam suggested.

"What if it's a girl?" I broke in.

"Bjorn could be a girl's name too," my mother said. "There's no rule. I had a beautiful cousin named Steve when I was growing up. A girl. Long blond hair, almost white. She married a man named Paul, so it was Steve and Paul on the wedding invitation, and they're still together, which is quite an accomplishment these days."

She said this in a way that suggested that a man's name on a beautiful girl could keep a marriage exhilarating. Jay and my sister, their set finished, their rackets zipped up, began walking toward us. "You're mean," Sarah was saying to Jay. "You're a mean player."

"Does anybody remember that record we had once?" Sam inquired. "When we were younger? The life of Beethoven? Narrated by Zoe Caldwell or someone like that? And the mother comes into his bedroom, and she says, Ludwig? Ludwig? And then you hear chords crashing and Zoe Caldwell goes: it was then she realized Ludwig van Beethoven was deaf. *Stone deaf.*"

"I don't really remember that," Sarah said politely.

My mother was worried about her, and when I saw my sister for the first time, all I could find to say was "You've shrunk." She'd always been slender. She'd begun a strenuous exercise program in her late teens— running, weight lifting, sit-ups—and before long, she'd boasted a narrow frame and a stomach as hard as any boy's. But now she was thin-thin— startlingly so—and her bare brown arms, obscured halfway up by the soft, childish, egg-blue ash of an antique, nearly buttonless jean jacket, looked pallid and wasted, and when I took her arm at one point, my fingers bit down into the skin as if into a fruit. "What did I just do to you?" I said, when Sarah cried out.

Her ribs, a lean shelf of lightly moving bone, pressed up against mine as she rubbed her arm, before she managed to let out a little pained laugh. "Jam, you don't know your own strength."

The most noticeable—exterior—change was her hair. She'd cut it all off and now it was an inch, maybe an inch and a half longer than mine, with a prosaic, squashed, flattened quality to the top, and the lack of it emphasized the fatigue in her face. I wasn't alone in my reaction to her appearance. Practically everybody had words, or a comment of some kind to make, except for Jay, who liked women bone-thin and who didn't see what the fuss was about. That night, my mother took me aside. "I'm concerned about Sarah, Jam," she whispered. "She looks terrible—have you talked to her at all? All she does is take long walks and wander around not eating and swim. Even her handwriting's changed."

"How can you tell that?"

"I asked her to make me out a shopping list. Of the things she wanted to eat while she was here. Wine, cheese, salad stuff, et cetera. But all she said she wanted was salad and Diet Coke. The letters were so little you could hardly read them. You'd need a magnifying glass. Sherlock Holmes." She fell silent. "I was hoping she'd said something to one of you. About what's *up*."

"What's up" was an expression of ours she'd recently adopted, and she stood there in front of me on the porch, swaying slightly, waiting for me to say something reassuring or helpful. But even if something were wrong, and I didn't know that there was, my loyalties belonged to Sarah. "I'm afraid I have no idea," I replied politely.

But I was concerned, too, though that visit I practically never saw her. She'd disappear for the afternoon, taking long hikes, once getting lost on purpose, ending up in the middle of some woods. "It was wonderful," she told me when she returned, "not knowing where I was. Everything looked the same. I had no idea if I'd find my way out." One evening she didn't bother to come home until four in the morning, and in the company of a stranger who'd seen her thumb and given her a ride. The next morning, I overheard my mother and she arguing, my mother urging her to attend the dance at the country club, and my sister resisting. "Just because you want me to end up marrying some dull businessman who drinks too much . . ." Sarah said. "Background is important," my mother replied. "For you, maybe," my sister replied sweetly.

Even her voice had changed. "You sound very democratic," my father put it, though Sam phrased it another way: she sounded like anyone, everyone. It was as though she were making a concerted effort to blend in, to shed any regionalisms that growing up might have entered into her speech, and when my father corrected her grammar once, informing her that "real" was not an adverb, she replied, faintly annoyed, "Well, it is for me." She brought up the name of her boyfriend in conversation shyly, incessantly, though none of us had ever met him, and even now I can't remember his name. "Maybe you could take —— out fishing when he comes to visit," she said to Tom, who'd come by the house with some fresh scrod. "He'd probably be really good at it." Or, "If —— ever comes here, he could help Father in the garden. He loves being outside." Sometimes it was a long shot, arbitrary and absurd, reaching its pinnacle when Sam materialized in the hallway one afternoon wearing a pair of white sneakers. "Oh," Sarah said. "—— has a pair like those."

Sam gazed back at her. "And?"

"Nothing. Just that, what I said."

His gaze didn't falter. "Um, is that supposed to mean there's a terribly interesting astrological alignment of stars going on, the fact that he and I have the same brand sneakers? I mean, Nike's a *huge* company, Sarah."

"You don't have to be sarcastic. I was just saying—oh, never mind, it doesn't matter," and a moment later she got up and left the room.

"They're a popular brand of sneakers," Sam called after her. He turned to me. "Am I nuts? Am I losing my mind? Don't a lot of people have sneakers like these? Nike's a big company, isn't it, Jam?"

The big news of that weekend, or rather, the news that reached my ears within the first six hours of my arrival, was that Sam had given up drinking. I was surprised at first to hear this; I hadn't realized the problem was anywhere near to coming to a head. But then it started making sense. I remembered a few times he'd called me on the phone, later into the night than was ordinary, and I could hear a clinking in the background, the sound of him breathing in and inhaling smoke, a cork twisting, as well as the bent, agonized, hissing pronunciation he gave to certain words. Once last summer, I'd walked into the kitchen as he was pouring a stream of vodka into his 7UP can; clearly he'd been planning on ambling out into the living room, casual as a deer, feigning a teetotaler's energetic innocence. He could always drink me under the table, but I'd accepted his explanation that because of his size—he was six-one, if he held himself up—his tolerance for alcohol was greater than most people's.

My first night home, Sam gave me a modified history of his drinking. He'd realized that it was a problem, he told me, when he discovered that once he had a beer with his midday lunch, he couldn't stop. "I'd have to drink two six-packs after that." He'd seal himself up at work, in one of the bathroom stalls. "It's like there wasn't enough beer in the world."

"At work?" I said.

"Yup. And then—" He paused, with solemn grandeur. "Nahh, you don't want to hear about it."

"Tell me."

He was glumly silent. "Well, I started getting these blackouts. Where you can't remember what it was you did the night before. I mean, people would tell me what a laugh riot I'd been at such-and-such a party, and I wouldn't have the foggiest idea what in the world they were talking about. Anyway, the point is, I joined A.A. It's great, actually. They have all these steps."

I had no notion of Alcoholics Anonymous other than a conventional and probably ill-informed one: I imagined a group of old crew-cutted men, retired mariners, no doubt, sitting around in a long-faced circle, smoking cigarettes. "So, are you the youngest person there?"

"Hardly. It's kind of hip, if you want to know the truth. There's lots of famous people there. There's—" and casually he named two television actresses and a well-known pop singer.

"I thought it was supposed to be anonymous."

"Oh, it is. Of course it is. But I just thought you might like to know who your little bro is keeping company with, that's all."

He seemed prouder of the fact that he was consorting with famous drunks than anything else, and I saw that the proximity to celebrity, even under the guise of recovery, still exerted a fascination for him. When I commented on this, though, Sam said, "No, no. I'm an alcoholic, just like they are. I have a disease."

"A disease?" I said.

"It *is* a disease, Jam."

"I thought cancer was a disease. I thought tuberculosis was a disease—"

"Well, alcoholism is too," Sam said crossly, adding, "Do you know what really brought me over the top? The thing that really made me want to stop?"

The news of his recovery, if that was the right word for it, traveled slowly through the members of our family; Sam seemed to be telling people shyly, one on one, and later he reported back the various reactions. "Mother said she was 'very proud of me,' quote unquote. Father didn't seem to give a damn," and when I told him that I doubted this, he shook his head. "It's *true*. He doesn't notice *anything*. He didn't notice I used to drink too much in the first place, so why in the world should he care if I've stopped?"

"Cut him some slack, Sam," I said. "None of us really knew. I mean, I knew you drank too much sometimes, but I didn't know it had become this big deal for you. You were always so secretive about it."

The word seemed to anger him. *"Private.* I was *discreet. Gentlemanly.* There's a big difference. Anyhow, Father didn't give a damn. Take my word for it. Jay didn't believe me. You're the only one who's listening to me. Who *cares."*

The idea of this made tears appear, unexpectedly, in his eyes, and a second later my own eyes followed suit; since childhood, I'd invariably been reduced to tears by the sight of one of my brothers or my sister in need. "I'm proud of you, Sam," I said at last. "I think it's great. I think it takes a lot of character."

The night before he stopped drinking, he told me, had been like most other nights in his life. He'd come home from work, having picked up two six-packs of Molson along the way, bolted the door to his apartment, turned on the TV and began to drink. He was supposed to meet somebody for dinner, but at the last minute he'd cancelled, pleading a migraine, which wasn't true. "Booze made me lie," he explained sheepishly. "I don't know why." He'd fallen asleep early that night, but not before leaving one or two empty sixteen-ounce beer cans by his bedside, next to his answering machine, "so if I had to take a leak during the night, I wouldn't have to get up and go all the way to the bathroom. Instead, I could just reach on over and pee into one of the cans."

But sometime during the night, he'd woken up, still half-drunk, his throat dry, and needing the relief of liquid. He'd reached for one of the beer cans, and forgetting that it was filled to the brim with cigarette ashes and his own urine, swallowed the contents. Since then—it had been eight months—he hadn't had a single drink.

"So what do you think's up with Sarah?" I remarked to Caroline later that week.

"*Up* with her?"

"Or is everybody just making stuff up?" Caroline, perched before the dresser in the guest room, didn't answer immediately. "You didn't really know her when she was growing up, but here was this person who had men *panting* after her. She exuded this—what's that word—*pheromone*. We're talking major cool cucumber. She slept with tons of men, and she seemed completely indifferent to all of them."

"You say that as though you're proud of it."

"Well, I was. *Once*. In a perverse kind of way. It's not an altogether unflattering thing when men find your sister attractive. And now she's what—" I paused. "What *is* she?"

"Well," Caroline said in a sensible voice, "you said she's changed but you haven't really told me how she's changed."

"Well, what about the thing with the camera?" I inquired. "Don't you think that was a little bit off the wall?"

A couple of nights earlier, my mother had ordered everybody outdoors. She wanted to take a group photograph, for posterity's sake, she told us, and so we filed out onto the porch, lining up along the bottom steps, where the earth begins to slope toward the marsh. The early evening was clear and beautiful, the water placid, the far islands washed with the sour yellow of a dying sun. "All right, you little rascals—" Sam began, but he was interrupted by my mother.

"Jay, you go in back because you're the tallest. Jam, you come down here in front. And put your arm around Caroline as though you like her—"

"I *do* like her," I replied, annoyed.

"Well—why don't you act like it? Put your arm around her. Take your glasses off, too, you look like your father. You're on vacation. *Relax.* Where's Sarah?"

Though she'd been with us at the dinner table only a minute earlier, she was now nowhere to be found. I was sent inside the house to find her, and did, finally, in the back bathroom. "Come on, Sar," I said. "They're taking a group shot."

"Tell everybody to go ahead without me" came her muffled voice.

"Yeah, but we *need* you. To be in the picture. That's why it's called a group shot."

"I don't want to have my picture taken."

I expected her to say more, and when there was a long silence, I knocked on the bathroom door again.

"Jam, *no.* Tell other people to go ahead without me."

"We *need* you, honey. You're indispensable." When there was no reply, I knocked one more time, and this time the door opened, and Sarah appeared in the glum light, toweling off her face. "John, look. I don't want to be in any pictures. I look too ugly."

"Ugly?" The word took me aback. "You?"

"No. Daffy Duck. Yes. Me. Your sister. Me."

"What are you talking about? You couldn't look ugly if you tried."

"Well, you *would* say that. You are my brother, after all."

Distantly, through various half-opened windows, I heard my name being called, faintly, shrilly. "It's just one picture," I said. "Come on. It'd mean a lot to everybody. We haven't all been home like this for ages."

"Jam, no. I said no. I look too awful. I don't want to be photographed looking the way I do."

Much later that night, I was sitting on the porch, sharing a beer with Jay and batting away mosquitoes, when I heard voices coming from the kitchen, and when I went inside to see what was going on, there were Sam and Sarah in front of the refrigerator. My sister looked furious.

"*Give* it to me, Sam. Right now. Sam, *give* it to me."

"Give what to you?"

"Give me the camera, please—"

"What's going on here?" I interrupted.

Sarah turned to me. "He took a picture of me when I wasn't looking. I *said* I don't want to have any pictures of me taken."

Sam tried to make a joke of it. "OK, what hand is it in?" but clearly Sarah was in no mood for games, and a moment later, tantalizingly, he produced the camera from behind his back. "What are you going to do with it?"

"I'll get the film developed tomorrow. I'll take out the ones of me and give you back the rest."

"Oh, Jesus Christ, what's the point?" Sam sounded disgusted. When Sarah didn't answer, he added, "Just don't expose the film or anything retarded like that."

Caroline was at the closet now, riffling through her clothes. "She's mad at him anyway," I went on, "because Sam borrowed some money from her six months ago and he hasn't paid her back yet. But he hasn't paid any of us back yet any of the money he's borrowed. I think he must wish there were still patronesses in the world. Perfumed women with pearl necklaces who'd give him a thousand dollars a week just for be-ing—" the words escaped me "—just for being *interesting.*"

"That was strange about the photograph," Caroline said. "I mean, granted. Then again, I don't really like having my picture taken very much, either."

"Well, you haven't told me what you think's going on with Sarah."

"I can't believe you're asking me that."

"Asking you what?"

"For a *diagnosis*. What do you think I do, sit around pathologizing everybody? Is that why you invited me here? And then write you up a report? I'm on vacation too, remember?"

"She's just so fragile, that's all. She's gotten to be so cautious."

"Well, that's what happens to women. Isn't that what they say? About women doing a lot of crazy, risky, fun things when they're young? Then something happens. They stop making waves. They go undercover. They quit excelling. The boys slide ahead. Even if they don't deserve to. How's this dress?" Caroline added. "Is it all right?"

I didn't really bother to look. "It looks fine to me."

"How do you think my hair looks on this side? Is it too pixieish and weird?"

"Whichever feels right," and I started lacing up my shoes, though after a minute had gone by, I realized that Caroline's eyes were fixed on me.

"You know," she said, "sometimes I don't like men very much."

Sarah was already up when I went into the kitchen the next morning, sitting at the table drinking some kind of dark tea, her hair damp and unbrushed, and she looked up surprised when I came in and poured myself a cup of coffee. When I asked her how she'd slept, she made a face.

"Terrible. I woke up at about three in the morning. Maybe you heard me. I guess it rained. There was a mist outdoors. You could barely see in front of you. I went for a walk—"

"You went for a walk in the middle of the night?"

She nodded. "And when I came back, I fell across Jay's car. It was that hard to see. I tripped. I crashed my wrist," though when she held up her bare, T-shirted arm, I couldn't discern any marks, and told her as much.

"I know," she said. "That's because I've quit bruising."

A terrible smell, like boiling algae, was coming from the stove. "What do you mean?"

"This program I'm involved with."

"Program?"

"Yeah, I go to this center out in Portland. And they make you up a program that's adjusted to me in particular. It's a control sort of thing. You take control of every aspect of your life, your body, what you eat, how you run things. It's a mixture of vitamins and lots of exercise and a formula you cook up. I call it the system."

"The system," I repeated. "It sounds sort of sci-fi."

"It thickens your blood, the formula. You take it three times a day. So if you fall down or trip or something it doesn't affect you at all. I've reached a point now where I could fall down a hundred flights of stairs and then get up, walk around. Remember when you squeezed my arm the other day? See, there are no marks—" and she held out her arms, both of which looked like dark, sanded wood.

"Maybe it's all a coincidence," I suggested.

"What is?"

"The fact your skin's so unmarked, but then you're also on this whacked-out system. The system," I corrected myself.

"Coincidences don't happen to me anymore, Jam. They used to, but they don't now. Not since I started on the system. And it's not whacked-out. In fact," she went on, "I don't think I've said the words 'What a coincidence' about anything for a long time. Then you realize all the expression was, was a way of making you think that somewhere there's a blueprint, and coincidences are its human expression. So no, in answer to that, no," and we were interrupted just then by my mother's arrival.

"What's everybody doing up so early?"

Sarah said faintly, "Hard sleeping."

"You couldn't sleep? Why's that? Why couldn't you sleep? Let's analyze this. Why that is. Your not being able to sleep," and she came up behind Sarah, and placed both her hands on the chair.

"Let's not analyze this, Mother," Sarah said in a pleasant, distant voice. "It was hot, that's all."

"You look tired. Do you feel exhausted?"

"I'm in great shape."

"I know you are, Sarah; I'm not, what's the word, challenging you on your good shape."

Later that morning, Sam disappeared into the basement and came back up holding a record album. "It's not Zoe Caldwell after all," he announced, "I was wrong, for once," and a few minutes later, the first chords of the Sixth Symphony filled the room, followed by a trained, slightly fatuous lecturing female voice. For the next hour, I learned more about Beethoven than I'd ever known before. That he had no close friends. That he was distrustful of women. That he was a shrewd businessman who died during a thunderstorm, clenching his fist. All Beethoven's brothers were played by one actor, and they kept saying things like "Ludwig, don't be so flinty and bearish." When the mother discovered her son's deafness, Sam's eyes widened. *"Stone deaf!"* he screamed along with Mrs. Beethoven.

Caroline and I spent the rest of the week sailing, swimming, playing tennis and miniature golf and eating out. The first night of our visit, I stole into her room, ostensibly to wish her a good sleep, gazing at her on the familiar guest bed, in her nightgown, and wanting more than anything to climb under the sheets with her, though it was just too risky. I was already keenly, slyly aware of how having her there had altered my relationship with my family. It was as though I'd brought home a representative, an agent, through which all future communication would now be filtered, and this was fitting and good; the bemused fatigue in my parents' manner signified to me an admission that after only three months Caroline knew me better than they ever could.

One night that week, all of us piled into the station wagon and drove the mile and a half to the country club, where a dance was being held in honor of the end of summer. People were supposed to show up in costume—the theme was freedom—and though none of us had bothered, several women in the crowd came as the Statue of Liberty—togas, cowboy boots, lime-green Styrofoam crowns and makeshift, foil-skinned lanterns. The clubhouse was packed, illuminated with yellow bulbs, the extra strands draped loosely in the branches of the surrounding trees and along the cottony tops of the tennis nets. Three black grills were set up along the porch. A group of children, the girls in long gypsy dresses, the boys with long light hair, were traipsing along the shoreline, chatting and giggling, though the tide was low. Five hundred yards away, I could smell the fermenting rocks and starfish.

Sarah, who'd earlier relented and agreed to come out with us, on the condition she could walk—she was contemptuous when the rest of us didn't do the same—made her entrance after dinner, wearing a tight black dress and huge copper earrings, and when she saw us, she waved disinterestedly, finding a seat not at our table but next to a muscular, black-haired, pale-skinned man who appeared to have come alone. Presently, he asked her to dance, because soon they both rose up and made their way toward the center of the room.

Sam leaned over to me. "I didn't know she was going through a foreigner phase. Where do you suppose this one's from? Yemen? What about her boyfriend?"

The two of them began dancing, and I don't think I'd ever seen a dance as peculiar as this one. The man, whoever he was, held my sister's wrists tightly, as though she infuriated him; then he ducked behind her, and when Sarah swung around to face him, he turned his back to her, before grasping her two wrists again, pumping them up and down in what resembled a parody of welcome.

Sam was revved up by then. "Actually, he's not from Yemen. I think actually he might be from Semen. A small Adriatic port, famous for its white sandy beaches. What the hell does that get-up she's wearing have to do with freedom? She looks like a goddamn mortician." A few minutes later, he excused himself, saying he was going back home, he'd walk. "Everybody's getting smashed. I don't think it's all that good for me to be here."

"Is it really hard not to?" I asked gently. Sam shook his head. "No." But a moment later, he pulled a chocolate bar out of his pocket. "They say when you feel the urge you should eat something sweet. It tricks your body. So I'll just down this baby and gain two hundred pounds, but at least I'll be a sober little fatso."

The rest of us stayed, ate dinner. Caroline asked me to dance, but I demurred, fearful other people might laugh at me; it was hard for me to let loose among a group of strangers, I told her afterward. We didn't get home until around midnight, and Sam met me in the hallway, his eyes huge, glazed. "You should have been here."

"Why, what?"

Sarah, it seemed, had returned to the house with her dance partner—Victor, his name turned out to be. Both of them seemed surprised, and faintly irritated, to find Sam at home, but they proceeded outside onto the porch, where they downed a few Molsons and, according to my brother, started kissing. They had the radio on loudly, and then, Sam said, "Victor stood up all of a sudden—"

"Wait," I said, "were you spying on them?"

"*Spying* is an ugly word. The marsh has good acoustics, that's all I'll say." Victor, he went on, stood up and told Sarah that the song playing on the radio was one that he'd written. "This is *my* song," he kept saying. "I wrote this song." Then, Sam continued, he claimed he'd written a bunch of popular songs, songs other people claimed to have authored— "We Are the World" and "Isn't She Lovely" and "Winchester Cathedral" and so on. He claimed he was going to sue all the guilty parties, and when the trial went to jury—he didn't know when that was going to be—heads would roll. "Oh, yes," Sam said, "he also told her he'd written the theme from 'Wagon Train,' that old TV show. So you know what I did?" He paused triumphantly. "I put on the Beethoven record, really loudly, and that did it. He left. He must have thought we were all nuts, though actually he was the nuts one. Crazies know Sarah'll like them, so they gravitate to her. And vice versa."

The night before we were scheduled to return to New York, Caroline and I went out to dinner at a local clam bar, and when we came back home, she took a shower while I ventured into the living room, where to my surprise my father was still awake, sitting at the end of the couch, leafing through a book. "Hey," I said, as casually as I could.

He glanced up. "Good fun?"

"Good fun," I said, trying not to sound as though I were mimicking him, and eventually taking a seat on the piano bench. We sat there in silence, long past the time when he should have turned the page of his book, and then he looked up. "Feel free to play, it doesn't bother me."

Slowly, I started to play "Skylark" by Hoagy Carmichael, trying to concentrate on the song and not on his reaction, though nonetheless I found myself glancing up every few seconds and checking his face. "So what do you think of old Caroline?" I inquired shyly when I was midway through the song.

"Caroline?" He paused. "She seems like a keeper. That's too fast," he added.

"What's too fast?"

"It's a melancholic song. You're playing it much too fast."

I abandoned "Skylark" and moved on to something else, a version of "Swanee," replete with flourishes, though when I was done, he didn't say anything. "Is there anything else you'd like to hear from my amazing repertory?" I asked gaily.

"Repertory?"

"You know, I've started playing here and there."

"What's here and there?"

"Oh, you know, parties. Weddings."

"You played at your brother's wedding. Is that what you mean?"

"Well, yeah, as a matter of fact," I said, annoyed. After a rapid courtship, Jay had been married a year earlier in Louisville, Kentucky, the bride's hometown. To my surprise and pleasure, he'd asked me to play the piano during the rehearsal dinner, and I had, though as the night progressed, the Southerners began calling out songs I'd never heard of; by the early morning, a group of them was clustered around the piano belting out Dixie beer songs.

Now my father seemed to be implying that nepotism had gotten me that job, as opposed to any innate ability. "And at a couple of other weddings, too," I went on stubbornly.

"Friends of yours?"

"Friends of mine?"

"The individuals who were married—were they your friends?"

"Well, yes." What was he getting at? "Friends, acquaintances, whatever." I brought my legs out from behind the piano and stretched them. "I mean, they may be my friends, but it's professional as well. It's not like 'We happen to know this guy who plays the piano, he's a friend of ours, wouldn't it be nice if he played.' It's not like that. I get paid for it and everything. Two hundred dollars each time."

The lighting in the room was such that half of my father's face was in shadow, the other half illuminated by the pale light coming from the kitchen. As if to reconcile both halves, he stood, and presently began to make his way around the room slowly, with almost deliberate courtesy. Halting in front of the sliding doors, he peered briefly at his own reflection, before turning suddenly. "Have you ever thought about teaching?"

The words didn't register at once. "Teaching?"

"Yes. Teaching."

"Teaching what? You mean, piano?"

"Or something else. Theory. Composition. Perhaps something more on the academic side of things. But teaching."

I was speechless for a long time, and when I opened my mouth, the words came out with a stinging, unintended harshness. "Why in the world would I ever think about teaching?"

"Why? Why not?"

"Father, I don't really see how we got from my sitting here playing the piano to *teaching*."

"It's simply that you have a young lady with you this weekend, and if you intend to get serious, as the lingo goes, I have to wonder how you intend to support yourself, as well as her."

I sat there on the piano bench, knotted, paralyzed. How could I tell him, without hurting his feelings, that I considered myself on the other side of teaching? The far side? The side of color, as opposed to the black-and-white side? That teaching represented the side of critics, and not artists? That I had no intention of becoming what he was? I was different. I was a musician, a man of the senses. "I don't know," I said stiffly. "I mean, I have some money, right?"

"Not enough to live on, certainly."

"Well, it's enough to—"

"Is music something you have plans to pursue?"

His interrogation was making me cagey. "Well, sure. I mean, I'd like to if I can, possibly."

"Certainly not as a career, though."

"Well, certainly *yes* as a career."

"From what I can tell, it's an insecure life."

"What is?"

"The life of a musician. And they're not very *nice* people. Or intelligent people." He paused. "You are."

"Oh, thanks. Thanks a lot. A lot of things are insecure, though," I added. "A lot of jobs and things and what people do in the world. And I love old music. You know, *your* music."

Lightly, he cleared his throat. "I might remind you that it was not old music when it was written, and when I first heard it. That what is a so-called 'oldie' to you was when I first heard it, what happened to be on the radio at the time. I'm simply trying to suggest to you that it might be useful to have a trade. A skill. Is all that I'm trying to suggest to you. For those times when the muse has left town, as it were."

It was as though he'd just set a part of me aflame, and I could only sit back helplessly, watching it burn. "A trade," I repeated dully. The word sounded vaguely Victorian, as though he'd suggested I think about becoming a scrivener. "Well, Father, we'll see what happens, won't we?" By then I was conscious of every nuance passing through my voice, and I attempted to steer the conversation away from me. "Why did *you* ever want to teach? I mean, didn't you ever want to do anything else in your life?"

As soon as I'd asked it, I wanted to repeal the question, touching as it did upon the possibility of receiving an answer I didn't want to hear. But I'd said it, and now I pressed forward in an appeal to his own early ambitions. "Mother told me you once wrote a book."

"That's correct."

"Well, so—didn't *you* want to do something with that, maybe?"

He didn't answer me at once. Instead, he crossed his hands in front of the buckle of his belt and gazed out the window; from behind, he looked as courtly as an usher. The night was black; I knew that he couldn't see past the glass, only the reflection of what was in the room behind him, his own form and whatever it suggested to him, the tools of the fireplace, the candles on the mantel, the coffee table, me, maybe, rigid on the bench. "I did not have what it took," he said finally.

He was addressing his reflection, and the words were rhythmic, clear, harsh. "I did not have what it *took,*" he said again, "and that came as a blow to my twenty-three-year-old self, but it was a fact I had to face."

"I don't understand."

"All I am saying is that plans can go awry. Ambitions can be leveled. And it's not an altogether bad thing when that happens. It sounds worse than one might think. One goes on. New interests come up, old interests die. These things mean less as you grow older."

"Yeah, I guess maybe they do. They must," I corrected, "have to." My stomach was weakly twirling. "Plans. Being unpredictable and all."

"I am trying to tell you, in the most charitable way I know how, and perhaps this is something that is not my responsibility or even within my ken to tell you, but in order—"

"I'm sorry, what?" I'd cupped one hand to my ear, hoping it would lighten the mood in the room, but he didn't appear to notice. It was a family joke that he could be long-winded at times.

"—in order to spare you any possible hurt later on, that you do not have what it takes either."

At first I didn't understand; it didn't, or wouldn't, sink in. "I'm sorry, *what* do you mean?"

"Jesus, it's hard trying to protect your children from life." His voice had risen again. *"Hard,"* he went on. "Life is hard." He turned toward the mantelpiece, his voice muffled. "I know a little something about music, you know."

When he didn't continue, I prodded him. "Yes? And—?"

"You don't have what it takes, that's all I'm trying to suggest. If I were to give you a grade as a pianist, which I know you did not ask me to do, I would give you a *B*-minus, C-plus."

He went on, the words blurring, thick and dim. He feared, he said, that I was too intelligent to pursue, as he put it, a quote unquote artistic life. Life was unpredictable enough without entering an unpredictable profession. There was a lot of competition out there, and not many spots. And it was not good to "lose" yourself in any art; your critical faculties became compromised. "You're too intelligent," he repeated, yet at that moment it was a compliment I took as the worst insult he could ever have delivered; it was as though he'd reached out and dislocated my shoulder. At that moment, I wanted nothing more than to be groping and stupid. "Well," I said at last, "gee whiz, Dad, thanks a lot for the vote of confidence."

His voice was polite. "I knew you would take what I said the wrong way. It's not a vote of no confidence in you, John Knowles, my son, but a vote of no confidence in the musical abilities you were born, or in this case, *not* born with. Like me, you simply don't have what it takes, that's all. It's something we have in common." Almost imperceptibly, he bowed in my direction. "If I've *wounded* you, as the expression goes, I'm sorry. But I'd rather you hear it from me than from a stranger."

"So you're telling me not even to try," I said slowly, after a moment. "Just to give it up. Everything I know. Everything I've learned. All the practicing I've ever done. Father, I've gotten into a conservatory—"

"Conservatories are businesses, just like any other business. They're in the business of making money. Feeding off the aspirations of people such as yourself. Piranhas, most of them are." He was silent. "I'm telling you that now is the time to consider other options. While you've still got the time. You're still young. There is nothing inglorious about the profession of teacher. It's not particularly remunerative—i.e., the pay's lousy—but it's been good work for me, and rewarding. I've always enjoyed it. Though it's hard, you know—it's harder than it looks." He made a little noise somewhere between a throat-clearing and a chuckle. "The good news is you get the summers off."

But I couldn't stand to look at him, even when in the reflecting glass of the sliding door I saw his figure come nearer to the piano. Nor, for some reason, was I able to look down at my hands, though I felt suddenly, passionately sorry for them. The keys stretched out in front of me like a mouth, a grin, a smirk, a thousand teeth. My father was by my side now, his breathing steady, so close that I could see myself upside-down in his glasses and watch as his hand, strangely warm, came down to touch my shoulder. "You get the summers off," he repeated.

Caroline and I stayed up late the next night, staring at the sky and the dark water from the protection of porch chairs. "You know, you shut down around them," she said at one point.

"Around who?"

"Who do you think?"

"I do not. Wait, *who* do I shut down around?"

"Your family," and when I shook my head, she added, "You don't even realize it, probably. I'm not saying there's anything wrong with it, I just notice it, that's all. Did something happen? Like did they take you aside and tell you they hated me?"

"Not that at all. It's like you've been here forever."

"Oh, like some old sock, you mean."

"I meant that as a compliment."

"Then what? Or are you always this moody when you're here? Because it makes me think I've done something wrong. Even if it has nothing to do with me. Maybe it's a girl thing."

"I'm always this way when I'm here," I assured her. "It's the heat. It's the hundred percent humidity. Nothing moving. Mosquitoes, heat, no breeze, no anything."

"Did something happen between you and your father?"

She was too acute for her own good sometimes. I gazed over at her in mock surprise, though her face showed she knew nothing. "Why?"

"Because you went out of your way to avoid him at dinner—"

"I did not."

"Well, then, if not to avoid him, to *not* address him."

"Maybe I didn't have anything to say."

She was silent. "Why doesn't he call you Jam, like everybody else?"

"Because he thinks nicknames are sentimental. And they are."

"Well, none of this is for me to say."

"What isn't for you to say?" Like most people, I was intrigued by objective evaluations about familiar things and people, by a stranger's take on us.

"He just tries to be nice to you," Caroline said a moment later, "and you don't let him. He tries so hard. Really. And I feel sorry for him. He tries, but you might as well have a No Trespassing sign on your forehead."

"He's the one who shuts *me* out."

"You wouldn't even play the piano tonight when he wanted you to."

"Well, Caroline," I said coldly, "I'm not a circus performer."

It had happened after dinner. We were settled in the living room, drinking coffee, chatting about this and that, when my father, who was standing rather carelessly in front of the darkened fireplace, spoke. "Wouldn't it be nice to hear a little ivory? John, will you indulge an old man's weakness?"

There was a long silence during which I shifted in my seat, meeting no one's eyes, before I finally met his firm, polite glance. In what perverse spirit was he asking me to play? Was this an attempt to humiliate me in front of Caroline and everybody else? A test designed to find out whether I'd taken his words to heart? Was he feeling remorseful about what he'd said earlier? No, I realized a moment later. No to all those questions. I think—or so it seemed—he genuinely wanted to hear me play. But so much of my identity was based on what I'd assumed to be my talent, and he'd convinced me I had none. "Nope," I said softly. "I'm a terrible piano player."

"You're a fabulous piano player, Jam," my mother broke in.

"No, I'm not." At that moment I wanted so much to glare at my father, but I couldn't; my eyes ended up scanning the rug. "I'm a lousy piano player."

"That doesn't mean you can't play right now," Sam piped in.

"Yes," I said, and I stood, as if distracted by an inspiration that had nothing to do with any of them, and stretched. "It does mean I can't play."

Now Caroline twisted around in her porch chair to face me worriedly. "You didn't mean what you said earlier about being lousy, did you? Jam, you're a *wonderful* pianist." I thought I heard, or imagined, a tentativeness in her voice, though that day everything in the world seemed to me tentative and askew.

"How do you know? Are you a music expert? Do you have a Ph.D. in musicology?"

"No, but I'm a listener. And I know I love what I hear when you play." Caroline looked confused. "But when did all this come—"

I told her I didn't want to talk about it, and for the next fifteen years we didn't.

4.

the temperature in the house was unpredictable. It rose and fell in minute bursts, sometimes changing during the night in midstream from hot puffy air to frigid gusting. Making my way around the house was a little like paddling along the shore of the bay in the summertime, with its liquid pockets of skin-cutting cold interrupted a few feet later on with regions of unanticipated warmth. Even when I toyed with the dial on the wall, it seemed to have little effect on the temperature.

Looking back on those first days at the house, I was no doubt in the midst of a kind of tribal dislocation. The sights inside the house—the old carpeting, the bells and switches of the old maid buzzer system high on the kitchen wall, the few cups and saucers in the pantry cupboard—filled me with the gingerly homesickness I felt as a boy staying overnight at a friend's house, except this time it was twenty years later, and I was at a house that I knew and loved. Several times, I had the sensation that I was seeing the house as it was not meant to be seen, but as it was meant to be imagined from a still point miles away, that the house should remain someone's idea of local scenery glimpsed from the back window of a car. There were other times, though, when I felt the heat of the sun—through the glass of the living room window, making a puddle on a patch of floorboard, like something spilled, or on one side of my face when I was sitting on the couch—and it made me feel so drowsy, and forgetful, that I could have practically fallen asleep.

I spent most of my third morning in town, where, among other things, I loaded up on more groceries and coffee and spring water (the water on the island is notoriously seedy) and a couple of heavy shirts, since I'd brought along with me no more than a single change of clothing. Afterward, I stopped at a small harbor restaurant for lunch. It was a cramped, dark-ceilinged place that in recent years had been claimed by tourists and day-trippers. Traces of the whaling tavern it had once been hung from the walls—shellacked models of swordfish and tunas, lips peeled back in sticky, ferocious grins, as well as a few artificially colorized photographs of island life around the turn of the century, back when there'd been a single stop sign, unpaved roads, a fish man and a milkman, and the island was of little interest to anybody but duck hunters. Irish girls came and went, softly padding in their white sneakers; in recent years they'd dominated the local year-round workforce, seeking sunlight, beer and a year or two in America. The color TV above the bar was still tracking the storm, whose center was thought to be hovering somewhere off Cape Hatteras.

I overheard a man at the bar say that that there were nineteen inches of snow on the ground, that the storm was expected to break a 105-year-old record, that the residents of the houses evacuated on Ames Point had set up temporary shop in the high school gym, that there'd been a three-car pile-up on Mann's Road, though no one was hurt, and that there was still no ferry or airplane service off the island.

After lunch, I lugged the groceries back to the house, and although

it had stopped snowing—the skies were overcast, the temperature dropping—the scent of fire smoke in the air created a festive feeling of
hibernation, of people hunkering down for the winter, not to show their
faces again until spring. In the country the snow tends to maintain its
innocence for a while after it's fallen, and the whiteness covering the
fields and the marshes and branches of the trees had the effect of blanket-
ing all my apprehensions.

Back at the house, I took a nap. The phone rang twice, an ugly,
unprotected sound that it took me a few moments to realize derived from
the scarcity of furniture and paintings in the house. I didn't answer it.
Nobody knew I was on the island, and even if they had, I had no interest
in talking to anybody. Later that day, I spent a couple of hours playing the
piano, though I no longer trusted what I heard coming from the keys as
great, or good, or even adequate. Not for the first time, it struck me that
not-very-good players such as me could fool themselves into thinking
they were just as good as the talented, and that the only difference between a successful man and an unsuccessful one was timing, or luck, or
insider's connections. I was too close to my life, too four-square within it
to be much good as an artist. How could a person hope to be any good, or
create anything, if he didn't see life clearly?

Tom, on the other hand, had always led what I considered an ideal
life for an artist. He was alone, unhindered by possessions and other
people. His life was clean, transparent. His war had been with himself,
not with strangers. He could see the world clearly, as it was, and I
couldn't, not in my vanity, not with the warm breath of friends and
family around me; and in the days and months after the conversation with
my father, I resolved not to be caught off-guard again.

they said it was a club, and it was. An unexclusive one, like a cabal of
dark-haired men, or dogs with collars, but a club all the same. Anybody
could join, and two years into our marriage, Caroline and I were signed

up. Afterward, we seemed to have traded in a public life, a dress-up-and-go-out-on-the town life, for something dowdier, shambling, bow-legged, aproned.

I made myself useful, or tried to anyway. When Ike was a baby, I scooped him up out of his crib in the middle of the night and carried him back into our bed so that Caroline could nurse, a messenger's role that the books suggested made the father feel more a part of things. I fed him, changed him, gave him a bottle and took him along with me on errands, continually surprised by how women who might have been fearful of approaching a single man had no qualms about coming up to a man inching along the pavement with a baby. By himself, the single man radiated sex, its wrinkle, its pirate's tooth. But the baby with his wide-eyed cartoonish features, his coin face a bolder declaration of sex than any vision of male solitude, softened you, detoothed and deboned you. As for the other fathers, backpacking or wheeling around their own kids, they grimaced at the sight of you, something humorous and rough in their mouths. Like you, they'd turned from rock and roll to folk, from city to country, the lines around their eyes and your mouth like the frets on some sweet brown guitar, though they didn't like admitting it, either.

Babies were like immigrants, I decided, just arrived from another country. A dark, emotional country, one characterized by blood, lamentation and extreme volubility. A country where everybody cried a lot. Bolivia, maybe, or Argentina. Like immigrants fresh off a boat or a plane, they were wobbly on their feet at first, but in time they managed to memorize a few fluky, hopeful phrases, short-handed idioms that could get them from, say, the airport to the hotel, or to the state department, idioms that they rehearsed tirelessly, hoping to get them right.

We'd found out Caroline was pregnant two days before I was offered a teaching position at a large Midwestern university. It involved three courses and the strong probability of tenure, and after some late-night soul-searching, we decided to give it a try. In August, I started off cross-country, meeting up with Caroline in Chicago and driving the rest of the way into Wisconsin, and three days later, we were reunited with our belongings. For the first six months, we lived in an apartment near the center of town, but by the end of the year, in preparation for the baby's arrival, we'd pooled what money we had and bought a rust-colored Victorian, the last house on a windy corridor of a road that dead-ended at the entrance to a park, less than five hundred yards from a lake.

Of the two of us, Caroline missed the East the most, and found the move the hardest. She missed old college friends; her own father wasn't too well, and after the first year, we were already discussing the possibility of returning home, despite the prospect of its numbing small-worldness— what Caroline called the 'Didn't We Throw Up Together at Hotchkiss Syndrome.' "You say the word, John," she'd told me more than once, "and I'll be shopping at J. Crew in my deck shoes before you know what hit you."

While I felt nostalgic for the Atlantic Coast as well, I wasn't prepared for the Midwestern habit of looking upon lakes as bodies of water as limitless and mysterious as any ocean. In the spring, following the melts, the water roughhoused against the shore, and sometime if you squinted, it was possible to believe you were on some ragged, wild-souled coast rather than surrounded on all four sides by arable land and dairy farmers and strip malls. Summer came, arid and inhospitable. The air conditioner in the back bedroom chugged and shuffled; the back lawn smelled like a pavilion crowded with dowagers holding ladylike drinks. The first snow fell in the middle of November, creating white-wire cages of the tree branches and phone poles; the roads leading out of town were silent and claustral, and ice hung down off the eaves and the sidings of the house. By the new year, the lake was solidly frozen, and ice fishermen worked its surface with drills and shanties resembling igloos.

But we stayed—teaching jobs in the east turned out to be scarce— and in time we even grew used to the Midwestern climate. Our second baby, a girl, Isabel, was conceived at the end of August, and then the fall arrived again with its swift, cool black days. I returned to teaching, experiencing the same addled, gusty sensation high in my chest that I used to have as a student, except that this time around, I was in front of the classroom.

We'd celebrated our fifth anniversary this past May, a Friday, and I remember this because Fridays tend to be my worst days, when I teach three classes back to back, with only a ten-minute break in between each one. It had been a busy week in general, with end-of-semester meetings and comments due, and I hadn't had time to buy Caroline a present, particularly something appropriate for a momentous (that is to say, divisible-by-five) anniversary. Nor did I really want to lie and tell her that I'd ordered something by mail that was late in coming, or that wouldn't be ready for another week, and so on the way home that Friday night, I'd stopped at a twenty-four-hour Walgreens, in the hope I could pick up something amusing that could serve as a substitute present before I found time to buy her something that she'd genuinely like to have. And I did find a few silly things—a bar of green soap carved to look like a frog, an eyeglasses repair kit with a tiny screwdriver and screws, and so forth—and with my purchases all wrapped up, I headed home.

It was sometime before the birth of our second baby that Caroline made the decision to stop working, and it had been a stormy adjustment for her. When we bought the new house, we'd rented a storage bin to hold all the things we no longer used or needed. "We have too many *things*," I told her as I surveyed our possessions. A few months earlier, I'd come upon Caroline on the floor of her office, pregnant and in tears, surrounded by piles of old college psychology texts and source books for her doctorate, some of which she'd already begun packing in boxes. "I'll work again, right?" she'd asked me. "It's all a compromise, right?"

The only thing I could think of to say was "They don't make it easy for working mothers," though I wasn't sure whether this was some prescripted pro-woman line I'd come up with to score points, or whether I really believed it. I knew that following Isabel's birth, Caroline had felt as though her brain were turning to rubber. "I don't have ideas anymore," she told me. "I forget to read magazines, I don't go to movies, I don't watch the news. My whole life is pee-pee and poo-poo and Raffi and Pete Seeger and people like that." She was gazing at herself in the mirror critically, and then all of a sudden she turned to me. "John?"

"Yeah?"

"I think I'm in mourning."

"Mourning for what?"

She turned to me suddenly and passionately. "For being a girl. I think I'm feeling that my days of being a girl are over. I'm a *mommy* now. I think it depresses me more than I know."

"Well, I'm sorry," I said, slightly formally. "I hadn't realized how miserable you were."

"Oh, come on, you know what I mean. You *must*. You must have it too, sometimes. With yourself. Getting older. Finding gray hairs. You know how much I love our kids. It's just that it means that a part of me, the girl part of me, is gone. It's disappearing." Caroline was silent. "I don't think I want any more children after this. I want us to travel. I want us to have freedom again. I want Ike and Isabel to hurry up and grow up so that you and I can both be free to do things again, and go to the movies, and go out to dinner, and take little vacations, and stay in weird hotels, and—" She gazed at me. "You look like you don't have the slightest idea what I'm talking about."

"You're thirty-one years old," I replied with a laugh. "You're hardly ready to be farmed out to the wheat fields."

"What day is it today?"

"It's the fifteenth. No, I'm wrong, it's the sixteenth."

"And you don't have classes until next Tuesday, right?" and when I nodded, her eyes sparkled. "Tell me if you think this'd be fun. We all drive to Chicago this weekend. See a show. Have dinner someplace nice. My treat. Just have fun. We could stay at the Ritz—"

"What about the kids?"

"We can bring them. I haven't been to Chicago in ages. And we don't even have to go to a show, we could just *be*. Talk—"

"If the kids'll let us get a word in edgewise."

"You never talk to me anymore."

"Yes, I do, too."

"Not as much as you used to. Do you remember when we were just married? You always used to tell me what was on your mind. You used to tell me what you *wished* for. All these things you wanted to do.''

"Well, that was back when I had things I still wanted to do," I replied cooly.

"Oh, come on, there's still some things you want to do, I'm sure there are."

I shook my head for a long time, and I could feel her eyes on me.

"See, you don't talk to me anymore. You nod and shake your head. What do you think about the Chicago idea? Doesn't it sound like fun?"

"It sounds expensive," I said, "and chaotic. Too much is involved. And we wouldn't be able to do much with the kids along. How would we get there, anyway?"

"Easy, we'd drive."

"Six hours round-trip. Listening to kiddie music over and over again. What a blast."

"They'd fall asleep. And we could find a sitter when we got there. A lot of these hotels have sitters, or know the names of one."

"Some other time," I said gingerly. "I just think it would be inconvenient right now. For everybody concerned." I began removing my pants. "We'd have to find parking, and the hotel would be, what, three hundred dollars a night—"

"It would be my treat."

"No, I couldn't let you do that."

Caroline gazed at me bitterly. "It doesn't matter, John. Some other time, then."

"Well, there will be other times, Caroline," I replied lightly.

She was home three days all week with the kids while I was at school, and I should have been more sensitive than I was at the time to her entrapment. When I came home that Friday night, I saw that she was freshly showered, and dressed, and wearing the earrings I'd found for her on our first anniversary, gold dolphins that clinked behind the mesh of two intricate silver cages. She looked beautiful to me, and while she was upstairs giving the kids' their baths, I went into my office and stretched out on the couch, a pillow propped up under my head. I didn't wake up until six hours later, at around two in the morning, and tiptoeing into the kitchen for a glass of water, I saw the table had been carefully set for two, but that dinner was in the fridge, under foil. Upstairs, of course, everybody was fast asleep. The next morning Caroline was perfectly nice about it. "You must have been wiped out," she told me in a light, distracted voice, as she ushered the kids into their coats and hats and mittens.

Ever since it had become general knowledge that Sam had stopped drinking, some of the members of my family had begun treating him as a kind of all-purpose substance abuse expert. "Mr. Recovery," as he put it, adding that several months earlier my mother had gone so far as to give one of her friends his name and telephone number; the friend had a son whose behavior was a source of concern, and could Sam recommend the name of a good rehab? "Jesus Christ," he said, yawning, "I'm surprised she doesn't ask me whether Mâcon-Villages is a decent wine or not."

Yet he seemed pleased by the attention, too, and it had struck me that in a family where you often had to clamor to be heard, here was something that was his alone; and whenever the subject came up, as it did several times during Christmas vacation that year, a distinct expression came into his eyes, a mix of superiority and jadedness, rancor and pride. On our first night back home he came upon a group of us in the dining room, sharing a couple of bottles of Bordeaux. "How's the wine, guys?" he called out from the doorway. "Stringent? Sardonic? Poignant?" and when nobody answered him, Sam added, "Jay, you have to swirl it around in your mouth so that people'll believe you know what you're doing. Then you have to say that it's amusing. Or oaken, or tree-lined, or thickly settled, or some other adjective like that. You're not being pretentious enough yet."

Jay ignored him. "This is OK," he said to my father, swallowing.

My father was wearing a matted blue down vest whose airless folds lay in softly zippered crinkles against his chest. He hadn't shaved that morning; the lower half of his face looked faintly charred, like the aftermath of a flash fire. He set down his wineglass, and from his vest pocket took out a soiled yellow napkin, which he crowded into the near corner of one eye, before gazing up at Sam, brazenly formal. "Does it bother you at all that we're drinking wine in front of you?"

"Sam, I got you some of that Moussy stuff," Sarah threw out faintly. "That's that nonalcoholic whatever, beer, it's in the pantry."

"Sweetie, don't slouch like that," my mother said to Sarah, who was resting against one end of the couch, Indian-style, a pillow propped behind her neck. My sister tended to decline all offers of couches and chairs when she was at home, most of the time preferring the floor, the rug, anyplace but up at face level. "Hold yourself up. Look how Doll's sitting."

"Oh, I'm not," Doll said weakly, "sitting in some good way." Jay's wife was nursing J.J., the baby blanketed against her chest. "I'm your basic beanbag," but by then Sarah had turned away and was pretending to study the tips of her fingers. "Boneless," Doll added, glancing over at Jay for help. "I'm like that noodle cat in all those 'Peanuts' cartoons."

"Well, that was very nice of whoever it was who got me nonalcoholic beer," Sam said, "but I frankly don't really see the point—"

"The point is so you won't feel left out," Jay said.

"I don't feel left out, actually. Not in the least. It's immaterial to me, if you want to know the truth. I can sit here and watch the rest of you get sluggish and repetitive and, you know—" my brother shrugged "—not mind in the least."

As I said, I think he enjoyed feeling set apart. The following day, a group of us decided to take a trip to a nearby mall to put the finishing touches on our Christmas shopping, and when we got there and split up into migrant groups, Sam insisted on heading off by himself; half an hour later I caught sight of him sprawled along one of the hard, blond circular benches, smoking furiously as he observed one of the holiday displays, a toy workshop scenario in which a red-capped elf slowly, jerkingly handed

over a plastic fruitcake to a Mrs. Santa Claus figure. "Isn't this unbelievably sinister?" Sam called out when he saw me. "These elves? *Jesus*, I
mean, have a nightmare for Christmas, why don't you."

Afterward, we decided to go to the movies. But something about
the smallness of the theater seemed to disturb Sam, and to bring out the
force of his disenchantment about being back home. He walked across
the parking lot hurriedly, with his head lowered, and inside the lobby he
made no effort to take off his dark glasses, even after Jay had remarked
that rather than appearing suave, Sam in fact resembled a blind man.
Clutching his ticket, he gazed sorrowfully at the popcorn, the bright pink
and green drinks sloshing around the glass cylinders, and when I made a
move to talk to him, he murmured something airy and noncommittal in
reply, as though if somebody were to catch him talking to me, his cover
might be blown. Later, driving back home, he seemed embarrassed to
admit he'd enjoyed the movie, as if that might signal to the rest of us that
he couldn't have done better himself. "Malls are so depressing," he complained. "All those tawdry, unhappy people. Coronary patients doing
circuits like piglets in lab experiments. Heavy metal teenagers with studs
in their tongues. The girls look as though they have a quart of maple
syrup in their hair. Plus, everybody looks so sore. What is it about life that
makes everybody so sore?"

The town's cardinal sin seemed to be nothing less than its localness,
that it was the place where all of us had been born and raised. His monologue more or less continued until a mile or so from the house, when our
car was halted temporarily by a crossing guard, a middle-aged woman in a
bright vest who raised her hand as a group of schoolchildren ambled
across the pedestrian walk. "*Hit* her, John," Sam said, and when I gazed
over my shoulder at him, I was taken aback by the ugly expression in his
eyes. "Look at her. Sanctimonious hen. Look at that little—"

"I'm looking," I interrupted soothingly.

"She's just a crossing guard, Sam," Sarah said.

"She thinks she's so unbelievably important. Here I am, some old-
bat crossing guard in a little orange tunic in a stupid little town, and I

think I'm the queen of the entire universe. Why, you ask? Because I can hold up my hand and turn you people into salt. I-Am-Crossing-Guard-Watch-Me-Halt-Your-Life.''

''Merry Christmas, Sam,'' Sarah said, touching his arm.

Then there was all the business about celebrity and recognition, which Caroline was the first to bring to my attention, whispering to me mock-warningly, ''If Sam tells our kids they have to be famous one more time—'' but I'd laughed, assuring her he was only prolonging a joke. But the topic kept coming up. At dinner, when my mother pointed out how long Ike's fingers were, Sam piped in, ''Maybe someday he'll be a famous sculptor.'' When Doll laid J.J. out on the changing table, and the baby kicked his legs, Sam, lurking behind her, blurted out, ''Maybe someday he'll be a famous Olympic diver. Maybe he'll bring home the gold someday.'' The next day, when Doll was encouraging J.J. to clap his hands, Sam frowned. ''Why in the world would you want to teach him how to applaud? To be a member of the great unwashed masses? J.J. should be the guy up there on *stage*. The applau*dee*.''

Finally, after he'd told Caroline that on the basis of the way Ike was stacking his books, his prediction was that someday he'd become a famous librarian, she'd had enough. ''Sam, why in the world does Ike have to be famous?''

''I didn't say he *had* to be famous. It's for *his* sake. I just want him to be able to get a good table in a decent restaurant, is that too much to ask?''

His latest avocation was taking pictures. He'd arrived bearing a brand-new Canon Eos, and when I asked him why he hadn't bought a less expensive model—it was a twelve-hundred-dollar camera, Caroline pointed out, the first one he'd ever owned—he replied that he hadn't seen any point. ''Why not learn on the most expensive one?'' he asked. ''You get better and better at taking pictures and the better you get, the more you should be using the best camera. So I just bought the best one to begin with. It'll save me from having to buy it later on.'' Later, he blurted out, ''I'm thinking of trying to get an exhibition of some kind going. Like in Soho or someplace.''

"An exhibit of what?" I asked.

"Pictures," though when I asked him what he knew about photography, he waved away the question as irrelevant. "It's not all that hard. All you have to do is have an eye. Which I happen to have, not to be immodest or anything, but people have told me I do. How do you think guys like Avedon, and Diane Arbus, and who's that guy who did those two French people kissing, Robert Doisneau, how do you think *they* learned? They read books. Then they just *did* it."

All of us had blind spots, and Sam's was his dilettantism, his flitting from interest to interest. His snobbery I could trace to an early social outsiderliness. He might have not been popular, but at least he had some money, and he considered his blood to be more sacred than other people's, and it was tempting to trace his dilettantism to the same sense of entitlement. He expected results at once. Apprenticeships held no interest for him. He expected to have a Broadway show mounted with him in the lead role; a book published; a screenplay bought; his photographs to be hung. More than anything, it was fame and recognition he craved; the work involved was no more than an inconvenient means to get there. And when he found out it wasn't so easy, he gave up. Socially, his glibness was his ally; artistically it was his enemy. He wasn't blind to this turn in his character, but acknowledged it with a peculiarly ironic, urban self-consciousness. "I know you must think I'm the sort of person who goes from one thing to another," he told me when broaching the subject of his photography; and the time before that, "I know, now you're thinking, This is a person who can't concentrate on one single thing . . ." as though naming people's unspoken accusations could ward off the truth.

And so when I asked him my first night home how his scriptwriting career was going, it was a test question; I already knew, I think, how he would answer. Screenplay-writing was for morons, Sam told me; it took too much time and work. It wasn't artistic; it was grunt work, literary carpentry, scaffolding, hammers and nails. Who needed it? Besides, a picture was worth a thousand words. "I know what you must be thinking," he said. "Here's just another thing Sam's given up on. He just must be so undisciplined, so scattered."

I didn't answer. "Maybe you should concentrate on your job for a while," I said finally.

"What do you mean, I should concentrate on my job?"

A couple of years earlier, he'd landed a job in the editorial department of a large midtown New York City publisher. It seemed a fitting profession for him, given people's general perception that editorial assistants couldn't possibly get along on a publisher's paycheck, and must undoubtedly have another source of income, which Sam does. Or rather did; I suspected he'd spent most of it. He liked his job, though, and was good at it. Aside from quotidian secretarial work—transcribing letters and answering queries, writing advertising and jacket copy for the books he was responsible for—one of his tasks was to scan the pile of unsolicited manuscripts that came flooding into the office at the rate of ten to fifteen a day; the slush pile, as it was known in office patois. Two or three times a month, he told me, he and the other editorial assistants stayed late into the night after their bosses had gone home, spreading out the manuscripts and cover letters on the floor, and laughing scornfully at the dreams of literary aspirants from around the country. While Sam invariably complained about this aspect of his job, I couldn't help but suspect that he enjoyed playing the bad guy, and I remember being dismayed the first time I heard that the naive, hopeful efforts of strangers were being monitored by a bunch of callow, badly paid gatekeepers.

"Well, and maybe not spread yourself so thin all the time," I went on. "Concentrate on one thing and work on that for a while."

"I'm not spreading myself thin. God, you sound just like Father."

"How do you mean I sound like him?"

"Just because you wanted to get someplace with your piano playing once and you couldn't doesn't mean you have to take it out on me, Jam. Whatever happened to that? Here one day, gone the next."

"It was hardly—"

"So you don't have to turn into this bitter, ossified critic person who puts down everybody else's attempts to do something remotely creative in their lives. Who sits on the top of some imaginary mountain finding flaws in other people's work because he doesn't have the guts to go out on a limb himself."

He knew; he wasn't stupid. He was talking about himself, of course, but he was talking about me, too. Though what passed between us then, between his oddly sunken-looking eyes and my own expression of disingenuousness, lasted for only a minute. "I didn't want to do anything with the piano," I said finally. "Give me a break."

"Hah, you give *me* a break."

"I didn't. It was a hobby. It always was a hobby. It was never going to be anything more than that." I laughed stubbornly. "I would hardly want to go into a world like that. Talk about an insecure life."

ᴍy father had always made it clear how much of a waste of money he considered buying a tree, and every year he waited until school let out for the winter vacation, at which point he enlisted the help of several Emery School custodians to haul the school tree from the back of the chapel to our house. But that year, Jay had hit upon the idea of driving out to a nearby farm and chopping down our own, and the next afternoon, he and I managed in short order to stake out a tall, aromatic Scotch pine. As Jay and Sarah prepared to hoist the tree onto their shoulders, Sam sidled up to our mother. "Doesn't Father like to do *anything* anymore?"

"Not too much. I don't—" He hadn't been feeling well recently, she added.

"Well, he could at least make an *effort*. Here we are, all of us at home, and all he does is sit around watching flipping college football games. Blue Bowl, Red Bowl, Orange Bowl, Cotton Bowl, Stupid Bowl."

"Fifty bucks for a tree?" my father asked once we were back in the car, the tree sawed and bound and sticking out of the back trunk like a limbless hostage. "Surely you must be joking."

"You can't take it with you, Dad," Sarah piped up, but he only grunted.

"It's all this selective frugality bullshit," Sam complained later that evening. "He'll offer whoever finds his glasses a hundred dollars, but then he'll rejoice at the fact that now that he's over sixty-five, he's entitled to some senior citizen discount at the movies. Go figure. Why would anybody want to rejoice over the fact that they're growing older? Poor Mother," he added.

While he set up the crèche on the mantelpiece, Sarah knelt down to untangle the vinelike strands of lights, plugging the ends into the wall socket to see whether or not a year later they were still working, before positioning the stepladder under the doorframe; presently, she asked Jay to hand her the mistletoe and the scotch tape. "Or would it be better to use thumbtacks?" Receiving no response, she tore off five or six scotch tape ends, tabbing them against the wood in a row.

She hadn't planned to come home at all. "I don't think I like Christmas anymore," she'd told me over the phone. "I'm too old."

"How can you be too old for Christmas?"

"If you're not married you can be too old."

"Not really—"

"John, *you* have a family, so quit complaining. I'm here at this limbo point. I'm too old to be having Christmas with *them*—" she meant our parents "—but I don't have kids, and so it's this point where it's like I'm waiting for something to happen. For Christmas to get fun again. Which I'm not sure it will get."

Up until the middle of December, she'd been planning on spending Christmas with a friend in Washington State, but my mother had convinced her to join the rest of us, emphasizing that lately she'd been concerned about our father's health. She had a point: since we'd been home, all of us noticed his haggard-looking appearance, the circles under his eyes, his slow walk. There was some irregularity with his blood, my mother said, though they'd know more, and more concretely, in the new year. Sam, for one, saw only that my father was neglecting his appearance. "Talk about not keeping the romance alive in your marriage," he'd told me. "The other night, I was in the kitchen when he farted. *Loudly.*

Didn't seem to care, just went on doing what he was doing. Mother shouldn't have to deal with that. I feel bad for her. We should get her tons of jewelry for Christmas. An evening gown. Something glamorous. Something to make her feel good about herself. She should be swept off her feet by somebody in a top hat and tails. I wish Fred Astaire were still alive."

We were lugging up the ornaments from the cellar, six boxes worth, oddly lightweight. "Well, Sarah's in charge of that," I said. At Jay's suggestion, each of us had given Sarah a certain amount of money, with the stipulation that she buy my mother something substantial that could be from all of us. It seemed preferable to filling up my mother's life with small, flashy, useless presents, and I trusted Sarah's judgment, assuming she knew my mother's tastes better than I did.

"Yeah, but she won't tell what it is. She says we have to wait until Christmas. It ought to be something good. At least I *hope* it's something good."

"Speaking of Father, what are you getting *him* for Christmas?"

"He says he doesn't want anything."

"So?"

"So when I asked what he wanted he told me that if I really want to get him something, then I can hire a van to cart away all the shit they already have. Well, he didn't actually use the word *shit*—"

"That doesn't answer my question."

"Jam, if you must know, I happen to be really tired of buying him stuff and then a year later I find—sorry, I happen to *come across*—whatever it was I gave him, and it's still in its package. Still in whatever wrapping it came in. Shoved behind his desk or in some dark room of the basement. It hurts my feelings. He doesn't have the grace to return it, or hide it. So I'm not even going to bother this year."

"Sam," I said, "he's not in terrific health."

"We don't know that. Nobody knows that for a fact."

"Well, yes, as a matter of fact we all do know that. He looks like hell, he's lost a lot of weight, he says he's cold all the time."

"Well, he should consider turning up the heat in this house once in a while. It's all this Yankee, stoical, the-cold-is-good-for-you-young-man nonsense. I have news for him: this cold does *not* make one into a better person. I mean, look at me, I'm a primo example of that."

Now, in the living room, Sarah stood back a few feet from the door, surveying the curling green taped to the molding. "There. Everybody, how does that look?"

"Beauty," Jay called over, and Doll applauded. "Brilliant," she called out lazily from the couch.

My new sister-in-law was a former Louisville deb, and Doll was her actual name, though at first none of us was able to pronounce it with anything other than a cumbrous, clubfooted irony. Our family was big on nicknames, but there was no way we could improve on the sheer beauty-pageant weirdness of "Doll," and so we respectfully backed off. An intelligent, acerbic, fiercely loyal woman, with flashing teeth and translucent, astonishingly white skin—you could see the light wiring of blue veins, another world, below it—her hair was already famous in our family for its length (it continued down her back, past her bottom, grazing the backs of her knees, practically; she usually kept it tied up in a thick braid, whose weight could knock a man out). Together, she and my brother—New England golden boy meets ex-Southern deb, or, as Sam referred to them, the Lug and the Teensy-Weensy White Girl—were a spectacular couple: gorgeous-looking, what Sam called "deeply sporty," each one as popular as the other, the envy of their friends, or so we all imagined; and they evoked in me a childish romanticism I didn't think it possible to feel for members of my own family.

Sarah began digging through one of the ornament boxes, and presently she held up a miniature penguin perched in a red cart. "I feel sorry for this one. It's so ugly. All these poor old ornaments sitting around all year at the bottom of a moldy box, waiting for their big day in life, and when it finally comes nobody wants to hang them up. We're out of those little metal ornament-hanger clip-on things," she added to my mother. "Are there any paper clips in this house? I don't live here anymore or else I'd go get them."

That year, I'd made a single, hopeless provision—that people go easy on presents. Was that too much to ask? But I'd been met with reluctance if not antagonism. "Don't be a killjoy," my mother had said, and so I'd amended it slightly by saying the children should get presents, but that the rest of us already had everything we needed.

"I'm not talking about need, Jam, I'm talking about *want*. Want is different from need. This is Christmas."

it was only when my brothers and sisters and I saw one another that I realized that when we'd left home each of us had gone on the equivalent of a sea voyage. That coming home provided a break in our traveling, a respite on the dock, a safe house. Like sailors, we sat around comparing notes. The scenery we'd encountered, the weather we'd experienced, how far we'd ventured out before turning back, notes on people we'd met along the way. Our parents, who'd quit the sea, looked on, listening, nodding, occasionally interjecting a note of caution or agreement, though like younger members of any venerable profession, we disregarded them; the water had changed since they'd sailed it.

Indirectly, we compared. How each of us was doing. Who our friends were. Whether or not we liked our jobs. What kinds of cars we drove. Our opinions on this subject or that. At first we circled one another, shy. The details of our lives and our appearances were declarations, casual but pointed—Jay's new overnight bag, a new band Sam liked, Sarah's shoes. Once we left home we became unknowable, familiar to one another yet unfamiliar.

Unfairly or not, and although we rarely saw him anymore, all of us had begun looking to Tom as the one who could give or withhold approval.

He wasn't even the oldest; Jay and Sarah held that honorific. And he wasn't really in the world, as the rest of us were, or fancied ourselves as being. His physical appearance inspired no more confidence than any other man's, and though he'd been practicing a martial art for ten years, it

wasn't something he discussed or had even had occasion to use; it gave
him balance, he said, that was all. One time, Sarah was with him on the
island when Tom had stumbled across another fisherman bent down on
the side of the pier, cutting his net. Jay, who was in the room at the time
she was telling us this, leaned forward avidly. "So what'd he do—did he
flip the guy?" But Tom had simply asked the man to please stop, and the
man, surprised, had walked away. "The world really doesn't need two
more people fighting," he'd told me afterward.

"Could you have kicked the guy's ass?" I asked.

"Who cares?"

I didn't have a good answer, and so I tried another tack. "What
about that Japanese thing you do?"

"That's not meant for fighting."

"It's a martial art, and it's not for fighting? What's it for, then?"

"Nothing."

"What does one fight matter?"

"It does matter. If a thousand people say that, then you have a
thousand fights."

He was punishing on himself. "I have to change myself," he'd told
me a few weeks earlier. "There's so much about myself that's false.
That's selfish. So much of me that's interested in the world. In all the
wrong things. That's interested in money, and achievement, and who I
am." That world had nothing to offer him, he went on.

"Tom, you happen to live in the world," I reminded him, but he
wasn't listening to me anymore. "I know," I went on. "I've finally figured
it out. You want to court pain and death and horribleness—"

"No," he said, "you don't understand. I don't find pleasure in so-
called worldly things, and I don't find pleasure in unpleasant things. My
only pleasure should be that this life, what I'm doing, is what's been
willed to me. I know the answer, you know? It's quiet. It's in seclusion.
Contemplation. But at the same time, I don't want to cut myself off
from other people. That's falling into a trap, too. Who wouldn't want to
set himself apart from other people? That's a trap, too."

"Tom, why don't you give yourself a break?"

"If I could I would. I can't. See, the obstacle is *me*. I'm the person who keeps myself from seeing things clearly. I have to detach myself, leave myself. To change. I don't want to find myself, I want to forget myself."

I reminded him of the time a few summers back when he'd pushed me over onto the lawn of the Menemsha house, and I held out my arm. "I'll bet you couldn't do it again."

"Right."

Standing, I waited there for a moment, but Tom was busy rubbing a faint spot on his pants. "So why don't you try it?" I went on. "Try pushing me over one more time."

"No."

"Why not?"

"Because it isn't a game. Or a demonstration. I did that before because I was saying to you that your grip should be loose. Light. Your grip in *all* things. Not just the grip in your arm."

"I'm afraid I don't know what that means."

"Well, you'll have to be patient with yourself."

I hadn't seen Tom in over three months, not since the end of the summer. Jay and I had met up in Boston and taken the ferry over to the island, and after dropping our bags off at the main house, we made our way over to Tom's. Afterward, we sat around eating and drinking late into the night. The silence outside was stupendous, the only noise the distant toiling of the waves and the buoys. It was obvious to me how much Tom loved living on the island, how at home he felt; even my mother seemed to have made a peace with his decision, though I still had my reservations. "Don't you go crazy living here sometimes?" I asked him.

He seemed surprised. "Actually, no, not at all. This is my favorite time of the year here, actually. There's nobody around."

"That's the problem, there's no *people*."

There was a silence. Then Tom's voice came in, patiently. "I'm not you, John. I don't need people in the same way you do."

The implication offended me. "I don't *need* people—"

"Of course you do. There's nothing wrong with that. I'm just different from you, that's all. I have what I need. Look," he said tiredly, "the life I'm living, for whatever it's worth, is not some reflection of you. Or of your life—"

"It's just not very real, that's all," Jay broke in.

"Why do you have such contempt for me?"

"Contempt?" Jay laughed. "Are you kidding? I envy you, are you kidding?"

"You go to church, don't you? People don't look at you strangely when you go to church, do they? For one hour a week? What if I want to spend more than one hour a week by myself? Why's that so strange? The problem is that people in this country have forgotten how to be quiet."

"But it's not real, Tom," Jay said patiently. "It's not life. This island is not real life."

"And life to you is what? Making money? Meeting the right people? Moving in and out of buildings? A good seat in a restaurant? Those are just shadows." Tom shrugged. "They're just shadows. They're nothing at all."

Jay thought of something else. "What about women? What about kids?"

Tom didn't answer for a long time. "Look, this is a compromise, OK?" he said finally. "Most people's lives are. But it feels right for me. I'd go nuts if I lived somewhere else. If I moved into what you call the world." He laughed suddenly. "I think it would just about do me in."

Early the next morning, we met up in the parking lot at Calumet Harbor. The night before, Tom said he had something he wanted to show us, and when we arrived at the pier, he was leaning up against one of the pilings, holding a Styrofoam cup of coffee and gazing down at the water. Except for a few dories, and three trawlers positioned drably dockside, there were no leisure boats; most of them had already been tabled and stored for the season. Beyond us, gulls hung floating like blown paper. "So," I said at last, "why'd you want us to come down here anyway?"

"I just wanted to show you all something. You see that?" He pointed to one of the trawlers. "That's mine."

"Yours?" I repeated stupidly.

The boat was enormous—I couldn't tell how long it was; forty-eight feet, I found out later—and Tom was already herding us on board. He'd commissioned a man in Texas to build it, he said, pointing out the net with its diamond pattern, ninety-four feet wide and eight feet high where it dragged along the bottom of the ocean; the top of the net attached to a rope that curled around the circumference of a drum, and at the end of the day you lifted the net, which was by then—you hoped—filled with groundfish, unloaded it and sorted out the contents, throwing away the small ones and placing the so-called "keepers" on ice in the cabin. "We can get fifteen hundred, two thousand pounds of fish on a good day." *We* meant him and a crewman; it took at least two people to man the boat, and Tom had hired a local boy to go out with him. Once they were on the water, they did a lot of waiting. "I listen to the radio a lot. Red Sox games. And I read a lot of books."

"What are groundfish, anyway?"

"Flatfish. Cod. Haddock. Sole. Gray sole. Hake." He went on like this for a while as Jay poked his head in the cabin, glancing around with faint distaste at the loose cables, the thick ropes, the flakes of rust already forming on the outside of the cabin. "What's that smell?" he asked.

"Blood," Tom said cheerfully. "Look at that," he added wonderingly, and as my eyes followed his finger, I caught sight of a dull-white bird diving with extravagant grace into the water. It was an arctic tern, Tom explained. "They're the best divers in the world. Look for a second, they're like little Olympians." He stood watching the pocked water for a long time until a volley of incoming waves made the spot indistinguishable from the rest.

Onshore, we made our way back to the car along a promenade; stacked on the land side were old lobster pots filled with refuse—empty cans of oil and motor detergent, a high heel, a thick rope like the leg of a long, rubbery child—and behind the promenade a low, shanty-roofed fish market. It wasn't until we were almost back to the house that Jay began his spiel. He didn't see the point of Tom knocking himself out the way he was doing. Maybe he should try something else for a while, at least give it a shot. "Come into the city," he suggested. "I'll help you find a place to live, introduce you to some people."

"No."

"Why not?"

"I know enough people. There's nothing for me in any city. Jay, I do this because I love it."

"What in the world is there to love about it?"

"The independence, for one thing. I can work my own schedule. I'm my own boss. I'm not accountable to anybody. Nobody tells me what to do."

"Why don't you just do it for a hobby?"

As we drove past the fort district, Tom held his tongue. "Look," he said as we approached the house, "not everybody can work out who he is in his life. In fact, most people spend their time covering up who they are. Everybody in the world I've ever met wants to have a passion of some kind in their lives. Wants to *love* something. Wants to feel as if there's nothing else in the world that they could have done but what they're doing. I have that. Do you have that?" Jay didn't answer. "Do you have that, Jay? John, do you have that?" A moment later, both of us shook our heads. Tom glanced down. "So I'm lucky, I think."

But I continued to miss him, and in a funny way, mourn him, though less so than before. I no longer saw him except rarely, when I happened to be visiting the island, since Tom didn't like to travel, didn't like to leave St. James, and claimed that cities spooked him. He even avoided coming home. "It's just not my world anymore," he told me after his last visit. "To me it's a series of false mystiques. False ceilings. Money, class, race, chitchat. It's not that I don't love everybody, I do. I just can't live my life in the midst of something that's so dead to me, and meaningless."

His was the life that I aspired to more and more, not only because he was doing precisely what he wanted, but because he appeared to be at peace with himself and to have an intuitive understanding of life. More and more my own life confused and disappointed me. It occurred to me that I was like most people that way, but this thought was hardly consoling; who, after all, can resist the idea of breathing air rarer than anybody else's? Things simply weren't turning out as I'd thought they would, though I kept this to myself, hoping no one would notice or bring it to my attention.

late Christmas Eve, all of us—except for Tom—sat around the living room staring at the tree and the fire, which was dying out but which nobody, including myself, had the energy to rebuild. It was a drowsy time of night. Low orange flames fluttered and snapped. The television screen grayly, passively gleamed back our faces, as well as a sampling of lamplight and furniture. Nobody had much to say, and since there was so little animation in the room, people had begun noticing little, strange things and commenting on them listlessly. "Jam, your socks," Sarah said to me earlier, "they're bright blue."

"Yes? So?"

"So—socks that are bright blue. That's all."

That was the general level of conversation in the room; all of us felt doped, sunstruck, as though it were midday in a sweltering country rather than close to ten o'clock on Christmas Eve. "I love eggnog," Doll remarked suddenly.

"I love eggnog too," Sam said. "Rather, I *used* to. Back in the good old days. Sorry, I mean, the bad old days." He was sitting beside the fireplace, and eventually he rose up and went over to the tree and, squatting down, picked up a red-and-white-striped package, which he shook from side to side. "I think we should all open one present tonight."

"Wait until morning," Jay said.

"Let's *not* wait until morning, actually," but sensing no enthusiasm in the room, he replaced the present under the tree.

"Jam, try looking at the Christmas tree without wearing your glasses,'' Sarah said a few minutes later. ''It looks even prettier than it does when they're on.''

I did; the tiny bulbs swam falsely, shimmeringly, blurry, exultant stars. A few minutes later, Sam yawned theatrically. ''Are we really going to church tonight? I don't know if I can last that long. I know—you all go and I'll stay here and baby-sit the kids.''

''No,'' I chimed in, *''you* can go and *I'll* stay here and baby-sit the kids.''

''We're *all* going to midnight service,'' Sarah said. Despite her reservations about coming home, she harbored an enthusiastic image of us at Christmas that she didn't like to see darkened. ''I love church on Christmas Eve. We can see all the people we knew growing up.''

''Yeah, we get to see what incredible messes they've turned into,'' Sam said. Sarah scowled at him, and eventually he excused himself. ''I'm going upstairs to get a sweater. It's freezing in here.''

Following our earlier conversation, Sam had disappeared, and later, when I went to inform him that dessert was served, I couldn't find him. Finally, I discovered him upstairs in his bedroom, the door locked. ''What—'' came his voice, muffled, irritated. ''I'm wrapping presents. Don't come in.''

''I wouldn't dream of it,'' though a few minutes later he ambled back downstairs into the kitchen. ''When you sit in front of the fireplace for a long time,'' he told Doll, who'd commented on his pink skin and red eyes, ''it makes your face as pink as a lobster's.''

''Since when is there a fireplace upstairs?'' Sarah inquired.

''I meant the one in the living room—oh, never mind.''

This time, when he returned to the living room, I remember being surprised by how much time had elapsed since he'd left, and when I remarked that I thought the reason he'd gone upstairs was to retrieve a sweater, he gazed at me insolently. ''Moths ate it.'' Wading with a forced and delicate expertise past our outstretched knees, he retook his old seat beside the fireplace. ''I wonder why Christmas is always so depressing,'' was the next thing he wanted to know. ''*I* know why. It's because I buy whatever it is I want during the year anyway, and so what's the point?''

"Well, the point is that Christmas doesn't really have to do with presents," I said lightly. "Or it shouldn't."

"In this family, it does."

"It does not, Sam," Sarah interrupted, scowling.

"Oh, and how many times have we mentioned Jesus in the past two days? It's not like he's been on people's lips around here. It's all Santa this, Santa that."

While I may have been imagining it—and retrospection often grants insight where sometimes there was none—Sam seemed to me different from the person who'd left the room. His gaze was shiny, and some stickiness in the center of his forehead caused his bangs to crack softly over his eyes, causing him to blink repeatedly, as though he'd just woken up from a disorienting sleep. His hair—somehow damp; had he run it under a shower for some reason?—rose up in the back like a rooster's comb, and as he squinted at Sarah and draped one long arm over his knee, his lankiness struck me, not for the first time, as both unruly and feminine. "It's freezing in here," he said for a second time, hugging himself.

By then Jay had roused himself from his seat. Did anybody want anything from the kitchen, he asked? and after taking orders, mostly for ice water, he turned to Sam.

"Seltzer water with lime." Sam answered. *"Por favor.* And ginger ale if there's no seltzer." He stared after Jay as he left the room, before turning to me with a pale, clownish smile. "I am completely wiped out."

Slowly, avoiding Sam's gaze, Sarah readjusted her skirt around her knees. She was sitting across the room in a hard-backed chair, a plant extending one of its fluid blades over her shoulder. Sam kept talking in a dreamy, disconnected way. Who remembered the Christmas when the tree fell down in the middle of the night, and on Christmas morning, the living room was a sea of choppy, silver glass? Or leaving an apple and a glass of milk for Santa Claus, and the surprise we'd felt as kids to see the milk gone and a bite taken out of the apple? Did anybody else realize that the fantasy reward figures of childhood—Santa Claus, the Easter Bunny, the Tooth Fairy—were all aerially inclined? "It's so they can fly right out of your mind once you wise up that they don't exist."

"The Easter Bunny doesn't have wings," I said.

"Yes, but it hops. You see? It hops straight up into the air. Hops over the fence and you never see it again."

Sarah began picking at a fleck of loose wool on her sleeve. His Christmas reveries now over, Sam gazed into the fireplace.

"God, wouldn't a cup of eggnog be good now." He shook his head "Oh, well. So it goes. In another life."

Sarah's response—a humorless, one-note laugh—escaped her mouth like a cap from a child's gun. "Hah."

"Hah what?" and when Sarah didn't answer, Sam said again, "Hah what? You just said 'hah.' Hah what?"

Sarah has always had a habit of yawning—or at least pretending to—whenever she's been faced with an emotion she doesn't like. Her voice was reproving, careful. "Oh, I'm not as dumb as I look, Sam. Don't think no one's noticed your little J & B cache behind the bookshelf in your room. Half-drunk."

My brother's eyes didn't flinch. "What J & B cache? What bookshelf?"

"Oh, right, tell me about it, *what* bookshelf."

"No, *what* bookshelf?"

Sarah mimicked him. "What bookshelf, Sam? Gee, Sam, I can't imagine what you're talking about."

A moment later, as if shooting down a vague discursion, Sam said, "Oh, you mean that thing in the upstairs." No answer. "The thing there." His voice was numbly, gently relieved. "That was there when I got here, m'dear." Hesitating, he turned, as if in slow motion, to me. "I just wanted to make sure—" he went on "—that thing, I can't remember whatever the details were, though . . ."

I was mystified. "What are you talking about?"

"I was walking past the bookshelf," Sam went on, "and it was there. So . . ." and his voice drifted off. "Who knows what goes on in this house when I'm not around. The shadow knows," he tacked on, lugubriously.

There was a long silence, and then Sarah said, faintly, "I don't care what you do with yourself, Sam. It's not *my* life." She turned to me. "There's this bottle in his room which I found. It was half-drunk. I know it isn't mine. I know it isn't anybody else's I know. Because nobody else in this family—"

"What were you doing in my room, anyway?" Sam demanded suddenly.

"I was looking for some scotch tape. Jam said you were wrapping presents earlier and you probably had some up there."

"Sarah," Sam interrupted, and for the first time I heard something in his voice that made me not trust him, "if that were mine, you would never have found it in the first place. What do you think I am, stupid?"

Her accusation appeared to have dumbfounded him. If she wasn't questioning his sobriety, she was questioning his—or someone of his stature's—ability to cover his tracks. An ancient frustration came into his voice. "Don't fucking *accuse* me, Sarah. I don't even *like* Scotch. You don't sit around here and fucking *accuse* me—"

"Then why do you smell the way you do?"

"Smell the way what?"

"Of booze?"

"I do *not* smell of booze. She should get her nose examined," he added to me incredulously.

"Sam, you don't have to yell," I said in a quiet voice.

"I'm *not* yelling." He was, though.

My sister's voice was strangely calm. "Sam, it's obvious. What do you think it is, invisible ink? I can smell that smell a million yards away. When you add mouthwash to booze, you just end up smelling like mouthwash and booze. It's not like we didn't grow up in the same family."

"Look," I interrupted, "he said it wasn't his, so why don't you give him the benefit of the doubt? It's Christmas Eve, for heaven's sakes."

"John, why don't you just be quiet? You're always defending him. It's time people quit defending him every other second."

"Sarah," Sam interjected in a rush, "if it were mine I'd probably—whatever I'd do. End up doing. The point is you wouldn't've found it. I'd probably hide it in the chimney. *Up* the chimney. À la Santa Claus. *Under* the chimney. No, that's too obvious. Look, I know myself too well to fall into *that* trap again. No. Hey. Here. Here's one. I would have hidden it, oh, I don't know, the way I used to, oh, God, oh, God," and then he was shaking his head, as if simultaneously comforted and repelled by memories of his drinking past.

He was relying on charm and on chance, now, as well as his ability to improvise. I could smell nothing on his breath, but then again, I was seated a good distance away from him. And when he stood a few moments later, briefly he lost his balance. It wasn't like a comic-book drunk tripping, but a sliding unsteadiness of his foot that might have happened to anybody who'd attempted to rise from a sitting position with grace and a modicum of control. Then he regained his footing, a piece of meticulous choreography that he managed to make seem inevitable and even graceful.

Sarah said, "Are you still going to your things?"

"Sorry, I don't talk to you anymore."

"So are you?"

"*What* things?" he snapped.

"Your meetings?"

"Uh huh. Yeah. Whatever." He was gazing at the mistletoe over the door as if hypnotized by its fragility.

"How many, though, that's the question."

"I'm hardly the sort of person who goes around keeping *count*, give me a break."

"Well, it's good for you to go, 'cause remember what happens when you don't."

"I kick ass," Sam said wildly. "I chase tail and I kick ass."

When Sarah spoke again, she sounded as though she were about to burst into tears. "Sam, if you can't stand being around us, you should *tell* us."

•   •   •

"The family that prays together stays together," my father remarked an hour later as we filed into a back pew of the local Episcopal church. The saying—I wasn't familiar with it—seemed to please him; he'd already said it a few times that day, the last time as we were fumbling into our coats and gloves in the hallway. Oddly enough, it was Sam who'd galvanized everybody into going to church, and he was the first of all of us to appear downstairs with his coat buttoned and his black watch hat stretched down so low it almost covered his eyes. Sarah's accusation seemed to have created in him a momentum, a quickening, based on a desire to show that he was just the opposite of somebody drunk—that he was alert, on guard, readier than the rest of us.

Which isn't to say she'd changed her opinion or softened it. As we were leaving the house, she eyed Sam. "You sure you can make it, Sam?"

My mother glanced back and forth between them. "Why wouldn't he be able to make it?"

"Why don't you ask him?"

She did, and Sam pursed his lips. "Because it's late and people are tired, that's why."

The ride to the church was short and awkward. Sam sat in the back, next to the window, one hand loose on the handle, as if he intended to burst out of the car at the first possible opportunity. The service was packed. As usual, my father sang loudly—"Silent Night," followed by a rousing "Joy to the World"—and with a quavering, angelic gusto that brought stares and half-smiles to our pew. Normally, I would've shrunk down in my seat, but tonight I couldn't keep my eyes off Sam, a sight that necessarily took in Sarah, since the two of them were sitting on the inside end of the pew, separated only by Caroline. In time, the first few rows began filing toward the altar to receive communion, and I noticed that my younger brother, observing them, wore an exotic, dismayed expression on his face. When it was our pew's turn, he craned his neck, gazing off into the crowd as though searching out friends who'd promised him they would be there that night but who hadn't, for one reason or another, bothered to show up.

Roughly, Sarah pushed past his knees. Locating Sam, my mother's eyes asked: *Aren't you coming?*

Sam shook his head, numbly urgent. *"I can't,"* he mouthed.

Troubled, her eyes searched his face, and as they did, his shoulders dropped in a pantomime of childhood defeat. His hand jerked up toward his lips and mouth, made a swigging, mimed gesture, followed by a loosely lolling tongue, and at once she understood: he didn't want to be faced with the communion wine. It was just too tempting, or for some other reason he knew to stay away from it. Relief came into her eyes then, a sudden radiance. "You don't have to," she whispered across the pew. "You can *pretend*."

"You *do* have to."

"You don't *have* to, Sam," she repeated.

"It's all the *same*."

"Well, do whatever you have to." She was so proud of him, she added in a stage whisper.

And so he stayed where he was, alone except for my father and for me—I'd never bothered to get confirmed, and my father had no interest in church or its trappings—at the end of the pew while the women went forward, kneeling in a softly uneven line at the altar. When I glanced over at Sam a moment later, his gaze was bright, frosty and distinctly smug. "What, Jamboree?" he whispered lazily.

He was lying. His whole performance that night had been a lie, and he knew that I realized it for what it was, that the luminousness in his eyes, the brightness that resembled lechery or, at the very least, knowing-ness, came not from the avoidance of temptation but from triumph, from putting one over on the rest of us.

He'd fooled our mother, convincing her, cynically, that he still needed her. He'd fooled me: I let this sink in, searching for a lesson to take from it, and finding none, I merely ended up shaking my head. He was an expert. He was to be perversely admired. But what else was he capable of? And as the women filed back into the pew, I knew I'd find it hard to trust him again, and I found myself lacing my fingers in front of me, surprised by how anxious I suddenly felt.

"What, Jam?" Sam said gently, without defiance now. "What are you looking at?"

In the past several years—since I left home for college, in fact—I've tended to sleep late on Christmas mornings. My recent Christmases have been leisurely, almost reluctant: coffee and a shower, and maybe a few phone calls to friends and relatives take precedence over the rush to get under the tree and start opening presents. So when a knock came on my bedroom door early the next morning, I thought at first that my brothers and sisters had decided to revive the helpless urgency of our childhood, when we'd jump onto our sleeping parents' bed and badger them to hurry, hurry, come downstairs into the living room and let's get started. But it was Caroline, holding a tray of coffee, trailed by Ike, languid and elfin in his red pajamas. After lazing around in bed for a few more minutes, we showered and dressed, and afterward made our way into the kitchen, where we were met by Jay, who'd just come from plugging in the tree.

Sam joined us downstairs before long. "Merry Christmas." His voice sounded slightly sheepish. "Happy New Year, many happy returns, and so forth." His shyness might have had to do with the incidents of the night before, or perhaps it was due to something else. All of us are uncomfortable with gratitude, with spontaneous reaction, and I wasn't surprised that when everybody was gathered in the living room, Sam lost no time in setting up residence underneath the tree, evidently having appointed himself as an unofficial Christmas distributor whose job it was to make sure everybody had a present in his or her lap at the same time.

His drinking. That, and the night before, still burned through my mind. He didn't look hungover, but what did a hungover person look like? Eyes red, head aching, sensitive to noise. I felt suddenly despairing, as if with a single act of camouflage and deception, Sam had caused our family to begin unraveling. The telephone rang then, interrupting this tortured reverie. It was for Caroline, and for the next hour and a half—for the rest of the day, actually—we fielded calls: Doll's parents and two younger brothers calling from Louisville, a great-aunt of ours from Delaware; a polite-voiced man looking for Sam.

In the interim, we'd begun opening up presents, setting apart Tom's, since he wouldn't be arriving until much later that day. Sam handed a present to my father, who set it down on the floor. "Aren't you going to open it?" Sam wanted to know, but my father replied that he wanted to extend the mystery of the moment. There were hardcover books and CDs and jokey knickknack presents, like a bag of black rubber flies from Jay to Sam, a pouch of Sea Monkeys from me to my mother, and from Sarah to Doll, a hot water bottle in the shape of a Heineken. Boxing gloves, calendars, finger puppets, toe warmers—I can't remember who got what now. Ike tore open all his presents and was starting in on other people's packages before Caroline told him to slow down; the baby, stolid and splayed on the living room floor, clutching her bottle between her lips like an angel with a trumpet, seemed satisfied with a ribbon. Then Sarah, unwilling to have her presents lost in the shuffle, handed Sam a long, flat package and commanded him to open it. At the same time, my mother passed a shiny red shopping bag over to Doll, who scrambled to remove her blue-socked feet from Jay's lap. "Oh, this is so nice of you—"

"You haven't even opened it yet," my mother said coquettishly.

Sam was jiggling Sarah's package up close to his ear, and hearing no recognizable noises, he started tearing at the bow. "Are we all supposed to save the paper? If we are, too bad." He slid out a low, dark tray. "Hey, weird. Qu'est-ce que c'est?"

"It's a Zen rock garden," Sarah said politely.

"Well, hey, I *know* it's a Zen rock garden, it says so right here on the

box, but what *is* a Zen rock garden?'' though when Sarah explained that
it was a plot of dirt and a collection of black, polished stones, fashioned
for the contemplation of nature, Sam seemed indifferent. "Maybe I can
lend it to Tom," he said after a second. "*Gracias.* Now open yours." A
minute later, Sarah pulled out a cruel-looking stainless steel machine with
a lever on one side.

"Neat," she said, confused.

"It's a pasta machine. You can make your own pasta with it. In all
different shapes. In whatever shape you want. Fettuccine or ravioli or
linguine or angel hair."

Across the room, Doll was exclaiming at my mother's present to
her, a fuzzy pine-green cashmere sweater.

"Do you like it?" my mother said. "I thought it was perfect for you.
With your coloring."

Sarah stared across the room at Doll and at the sweater. I can't say I
know what passed through her mind, and yet when she opened her own
present from my mother, the slip of paper, with its attached black-and-
white photograph, seemed clumsy in her hands. "Adopt a Timber-Wolf?"
she inquired a moment later.

She'd gotten each of us an adoption certificate from the Timber
Wolf Information Network, my mother explained—it was a not-for-profit
environmental agency in Alaska. "Each of you has a wolf of your very
own," she said. The kit included a picture of your wolf, as well as a
videotape of the Northern Canadian wilderness where the wolves made
their home, bred and hunted. "There's a newsletter that'll be coming to
you every three months. It lets you know how your wolf is doing."

"What if my wolf's been shot and killed?" Sam said. He'd un-
wrapped his own Adopt-a-Wolf certificate, as I had, and of all of us, he
seemed the most deflated. "I don't know, Mother. *Thank* you, I guess."

"He's cute-looking," Sarah said, "my little wolfie."

"This sweater is so gorgeous," Doll interrupted. She'd slipped it on,
and now she burrowed up next to Jay. "I love it. I can't thank you
enough."

"I thought it was you," my mother said. "Beautiful. Stylish. The right color." She looked at Sarah. "See how the green brings out Doll's eyes? Since your eyes are hazel, you should think of wearing something a little lighter, but maybe in the same color."

"Well, I'm not her, am I?"

My mother hadn't noticed the sharpness in her voice. "You *can* be. It's easy with a little sense."

"Well, Doll's perfect, after all, right? I'm not."

Startled, nobody said anything for a moment, and then Doll let out a faint laugh. "Oh, please, Sarah, I'm *hardly* perfect."

"You are," Sarah said. Her voice was clear, bell-bright, though she was avoiding looking at anybody. "The perfect woman. Everything you do is perfect."

"Where in the world did you get that from, Sarah?" Doll said. "That's the dumbest thing I've ever heard."

"Oh, I can't imagine where I got that idea. *Mother*," Sarah added. She mimicked my mother's chiding voice. "Hold yourself up like Doll. Sit the way Doll sits. You should wear such-and-such color just like Doll. Then you can be beautiful too. How do you think that makes me feel? You give her this great sweater, and I get a pet wolf."

"Hey, Sarah, I got a pet wolf too," I started to say, but my mother interrupted.

"Sarah honey, I would have given you a sweater too, but I'm not sure of your *size* anymore. Because I never get to see you anymore." My mother looked genuinely distressed. She thought the wolf could be like a baby, she went on. "Since you're not married yet, and Jam has a family, and Jay has his family, and—"

There was a silence.

"Oh, that was a *really* nice thing to say," Sam said.

"Sarah, I'm *not* perfect," Doll repeated. Clearly, she was at a loss for words. "I'm, like, *not*. I'm the least perfect person I know. My tits are too small, my hips are too big, my neck is too long." She began to chatter. "You have this gorgeous hair, you have a kind of grace about you, you're popular."

"I'm hardly popular, Doll," Sarah said, and then Jay broke in.

"This is getting totally ridiculous. What is this, the Miss America contest?"

"I don't know what to say to you, Sarah," my mother said. "I'm at a loss here. Truly I am."

Doll thought of something. "Here, you take the sweater. I have lots of sweaters at home. I'll trade." She started removing the sleeves. "I'd *love* to have a wolf, actually. It can be like Jay's and my foster-wolf."

"I got that sweater for *you*, Doll," my mother said in a hurt voice, "and I wouldn't want you to give it away."

"No, I'll keep my wolf. It doesn't really matter," Sarah said. There was a plainness in her voice I'd never heard before. "It doesn't really matter."

"I think I'll play with my so-called Zen rock garden now," Sam announced in the silence, and as the rest of us looked on, grateful that he'd taken the spotlight off Sarah and Doll, his fingers toyed with one or two of the odd black rocks. "Gosh, this is such fun. It makes me feel so holy and impermanent."

Sarah's mouth seemed to be swirling. "Well, gosh, Sam, it's probably about as much fun as the pasta machine you gave me. Where'd you get it, at the airport when you landed here? Or did somebody give it to you and you didn't want it so you just rewrapped it for me?"

"Well, fuck you, Sarah," Sam said, sounding genuinely surprised.

"Will everybody please stop it?" my mother said.

"Open your present," I said to my mother. "*You* open your present," and Sarah, who seemed not to want to have anything to do with any of us at that point, passed the package to me, and I handed it over to my mother.

The gift, whatever it was, was enormous yet surprisingly light-weight. My mother took it into her lap, and a look of a much younger woman, playful and intent, came over her face as she began to undo the paper. "It's from all of us," Jay chimed in. "Well, Sarah picked it out, but we all chipped in."

As we all looked on, she separated the thin tissues and a moment later she brought up from the hectic swirl of paper an enormous brown-and-white stuffed animal. At first she looked perplexed: what exactly was she holding? Then, beaming, she hoisted it high up into the air. The dog—it was meant to be a Saint Bernard, I think—gazed down at us with foolish, popping button-black eyes. "Oh, I love it, you all," she exclaimed. "Thank you all!"

She was disappointed, and was I imagining it, but as Sarah rose to discard a pile of wrapping paper into the fireplace, did she have a look of placid satisfaction on her face? Why hadn't she gotten my mother what she was supposed to have gotten her? Clothing? Or jewelry? A skirt? A necklace? A trip somewhere? Something that could take her away from what she was being asked to live with—a sick man, the frost on the walkway, winter? Oh, we'd blown it.

"I just love my Saint Bernard," my mother said for perhaps the fourth time.

"You can sleep with it," Sarah said helpfully and, I thought, unkindly. The assumption, that a stuffed animal might provide her warmth now that my father might be too sick to, nervously suffused the room, and Sam quickly changed the subject as the dog—wide-eyed, a black chip for a nose, a blank snowman's face, a wooden beer keg clinched under its chin like the knot in a noose—was passed around for acclaim.

"It's so cuddly and warm, and I just love it," my mother went on, and she rose up and went around the room, kissing all of us on our foreheads. "This was an absolutely terrific Christmas. Absolutely wonderful. Thank you, everybody."

"A good Christmas," my father would proclaim later, as he sat in front of the television next to Jay, watching the first of three college football games. "Low in the crap department."

Presently, Caroline left the room. She'd forgotten something, and ten minutes later, when she hadn't come back, I headed upstairs to our bedroom. "Do you hate our family as much as I do?" I said, shutting the door gently behind me. "Am I imagining it, or are we just awful people?"

Caroline didn't answer. Instead, she handed me a package that she'd lifted out from under the bed. "I forgot to give you your present, John. Imagine—you, the most important person in my life, and I forgot to give you your present," and a moment later she hugged me, and wished me a Merry Christmas.

the night before Thanksgiving, asleep on the living room couch, I had a very strange dream. And while I know dreams are of zero interest to anybody except the dreamer, and the professionals who are paid to analyze them, I couldn't help thinking when I awoke that the dream was connected to Tom, and to whatever murky impulses had brought me onto the island in the first place. In it, a man—me?—was standing on a hillside alone. The landscape around him suggested some ancient British isle, replete with stones and sea, and from a distance, the man looked crazy. He was naked, shoeless and grabbing pointedly and frantically at the air around him, as if hoping to snatch from the dusk, what? Gnats? Seeds? Pollen? Rain? Snow? But the moment he managed to grab one of whatever it was, it vanished, and his hands flew back out in continuation of this charade, whatever it was.

Seconds, I realized the next morning. The man was grabbing at seconds. Just when he thought he had one safe in his hand, it disappeared, similar to a boat whose sharp, plowing nose turns the waves backward into the past, the only present time the moment when the boat's nose briefly touches the water. What all this meant, I had no idea. The present was like a drawing, perhaps, such as those paintings of mild attic-chest interest that you discover actually reveals something exquisite, done long ago. And yet unlike those paintings, the present was single-edged and reluctant to reveal what once lay behind the lawn, the stairs, the tar, the wood. If you scratched hard enough, though, it was there— layer upon layer of men, women, children, noises, murmurs, footsteps, people rustling into life and out again.

The house had begun to remind me of my father.

Our mother had arranged the July Fourth weekend well in advance, and was looking forward to having all of us around. Although Father had died on a cool, blue-eyed afternoon a year earlier that September, the long weekend of the Fourth was more convenient for all the members of our family, and since most of us were coming in from a fair distance—Sarah from Oregon, Caroline and I from Wisconsin, Jay and Doll and J.J. from the north shore of Massachusetts, Sam from New York—the weekend appeared to afford us an ideal opportunity to commemorate the anniversary of my father's death in whichever way we agreed upon, and also the rare chance to spend some time with one another.

Caroline and I had choreographed our trip to coincide with Sam's arrival at Logan Airport in Boston (I'd remarked to myself, with some amusement, that now that Father was dead, neither Sam nor I no longer felt any guilt about spending extra money to fly home), though I was slightly put out by having to drive an hour out of our way to pick him up. There were connecting buses he might have taken that would have deposited him much nearer the island, but over the phone he reminded me of the times he'd put aside important things he was doing and come to collect me at train stations, bus depots, shuttle terminals or familiar family drop-off points, such as the Howard Johnson's that stands halfway between the house and the airport.

"I dread this weekend, Jam," he told me as we drove. "I don't even *want* to be here. What are we going to do, anyway? Have some creepy little pre-ballgame-like moment of silence? Lower a flag? Recite verse? Father would *hate* that."

He laughed uncomfortably and proceeded, as though it pained him to bring up so sensitive a topic, to stumble over his next idea: that patriotism—specifically, the attention that a particular person or family pays to national holidays—was a stonily reliable class indicator, and so it followed that being Knowleses and all, we didn't, *wouldn't* care anything about ceremony, particularly as it related to death and Independence Day. Flags were tacky. They implied loyalty to a system rather than to the individual. We were above all that. Hell, we didn't even own a flag.

"Father was extremely patriotic," I pointed out. "Most people of that generation were."

"Yeah, but he didn't stick a flag up over his front door. He didn't march in parades up and down Main Street. Or prattle on about the wonders of Korea."

"That's because he wasn't *in* Korea."

"Well, wherever he was."

"He didn't talk about it all," I said. "Remember?"

"Well, that's my point here, right? Extreme discretion."

He fell silent as we drove past what had once been the Howard Johnson's. "A Christmas tree shop? When in the world did that happen? What happened to—"

"Last year." New management, I added; it had been in the local papers.

"This place—" but he didn't bother to complete his thought until after we'd reached the ferry landing "—it's getting completely ruined. The good thing about this island used to be that everybody looked familiar. Even if you didn't know the person, he or she still looked familiar. Now look at everybody. You know what? There's too many people in the world. They ruin one place after another. They ruin one place and then they go, Hey, there's a place over there that's temporarily unspoiled, let's ruin *it* too. Speaking of ruining things, are Jay and Doll coming this weekend?"

"Well, yes, I'd assume so."

Sam made a face. "Oh, well. And the brat?"

"I don't think they can very well leave him behind."

Caroline had been surprised at how well Sam had taken to his new status as an uncle. Over the past two years, he'd showered our kids with gifts—books, Etch-A-Sketches, trains, cassettes, cannisters of Play-Doh—though at the same time, the fact that we had families and he didn't, the forward momentum this implied, seemed to have made him more self-conscious than ever. "The perfect family," he liked to say about Jay and Doll. "House, Volvo, garage, sprinkler, babysitter, dog, Alpo in the bowl. Yuppie trash—you gotta love 'em. After all, what more could you want out of life?" He answered his own question. "How about *culture?* How about *fun?*"

Although the question of Sam's ever marrying, settling down or, for that matter, leaving New York no longer came up, my mother hadn't given up hope. "I wish he'd bring somebody home for us to meet sometime," she'd told me, almost poutingly. "We don't *bite.*"

"Well, there's a lot of us," I replied, in his defense. "The poor girl would probably get intimidated."

"Well, then, she's not the right girl."

"Would you mind driving in a more leisurely, opportunistic fashion, Jam?" Sam said as we neared the start of our road. "Can we maybe try and delay getting there as long as possible?"

*M*other was out in the garden, yanking up parsley, when we pulled into the driveway, and as she strode across the front lawn with one bony, dirt-stained hand raised in greeting, I marveled at how youthful she looked. Since Father died, she'd been leading a fairly isolated life; though, like most people who lived on the island year-round, she insisted that just the opposite was true—that it was hard for her to capture a moment to herself. Her days were filled, she said. She volunteered at a local animal shelter, organizing an auction that helped defray the costs of anything from taping up the broken wings of starlings to rescuing bats from people's attics. She walked for miles along the ocean in the early morning. She gardened—"violently" was the way she put it—ran a contemporary-reading group, worked part-time at the local gift shop and, all of us suspected, drank a great deal.

"Darlings!" she exclaimed when we got out of the car and embraced. "Isn't this serendipitous? Jay came thirty minutes ago, Doll is out to *here*—" she held both her hands a foot away from her stomach "—Sarah's down taking a swim, though the water's *bone*-chilling, and she's made margaritas in the blender for everybody, the table's all set and—"

At age seventy-three, I knew that Mother came across to most people as fragile and elusive, though I think only the latter word could be used about her. In the past year, she'd embarked on an exhaustive organizational binge. She'd sold the other house, apportioning much of the furniture into the attic and cellar of the St. James house. Each of us now had a corner of the basement filled with his or her old possessions. Books. Old theme tablets. Record albums. Shoes, sneakers, pants, T-shirts we'd outgrown, clothes and baseball caps left behind by weekend guests that she assumed must belong to one or the other of us.

With my father gone, she was able to see her life in segments. I was driving her to the airport after her first visit to our new house when she turned to me in the front seat. "I remember when your daddy and I moved into our first place. All the mismatched furniture. The paintings on the wall—just like you and Caroline."

Her voice was charitable and if not faintly absent, then logical. That particular time for her was over, she was saying. We—or someone our age—had taken her place. During her week in the Midwest, she'd dis-

played an obvious, dark-eyed pleasure in recalling the men and women—
the Jocks, Piesies, Bunnies, the women who "were" Hallowells, Phippses,
Forbeses—with whom she and father crossed paths/consorted/traveled/
drank/quarreled/reconciled, people whom she now said they loved. Some
she was still in touch with, others she wasn't. "You really find out who
your friends are at a time like this," she'd told me several times, her voice
sharp.

And yet despite her nostalgia for more nearly perfect, familiar decades, an unfamiliar hardness seemed to have crept into her manner.
After one visit home, Sarah had reported to me that she'd even concocted
a new laugh: rough, jovial as an emcee's, faintly mechanical—a laugh that
came not from a heart we recognized but from a distant place that
seemed to repel both intimacy and further interrogation. While Mother
was a naturally witty woman, this laugh had little in common with happi-
ness, and I cringed whenever I heard it.

"My bird feeder's missing," she said. Her cigarette, a Virginia Slim, was
smoking beside her in an ashtray made out of a quahog flap, and her
words landed softly and accusingly. "I have a feeling raccoons might have
rolled it down into the marsh. Or cats. I heard yowling and all this hissing
late last night, and I thought immediately, it must be cats. There's a
footprint in the kiddie pool that doesn't look human. And now the bird
feeder's gone. Disappeared."

On the porch, for the benefit of his son, Jay had shaken lighter fluid
over the coals and was igniting them, stepping backward as the flames
shot up, jiggling and flowering around the wet, black pan; he tore off and
struck the matches with the fingers of one hand—a trick he knew. Jay, Jr.,
who'd just turned three and a half, and whom all of us called J.J. for
short—was swinging in the oversized hammock not fifteen feet from the
grill, snapping out little-man orders, which Jay was following conscien-
tiously, though with a slight frown on his mouth. J.J. was a bright, blond

child who had his parents' good looks (Sam's nickname for him was
"Perfect," though he'd never used it in front of Jay or Doll; alone with
J.J., however, I'd seen him squat and beckon, heard him call, "Come
here, Perfect. Come to Sam," and the poor kid obeyed), and Mother
doted on him.

Doll was seven months pregnant, and now she adjusted her bulk,
drawing her knees up close to her stomach. "Oh, will you cut it *out*," she
said to Jay, who'd thrown another match down onto the coals. "Don't
blame me if you end up in some hospital. And don't expect me to come
visit you there, either."

"Have you ever had okra?" Sarah threw out to Doll. When no one
answered, she added, "It's foul. It's like eating algae. Or peat moss or
something." Back from the beach, her hair wet-combed, she was sitting
hunched on the top porch step, an empty brown grocery bag between her
bare knees, coolly stripping silk off the corn and chucking the ears into a
colander—a ghost version of my father.

Sam ignored her; in his opinion, Sarah, in fleeing New England for
the Northwest, had sold out our family years ago. The direction her life
had taken since then—lately she'd been working for an independent environmental group in Oregon—mystified him. "Rocky Raccoons they must
have been," Sam remarked. "Sorry, I mean *Rambo* Raccoons." He was
leaning against the blue lattice that protects the outdoor shower, and his
long bare feet slid through the overgrown grass. He aimed a hard, stubborn stare at Mother. "If you think raccoons can lift up a twenty-pound
bird feeder and launch it into the marsh, Mother, well, then, there's some
nice marshland in Florida I'd like to interest you in."

Then abruptly he raised his hands and shouted unintelligibly at a
rabbit on the lawn. His soda splashed through his fingers and onto the
sleeve of his New Orleans–bought T-shirt ("Shuck me! Suck me! Eat me
raw!" the T-shirt said—a reference to Gulf Coast oysters, and an old
birthday present from Doll). The rabbit moved as far away as was safe
and no farther. "They're just like the pigeons on my street in New York,"
Sam announced. "Disgustingly tame."

"Aren't they just the *pits*, Sambo?" Mother said. She liked that expression, "the pits"; I can't remember which one of us gave it to her, most likely Sam. "They've eaten *all* the lilacs . . . and they're adorable, but . . . it's 'cause your father's not here. I think they must know your father's not here—"

"You should get a dog," Jay said affably, but Mother shook her head.

"I hate dogs," she said.

"What about Judy?" Sam said, and then everybody joined in: "What about our other dogs?" "What about Bob?" "What about Lucy?" We'd always given our pets human names, as opposed to say, Spotty or Skippy or Snowflake.

"Get traps," Sarah said faintly. "They have those Havahart things—"

Jay tossed the empty matchbook on the fire and took a step backward. "Hey, man, can I borrow your matches?" he said to Sam.

"No, *man*. You may not borrow my matches, *man*. I need these matches, *man*," Sam said, and then relented. "You may have them on condition you don't call me *man*." Then he added needlessly, "Man."

"I loathed Judy," Mother said. "Bad dog. Smelly. No, I did. I'm not going to get a dog. And besides, what would I do with her if I went someplace—traveling, I mean? Your father was the dog person." She had a thoughtful, warlike look in her eyes—nostalgia, as well as a resistance to its soft trap. "Here, Jay, you need matches?" Mother held some out, like a flirt too Old World to light her cigarette herself.

"J.J.," Doll called over, "don't go near the marsh without me."

"Let him go," Jay said. He made a sudden, rude gesture with the spatula. "He's old enough to go down to the marsh. There's nothing in the marsh. He's not going to get mugged."

"Except by a horseshoe crab," Mother said.

Jay laughed. "Right."

"Ever heard of drowning, Jay old boy?" Sam said. "Glug, glug, glug?"

"Sam, be quiet for once," Jay said. He faced his wife, missing Sam's brisk, flabby salute. "Let him go. What's going to happen?"

"I am *not* going to let him go, there are *ticks*."

It was the second or third time Doll had brought up ticks: she'd read an article in that morning's newspaper that confirmed all her fears about Lyme disease. It reported, among other things, that ticks had infested the Northeast and that everyone should take precautions—especially in high grass. Before coming out onto the porch she'd changed into white pants, tucking the hems under short pink socks; she'd sprayed her upper body with something called Tick Garde, then insisted on doing the same for J.J.

"Judy was a fool," Sam said. "And she smelled rotten, like an old egg. Judy had the breath of a dog who'd died, like, two years before she actually did. Death-breath. And Lyme disease is a complete invention of the media, Doll. Like most things. It's completely distorted. It's so tick-and-insect repellent guys can make caseloads of money." Brightly, he added, "Hey, *here's* what we can do—we can somehow get the ticks together *with* the bunnies, then the ticks can *bite* the bunnies. Then all the bunnies will get rheumoarthritis or whatever it is they get, and so—" Sam stood back, awaiting laughter and acclaim that didn't come "—so we can wipe out the whole population at the same time. How's about it?"

His mood, grimly merry, was accelerating. Someone was about to get insulted or hurt; and in the general interests of prevention, I made a move to herd everybody indoors. When no one followed, I lingered in the doorway, challengingly. "Sam, do you have any interest in going with me to the market to get some ice?" I said finally, but my brother, wandering distractedly around the lawn, barely bothered to shake his head.

"I *know* somebody who has Lyme disease," Doll said after a moment. "She can hardly move her arms. Her nervous system is completely shot. And—"

"Whosat?" Jay looked up. "Who do you know?"

"Someone you don't know," Doll replied tartly. "We do know different people, if you hadn't noticed. And if you don't introduce me to any of your friends, don't expect to know mine." She turned to Sam; she looked small and ferocious, a wren on the warpath. "It's real, Sam," she said. "It's not just some newspaper stunt."

"Uh-oh." Sam waved a finger mock-warningly. "Trouble on the home front, you guys? The woe that is marriage, you guys?"

"Marriage is terrific," Mother said, with great feeling. She'd donned the familiar white apron whose front read, in oversized, thick red letters, "Bitch, Bitch, Bitch." "I *adored* my marriage. Your father gave me forty-five wonderful years."

But everyone was looking at Jay; he'd taken his place at the center, but this time not for the habitual reasons. Did he really not introduce Doll to any of his friends? Who were Jay's friends—of course there were hundreds of them, but who were they? My brother, though, was more interested in getting on with the business at hand. "Anyway, who wants rare, who wants well done?" he asked.

Jay looked as well as I'd ever seen him, and when we'd hugged hello earlier—something we'd started doing only since Father died—I was reminded that we didn't see each other nearly enough, and I was happy to see that his good looks—he was still the handsomest and least tarnished looking of us brothers—were in no way diminished by age, marriage or, most miraculously (to me, at least), fatherhood. Where were the pot-belly, the pipe, the self-absorption, the dull irritation I'd expected to materialize? Nowhere I could see; he looked good—huge and healthy. For the past several years, he'd been in the business of selling commercial real estate in Boston. He lived in a suburb north of that city that managed the trick of combining both ocean and horse pastures (Doll was a big rider), and he was, from all reports, a big deal at his office, where, among other perks, he was the beneficiary of a seemingly infinite number of hard-to-get tickets—Celtics, Red Sox and, most recently, the Rolling Stones—which he was more than generous in handing out to his friends.

"Pete and Patricia McPerfect are back in town," Sam had whispered to me earlier. "And that child of theirs, he's a *genius.* Why, not since Jesus or the baby Buddha have I seen a child with such extraordinary grace and aptitude. Just like his *amazing lug father.*"

That made me laugh, his sarcasm a clear indication that we were all, for better or for worse, under the same roof again. "Well, you don't have to talk to him," I said. "You only have to be his brother."

"Thanks for reminding me."

Sam was furious when Mother sold the house in the city—less because of nostalgia, I think, than because he must have imagined the sale diminished him in other people's eyes—and while Jay and Doll were getting ready for dinner, he wandered around seeing what had been altered or defiled, now and then coming back onto the porch, his voice lightly cutting. "Where's the cockfight print that hung in Jay's room?"

"Frame's being cleaned."

"What happened to the chest of drawers that Father told me was *mine?*"

"Basement, Sam—a family of mice was living in the sweater drawer."

"Ping-Pong table?"

"Basement again. Why don't two of you handsome men take a side each and we'll set it up on the porch?"

"Why does the house look so little?"

We'd gathered from far-off places; now, on that first night home, on a more provincial level, all of us came floating and traipsing into the dining room. As Jay and Doll emerged from the rear of the house, Sam, still wearing his jean jacket, hovered before his placemat at the table and began to bite his nails.

"Caroline, you're in charge of the music department," Mother sang out—on the theory, I imagined, that assigning her in-laws tasks made them feel at home, "and Jay gets to carve."

"Put on Lou Reed," Sam ordered. "Put on some Pearl Jam or some Lou. Let's have some Lou. Let's get this house *going*—"

"Anybody but Lou Reed," said Sarah, staring down at the steaks. "Jay, I want mine rare. I want mine still breathing."

Doll had her hand on her purse. "Can we contribute any to the food?"

"Oh, absolutely not," Mother said. "Don't be silly."

"What do you think we are?" Sam said to Doll. "Indigents?" He looked terribly offended. "And it's *may* we, by the way, contribute any to the food. Someone put on Lou Reed," he insisted.

"Oh, darling, no, please," Mother said. "This is dinner music. Let's all be *civilized*. Put on that black I like." She stood in back of Jay, watching as he transferred steaks onto the platter. "Roberta," she pronounced it "Roberti," "Flack. And no more talk, Sam, really."

"Lou, Lou, Lou," Sam chanted.

Sit-down dinners are rare for us, but tonight, with all of us gathered in one place, my mother had made, I thought, a splendid, detailed effort. The table in the dining room, its glowing ceremoniousness, made all my reservations vanish, and even when Sam sidled up to me and said, "Looks like a funeral parlor in here—where's the body?" I grinned idiotically; I couldn't keep my eyes away from the table. Lilies of the valley floated in white saucers; wildflowers drooped from a shallow drinking glass on the sideboard; there were candles and our good silver and, beside each setting, place cards my mother had meticulously inscribed.

Yet, despite the gorgeousness of the table, dinner was strained, and there were moments when I think each of us was grateful for the distracting sounds of silverware. The steaks were tough, and Doll smashed a wineglass by accident. "Please pass the embalming fluid," Sam kept saying during the first course, referring to the cucumber soup, though only I grasped what he meant.

"Could you translate that into English?" Caroline asked at one point. Sam smiled flirtatiously and fluttered his eyes at the ceiling.

"Does my cucumber soup taste like embalming fluid?" Mother said. "Is that it, Sam?" She added, "Honey, why don't you take off your jacket and stay awhile?"

"I defer to the brothers o' mine," Sam croaked, with great, obnoxious politeness, his look sweeping back across the table and landing on the centerpiece. He pretended to shiver. "Plus, it's absolutely freezing in here. Certain things never change, I guess."

"Why can't anybody in this family ever say what they mean?" Sarah said loudly. "It's like everybody's talking Esperanto or something—"

"Let's ask the Good Doctor," Sam said. "Caroline, you're on. Five seconds." But before Caroline could reply he barked out, *"Bzzzt!* Time! Sorry, Caroline, as the runner-up you win a case of Turtle Wax!"

Normally Caroline finds Sam amusing—even when I don't—but this time I could tell she was annoyed. At a loss for an appropriate response (with your in-laws, as with other people's children, your rights are never entirely clear), she shook her head, looked questioningly across the table at me, then out at the darkening bay water. "Simmer down, Sam," I said in a voice much too low for him to hear, then felt ashamed that I hadn't come to Caroline's defense more authoritatively.

By then, though, everybody's attention had passed to J.J., who was grabbing at the asparagus spears with his fingers, biting off the dully beaded heads and replacing the stems on his plate. "Caveboy child," Sam murmured, without affection, and as he spooned rice onto his plate Caroline gazed at his slack, prematurely lined profile with an expression— neutral, serene, shut-off—that I imagined she used to maddening effect at work.

None of us, for some reason, was in full voice. "Just another night at the Knowleses'," my mother kept saying, as though a cheerfully unmanageable chaos were taking place in her dining room. The implications rang hollow. How were we to know what nights at home were like anymore? She talked at length about her plans to take a cruise down the Nile in December with a group of British bird-watchers. It was the first time any of us had heard mention of this trip. "I've always been mad for Egyptian artifacts," she said.

"Oh, have you *rally?* Since when?" Sam wanted to know.

"Well, since always." Mother looked embarrassed. "Since I was a little girl. But, you see, your father never really liked to travel." There was a silence.

"So?" Sam said, almost rudely. "Some people don't like to travel. I mean, *I* don't like to travel. *I* had two parties to go to in New York this weekend—"

I interrupted. "Well, I think all of us wish you'd gone to them and spared us. I think Egypt's a terrific idea."

"Mother, don't you think it's a little soon?" Sarah inquired flatly. My mother stared across the table at her.

"Soon?" she repeated. "No. No. I don't think it's too soon. Do you all think it is? Too soon for what?"

When Sarah didn't answer, Mother said, "Dearie, you don't expect me to sit here and watch the fog come in for the rest of my life, do you?" Then she added, "Sarah, I may be no spring chicken, but I can still *cluck.*"

Doll was silent during dinner except to acknowledge, briefly, under questioning, that she hadn't any idea what she and Jay were going to name the new baby girl (they'd had the test, and already knew the sex). She liked the name Suzani.

"Don't you think that's, uh, like, just a teensy bit precious?" Sam inquired.

"I like 'Molly,' " my mother interrupted. "And I like 'Sarah,' of course, and I like 'Katherine' with a *K.*" She glanced around her, confused. "For some reason, I like 'Allegra.' "

"I like 'Kate,' " Doll volunteered.

"Oh, yeah, right. That's like your basic free-spirited *heroine's* name. That and 'Maggie.' Just pretty please, guys, for my sake, don't give her any of those fake-o, wishful-preppie, Anglophiliac Ralph Lauren kinds of names—you know, like 'Chelsea' or 'Tyler.' "

"One thing I know, heart," Doll said, smiling gamely back at Sam. "We're sure not going to name the baby after you."

J.J. was acting like a complete pest; he was as spoiled a kid as I'd seen, and his parents had always seemed either unable or unwilling to set any limits for him. He looked pale and frantic; a connection, a warmth was missing in his eyes. When he wasn't switching the overhead lights off and on, or applying pressure to the maid's button on the floor, causing a rusty bell to cry out weakly in the kitchen, he was meowing with his head in his mother's lap. This was funny and ingratiating at first, but when he kept it up Jay snapped at him, "For Christ's sakes, buddy, will you just put a *lid* on it?"

J.J.'s face twisted, and, lapsing into sudden, loud tears, he buried his face even farther in Doll's lap. At that, Sam clapped lonesomely, sarcastically—whether at the effect or at the words, I wasn't sure. "Oh, my God, Jay," he groaned, "maybe you *shouldn't* have ol' Chelsea Tyler—" and then he stopped short, glancing first at me, then at Sarah, for help in finishing.

"Minor crisis," Doll murmured, smiling grimly, rubbing J.J.'s scalp. "Minor crisis." Then she said something that staggered the table. First she asked Mother to pass the pepper, her voice faraway and affable, and then when she was halfway through shaking it onto her rice she looked up very calmly at Jay and said, in a smooth, reasonable voice, "If you ever talk to him like that in front of other people again, I'm gonna put your balls out on a tray and crush 'em. *Buddy.* OK?"

She wasn't in the least bit drunk—like most pregnant women, she'd sworn off the stuff. (She'd also given up her formerly ever-present pack of Merit Ultra Lights.) Yet, looking around, I didn't think anybody at the table, including Jay, could believe that any sober person would be capable of making a remark such as that in front of her husband's whole family— on a weekend, no less, supposedly dedicated to good feeling, to nostalgia and to reassurance that although we were missing a person at the table, we were still recognizably the same family.

Sam tried to joke the table back to sanity. "Really?" he said to Doll. His eyes were as wide as Sarah's, though he was clearly amused. "Crush 'em? You mean, crush 'em like lobster claws? *Aggghhh! Aggghhh!*"

Sarah giggled, then glanced at Jay, who looked hurt and embarrassed. I was aware of some shift in his eyes and his chin. Subtly, he eyed us all. An increased politeness in his manner signified to me that he was now playing to his family, almost as though he'd never left home; he was ours again and Doll merely a teenaged date he'd brought home for inspection. "Well, honey, we're all trying to eat here, and he's tired," he said.

"So *show* that when you're talking to him," Doll said. "Show a little understanding sometimes, it won't *kill* you, Jay."

"Oh, I think we can eat and play with the lights and meow and do everything at the same time," Mother said tiredly. "Who wants more pilaf?"

"So," Jay said to Sam in the silence that followed, "how's life treating you in the Big Apple?" Jay can refer to the Big Apple without realizing that he's uttered a rube's faux pas.

"Fine, Dad," Sam said, absently, solemnly. "Oops, I mean, Fine, Jay. 'The Big Apple'?" His tone was withering.

"Sam, why do you hate me so much?" This, the next thing Jay wanted to know, landed on the dinner table like an unspoken assumption—so much so that I wondered whether Jay had actually said anything.

There was a silence. No one laughed. Then, slowly, with a politeness that hung over our heads like a thick, pea-green obscenity, Sam said, "Why, I don't hate you, Jay," and I think that, despite his dumb, belabored irony, he really meant it. Then he had to add, "What makes you say-slash-think that?"

My mother politely bothered to groan, "Oh, Sam, you're *too much*," and then, rather officially, she stood to announce that she had a surprise—would we mind gathering in the living room? None of us, I think, was in the mood for any more surprises, but we did as she said, taking seats on the enormous white couch against the far wall: boy, girl, boy, girl.

Nothing in that room had changed very much since my last visit home. The Oriental rug with its jagged slice across one corner. Books on sailing, wildflowers, the history of the region, the bound logbooks of long-dead whaling men. Father's old hardcover G. K. Chesterton and Mr. Fortune mysteries. The antique turntable, with its wind-up crank and assortment of dusty cubbies filled with wooden needles, a stash of seventy-eight-rpm jazz records erect in their old green sleeves. The two prints on the wall over the couch, *The Tree of Life* and *The Tree of Death*, with their fertile, puritanical blossoms. Purity and Godliness swelled on the branches of the former, while on the latter fruits as round and black as bombs bore labels like Deceit, Vainglory, and Love of the World.

Doll excused herself, with J.J. in tow. Jay called after her, offering his assistance in putting J.J. to bed, and when she shook her head he gazed at her retreating figure with a quizzical, oddly self-satisfied expression. Sam started crooning "Try a Little Tenderness" in a deep, hammy, dinner-theater voice, and Caroline suddenly pitched a pillow at him. More amused than indignant, he threw it lightly back, missed Caroline and instead hit *The Tree of Life*, which rocked tremulously on its wire.

"I'm sorry," I whispered to Caroline. "I've never seen these people before in my life. We must have taken a wrong turn back somewhere." She smiled and squeezed my arm, yet when she whispered back, "How are *you* doing, my sweet?" I felt mildly insulted; was she criticizing us?

When my mother spoke, her voice was firm and excited. She announced that she'd unearthed a carton in the basement, packed with tapes, the reel-to-reel kind. None of them were labeled, and she'd spent the past week playing them all, trying to identify their contents. I could see Sarah not exactly stiffen, but a glazed, formal and almost forlorn expression—her version of preparedness—came over her face, and she crossed and uncrossed her legs. "Oh, God," she said, placing both hands over her ears. "If it's what I think it is, I'm going into the next room."

The fear, I think, in everybody's—not just Sarah's—mind was that Mother had uncovered a recording of Father's voice, and the anticipation of hearing it was unsettling, spooky. It was impossible to predict the impact of his low, correcting voice on our ears nearly a year after his death. Was this what she'd planned for the long weekend—was this the big event? But, no, it was, Mother announced, a recording of all our voices when we were young. "Now, it's *adorable*. Wait till you all hear."

She left the room and came back lugging the seven-inch reel-to-reel recorder on which Father used to play his music tapes, and with Jay's help set it up on the mantelpiece. At the time the tape recording was made,

Jay must have been around eleven, Sarah was ten, Tom was a year younger, I was seven and Sam five. The tape began as a jumble of high voices; then, before long, I could discern Sarah's voice. She was going on, at some length, about one of her dolls when she was interrupted in the background by Jay, who was making the roaring, sputtering sounds of a race car. Soon we heard a strange, shockingly kind voice: Sam's. Sarah could be heard offering him a doll. "You can play with it if you want," she said.

"Thankth," said the Sam voice. He had a lisp when he was little.

On the couch Sarah, relieved, made a face and poured herself some more wine. "This is a nightmare," she began lazily, but Mother held up her hand.

"Ssshhh!"

"Sam! Sam!" the ten-year-old Sarah was saying. "D'you like dolls?"

"That's *you*, darling," Mother said to Sarah, helpfully.

"Yeth," child Sam replied in his lisping voice. "I *love* dollth."

"So Sambo loves dolls," commented the thirty-four-year-old Jay. He was hunched forward on the couch, with a broad, fractious grin on his face. "Christ, no wonder you're such a fuck-up."

"*Sshhh*," Mother said. "There's more. Jammer, that's you."

In retrospect, I think Jay was genuinely delighted to hear our ardent, disembodied younger selves and, embarrassed by his own enthusiasm, was attempting, in his clumsy way, to interrupt the spell that had fallen over the room. Perhaps he'd had too much wine; perhaps he was as annoyed as I was that barely a day into our visit, old frictions had already begun resurrecting themselves. And Sam, for his part, had been acting provocatively since he'd walked through the door. Earlier, when my mother had asked him to make his famous salad dressing, he'd stared at her disagreeably. "What famous salad dressing?"

"Your famous salad dressing," Sarah had echoed. "You know, with honey or sugar, or whatever it is you add."

"I've forgotten how to make it," Sam had snapped. "Use that Paul Newman crap." The bitterness in his voice had surprised me at the time, but in retrospect, I presumed that Sarah's request had served only to remind him that a year after Father's death, he was—still—famous only for a mixture of oil, balsamic vinegar, mustard, pepper and honey; in the same vein, he might have been disgusted that our standards for celebrity were so slight.

The truth is that people sometimes hear what they fear hearing, and Sam, drifting in and out of the doorway, his bare feet crackling against the floorboards, heard, I think, only something that panicked him: no matter how much trouble he'd taken to invent himself as an attractively careless scion of the Knowleses and a credit to his father, the members of his family still saw him as a sad, lazy, effeminate, dilettantish, slightly shifty lunk.

"Isn't that marvelous?" Mother said as the tape came to a close and the oven buzzer, as though precisely timed, rang out from the kitchen. "Isn't that the most marvelous thing you've ever heard in your life? To-morrow, I'm going to make copies for all of you."

We went onto the porch for salad, coffee and two pies, pecan and apple. On the way out, I swatted Sam on the butt as a gesture of sympathy, but he misinterpreted the impulse, whirling around sharply as though I'd made a move to undress him. Although I told myself that disagreements were inevitable on a weekend such as this, I felt dismayed by my unsuccessful attempts at peacemaking, and I came out onto the dark porch feeling hopeless. Yet the night was one of the clearest I'd ever seen, the stars so sharp they appeared to be nicking the sky. The air was mild and sweet. There was a light, salty breeze. On the water, buoys were clinking—a woeful sound, which I love—while on the outer beach a few stray fireworks rushed the holiday and poufed delicately apart in the sky. Caroline linked her arm through mine, and the look on her face was loving and consoling.

"I just had an incredible déjà vu," Jay interjected. He was standing at the edge of the porch, his stomach slightly protuberant, as though stuffed with straw, his hands buried in his pockets. "Wow. That was intense."

Sam had been waiting all night for an opportunity to pounce, and now, from the protection of the doorway, he did. "I doubt it was an actual déjà vu experience, Jay. I think it's probably just the dulling and rote, unimaginative, accumulative repetitiveness of your banal existence. I think it's more you *wish* it were déjà vu."

"Sam's getting back at me now." Jay sounded as though he were explaining a predictable natural phenomenon to an auditorium of college boys. "I apologize, Sam." He bowed, slightly formally, and in fact, he did seem contrite. "I've been acting a bit—"

"A *bit?*" said Sam, but shrugging, he didn't wait for Jay to finish and instead vanished inside the house. A minute later, Jay turned toward the dark lawn and sighed. "It's hard being back, everybody. This place is so associated with Father, you know? At least it is for me."

Whether it was his attempt to bring up a subject that we'd been avoiding, or his gently stumbling attempt to put expression to it, his words had a silencing effect on the rest of us. "Don't start," Sarah said in a low voice, "or I'll burst into tears. I swear to you. I'll turn into a basket case."

Caroline came to the rescue then, and began talking about a degenerative disease, caused by brain lesions: every few minutes the sufferer experienced déjà vu. This sounded nightmarish to me, and I said so. "Wouldn't you go mad after a while?" I asked.

Caroline was answering, "No, because of course you'd feel you already *had* gone mad," when Sam, hugging Father's tape recorder in his arms as if it were an overlarge infant, sauntered outside.

"Come join us, darling," said Mother, who'd come out onto the porch herself a few minutes earlier.

"Hey, everybody, listen . . ."

Gnats were raining down on the porch screen that opens out onto the lawn, and June bugs, fat and hard, kept smacking against the door like strikes into a catcher's mitt; in the dim light of the porch under the Chinese lantern, breathing the air fragrant with lilacs, grass and Cutter insect spray, we stared up stupidly at Sam.

"Have you found another tape?" Mother said, with some trouble. She was quite drunk, I could tell, but with the excitement of everybody's coming home for the weekend none of us could really begrudge her. A moment earlier she'd wondered aloud, "Which one of you marvelous creatures has absconded with my wine?" gazing at us, her mouth slightly open.

"Haven't we done this?" Sarah asked. Her thin body was slung across the porch swing. "Sammy, it's OK once, but I think *twice* is a little hard to take. I don't really like myself as a brat quite as much as you do. I have the hiccups," she added ruefully, to no one in particular.

Sam had changed into canvas shorts, long blue boxers underneath them, ragged hems peeping out: a carefully untoward look he'd never been able to get away with at Emery—he'd been too shy, not the right type. "No, no. *Listen*," he said, and as the reels began to spin slowly around—spellbound cartoon eyes in their huge, formal sockets—Mother came forward slightly in her seat, a rapt, perplexed expression on her face.

The tape was the same one we'd listened to just fifteen minutes earlier. Again we heard Jay making roaring noises with his lips, and Sarah offering Sam her doll. This time, though, in response to her question about whether he liked dolls, the texture of the tape changed and a new voice, a jaunty twenty-eight-year-old's, thick enough to suggest a head cold, came forth. *"No,"* it said, deep, sour, stuffed up. *"I hate dolls. I want to shave their heads with a straight razor."*

I was so startled and outraged that I actually laughed out loud. Sarah dropped her fork ("Like in some dumb 1930s movie," she told me later, with a faint note of self-admiration). For a moment nobody said a word, not one, though I'm certain that the naive, surprised expression on Sam's face struck not only me but all of us as unbelievably foolish. At the end of the table, my mother looked as though someone had slapped her face. She rose, and for the first time, Sam looked scared. "Son," she said. Her voice was passionate; only my father had ever called him that. "You have a *talent* for breaking my heart. A *talent*. You should go onstage with it.

You'd be *brilliant*. Go right ahead." She picked up her small, rounded pie knife and held it out. "Cut my heart. *Cut* it."

As usual, Mother had gone too far. With one gesture too many—actually picking up the absurd pie knife, waving it around—she'd diminished the effect she had intended, and, seeming to realize this, she stood there swatting at a bug with her free hand, gradually lowering the knife. "You are the *pits*, Sam," she added angrily.

"What?" Sam said. He glanced around the table carefully, courteously, taking in each one of us, a school prefect mutely counting heads. He sounded indignant. "No—what? What's the big deal? I hate dolls," as though this were a basic truth that should surprise no one who knew him well, which, quite obviously, none of us did.

it was with an optimism that descended rapidly into weariness that I awoke early the next morning, and tiptoeing around the sleeping bodies of Caroline, who was tangled up in the sheets beside me, and Ike lying S-shaped in his Portacrib, I stole into the kitchen, and after brewing a pot of coffee and pouring almost half of it into the largest mug I could find, I set off across the marsh for a morning swim. Once on the beach, I stripped off all my clothes and waded in. The water was black and misty, and its gelatinous warmth enveloped my neck and shoulders like a pleasurable mediocrity. I paddled out to the tiller of a moored cruiser, as if in an attempt to wash the events of the night before off my skin—to outswim them, as it were—and yet when I found myself back on the shore toweling off, no real transformation had taken place, and in fact the events of last night had come into even sharper focus.

We'd remained outdoors on the porch for a few minutes longer, eating our pie and ice cream and sipping tepid coffee. Sam had taken leave earlier, not abruptly but with the same obnoxious languor with which he'd delivered his pièce de résistance remark, and an hour or so later I found him in the kitchen with his sleeves rolled up, assiduously washing all the plates, cups and silverware from dinner, soaking the pots and pans in the other side of the sink. While he pretended not to notice when I came into the kitchen, it was clear to me that all this industry—as well as his voluntary setting-up of the Ping-Pong table on the far side of the porch, while the rest of us were gathered around the VCR preparing to watch *Body Heat*—served as a kind of atonement, one, however, that failed to convince anybody of his remorse.

I wanted to understand him. He wore the characteristics of fatherlessness—muddy silences, odd angers—even more acutely now than he'd worn them when our father was alive, and I felt keenly sorry for him. "How are you doing in here, Sam?" I said.

"OK." He didn't look up. He'd put on his glasses, I saw, and the lenses were wetly clouded from the water.

"Just OK?"

"Yup. Just OK. Actually," he went on, still not looking at me, "I think I may go home early. Like tomorrow morning."

"Why?"

"Why do you think?"

"I don't know," I said, then, "Because we're all having such a great weekend so far?"

"It's depressing." He was speaking over the sound of the water, and his voice seemed to have taken on its characteristics—a monotonous pulling downward, a gravitational drag. "Isn't it at all depressing for you being back here? With everything changed? All the rooms looking so different? None of our old stuff where it used to be? Am I completely alone in this as usual?"

"Well, it's hard, if that's what you mean. I mean, he's everywhere in this house. Father is."

Sam shut off the faucet, wiped his hands on a paper towel and turned sideways, so he was gazing out the window at the darkness, the floodlit lawn, the black-helmeted bulbs cocked in the branches, and when he spoke his voice was tedious, blunted. "I found his fingerprints in the basement."

I didn't understand. "His fingerprints?"

"Father's. When they came down here last winter. They had sand to put on the walkway so they wouldn't slip. There's this perfect, exact imprint of Father's hand in the bucket of sand. It *must* be his. Mother has nails. These are fingertips with no nails on them. His hand is bigger than hers. What are we supposed to do with that? With his palm in the sand? What are we supposed to do with his writing? All the ex libris tags he has in his books? With his writing on them? What are we supposed to do with that?" Sam's voice rose. "Dammit, I can't get mad without crying!"

My mother had fallen asleep on one of the couches in the TV room, and we'd treated this with an amused equanimity—she was snoring a little bit—but in our attempts to tiptoe around the room, we accidentally woke her up, and she called out my father's name. For a moment, none of us knew how to respond. "Actually, *no*," Jay replied finally. "It's Jay. And John—"

"And everybody else," I added.

She opened her eyes, surveying us in an unfocused way. There we all were on the couch, or slumped in chairs we'd pulled in close to the TV. What did she see, I wondered? She'd always wanted a flirtatious idiot for a daughter, and instead she'd gotten one in her youngest son. Another son was a commercial fisherman, but we'd barely laid eyes on him that weekend. Her oldest son lived a life as serene and successful as a child's heartbeat. The fourth taught the same things over and over again, year after year, to college freshmen. There were two wives, assorted children. Who were we anymore? She remembered to smile.

That was how the evening had ended, except for the rain that came down after midnight, soaking the inside of the sills and flushing the corners of our bedroom with a wind that toppled the wastepaper basket and flipped over the lampshades.

And yet the rest of the morning passed without incident. We—Jay, Sam and I—began playing tennis at a neighbor's court, which we'd walked half a mile to, so all of us were in moods that embraced our own illusory satisfaction at living (fleetingly, at least) what felt like bracingly athletic, sanitized and morally fit country lives. The day was cool and cloudy, and the clematis bordering the road was in snowy, uproarious bloom. Caroline joined us before long, and the team of Jay and Caroline won their set so effortlessly that we all agreed to switch off, with—this part was unspoken—the best and worst players paired. It was decided that Jay and Sam should compose one side, Caroline and I the other, and when Sam realized that he was unanimously considered the worst player he quit, saying he had a blister on his left heel that was on the verge of exploding, and leaving the rest of us to play three lopsided games of Canadian doubles.

The court—a good clay one—belonged to a huge Irish-Catholic family named Flaherty, and, as Sam was absently sweeping out a puddle in the backcourt, Francesca, the middle Flaherty daughter, took a seat on one of the low stone benches overlooking the court. I hadn't seen Francesca since we were teenagers and our families practically insisted that the children be friends, but I remembered her affectionately, as I did any familiar figures from the road, no matter how noisome or bizarre they used to be as children. The small, gleeful, dirty-faced girl who used to dash out naked into the road and perform a wriggling dance for passing drivers had become a slender, wide-eyed beauty whom I didn't recognize at first; and, since Sam had removed himself from active tennis duty, she accepted our invitation to play a set, which the team of Jay and I won—barely scraping by—in a tiebreaker. The four of us had been instantly compatible on the court, and when Caroline suggested another set everyone was eager. Now and then I glanced over at the sidelines, where Sam was standing between stone benches, with his arms tightly crossed.

I could tell Sam's interest was aroused by Francesca, and I also knew how badly he wanted to play, if only because she was playing, but I still hadn't entirely forgiven him for the night before, and I felt a certain sadistic pleasure as I watched him stewing courtside.

But, after the second set was over and we were debating whether to play another, I took pity on Sam and held out my racket. He shook his head. He was pinned to the wall by his blister excuse, and also didn't want to appear in any way uncoordinated or pitiable—I couldn't blame him—in front of a player as graceful and experienced as Francesca. He was rescued by, of all people, Jay, who announced that he'd had enough tennis for the morning and that if we wanted to go to the beach we'd better start off before the parking lots got too crowded. Before leaving the Flahertys', Sam jokingly invited Francesca to join us, and to everybody's surprise she accepted without hesitation.

"So how're your parents doing?" Francesca wanted to know. She was zipping up her racket in its snow white rubber sleeve.

Sam said, "Well, actually, if you hadn't heard, my father *died*." He glanced around him quickly, to see whether the rest of us minded his using the "my." When Francesca responded, "Oh, God, I'm so sorry, I didn't know," Sam added, hastily, "No, just kidding, he didn't die, just putting you *on* here. Little summer *yoke* here."

"Wait," Francesca said. Then, "Did he?"

"Did he what?"

"Did he . . . pass away?"

"No, Francesca, he *died*. See, 'passed away' is a euphemism that's used by people who can't face facts. He *died*. As in rigor mortis. As in six feet under. As in 'Sayonara, baby.' "

This exchange with Sam seemed to perplex her thoroughly. She stood there, her small dark fox face looking mildly offended, as though my brother had introduced a language he knew perfectly well she didn't speak.

Finally, Sam said, in a casually self-pitying voice, "No, really, Francesca. He really did die. Or pass away, whatever you want to call it. Really."

"Boy, that's very funny, Sam," Jay said.

"*I am hilarious!*" Sam shouted, his voice echoing up the road.

As we walked along he sustained a loud and critical monologue about the recent construction on the island. He barely recognized the road he'd grown up on anymore—*his* road. He snorted at houses with names like Sea Song and Wind Chimes, at certain well-tended lawns (excessive neatness, Sam had decided, or read somewhere, was emblematic of middle-class desperateness), and at a sign that read DEAF CHILD. "What am I supposed to do?" he inquired. "Scream?" Clearly he was performing for Francesca, testing her, and whether or not she was aware of it she'd get plus or minus points on the basis of her reactions to his outlandish statements.

"Hold on, hold on here, please," Sam commanded as we neared the end of the road. "We absolutely *must* pause, we simply have to halt our little feet *ici.*" He'd pulled up in front of a sign that read, in black letters, MAYFLOWER MANSION, and, under it, L. YANKELOVITCH, PROPRIETOR, and now he heaved a giant, pedantic sigh, and gestured at the pretty red saltbox set back beyond the hedge.

Much of Sam's attractiveness to women, I've always felt, had to do with his soft, studious inflections, the actor's timing with which he delivered his words. He's no good, for example, in a loud setting, where the tidal rip and flow of his voice can't be easily appreciated, but in the dull root silence of the old road, he appeared to be in his element. He amused Francesca, I could tell that plainly, but, then again, she seemed like the kind of girl for whom flirting and laughing at boys' jokes were acts as natural and necessary as breathing. "So, Sam," she said at one point, "if you're going to be here for the weekend, you'll have to come over and *play.*"

She was clearly Sam's type, at least in a woman: tanned, attractive, from a rich family, slow-witted enough for him to manipulate, except—horror of horrors—she was Catholic. I wondered whether anything would come of it, and I had a feeling this had occurred to Sam, too. By the time we reached the house his mood was buoyant and careless. He kept touching her shoulder. "Y'know, Francesca," he said chastely, "someone asked me, Jam here, I think it was, a couple of months ago, 'If you could ask your father *one thing*, what would it be?'" There was no sun, but he squinted anyway. "Y'know what it'd be? It'd be, 'Dad, excuse me, Dad, but is your watch waterproof?' See, when he died I got his *watch*. It turns my wrist all black when I sweat or if I get wet—see, you can see—but I'm always forgetting to take it off in the shower, so that's why I'm so *curious*, y'know?''

*b*ack at the house, we packed a picnic lunch and drove to the ocean, where we used to go as children. We were all squeezed into Big Red, Mother's giant, broken-down station wagon, since it was the only car with a beach-and-dump sticker on its back window. The parking lot was crowded—mostly with BMWs and new Mercedes—and then, since Mother's sticker turned out to be from the previous year, the attendant told us it would cost seven dollars to park. From the backseat, Sam announced he wasn't about to pay money to sit on a beach he'd been going to all his life. I don't think he actually cared a lot—he hadn't brought his wallet with him anyway—but his self-righteousness infected everyone in the car, and we ended up parking illegally on the fringe of somebody's marsh. Though first we dropped Doll and J.J. off at the attendant's booth; Doll, the can of Tick Garde tucked under her armpit, wasn't about to walk through any marshes. "There might as well be a sign there saying 'Tick Farm,' " she announced peevishly, sounding more like the daughter of a chaplain than of the man who owned practically every radio and cable-TV station in Kentucky.

Behind the wheel, Jay sighed. "I'd like to put a tick in her Raisin Bran," he commented. Everybody laughed.

Sam said, "There was an ant floating in the thing of honey this morning. There are leopard slugs on the porch and spiderwebs in the shower. It's really charming to look up and see a spider reaching down trying to squirt conditioner in your hair." His voice was accusing. "When was the last time anybody bothered to clean out the pantry? Or clean anything, for that matter?"

"Doll hates our guts," Sarah commented from the backseat, glumly good-natured. "She thinks we're all crazy." It was hard to miss the showy note of pride in her voice.

"Oh, she does not," Mother said quickly. "Does she, Jay? I don't think Doll hates our guts. If anything, I think she hates not being with her *own* family during the holiday."

"July Fourth is hardly what you'd call a *family* time, Mother," Sarah said.

Mother sighed heavily. "Will everybody stop criticizing me, please? Just *stop* it. I mean it. Really. You kids are acting like a bunch of *vipers.*"

Sam got out of the car and laid his head down on the hot roof, his arms stretched in front of him like a child at peace. "This town's going completely to seed," he complained, his point being, I think, that probably only in New England would the presence of the latest-model foreign cars—supplanting those lame, ancient, wood-studded station wagons—be a sign that the Devil was near. "Dis town be such a ley-mon, mahn."

On the way to the beach, Led Zeppelin's "The Lemon Song" had come on the radio, and Sam had reached over the seat to crank it up loud, though Mother kept repeating, "Who is this man? He's like an angry hornet."

The beach was crowded, the pale sand covered with pine needles and cigarette butts and drinking straws. On some level I'd expected summers to come to a stop once I'd left the island, and naturally they hadn't, and wouldn't, but it was still unsettling to stumble upon the ongoing vacations of strangers. The beach looked dashed and worn out. There was an oddly limp, poisoned and colorless quality to the sand and the sky that I associated with exhaustion and desuetude. The dunes had EROSION signs all over them. The green trash cans were spilling over with garbage, which attracted yellow jackets. The ramp down to the beach was shabby and weakly sand-swept, and the hot dogs and fried-clam platters for sale at Tod's Snack Hut seemed less like timeless summer treats than summary invitations to a coronary. The coast guard boat, deadly still, lay on the horizon—the old target ship the one recognizable constant of the beach we had known all our lives. Our own spot, thirty feet from the shoreline, resembled the crowded interior of a vacation hut; Mother had brought along gaily covered lawn chairs, towels, a picnic basket as well as several thermoses, a transistor radio, a parasol and pillows from one of the guest room couches. "So where's the television?" I whispered to Caroline.

Already there seemed something slightly ill-fated about the excursion. On the way down to the beach, we'd passed an elderly woman in a wheelchair, wearing a white terry cloth bathrobe, her arm and hand raised in what appeared to be a general greeting. Doll waved back, as did Jay, and when the woman gazed back at them nastily, all of us realized at once, I think, that she wasn't waving at all, but that her arm, her hand, her shoulder, probably her entire left side was paralyzed.

Another problem was insects. Something about the wind, or the lack of it, had brought out scores of green flies. They targeted not only the skin on our exposed bodies, but anything that seemed wet and hospitable—mouths, eyes, ears, nostrils. There was no escaping them, except in the water, and minutes after we'd junked our stuff on the sand, everybody, including Caroline and me, piled into the waves; then we came back up the beach, leaving Sam and Francesca still submerged, though when Francesca began a vigorous crawl out into deeper surf, Sam angled his way back up the beach to where we were sitting.

"Angled" isn't a word that I use loosely. Ever since Sam lost weight he'd seemed unsure about how his body looked to other people; he still moved with the careful, guarded posture of a man forty pounds heavier and considerably less assured. His selection of bathing suit—a pair of ratty trunks pulled up high, with antique gray strings in front—comically confirmed his modesty. Never once did he turn and face us; he made his way up the beach sideways, like a man favoring an old injury. Finally reaching our spot, he collapsed onto his blue towel, stuffed himself into his shirt and grabbed his book.

"So how's dat ol' patriotic, cholesterol-ridden Midwest?" he said to Caroline. His voice was profoundly lazy. "Played midwife to any ewes recently? Seen any Satanists at any cheddar festivals?"

Sam claims to have an aversion to our part of the country, in fact, to any part of the country that's not coastal. On his last visit he'd complained about the disproportionate ratio of traffic (too much) to actual excitement (too little). "It's too claustrophobic here," he told me before leaving. "There's too much blue-collar blubber. At least people on the two coasts care what they look like."

"You ought to come back and visit us, Sam," Caroline said, for what seemed like the tenth time in as many years. "We have plenty of room."

Sam's eyes showed no indication that he'd heard her. Then he said, "I can't, I'm busy that day, sorry," and turned over onto his stomach.

"Fine," she replied coolly. "Well, neither can we."

"Oh, Liner, I was just kidding you. Lighten up."

"B-E-" Sarah was trying to read smoke letters from a small airplane's exhaust. "B-E-something . . . B-E-G-something . . ."

"There's fireworks at Carey's Landing later," Mother said. "They're madly illegal, but they still take place, even though that Kramer boy lost the tip of his finger last year." She rolled, with difficulty, onto her back. "I think we should all go see the fireworks. Who'll come see fireworks with me tonight?"

When no one answered she passed the lotion to Doll. Poor Doll—with the exception of Sam, she was the only one of us not drinking, and she sat in the hollow of a dune, in a white floppy hat and sunglasses, randomly picking at her onion rings, looking for all the world like a tiny, fragile, good-luck trophy you might win after riding a carousel twenty times in a row. Nobody had mentioned the scene at the table the night before, and I had noticed that, by the time Jay had woken up, Doll, J.J. and Sarah had gone into town to shop. And when they returned Doll hadn't wanted to come to the beach at all.

"How are you feeling?" Mother said to Doll. "Are you comfortable? Can I get you anything?"

"You can get me a lobotomy," Doll replied. "I'd like a full-frontal lobotomy." She rose to stretch, and proceeded to head toward the shore. "But, since none of you can give me a lobotomy, I'm going to get my feet wet. Will you keep an eye on J.J.?" she added over her shoulder. "I worry about people kidnapping him."

"The kidnappers would live to regret their incredible error in judgment," Sam said, low enough so that my brother couldn't hear.

"Why does she want a lobotomy?" my mother demanded when Doll was out of earshot. "Jay, why does Doll want a lobotomy?"

He shrugged. "Don't ask."

"Why'd you get one, big guy?" Sam drawled. "Peer pressure?"

"Is Doll all right?" Mother said, and without waiting for him to answer, she answered herself. "Well, being pregnant is hard on *anybody*. On the nerves. Not to mention your mood, I mean. It's no fun. Really. Even for Doll."

"Well, it's not fun for me either," Jay said, and then he jumped up—he wasn't for keeping still for very long—and proposed a game of Frisbee, and all of us except Mother and Sam took positions in the sand. After a few rounds, Jay and Francesca jogged down to the water.

"Oh, are those crazies going swimming? I find it just too *hot* to swim," Mother said. "The waves are so rough. And the tide's high. Last week there were jellyfish rushing around stinging people. I think *I* will stay right here where I am, and enjoy my drink and having all you wonderful people around me."

Across from me, looking stodgy in the sand, his calves soft and veined and wintry white, the only one of the boys not just wearing a shirt but with it tucked inside his trunks, Sam stared after Jay as he plowed into the water; before long it became obvious that Jay had taken it upon himself to instruct Francesca on the finer points of bodysurfing. She stood ankle-deep in the water, both hands on her knees, laughing her high laugh. Her figure was terrific, lithe and brown-skinned, if slightly over-Nautilused, and at that moment, with the waves softly slugging her legs, she seemed to me the tanned, freckled and adorable essence of a summer girl.

My younger brother looked terribly gloomy. "He's going to swim out to sea," he said in a low voice, "and take her with him on his shoulders. Watch. It's so banal. He's showing off for her. Mr. Athlete's Foot. Oh, gee, let's all be the Kennedys or something. Hey, John-John, catch. Hey, Bobby, hey, Eunice, hey, Caroline. Just watch. Oh, it's so ridiculous. It's just all so trite and predictable and pathetic—"

"What are you talking about?" I said.

"Just because his bitchy wife's out of commission, that asshole's going after her. And she's *my* friend. *I'm* the one she likes."

This seemed to me so ludicrous a translation of the situation that I just gazed at him in disbelief. "Sam," I said, "you're dreaming. You're having a hallucination. You're having an acid flashback."

Sam had a match between his teeth—now he was sucking off the head. For an accuser he seemed nervous. "It's not as though he hasn't tried it before. Remember—" and he named a girl he'd brought home for the weekend a long time back. "Remember when he tried to take her miniature golfing with him when I had a cold and I couldn't go?"

"He's just being *nice* to her, Sam," I said. "For God's sake, we've all known her since she was two. And the only thing you've been doing is putting down the place where she's lived all her life. All that about what-ever-their-names-are—the Yankelovitches, I mean. Consider how that might make her feel."

Hearing this, Sam seemed to cheer up a little. "That's right," he said. "That's right." I thought at first that he was regretting what he'd said, but I was wrong—he was merely preparing a more detailed case against Francesca, like a lawyer jumping sides midway through the trial. "Her father's a *construction executive*," Sam said sourly. "I mean, we're talking about a guy who lives in a *mock-Tudor* house. We're talking major mafioso R.C.'s here. *Mock Tudor*. That guy might as well keep his speed-boat in his front yard. No wonder she's been hanging around him. Jay. *Lughead* over there—I mean, with his *balls* hanging out of his bathing suit? He's not wearing underwear." He cleared his throat. "Guess he forgot. Now that bitch wife of his can *really* put 'em on a tray and smash 'em. I mean, geez, what a gigantic turn-on."

I'd noticed the same thing, had in fact silently rehearsed making one of several collegiate-sounding comments to my brother on the order of "You're losing something, pal," but I'd refrained, and then I forgot. Sam was right: at certain angles, in certain sand-straddling beach positions, Jay's glamorous balls dropped out of his suit for all the world to see and remark upon. Did Jay know? If he knew, did he care? Francesca had no doubt seen them, too, but hadn't said anything, either. What was there to say? "Nice balls"?

Why didn't I say something to Sam? Probably because I thought—hoped, rather—that each time would be the last. And his humor, if you could call it that, was strangely restorative; it underlined an exclusivity I'd once thought unique to our family. "Give it a rest," I said at last. "They're *swimming*, for heaven's sake."

"She's darling, Sam," Mother called over. "Francesca. Like her a lot."

"I'm hardly going out with her," Sam replied, but he seemed pleased and flattered that Mother had perhaps picked up something amorous or lustful in Francesca's eyes that another woman might notice, even if that other woman was his mother. The subject of Jay and Francesca was dropped; Sam concentrated his attention on an old man trolling the upper shore with a Geiger counter, and eventually we ate lunch and broke open another bottle of wine. The sky was cloudless by then, the overhead sun painful, and before long my neck and shoulders began to redden.

"So, Sarah," Mother said at one point, "are you absolutely *loving* the Northwest?"

"B-E-G-O-O-D, Sareeta," Sam said absently, staring up at the sky letters. "It says, 'Be good.' Uh-oh, Father's mad at us."

"It's a brand of blue jeans, actually," I said.

Sam shook his head faintly, solemnly. "Nope—Father's mad at us."

When Sarah didn't respond to my mother's question, she kept picking. "Whatever happened to that nice guy you were going out with? Paul. Why isn't Paul here this weekend?"

"Mr. Locksmith?" Sam inquired acidly. Paul Buyers was a recent boyfriend of Sarah's whose father ran a chain of spectacularly successful twenty-four-hour lock-replacement stores—Mr. Locksmith. That nickname, inevitably, stuck.

"That boy could fix anything," Mother said, her voice grand, nostalgic and a little husky, as though Mr. Locksmith *fils* were a towering figure of the twentieth century whom we'd all been lucky enough to brush up against. "I don't think I shall ever forget . . ." and she began a long, uninvolving story about some fuses that had blown one night and how Mr. Locksmith had borrowed her blue rubber kitchen gloves and disappeared into the dark basement, and before she knew it the house was lit like a riverboat restaurant.

Sarah finally looked interested. "Well, Mr. Locksmith was good at things like that. In fact, that's about *all* Mr. Locksmith was good at."

"Mr. Locksmith was *superb* at things like that," Mother replied. "I don't know why you put things like that down, Sarah. I love a man who knows what he's doing. Who's good with his hands."

The thought must have been in everybody's mind, not just in mine, that Mother's last comment somehow reflected badly on Father, who wasn't particularly adept with his hands, and who'd spent most of his life bent over a desk.

"*I* love a man," Sam interrupted, "who smells clean. Just like soap and water." He glanced around him. "Isn't that what women say to each other when the guys aren't around?"

Sarah ignored him. "Nope, Mr. Locksmith's all gone. And Mel Gibson hasn't called. Not once. I'm so insulted. I guess I'm just a sad, pathetic old spinster."

"Oh, now, you are not," Mother said quickly. "Now don't use that word, Sar—it's ugly."

A signal had been missed. Sarah had been joking. She'd assumed, I think, that no one could possibly take her words another way. She'd even given a mock-sniffle, to accentuate the put-on. But under the hot sun, along a familiar but almost unrecognizable beach, something had gone wrong. Mother, who saw Sarah rarely those days, and who hunted for clues to her life whenever she did, had taken her at her word. Sarah's expression turned suddenly, markedly unpleasant.

"Oh, I just want more grandchildren," Mother went on obliviously. "J.J. and Ike and the baby are so marvelous—they whet the appetite. I'm *spoiled*." She turned to Jay and said, "Thank you, darling, for spoiling your mother. I don't feel like I deserve it. Thank you, Jam, too," she added, "for Ike."

Sarah spoke up, not realizing, I think, quite how savage she sounded. "I already *have* three children, Mother; I'm just keeping them away from you so they won't get *ruined* beyond belief."

"Oh, Sarah, how *mean*. That's mean of you to say. I didn't ruin *you* all, did I?"

Sarah closed her eyes. "Mother," she said softly, patiently, "I'm not doing anything wrong with my life." She rose. "You think anyone who's over thirty who's not married must be doing something wrong with her life. Well, I'm not. I'm just not. I'm *not* doing anything wrong with my life. My life is *great*." Pointlessly, she added. "Mother, you're the one going off *gallivanting*." She was going to Tod's to get a Diet Coke; did anyone want anything?

No one dared place an order. That would have seemed to be taking sides. We watched Sarah disappear down the sand. She hadn't meant what she said—Mother, who had nursed our father uncomplainingly during the last three or four years of his life, deserved pyramids and a good, free life now—but Sarah had said it; the deed was done. "Maybe bug spray," Jay called loudly after her, and Sam, squinting at her retreating figure, said, "Well, she'd better hurry up and get married. See how incredibly bitter and hateful she's getting?"

"Oh, dear, now I've upset her," Mother said, staring after her. "Oh, dear." She turned to Caroline with a pinched face and took a drag on her cigarette and said, "I didn't mean to upset her, Car. What should I have done differently?"

It was a joke in our family how often its members turned to Caroline in their moments of upset, expecting her to react with a wise, beatific calm, as though we had an unpaid shrink on the premises—which in a sense we did. But Caroline, as a rule, didn't stick her nose into our family dramas. Now she merely gave Mother a slight smile. "You should see me with my own mother" was all she said.

*t*here were usually three stages involved in returning from the ocean, and that afternoon we honored all of them, though more in tribute to tradition than out of genuine enthusiasm. The first was ice-cream cones at the Friendly's off the rotary, the second was a stop at Mill's Lake (Piss Pond, as certain members of our family called it—a reference to its suspicious yellow plate-glass stillness) to wash off the accumulated salt and sand, and the third and final ritual was the outdoor shower. Built onto the side of the house near the kitchen stairwell, the shower was simple, even primitive: a sleeve-shaped stall with a peeling, light-blue lattice, after all these years still miraculously intact. Inside had always hung the same objects: a length of old hose resting on a nail, several rusted gardening tools, a sticky brass soap dish and a shelf of bottles of Head & Shoulders and Johnson's Baby Shampoo filled with assorted heights of old soapy water. A spray jet sent the water down in a rapid, tortured, highly satisfying stream. "The best showerhead on the island," Father used to brag.

Jay showered first; like many former athletes, he tended to attach an almost fetishistic importance to cleanliness. A half hour after he was done and was still wandering around the kitchen shirtless, a towel around his waist, one hand buried in a box of Triscuits, Mother asked me to fetch two or three bottles of good Chardonnay from the cellar for dinner. First I went upstairs in search of some lotion, since my shoulders were burning from the sun, and then I trooped downstairs. When I snapped on the overhead light, I was surprised to see the figure of my younger brother. He was standing on a toolbox, staring out the dim, spiderwebbed window at the back of the room, and when the light came on, he whirled around.

"Jesus, you startled me!"

"What are you doing?" I said.

Sam looked embarrassed. "Getting wine. Getting *vino* for dinner."

"In the pitch black?"

"Well, it's gray, actually. I couldn't find the light. Where *is* the light—oh, you got it."

I told him I was on the same mission, and he mumbled something about great minds thinking alike. Then I noticed something I'd never noticed before, and it made me stop: the window Sam was peering out looked directly into the outdoor shower. Through it now you could clearly see the torrent of water as it cascaded down onto the ground, and

Caroline's bare ankles rubbing against each other. Sam's eyes followed mine. When I came up beside him, he sprung down off the toolbox and started jabbering about how dusty the cellar was. Where in the world was the Sunfish? And Father's old ham radio kit? And all the slickers? Everything had changed.

I wasn't listening. I'd moved closer to him, and I could see my naked wife; it was a young boy's view of a woman—strange, knee-high, mysterious. Through the narrow window I could see all the hot spots: calves, thighs and (shifting my head sideways) the soap foam as it caught and wet-braided her pubic hair. For a moment I stood frozen in place, barely breathing.

Sam seemed anxious to leave. His voice was a drawl—bored, ordinary. "If you're going to get the wine, Jam-Bo-Ree, then I guess I don't have to, so I'll—" but as he was passing I grabbed his wrist. He was right: the slender, slippery wrist was newsprinted black with our father's old watch. His breath stank of wine, and when I glanced around for the bottle, I found it, three-quarters empty and half-hidden on the rough floor beside the toolbox.

"Listen," I said. "I know what you're doing down here—I mean, what, did you have your hand on your dick the whole time?"

Sam tried to make a joke. "You mean, squeeze my ley-mon, mahn?" But when I didn't laugh and instead increased the pressure on his wrist, he tried to shake off my hand. "Don't touch me. I don't like being touched."

"Cut it out, Sam. And you're drunk."

"I am *not* drunk, Jam. *You're* drunk."

"Then what's that bottle of wine doing?"

"It doesn't mean I'm drinking it just because it's *there.*"

"Then what does it mean?"

He cupped his ear, as though he hadn't heard me. "What? Look, Jam, it was a joke. So I heard you coming down the stairs. I got into place—easy, right? It was a joke. OK, so a *dumb* joke, but—"

"Look, Sam," I said, "am I so goddamn stupid that—"

"Well, I just don't know, buddy, are you? I mean, you tell me." Sam's arm and wrist were relaxed under mine, but his eyes were hard. "Hey," he said, laughing, "your wife is very attractive and all, certainly, very *smoldering,* et cetera, I mean, if a little *Rubenesque,* but I mean, hey, Rubens is like my absolute *favorite* painter in the world, after all, no offense, next to, like, Andy Warhol, that is, but—"

"Stop it," I said, oddly calm. "Just stop talking for one second."

Like a fishing line, his wrist suddenly jerked under mine, but I managed to hold on. "What do you want from me? I *told* you I was just down here getting *wine.* Wine, you know, *vino?* So Mother can drink herself into a complete—let go of me!"

I am no good at scenes or confrontations, but at that point I lost my temper and began yelling at my brother. I was furious; Sam's assaults on our family diminished all of us, and forebearance on my part seemed only to incite brand-new violations. I kept hold of his wrist and shouted into his face, six inches from mine. I called him a name—"faggot"—I'd once promised myself never to use with him. "Knowing," I said cruelly, "your *extreme* sensitivity to the word."

I told him he was nothing more than a sleazy Peeping Tom, that what he'd done with the tape of our childhood voices amounted to an assassination and that he should be thoroughly disgusted with himself. "Ever since I picked you up, you've been acting like a complete *shit,*" I said. "If Father were here—"

"He wouldn't do a thing! He wouldn't even notice!" Sam looked near tears. I've always been able to make him cry, and I was perversely pleased that I hadn't lost the knack. "You're so pitiful, John! I feel totally sorry for you! I think you're crazy! You're crazy and you're *pitiful!* You should get your fat, stupid wife to shrink you! You're just this brain-dead arid academic *psycho!*" And then he couldn't control his tears any longer and he ducked out from under my grip and ran up the cellar stairs.

What was the matter with all of us? Had we all died at the same time our father died? Disgusted and still furious, I left the cellar, completely forgetting about the wine. Passing by the porch, I could hear the hollow click of the Ping-Pong ball on the moldy table; it seemed to echo through the hallway and the blank rooms like a threnody of disapproval. The telephone was ringing but no one was answering it, and when I reached the console on the eighth ring, whoever was there had already hung up. "Why doesn't anybody in this house pick up the phone?" I shouted to no one. The ringing phone seemed symbolic of something else, a slackness, a passing-of-the-buck, which only added to the toxicity of my mood. Upstairs I showered, shaved and changed for dinner—the outdoor shower was spoiled—and when Caroline came into the bedroom, her wet hair wrapped swamilike in a blue towel, her body wrapped in another one, I debated telling her about Sam. She seemed, impossibly, not to have heard us over the racket of the running water. But instead we started making love.

Whether it was the strength of the sun, or the island wind that brings on a profound bone fatigue, or whether it was the scene I'd just witnessed in the cellar, and the idea of my brother, drunk and observing my wife taking a shower, sex was hasty—uncoordinated, a disaster. When Caroline reached around to touch my back or my neck, the skin stung, and I snapped at her. And yet such vulnerabilities seemed to make her affectionate, and as we were getting dressed for dinner, she told me that she loved me, and that I was her best friend. "I feel so lucky," she said. "I feel like I can tell you anything at all. Do you know how rare that is for me?"

"No," I said, "I don't."

"I'm lucky."

"Lucky?"

"Lucky to have you as my best friend."

I tried to joke this away. "Believe me, you're not all that lucky."

"Am I *your* best friend?"

I was buttoning up my shirt. "Well, you're certainly *one* of my best friends," though I regretted the words as soon as they came out.

"What do you mean, I'm *one* of your best friends?"

"Just that. One of them. I have other friends, too," and I listed off a few of them, aware of her eyes on me.

"Well, so do I, I have lots of friends, too, but . . . oh, never mind. Forget I said anything."

"OK, yes," I said, "you're my best friend. You *are*." I came up behind her and squeezed some skin on her side. "Puttin' on the pounds, eh?" I added.

"Am I?" Caroline said. "Am I getting fat?"

She wasn't fat; she was just fine the way she was. I said I was sorry. "I was joking," I said, aware of a dull, crumpled-up, sick feeling in my stomach.

"I thought I'd lost all the weight I put on with the baby."

"You *have*."

"Well, so, what am I doing wrong, then?"

"Nothing," I said, "absolutely nothing. You're the only normal one in this whole house. On this whole *island*, actually," but Caroline still refused to meet my eyes. "You're not fat," I kept insisting. "You're *not*. I don't know why I said that. *I'm* fat." I sat down on the edge of the bed and took hold of my stomach. *"I'm* the fatty here."

downstairs, the sliding doors were open onto the bay. A stiff, battering breeze was blowing in from the narrows, and the wind-swollen screens were flapping. The confident buzz of a power saw droned from a nearby development, and I had an image then of my father, one as vivid as though he'd merely stepped into another room to get an extra ice cube: an image of him standing in front of the summer doors—large, red-domed head cocked, glass of wine warming in one palm—and announcing with no room for contradiction that the wind was coming in from the northwest, or the southeast, or whatever. How he knew this always struck me as a mystery. Though the grass was slanting, how could he tell what direction it was coming in from? No flags or pennants waved from the hillsides. He'd call one or all of us over to the window, and when his audience was gathered, expecting a lecture or at least an interrogation, he'd gesture with a hand that took in the water, the shoreline, the sand, the boats from the nearby sailing camps, the view whose very simplicity seemed like an opulence, and he'd look at us with great surprise—what were we doing there?—and say, "I just wanted all of you to remember this."

My eyes were damp. I missed my father; I think we all did. I found Mother in the pantry, preparing dinner, and I came up behind her and put my arms around her middle until my fingers were touching. I could feel her smile. "Jam," she said. "Hello."

I said, "You know those times when Father would say that such-and-such a wind was coming in from such-and-such a direction? From the bay?" When she nodded, I let go of her waist. "So how'd he know that? I mean, did you all have some kind of weathervane hidden someplace that he'd look at every time before he'd say that? How do you get to know that?"

Mother turned. Her hands flew, dully shelling. "Air Force, I think," she said mildly, "from when he flew. You know about that. You know he was a flyer. Navigator. D day, Normandy, all that. That's how he knew. I think you have to know all about the wind if you're a navigator." She laughed. "Really, I don't know very much myself. I think I know about as much as you know. Which is to say not very much at all. You might remember communication wasn't his strong suit."

"Well, you look great, Mother," I said awkwardly, after a minute. "Really, I think you look great. You're doing well for yourself."

"I'm doing fine," she said. "Just fine," she repeated. "The first year's almost over. One more season to go, and the first year'll be over." She fell silent, as though counting off to herself. "Right?" she added.

That night she'd prepared what for Father's side of the family is the traditional July Fourth dinner—fresh, barely steamed peas from the garden and a cold poached salmon. And afterward it was decided, by consensus, that we'd go watch the fireworks off Carey's Landing, about a fifteen-minute drive from the house. "Francesca's coming with us," Jay announced in the hallway. He seemed embarrassed; it turned out he'd offered her a ride earlier. "If it's all right with everybody."

I didn't think this was such a good idea; I thought we'd had quite enough of Francesca for one day, but it was too late to back out. Jay asked Sam to call Francesca and tell her to meet us at the entrance to her driveway, but Sam refused. "I'm not going to call that airhead," he said. He mimed dragging an imaginary cloth through one ear and, finding no resistance, out the other. *"You* call her. She's *your* honeybunch."

"Sam," Jay said tiredly. "Sam."

Mother, to my surprise, begged off. She said she never got to see J.J. and Ike, and that night she wanted to stay in and read to them. "In the attic I have all these wonderful kids' books I've saved for *your* children," she said brightly. "Now make a good-luck wish on the sky for me. And when you come back we'll have our own little fireworks display." She returned from the pantry a moment later holding a shallow carton filled with various pink and blue sticks, cubes and sparklers, all loosely tossed in together, which she handed over to Sarah.

Jay and Doll went into the other room. I could hear them arguing. "I don't want to leave him," I could hear Doll say. "If he stays, then so do I. You just go off with your—" Family? New girlfriend? I couldn't hear. Her laugh was hard and transparently unhappy.

My brother said, "Jesus Christ, what does it matter?" There: he sounded like a father—I knew it! And the door slammed shut. Yet when they emerged five minutes later it appeared that Jay had won; Doll merely kissed J.J. on the head and said she'd see him bright and early in the morning. We all piled into Jay's station wagon.

There was no moon; the soft summer night air reeked of skunk and salt, and Jay switched on the headlights to reveal in front of us perhaps half-a-dozen rabbits, of all shapes and sizes. They were parked on the dewy grass, their heads were bowed in a tense, sanctimonious rapture. When Jay honked the horn, they didn't stir or even react. "Kill 'em," Sam ordered, but nobody paid any attention to him.

After picking up Francesca—she entered the car breathlessly, smelling faintly of jasmine and toothpaste, and, because space was tight, proceeded to stack herself on Sam's lap—we drove the twenty or so miles to

Carey's Landing. The parking lot was jammed with jeeps and cars and with couples and single men milling around, clutching beers. We got out of the car and took seats on our hood, in imitation of the other pilgrims, and at midnight the most spectacular display began: parabolas, lazily dancing circles, cones and floral bouquets leaping up and dripping back down again. Francesca yelled, "Happy New Year, everybody!" and then she kissed all the Knowles boys hard on the mouth.

Then Doll, quite out of the blue, burst into tears. No one knew why—nothing had preceded it—but Jay was quick to respond. He got down off the car hood and came up behind her and put his hand on her shoulder. Doll wasn't having any consolation. She pushed my brother away roughly, calling him an ugly name, and got down off the hood herself and covered her face with her hands. Then she commenced a brisk waddle across the parking lot, trailed a moment later by my wife. Jay, standing there in the dark, stared after both of them with what seemed like revulsion.

"Boy, oh, boy, oh, boy, oh, boy," Sam commented. His back was pressed up against the black, shiny windshield, and he was holding a beer in one hand. "That gal must've been *profoundly* moved by the fireworks."

I wouldn't say that I didn't see Jay coming, but I was surprised and strangely exhilarated by how quickly he moved. He hit Sam twice across the face—so hard that the whole hood of the car seemed to resound. He'd used his open hand, and, on the backswing, his knuckles. The force knocked Sam partly off the car hood. The whole thing seemed to take only two astonishingly graceful seconds—and then Sam was lying on his back on the hard concrete. It was Jay's wedding ring that had done the greatest damage: Sam's nose and lower lip were bleeding; there were red marks on both his cheeks. Instinctively, I started over to help him up, but Francesca was there first. "What the hell's the matter with you?" she yelled at Jay.

My older brother leaned the heels of his big hands against the top of the car and stared down at the sand-dusted pavement. He looked so, so much like a Knowles just then—so like our father and grandfather, in all the old photos hanging in the basement and throughout the house—that I wanted to burst out laughing. Yet when he spoke I realized I'd never again be sure of him. "Fuck you," he said to Francesca; his voice was low, horrible. "You don't even know us. Get out of here. Get *out* of here." Now he was shouting at her. *"You don't even know us."*

On the day our father died, the pollen counts on the island were the highest they'd been all summer—this according to the local news, which was concerned about the effect that allergens might have on senior citizens and people with breathing problems. He lay in his bedroom, in the back of the house, as he had for the past two weeks, surrounded by all his favorite things. Or rather, things we associated him with—*favorite* was a word I didn't. Books, a tape recorder to play music, tapes. My mother had rigged up a sequence of pictures of us snapped through the years—as babies, kids, teenagers, in college—and tacked them up against a bulletin board. The children had fashioned leaf collages, as well as animals made out of rocks and shells they'd found on the beach, arrowheads for beaks, pebbles for eyes, mussels for ears, which we'd helped them glue onto shingles. From anywhere in the house, you could hear them squawking; they'd taken over room after room with their toys and equipment. The intercom near the crib was left on all the time, which meant their voices echoed not only in the room they happened to be in at the time, but in the living room and the kitchen and the hallway, so their presence seemed quadraphonic. They were colonizers, chatty, steadfast marchers, though instead of tanks and bullets and flags, they left behind trains and stuffed animals and pieces of train tracks and milk and juice bottles discarded like worn-out wind instruments.

The shades in my father's bedroom were half-open, letting in the hard, heightened light of early autumn, though maybe on the day you died, no weather was appropriate. But the weather on the Friday before the long weekend was glorious, with transparent clouds and that quiet, precise sense of emptiness that fall brought to the region, a vacancy that magnified the sounds of voices and distant cars and birds. The roads were practically empty. The grass had a gallant, vacant slant. The up-top branches of the trees on the lawn tossed like a girl's hair, while the snapped-off, limply hanging ones rubbed and squeaked against the bark. Outside on the lawn, the kids had begun playing pirate, tumbling in and out of the old rowboat that Tom and I had dragged up from the marsh, though inside the house, things were hushed, cradled in a mahogany silence.

All of us were taking turns at the side of my father's bed, some of us kneeling, others sitting, perched, casual, on chairs borrowed from other rooms. Or we stood in the doorway, soldierly, on guard, looking down the hallway as though awaiting extra provisions. Sam kept leaving to do errands; we'd hear his car distantly roar to life, then the crunch of drive-way shells. He returned bearing unimportant things. "I thought we might need this," he'd say if asked, holding up a bag of ice cubes, a bottle of seltzer water, English muffins.

I didn't know what to do with myself either. I found myself prowling from room to room in search of some dim, fleeting satisfaction. More than once I ended up in the kitchen, gazing into the open refrigerator, hoping that the contents might have shifted since the last time I'd looked. Mostly I kept to myself, creating odd jobs to do around the house— restoring an old desk, sanding down a pair of oars, sharpening the kitchen knives on the millstone in the cellar, raking leaves into piles.

We needed the women.

Unsure of their place, our wives were keeping their distance. At the same time, they were there if we wanted them. My sister needed them, too, needed someone outside her own family—the women who slept with her brothers, who knew her brothers better than she could. Doll and Caroline, united by their status as in-laws, had taken charge of the kids, though when I wandered out into the living room, both of them searched my face for clues. "Why don't you guys come on back?" I said at one point with a deceptive casualness. "Poke your heads in if you feel like it?"

We needed them. They were necessary at birth—that went without saying—and crucial at death. There were too many men in the room; like sticks or brass rods, we damned things up. When we were in it, the air in the room hardened, spiked. But when the women came in, even if it was just to touch one of our shoulders or bring us a cup of tea, the slatted air wavered, defeated. Earlier, I'd ventured into the kitchen where Caroline was starting dinner. "I know you all, you'll forget to eat anything," she said, and the sight of her in a borrowed apron, the prospect of kindness, made me burst into chest-rattling sobs, a storm that lasted for no more than a minute, and then I went back into my father's bedroom, where Jay was chattering about a property he was developing in southern New Hampshire. "You'll have to see it sometime, Father, next summer, maybe. I think you'd get a kick out of it."

My father's eyes were closed, his breathing light; it was unclear whether he could hear us. Sam looked up. "Jay, do you really think he's interested in the projectory of your career at this particular moment in time?"

"I'm just trying to keep—"

"Well, don't try and *keep*. Whatever it was you were going to say. Do you really believe he's even going to have a next summer?"

Jay gazed over my father at Sam with pity in his eyes. "Can we not fight this minute?"

My father's chest rose and fell. And then the children came into the room for a last time, confused, solemn-faced, tiptoeing, before retreating to the kitchen where they'd been promised ice cream cones. That gave me something to talk about—kids. Ike had begun day care. In the mornings, it took Caroline and me forever to get him ready. "First I get him a waffle, Dad," I said, my voice as hollow as a mobile of stainless steel spoons. "Maybe a pear or a peach or an apple, all cut up. Or toast, but it has to have a very specific type of jam on it. No substitutes allowed. And no crusts. Then we get him dressed. Diaper, socks, shoes. It's like trying to dress a tomcat or a beetle. Caroline and I spend most of our lives getting him ready." I gazed down at my father's face helplessly. "Maybe that's a metaphor for something or other, I don't know." Sometimes before dinner, I went on, we danced around the living room. "I put on something like the 'King Porter Stomp.' Or 'Sing, Sing, Sing.' Or 'Big Noise From Winnetka.' The kind of stuff *you* like. Then we all just sort of galumph around the room like a bunch of bears." A minute later, I laid my hand on his wrist, and Sarah, who'd come in a few minutes earlier and who'd been sitting expressionlessly on the other side of the bed, reached out and laid a hand on the other one. *Copycat*, I thought, with a pettiness that almost made me burst out laughing; she didn't know what to do either.

Presently I joined Tom and my mother in the hallway. "I'm not going to cry," my mother was saying. "He's not going to see me cry."

Tom put his arm around her shoulder, and that did it; she cried. "I think he must be waiting," Tom said gently when her sobs had quieted down.

"Waiting? For what?"

"He's waiting for one of us to say that it's OK. To go." I must have looked perplexed. "He needs to be told it's all right, John. That we'll all be OK. That we can take care of ourselves and look after each other. He needs to know that so he can leave."

"How do we do that?"

We entered the bedroom again. Tom said something in a low voice to my mother; silently, she nodded, and he knelt on the floor beside the bed.

"Father?" Tom began, and then he changed it. "Dad?" Then, more infantile, "Daddy? You remember that boat we all used to have? The one you built? The one we used to sail on as kids?" Now Tom was stroking my father's arm. "That was such a good boat. Well, hey, you'll never guess what." He hesitated, took a deep breath and gestured for me to open the shade, which a moment later, I did.

"Look at that, Daddy!" Tom's voice was urgent. "The boat's right out there. Right outside the window. I know you can't see it from where you are, but it's there. It's anchored right offshore. It's ready to go. The sails are up. The jib is up. The wind is just right. What a day for a sail it is. There's a great wind, the tide's high. And so all you have to do is get aboard now."

There was no answer; Tom's knees shifted against the floor. "Daddy, take the tiller, it's right there. Take it, you know how. You taught me everything I know about sailing. Just grab it. Grab the tiller and you'll be off." But my father had already stopped breathing, and a moment later, Tom rose up slowly to his feet. "He *took* it," he said. "He *took* it."

Later that night, we all stood around in the backyard of the house, with glasses of wine in our hands, toasting him. It felt so unreal—no one to call us back inside. For whole minutes it was fine, then I remembered again the word "dead," and the words "He's dead," which became the new words "My father's dead," and it was then that I felt a sudden, amazed, unfamiliar tightness deep in my stomach—as though I were going to be violently ill. This was something that happened to other people, but not to us. The night was cool; fall was coming. The small, bright, audacious light glowing from the tiny cupola on the outer beach blinked once and then all we heard were crickets and the waves, loping. We were silent for a long time. Then Sam glanced up into the bright sky and said, "So where's your basic star?" Someone asked him what he meant— maybe it was me, I don't remember; it was probably me—and he replied, "Well, for chrissakes, when people die, you're supposed to look up at the sky and then you go, 'My God! Hey, man! I've never noticed that star before! There, see? Over there. That new star must be *him!* Watching over us.' And there's no star. I don't see the star. So where's the star." It wasn't a question.

6.

as a boy, I could remember times when I'd all but willed my father to die. To be hit by a car, a bike, a train, or simply not to wake up. He'd embarrassed me, put me on the spot. During the day, when most kids escaped their parents, I'd always been aware of him roosting upstairs in his office as I filed in and out of classrooms a floor below. During the time he was sick, I was a kid again, chiding him toward his death. I was restless, impatient, sick of waiting. *Die*, I thought to myself sometimes, with a strangled, obdurate meanness, as though the word had the force of a command. Illness was tedious, predictable. I was tired of the trips home. The classes I'd had to cancel time after time. He'd pull through again. I'd go back home. My traveling bills mounted. "I have a life, too!" I shouted one night, to empty rooms.

And then it had happened, with Tom at the side of the bed, as if steering a boat of his own into some uncertain wind, my father the only passenger, the sheets like fallen-down sails.

At his request, he'd gone simple in his death, "cheap to the end," Sam joked afterward: cremation followed by burial in a narrow graveyard overlooking the ocean along a lonely stretch of the island known as Quinconet. A hundred feet below us, the tide drenched implausibly white sand. We were surrounded by gravestones that anticipated wives. The block letters spelling out a man's name, and below that, the woman's name, with her dates to be filled in later. "Poor Mother," Sam whispered into my ear. "I wonder what's it like to see your name on a gravestone, and you're not even dead yet." My father's ashes went into a box, and the box went under; each of us took turns shoveling dirt onto the lid. A salt wind blew in, and Sarah's shoulders stiffened, her teeth lightly chattering, and a second later Tom reached out and put an arm around her. We all stood there for a long time, not saying anything but staring down at the dirt, the box, wishing it were later that day or even the day before—any time was better than this. Then we went home.

I cried a lot that year. Tears came into my eyes at funny times. Shopping for Christmas presents, I found myself searching for things my father might like, books on history and the war, socks, boxer shorts, before I'd remember. Hearing certain kinds of music or having someone express sympathy could make my eyes well up.

As a child, I was once amazed by the ease with which my parents could prattle on about their own parents. My grandparents, that is to say, people who'd been dead for years by the time I was born. They'd bring them up in conversation now and again, and then they'd go on to other things, other topics. I always used to wonder, Where's the tug in their voices? The choking up? And it wasn't there.

A couple of years after his death, there were times I realized that my memories of my father had drifted off, fogged over. It was hard for me to picture his face sometimes, and this made me ashamed. I could recall him in the twist of various poses—leaning up against the mantle; gazing out at a particularly Byzantine-looking sailboat furrowing the water, standing in a doorway—but that was how he remained, vague, defiantly sculptural. One morning, frustrated, I pulled out a photo album. There he was. Hair, cheeks, glasses, neck, bluff nose. And ways. A way of standing. A way of holding a pencil, a glass of wine, a receiver, reluctantly and angled, since he didn't like talking on the phone. But a few days after closing the album, I'd be back to remembering poses.

Tom was, of course, more philosophical. Think of a family, he told me—our family, any family—as a shape, a pyramid, maybe. And that one of the sides of our pyramid had come undone and fallen off for good. "The object here," he said, "is for all of us to compensate for the tilting side, and get it so the pyramid looks like itself again. The way it always did. Think what it was you got from Father, and take it upon yourself to give that quality to yourself. And to the rest of us, if you feel like it." His glance was sympathetic. "You'll have to give yourself some approval, Jam, probably, among other things."

And so we divided up the emotional spoils. All of us took on our father's quiet, seldom discussing his illness or his death. For a long time, Jay seemed to lose his entrepreneurial enthusiasm. "How do most people get up in the morning?" he asked me once, to my surprise; I'd never heard him say a thing like that before. Tom descended, if possible, even further into himself, and one time when I brought up our father in conversation, he seemed impatient. "Why do you keep dividing things up the way you do, Jam? It's all life versus death with you. It's not like we don't drag our own corpses around with us every minute of our lives." Sarah stayed out west, refusing to even entertain the idea of visiting the island, though whenever one or the other of us discussed disposing of the house, she was adamantly opposed to the idea. There were arguments, asperities, a new metal in my sister's voice. "I think it'd be nice to have the grandkids playing here someday," she told me during one brief, two-day visit late the following summer. "Ike and J.J. and Isabel, and whoever else—"

"Why don't you have your own kids," Sam interrupted, "and *they* can play here? Then you can stop picking on Jam's and Jay's kids to satisfy whatever golden need for this house you have." He'd run out of money and was hopeful for his share of the proceeds. Another time, he overheard her on the phone counseling a friend whose own father had just died. "Well, I've been through it," my sister was saying.

"She acts," he remarked sourly, "like she's the only person in the history of the fucking world to have one of their parents die."

Sam, for his part, seemed mostly preoccupied by the differences he found on his visits back home. A girl had accompanied him to St. James one weekend, and not only had my mother put them both in the same bedroom—"It doesn't matter where people sleep," she'd told Sam, to his surprise. "There are more important things in the world."—but later the next day, after she'd heard him dialing his answering machine in New York to pick up his messages for perhaps the fifth time, she announced she was no longer willing to pay for his long-distance calls. When my brother came out to the Midwest a few weeks later for Ike's third birthday, the first thing he'd wanted to know was, "Is Mother broke?"

"Not that I know of," I replied.

He took a deep breath. "Father would never have made us pay for our phone calls. I thought it was deeply tacky and graceless of her."

I didn't quite know how to respond. "Well," I heard myself say at last, "that was then and this is now."

"Oh, thanks, Jam. 'That was then and this is now.' May I quote you? What's it like to be such a genius?"

The second or third night of his visit, I found him standing at the foot of our driveway, gazing down the block at the other houses; when I joined him, he told me he'd been envisioning all the empty bedrooms of all the children who'd fled the Midwest because they hadn't toed the line. "No wonder people leave here," he said in a sour voice. "It's all this conservatism. Meanness disguised as morality, as *niceness*, as family values. I suppose they actually *are* nice, these cheddary, milk-fed, butterheaded neighbors of yours. They're just fascists, that's all. And it'd be a nightmare for anybody who wanted to do anything different with his or her life."

"Someday when you're famous, Sam," I said loyally, "people'll be asking you to autograph your old bedroom. Your bedsheets. Your pillow-cases. Any old remnant of—" and I was suddenly at a loss for words "—unusual you."

He turned on me, gently and seemingly without bitterness. "Is that all I am? Unusual? Is that what it's come down to, what people go around calling me? *Unusual?*"

"Hardly—"

"Jesus, it makes you want to kill yourself."

Despite the cold, he remained where he was for a while longer, his hands thrust in his pockets, his old watch-plaid scarf wound around his neck. Then, lightly, he cleared his throat. "I think fame and being famous is tacky."

"Really? That's a new one for you."

"Hardly. *Hardly.* It's hardly new for me." He seemed to want to go on record with this. "Actually, I think fame is for nobodies."

"Nobodies?"

He took a deep breath. Fame was for lowlifes, he'd decided. It was their revenge for having been born with so little. "Fame is for under-educated trailer-park people," he said, "who flee their horrible little Southwestern hometowns and go to Hollywood and end up dying of drug overdoses in the middle of the sidewalk. It's for actresses with borderline-personality disorders. It's for gay actors who pretend they're straight and have to get married to protect their careers. It's for ambitious people. It's for hustlers. It's for shrimpy men with beards and cellular phones. It's for wannabes. They buy Italian suits and pretend they always wore Italian suits. They make themselves up like ideas. Then they get really snobby about people who *aren't* famous. They start to believe everything the world says about them."

"Well, look, Sam," I said after a moment, "most everybody's apt to believe what other people say about them."

"Yeah, but it's the wrong kind of snobbery. It's the kind of snobbery that's based on success and achievement."

"And what's the right kind of snobbery?" I asked dryly. "Your kind?"

He didn't answer. "It's for not-very-nice people, I don't think. Fame is. And the worst part is, then people get addicted to it. And to publicity. They become overly susceptible to it. It's like flies stuck to a No-Pest strip. I wish I were more ambitious. I wish I were tougher. Less *nice*. I wish I hadn't been born with anything. That's my curse, you know?"

"You *weren't* born with anything."

Sam seemed to rise up a few inches. "We were born with a name, Jam. And a lineage. In case you've suddenly developed chronic amnesia. Everybody wants to be us."

"Not anymore."

"Yes anymore."

"No." For a long time I didn't say anything. At last I said, "The party's over, Sam. They're sweeping up people like us and putting the chairs on the tables. People like us don't control the world anymore."

"What do you mean, we don't control the world?"

"Look around you. It's all over. There's not an aristocracy anymore. That is, if we were ever a part of it. It's a meritocracy."

"They should bring the aristocracy back, then. Who needs a meritocracy? A meritocracy is just based on stuff you do *during* your lifetime."

"What's wrong with that?"

"You can't control it, for one thing."

"They did themselves in, Sam. It's their own fault. They got weak and lazy and spoiled. They acted like idiots."

"It's not fair." We'd been brought up in a certain way, Sam went on; why couldn't that way last?

"There was never any promise that it would last."

Now he was cross. "It was *implicit*. And if there wasn't, then they shouldn't have brought us up that way. If they couldn't make sure it would last."

His logic was bewildering, if not completely bizarre. "Sam, if you want to live a life as good as the one we had when we were kids, then you'll have to get out there and *do* something.''

''But why do I always feel as though I'm swimming against the current? You know what the funny thing is? People like us used to *be* the current.'' He paused. ''I guess we're just penniless aristocrats then.'' The sound of this seemed to please him; it was a way of being broke and feeling superior at the same time. ''Kings and queens banished to the carriage house while the cigar-smoking vulgarians live it up in the big house. Here we sit with all our old silver and our beloved Rosemedallion bowls.'' He let out a sigh. *''God,* I wish I were black. I wish I were a Jew. I wish I were a woman. I wish I were handicapped. I wish I had more to prove. So I could walk all over people and have a chip on my shoulder, et cetera. You know the type. Angry. Vengeful. Pissed off at their lot.'' He was silent. ''Brooklyn is the way to go,'' he said at last. ''Brooklyn is the place to be from if you want to make anything of yourself. I should've been born in Brooklyn.''

''Well, you could always move there,'' I suggested.

''Who the hell wants to move to Brooklyn? That's counter-intuitive. You have to *have been* from there, or it doesn't count.''

That he seemed to be mining new levels of self-deception—blaming his lack of success in the world on anything but himself—distressed me, but I kept my mouth shut, pleased at least that he wasn't drinking. He'd proven in the past how skillful he was at subterfuge. Now the rest of us watched him and assumed the worst. I'd gone so far as to attend a few Al-Anon meetings, urging Jay and Sarah to do the same, crowded, smoke-filled gatherings that took place in church basements around town, where I learned (to use the lingo) that I was ''powerless'' over another person's drinking, as well as over their behavior. I'd sent away for various materials on rehabs and interventions—the latter where family members and friends confronted a person about his drinking—though I'd done little more than skim them.

My mother called me up one night six months later. She'd been cleaning out my father's files, and she'd found one containing ''all the letters you kids ever wrote him. As well as letters *about* you. When other people mentioned you guys in their letters. He was so proud of you all."

She fell silent, her breath wafting in and out on the other end of the receiver. She'd told me this, I knew, as a lawyer puts forth evidence, proof of something, attention, love, good faith, even if, like a secret crush, it had had to be hidden, so as not to hurt or destroy anybody, a friendship, a reputation in the community, hidden until its participants were all dead. But I'd already, always known that about him.

And a year or two before he died, I'd managed to make a kind of peace with him. Our good-bye, as I mentioned, was marked by the same silence and grieved, impersonal understanding that had always characterized our relationship. But by the end, some circle had been joined, a link reconnected, and it was one that took place, strangely enough, on his home turf, during my twentieth high-school reunion.

I wasn't a nostalgist. Not in the least. I never had been. Nostalgia brought with it certain distortions and sentimentalities, and I liked to keep my backward eye clean and sharp-seeing, as a first-line defense against self-deception. Since my graduation, I'd glanced through my high school yearbook maybe three times, and replaced it almost immediately on the bookcase shelf. At parties, guests would notice it sometimes and pull it down. "What page are you on?" they'd ask, riffling through the photographs of the graduating seniors, the quotations or fragments of song lyrics that had seemed timely and self-explanatory then, and which now seemed posturing and absurd. Those days made me wince. I felt unforgiving, even sadistic, toward my thrashing teenaged self, all his affectations and uncertainties.

Even more, I felt as though I had little to show after twenty years. What had I done? I'd gotten a couple of degrees, been married, moved around several times and now was helping to raise two children. I taught. I spent half my life in the cold, and the other half asleep. If I had enough money at the end of the year, I took my family on vacation somewhere—a dude ranch in Arizona, a resort in St. John's, a bike trip through southern Canada. Was that a life you could chat about at length at a cocktail party? Was I a failure? A success? A little of both? When I considered what my classmates were doing—or at least what their alumni notes claimed they were doing—I felt jealous and diminished. One was a publicist on Broadway; another ran his father's Fortune 500 company. They worked in television; they were doctors, lawyers, bankers, architects, commercial artists. One played a gigolo on a soap opera. There were two playwrights and a movie director and the head of an inner-city hospital. Three were missing; one had hung himself, the second overdosed on pills, the third died in a fire. The rest of us were still alive, going on.

Make no mistake—I wasn't averse to the idea of attending. In fact, I'd showed up at one reunion, five years after I'd graduated, a meeting that provided all of us who went with the ambiguous and occasionally melancholic opportunity to compare notes on the world so far as we'd found it to be. A classmate, known when we were in school for his raucous parties, had offered up his house and beach on the tip of Cape Cod for a daylong clambake. It was the same spot where we'd spent illicit time as seniors, due mostly to the permissiveness of his parents, and I'd stayed only briefly, long enough to drink a cup of beer and polish off a hot dog.

"I'm not going," I said to Caroline when I received the invitation. "They'd have to pay me a million dollars to attend that thing. Sitting around drinking sherry and making small talk with people who I don't care about in the first place."

"John, that place was so much a part of your life."

"It's part of my father's life. There's a difference."

"Right. And so it's part of *your* life too. You went there for half your life."

"I don't see you marching triumphantly back to your high school reunions, sweetiepie. I don't want to be one of those *people*," I added.

"What people?"

"The kind of people who had their best years in high school. Some pathetic old alumnus who clings to the past. To the golden years of cleats and jockstraps and slow dances to Stones songs in the gymnasium. Who simulates all the touchdowns he scored on Saturday afternoons, all his erstwhile glories, and then gets smashed and starts telling other people what he *really* thought about them. The sort of person who needs to attend reunions because nothing in his life's happened since."

Caroline gave a short laugh. "I don't think you'd ever be confused for a person like that. You never scored a touchdown, for one thing."

"It wasn't because I didn't want to. Anyhow, then give me one reason why I should go."

She was silent. "Your father's sick. I'm sure he'd like to see you. And because no matter what you think of them, you'll never have friends like that again. Because it was such a vulnerable time for all of you."

"Precisely," I said. "And now that I've become invulnerable, I think I'll stay right here and mulch the lawn."

It was easy—too easy, in fact—to take note only of the marks of time on the faces and bodies of my classmates, to see their aging, as well as my own, as evidence of something *sad*, as Sam was wont to say; to take notice only of the gray in their hair, or the absence of hair, the stiffness in their gaits, the bulges over their belt, the lines in their faces, the disappearance of their youthful forms into something more solid and at the same time more fragile. But as I greeted my laughing, chattering classmates first at a coffee reception, and then following a lecture, at a midday cocktail party, I found myself overlooking their obvious physical changes—I was hardly the same myself—and attending instead to the staggering variety of professions they'd chosen, or, in many cases, backed into. Boys whom I'd expected to remain locked in a holding pattern all their lives had managed along the line to break out. Athletes were actors. High school actors were sports agents. Poets had become ministers on Indian reservations. Of course there were a few inevitabilities—a few scholars had become full professors, the computer nerd was now the president of a software company—but gone were most of the old, divisive camps common to high school society. Even the unpopular boys had come back for our twentieth, putting ancient hurts and anxieties behind them, and so had the techies, the car nuts, the speech team people and the downhill skiers.

In front of a silver tray of sugar-dusted cookies, I greeted Tony Munroe, once a jock and a bully (he'd hung boys who weren't face-high on hooks from the elastic of their jockey briefs). Now, bald, loafered and plump-faced, he sold insurance in Washington State and appeared in amateur theatricals. "Coriolanus," he told me with a gleam in his eye, "and Jonathan in *Arsenic*. Mr. Applegate in *Damn Yankees*." Next, Chris St. George came up to talk to me. In high school, he'd resembled a leprechaun, with his sharp, knowing, almond-eyed face. These days he had the broad, planetary forehead of a marathon runner, and I wasn't surprised to discover that he was the manager of an athletic shoe store in a suburb somewhere in Connecticut. He introduced me to his wife, whose name I forgot instantly if I even registered it, so intent was I on presenting myself in the most confident light possible, as someone who'd never known even a second's career hesitation.

This fleeting tentativeness didn't last long. As the cocktail party was coming to an end, I ran into Laura Singer, the heartthrob of our sister school and now, she informed me, the mother of two little girls, two and four. She was drunk and happily emotional, and she hugged me for a long time. "I *had* to come back here," she told me. "We have our own reunion, but so much of my time in school was spent around you guys." After a few minutes of small talk about the past and the present, she admitted to me, in a burst of sherry-tinged candor, that during my senior year, she'd had what she called "a sneaker" for me. "You did your own thing. Everybody else was in a group of some kind. You played the piano. I loved that. That was really great. I was too scared to do something nobody else did."

I stared at her for a long moment. "I feel like strangling you," I said cheerfully, and when she looked back at me, surprised, I added, "I just mean life would've been so much easier for me back then if I'd known that."

Her warm, tense hand touched mine with great sincerity. "You remember how it was."

She didn't need to say anything more, and when I nodded, she kissed me softly on the lips before vanishing into the crowd.

That these little, dated passions and desires were being admitted to after two decades seemed extraordinary to me, and I felt a sudden and unfamiliar affinity with the other men in the room, those who'd gotten as far as they had, as well as those of us who hadn't. At the same time, as I looked around the room, I knew it would be probably the last time I'd come back to the school. I preferred to guard the school in my memory, as part of the jagged geography of my emotional coastline, than to revisit the actual place it was and would probably always be; the bells; the rugs; the worn unread volumes squeezed tightly into the bookshelves; the tea service, as huge and gleaming as a tuba; the hen-women with their firm fingers on the spigot. And the idea of not coming back made me strangely lighthearted, though perhaps that had to do more with the effects of the sherry in my stomach and thanks to Laura Singer, still faintly scenting my mouth.

Earlier that day, we'd sat on lawn chairs watching the boys varsity lacrosse team beat their chief competitor. There I sat, my knees angled to one side of the bleachers like the turned-in wheels of a curbside car, my hands tight in my pockets as a defense against the chill, watching the boys do sprints, their thick sweatshirts lying in ripples on the just-mown grass as they performed feats for the girls, just as boys had always done.

Four years earlier, for the first time in their history, Emery had decided to admit girls. At first, there were only thirteen; the next year admissions nearly doubled, and then tripled, to the point where now almost a quarter of the students were female. It was the girls who'd provided the most obvious change in the school, but there were subtler changes as well. A hundred small extinctions took place in the world, day after day, but since I knew the school as well as I did, I found myself noticing things other people might not have. There was a sameness to the hallways, the carpeting in the jetties, the chairs, the mailboxes. But the old photographs of teachers past and present had been taken down and replaced with a mural that represented several hands of different hues holding what appeared to be a stalk of something leafy and fertile and still growing. Judging from the school calendar hanging on the faculty bulletin board, the world had begun to intrude.

My father clearly disapproved of all this. When I'd shown up at the house the night before, he was waiting up for me in the kitchen, and after getting settled upstairs, I rejoined him. "So," he began, "you'll be on campus tomorrow."

"Yes, sir." Coming home had been an impulse decision on my part; rather, decisions like that are probably already made, they just need airing, weighing and even turning down before they begin to seem attractive.

"It's a changed place."

I waited, but that was all he said. "Wine?" and when I nodded yes, he poured me a glass. "There's a lot of talk these days about *feelings,*" he went on presently. "How people *feel.* And *sharing.*" Wearily, he leaned back against the stovetop. "Everything is spelled out nowadays. I fear that the implicit has become explicit."

When he asked about my life, I answered his questions as clearly and formally as I could. Caroline was fine; the children were fine; the Midwest was fine, though on the chilly side, and of course I was relieved that another winter had gone by.

"Nonsense, it toughens you up. School?"

"Fine, sir. Classes're going well."

"It's hard, isn't it? Harder than it looks?"

"What is?"

"Teaching. Nobody tells you how to do it. It's like most things. You just go in and do it. In the dark. You against them. It's nerve-racking." He fell silent. "It's a little like being a parent. A father. Nobody tells you how to do it."

There was a long silence in the room. He poured himself another glass of wine, then offered me one, and though I'd had enough, I accepted a refill anyway. His words hung between us, fond and helpless, though presently he went over to the fridge and started removing things. A stick of butter. A collander holding four ears of corn, shucked. These he laid down on the counter, and then he went over to the side cabinet and brought down a jar of peanuts. He put on a pot of boiling water for the corn, dropped them in a few minutes later, then snapped open the peanut jar, which produced a low gasp. "Nut?" he said to me, holding out the jar, his mouth full.

They were all the foods that he wasn't supposed to eat, and which, when my mother wasn't around—she'd gone out that night—he consumed with ardor. When the corn had finished boiling, he transferred the ears to a plate, sprinkled two separate piles, one of salt and the other of pepper, onto a separate saucer, and then cut off a nearly half-inch slab of butter, which he dredged in each pile, before popping it into his mouth. Then he picked up the ear and started eating, evenly, almost comically, left to right, like the moving cartridge of a typewriter.

"Why don't you have some corn with your butter?" I asked jokingly after a moment.

My father glanced up, his chin glistening. "Sure you won't have some?"

"Sure. I mean, yes, I'm positive."

Still standing, he ate in silence, refilling his wineglass several times. "There are not any models for being a father," he said between bites. "There are models for being everything else having to do with being a man, quote unquote. With being a smoothie with women. An athlete. A fighter. I can't think what else. An *artist*, so to speak. But not for being a father." He was silent. "The point of things, I suppose, is to improve on the model you had."

The topic was making me uneasy. "So—*you* still get nervous when you teach?"

"Yup. Before every class. Yessir, I do." Gazing meditatively into his glass, he jiggled the stem so the wine made rippling waves against one side. Setting it aside, he grasped the brown polished cones of a high-backed chair, seizing them like controls. "It's a changed school. At one time it used to be gentlemen teaching gentlemen how to be gentlemen. Now it's . . . well, how can I put this without sounding like a snob, or an *elitist?*" The word seemed to amuse him. "*Elitist* means 'the best.' But they won't have any of that." When he came to the school after the war, he said, he and his colleagues were interested not only in disseminating ideas, but in decorum. In honor. In valor. In teaching courage and modesty and character. Words he feared no longer meant a lot. The boys were barely interested, and as for the girls? He sighed. What else did he fear? That what he represented no longer had currency in this world. Things that were lasting, that he knew to be lasting, that had withstood time and testing, were referred to these days as old-fashioned. "Or to put things in cruder, B-movie terms," he went on, "I fear my money is not good here anymore."

"Oh, Father, I doubt that that's true," I said helplessly, but he merely lifted his eyebrows, grimacing.

An hour or so later he peered into the living room, where I'd taken up casual residence with a book. "May I take a few moments of your time?" he inquired, and when I looked up, he came forward into the room, assuming his usual position in front of the mantle piece. In one hand he was holding what looked like a loose sheath of papers, an inch or two thick, but rather than asking him what it was, I waited for him to say something. When he did, he told me, haltingly, that he'd been working on his memoirs.

"Your memoirs?" I repeated.

"Yessir." They were by no means finished, or even halfway there, but for the past few months they'd taken up most of his free time. "A lifetime," he said, not looking me in the eye, "spent in service to an institution."

"Which institution?"

"The Emery School, of course."

He wondered, he went on, whether or not I might have time before I left to take a look at them. "I know you're busy, that you have a lot on

your plate and so forth, but if you could do me this favor, I would be—''
here he hesitated ''—over the moon, as it were.''

''Sure, Father,'' I said a moment later. ''I'd be happy to. Though I'm
not an expert on—'' and it was my turn to hesitate ''—anything having to
do with things like that.''

''You're an acute reader, you're intelligent, and I would value your
opinion.''

''How's your health, by the way?'' I asked before retiring upstairs to
bed, the pages tucked under my arm. ''How are you feeling these days?''

He squinted at some small thing beyond my head; I almost turned
to see what it was, but there would have been nothing there. ''I'd say I've
felt better, John old man,'' he replied at last, politely. ''I appreciate your
asking.''

i didn't want to like or dislike what he'd given me; I wanted the pages to
disappear, that was all, and I spent a long time avoiding them, thinking up
last-minute tasks to do before going to bed—did I really need to shave? To
floss my teeth? No, but I did—and finally, I retrieved the pages from the
dresser, where they'd been sitting in a messy, desolate stack, though not
before first calling Sam in New York. ''Father's just presented me with his
memoirs,'' I said.

''Oh, God, Jam, I'm sorry, how fucking embarrassing.''

''Well no, not really.'' Hearing someone else utter my worst
thoughts made me oddly defensive of the unread manuscript. ''I was just
wondering if he'd shown them to you, you being in publishing and all.''

''God, no. Is he going to? He and everybody else. Why do people
think their own lives are remotely interesting? So tell—are they any
good?''

My father asked me the same thing the next morning, in his own
way. He was already downstairs when I came into the kitchen the next
morning and fixed myself a cup of coffee. For the next fifteen minutes we

discussed anything but the topic at hand; the *Farmers' Almanac* and its never-to-be-trusted predictions, Chicago's hoarse greatness as a city, the broken or diseased trees on the St. James property and how they'd have to come down, and that would be expensive, though the local tree man was honest, a friend. Father kept the hood of his bathrobe on as we spoke, and that, mixed with the long tail of his bathrobe between his legs, gave the impression of a monk mated with a threadbare lion. He stood up at last and announced plans to take a shower, but before leaving the room, he turned in the doorway. "Any reaction to the material I gave you last night?"

The memoirs, and what I'd been planning to say about them, had weighed on my mind all morning, though at first I didn't understand what he meant—or rather, given the inviolate rules of our old game of subterfuge and indirection, I feigned a confused deafness—and when he told me he meant the pages he'd given me, I sat down at the kitchen table as still as I could, collecting my thoughts. Five feet away from me, Father's face was questioning, and at the same time shut down. He stood in the doorway with ginger dignity, something faked and quiescent in his eyes, reminding me of nothing so much as a schoolboy waiting to be flogged.

I could have told him anything. In the name of honesty, he'd discouraged my ambitions once; surely he must have expected the same in return. His words had upended the person I thought I was at age twenty-two, and even though the sting of that night had faded a long time ago, it would have been simple to tell him he had no talent, and that his life was of no interest to himself and to us; but I wasn't sure if that was true, and if it was, it was not for me to say. Once the sadism in me had been a waterfall; these days it was only a trickle, a flutter, barely damp.

It wasn't until much later that I realized he'd given me the memoirs not for the purposes of any payback I might exact, but to fill me in on things he was too shy to say in person. Like a mute boy, or some primitive organism snatched from the lightless jungle of his own formality, he'd written them down instead. And now he was allowing me, a teacher, to grade them.

"I really loved what you showed me, Father," I said at last.

He seemed pleased. "Really?"

"They were really fantastic," I went on. "Beautifully written. Totally absorbing and believable."

"Believable perhaps because they did happen."

"Well, even if they hadn't happened, they were totally believable. And totally great. I loved everything about them. Thank you," I went on, "for showing them to me. *A*-plus," and when he continued to look pleased, and even relieved, I began enumerating all the various things about them I'd liked best.

*a*s part of the festivities of alumni weekend, the old boys were invited to sit in on classes, and later that day, when I was handed a schedule paper listing the various options, from a German colloquium, to a beginning French class, to a dress rehearsal for the next night's jazz ensemble concert, to an intermediate Italian course, I saw that one of the classes that alumni could attend was my father's Victorian Poets seminar. It met from two-fifteen to three that afternoon, though I had no intention of showing up for it; my heart was set, or so I thought, on the concert.

But when two o'clock came around, I found myself in the same place I might have been twenty years earlier, my forehead pressed against the glass of my father's classroom door. Time, it appeared, had left his classroom alone. Downstairs there was a feel-good mural and therapeutic meetings for beer-drinking kids; a few minor wars had passed; music that had once seemed lasting had faded into quaintness; most men, I'd learned, stood around watching as the world they knew once vanished; but his classroom was the same. The same desk. The ink-black stapler, the cup of pens and pencils. Over the doorway, the industrial clock with its off-white face. From this room to the rooms of our house, to the rooms of St. James—that was the circuit of a life, the rooms he traversed and lived in. And there were the students, sitting in crookedly aligned chairs, mostly boys but several girls, too, waiting for another class to get underway.

The bell rang and I pushed my way awkwardly into the back of the room, taking a seat in the far back row, next to two girls who were chattering in low voices. "He'd *kill* me," one of them was saying. The other girl shrugged. "So?" and I leaned forward in my seat.

"How is this class, anyway?" I inquired.

The first girl turned around. "It's OK. Kind of interesting some-times," though the second girl broke in to say that the teacher left some-thing to be desired. "He's kind of losing it, actually." She tapped one side of her head. "We think he has Alzheimer's."

"We?"

"Everybody."

I was about to say something, but just then the door opened, and my father came into the room and took a seat behind his desk and began shuffling the papers in front of him. After a few introductory remarks welcoming back the alumni, "some of whose faces look very familiar to me," he said, he stood and began his lecture, now and again pausing to clear his throat or to scribble something on the blackboard. At one point when his back was still turned, a boy in the front row yawned with exaggerated volume, followed by a hasty, gulping "Sorry, sir."

The students seemed restless. Since the dress code had been aban-doned, boys could wear whatever they wanted, so long as they gave off a general impression of neatness. But that day at least, they seemed bored; there was a lot of glancing at watches, then at the wall clock, most likely in the hope that the later time was more accurate. When the class was nearly half over, my father aimed a stare at a boy sitting at the end of the second row and demanded his gum, but I could tell the boy wasn't fright-ened of him, and not only did he keep the gum in his cheek for a moment longer than I expected, but he spat it out onto my father's hand with an almost mocking propulsiveness.

After discarding it in the garbage, my father retook a seat behind his desk. " '*Ulysses* . . .' " he began, and when I heard that word, an uneasy impatience overcame me. Why was he still teaching what he'd taught twenty years ago? His eyes settled at last on the girl next to me, the one I'd spoken to earlier. "Miss Chandler, what is Tennyson's ambition here?"

"His ambition?"

"What, as it were, is he after?"

She hadn't read the poem, she said. Sorry.

My father's gaze found another girl with a face like a mean doll's, whose hands flew out in flustered submission. She hadn't read the poem either; she'd lost her book and had meant to borrow a classmate's, but then she'd forgotten.

"Where did you lose it, my dear?"

"I can't remember. And I'm not 'your dear.' " The bitterness in her voice startled me, but my father had already turned away from the class. "What does the poet say in his last fifteen lines? Did anybody do the reading?" He gazed out again, mock-disappointed. "Mr. Hart?"

Mr. Hart, whose long blond dirty hair was parted spaniellike down the middle, grazing scarred and lotioned skin, hadn't read the entire poem, just parts of it.

"I'll start you off, then. 'Come, my friends. Tis not too late to seek a newer world. Push off, and sitting well in order smite—' " He hesitated. "Has anybody done the reading? Does anybody know what comes next? I'm not altogether sure if I remember myself." There was light, general, nervous laughter. " 'Push off,' " he began again, " 'and sitting well in order smite—' " and then his own memory failed him.

Nobody knew what came next. Practically no one had done the reading. And worse, nobody seemed to care, and in a fleeting moment of panicked paranoia, I wondered whether they'd all conspired to leave my father embarrassed and flat-footed in front of the visiting alumni. The students were whispering among themselves now, and behind me, I could hear theme paper crackling, the kind of crisp, irritated sound you heard sometimes in the aisles of movie theaters.

He'd become a figure of fun, clearly. To be humored more than admired, or liked, or loved. An eccentric. And not a good eccentric either.

He was as old-fashioned to them as calligraphy, or a quadrille, or a bill-board from the 1930s that advertised the cost of Coca-Cola at three cents a bottle. From my experience, I could recognize the times when a class-room was lost to a teacher, and just then, I could've happily pushed aside my chair and taken my leave of the room. Yet I felt no satisfaction. Yes, he'd embarrassed me plenty of times in my life, but I couldn't bear the idea of the same thing happening to him.

Now he was leafing through his anthology, in search of the poem, while murmuring to himself some faint interior narration intended to show he was in control of his own memory. Every second that went past deepened and lengthened my anguish, and a moment later, I rose up unsteadily. "I know the poem, I think, sir."

There was a shifting of paper, a squeaking of wood as all the eyes in the room turned to me.

My father's bottom lip seemed to move slightly. It was the first time he'd acknowledged me. "Which poem are you referring to, sir?"

" 'Ulysses.' "

He bowed formally at me. I think his eyes, or at least one of them, flickered. "Let's have it, then, sir."

I can't tell you where the words came from. Nowhere, everywhere. Where do words like that live? I'd thought of that poem no more than twice since I'd memorized it twenty years earlier, and when I did, it was with a distaste and a humiliation as keen as it had been that day in class. Why was it still fresh in my memory, then? But under the harsh institu-tional lighting of the present, the old, dim words came out of my mouth as though I'd committed them to heart only the night before.

" 'Push off, and sitting well in order smite the sounding furrow. For my purpose holds to sail beyond the sunset, and the baths of all the western stars—' "

My father's voice broke in suddenly, raspily. " '—Until I die. It may be that the gulfs will wash us down. It may be we shall touch—' "

" 'The Happy Isles. And see the great Achilles whom we knew—' "

His voice was with mine now, like two ropes entwined around each other, tumbling and occasionally snagging, as we raced toward the finish. The last few lines we recited together. " 'Though much is taken, much abides. And though we are not now that strength which in old days moved earth and heaven, that which we are, we are. One equal temper of heroic hearts, made weak by time and fate, but strong in will. To strive, to see, to find, and not to yield.' "

I retook my seat, shakily. My father stood for a moment in front of his desk, and then he turned his back to the room, propping himself up against the edge of his desk. There he sat, displayed, saying nothing, even when the bell rang out a few minutes later, signaling the end of class.

7.

I'm not as good at being alone as I was when I was younger. I can date this betrayal—and that's what I think of it as, the defeat of a proud, boyish self-sufficiency—to marrying Caroline. Over time I found myself uncomfortably used to company, and to chatter, and comfort, and art on the wall, and the sighing, rattling sounds of cooking from the kitchen. And for a long time this bothered me, since I'd always been convinced that in solitude and contemplation lay something akin to an artistic life. In the coast lay that life; by the water lay that life; in stillness lay that life; in simplicity and in calmness and by yourself lay that life. Art wasn't land-locked or hilly or bloated; it was bladed, crevassed, creeked, ragged, cal-loused, coastal. No wonder I'd failed at the piano; my day-to-day exis-tence was stuffed with things that were lame and inessential. I was hostage to people and to my possessions, to a house and a garage and a front walkway that had to be shoveled unless I wanted to be given a ticket by the town; all the rules and systems and geographies in place when a person comes into the world.

"You have so much time to think about things," I remember once telling Tom, and he gazed back at me curiously, before remarking that if a person spent his life in contemplation—with a big C—then it, contemplation, was no longer anything special, neither something you thirsted for or that you were willing to lay aside a few minutes a day to perform; in not talking about it, you became it. I sentimentalized him, Tom said, adding that there was a lot less to his life than I probably thought. The problem was that I hadn't found my vocation yet, and when I reminded him somewhat curtly that I'd been a tenured professor now for four years, Tom smiled. "You're still thinking about other things, Jam. About how you should be living. How you want to be living. You're like Sam in some ways. You haven't begun to just *live* yet."

"Well, aren't most people like that? And how am I supposed to accomplish that? To just live, as you say?"

Tom grimaced. "Sell all you have, give to the poor and come follow me. How should *I* know?"

"Well, frankly, Tom," I said, slightly annoyed, "I don't have the time to quit civilization and spend the rest of my life watching herons balancing on one leg. Most people don't have the time. And I certainly don't have time these days to be by myself."

"Do you think you have to live the way I live in order to be alone? That's crazy, Jam. And stupid. You're alone all the time. You can have three hundred people around you and be alone. People carry their solitude *with* them."

But now, contemplating, as it were, my solitude, in the empty, silent house in which I found myself temporarily squatting, I felt diminished, eager for some kind of commotion. I'd made a nest for myself, or rather a series of nests, on the living room couch and at the kitchen table, as one is humanly prone to do when confronted with too many rooms; the rest of the house I left alone. I hadn't gone outside since my excursion into town the day before, though glancing out the front bay windows I could see that a fog had floated in from somewhere offshore and was refusing to lift. It was as though summer, or rather the languor and slowness that I associated with it, was paying a visit, and for the next few hours the lawn was obscured under an eerie whiteness like fat or feathers. It wound around the trees at the start of the marsh, darkening their barks, coating all the cracks and corners of the lawn, cottoning the marsh. From somewhere in the middle of the water, the hull lights of some passing or confused boat gleamed dully through the mist like the currant glaze in a pastry; occasionally a single steel mast would appear for a second, harsh, tilted and keeling forward, before retreating again. But otherwise the island was completely silent.

It was Thanksgiving, a fact I'd realized only when calculating the number of days I'd been on the island—four—and while I hadn't been looking forward at all to the holiday, I wasn't prepared to spend the day alone, either. Roaming around the house, I was overcome by a few loose strands of self-pity. Back home, I imagined Ike struggling into his wooden chair with the four-inch-thick Yellow Pages on it, Isabel in her higher, plastic one, in her bowl a few strips of turkey, a spoonful of mashed potatoes, a few soft trees of broccoli. The Thanksgiving following Ike's birth, I remembered, Caroline, accustomed to straining food for the baby, had mashed our entire Thanksgiving meal. We sat at the table devouring creamed spinach, puree of celeriac, sweet potatoes, stuffing; even the turkey tasted pureed. "Is there anything in the kitchen to eat that's hard or crunchy?" I remember asking, though at the same time, observing the small, already familiar life we'd created in a strange city, I felt supremely blessed, but it wasn't to last.

Six months later, in the days and weeks after Tom's death, I found myself in a fog. The days seemed cold and brusque, like playing cards being dealt by a bored dealer. I'd be flipping through the TV channels and see that a certain show, a comedy or a drama, had come on. Wasn't this on just a couple of nights ago? I'd ask Caroline, and she'd tell me that a week had gone by.

The consolations of church missed me. In the wake of one Sunday service, I approached the minister in the vestibule. "So what would you say about somebody thirty-five years old dying? How do you explain that in terms of there being a God?"

The minister was a Vietnam vet; several times during sermons, he'd mentioned shrapnel still lodged in his back. "How did the person die?"

"He killed himself, as far as I know."

The minister was taken aback. "I'm sorry." For a long time he said nothing, and at last he touched my shoulder. " 'Thy kingdom come, Thy will be done.' Are you able to say 'Thy will be done'?"

I didn't even have to think about it. "No."

In the early fall, I fertilized the lawn, the blades spitting out white beads onto all sides. Twice a month, I raked the leaves clustering our lawn. In the winter I shoveled the walkway free of ice and scattered the asphalt with a distillation of sand that might have come from a summer beach. Sometimes the snow would roll off the roof, a faint, distant rumbling like an army making its way over a mountain. Mostly we stayed inside, as the snow gradually separated the house from the street, until finally the sidewalk seemed unimaginably far away from the door, and the house resembled an island that had broken off from the mainland. Then one day I saw on the surface of the lake what I thought were clumps of frozen snow, but which turned out to be water, easy and white and roiling, and I knew the lake was finally melted.

I'd intended to spend my spring break puttering around the house, putting up bookshelves, but Caroline surprised me with a trip to Paris. She arranged for her mother to come take care of the kids for a week, and reserved us a room at a small hotel on the Rue dès Saint Pères on the Left Bank.

It was dark when we boarded the plane, a darkness that seemed to follow us to Paris when we arrived the next morning before breakfast and made our way through customs. Paris seemed elderly and unchanged, the same place we'd gone on our honeymoon, as if the city were merely continuing a conversation it had begun ten years earlier. The French

seemed dark, hurried, tinted. The women had a tousled, unhygienic quality. The faces of the men resembled latex masks. The weather was tropi-
cal in its moodiness. It rained a part of every day, and with it came great
gusts of wind, damp and sudden and sour-smelling. At night, after dinner,
as Caroline slept, I'd sit by the window, listening to the police sirens and
their blurted, sawing, vertical rhythm of dread.

For the first few days, we were tirelessly cultural. We went to muse-
ums; we bought rolled-up wall prints of leaves and fruit and seashells
from the stalls along the Seine. We roamed the cemeteries. We found
Chopin. Graffiti led us to Jim Morrison and a row of faithful teenagers. A
tender-eyed old woman led us to where Edith Piaf was buried. I could
feel myself sinking. Each day felt dimmer and more obscure than the last.
By the middle of the week, I'd retreated into privacy, thermal and wordless and discouraged. At the same time, some aspect of Tom's dying
seemed to have unleashed in me a cartoonish carnality, a satyr's dumb,
turbulent, jelly-eyed desire. Joyless lovemaking—that was the only thing
that gave me pleasure, though not much of it—and afterward Caroline
would gaze back up at me, surprised and confused.

On an overcast morning a day before we were due to leave, we took
the Metro to the Bois de Boulogne and walked half a mile to the small
zoo inside the Jardin d'Acclimatation. We were snacking on *gaufres*, fragile pancakes dusted with confectioner's sugar, and we'd just strolled past
a family of brown bears when I found myself in front of a birdcage.
"There's a *seagull* in there," I said. "Do the French actually think a
seagull is something to write home about?"

"Maybe they don't have seagulls in Paris."

For some reason, I couldn't stop laughing. "*Seagull*," I managed to
choke out. "*Seagull*," and a moment later Caroline glanced at me
strangely.

"John, it's not *that* funny—"

"I think it's very funny. I think it's hilarious, actually. A seagull? A
seagull in a cage? In a zoo? While they're at it, where's their *squirrel*?
Where's their *ant?*"

When I stopped laughing, I saw that Caroline was gazing at me with the same slack, exasperated patience I'd noticed on her face several times since we'd arrived. And that night, at dinner, she told me she was concerned about me, that I wasn't taking care of myself. "You haven't shaved in a week, John."

"It's that stubbled French *je m'appelle*-the-wolf look."

"Be serious, please, for just a minute. And you're drinking too much, too—"

"Anything else?" I inquired lightly.

Later, over coffee and cheese, she asked me what I remembered about Tom.

"Nothing."

"Oh, you must remember a lot."

"Nope." Presently, I raised my wineglass. "Look, the French have the right idea. Why should we sit around bothering ourselves with what goes into our bodies? Why should we be enslaved to our cholesterol level? To bran muffins and cabbage and what do they call it, roughage? Fiber? No booze? And no cigarettes? And eight glasses of water a day? We should do what they do, sit around and shovel cheese into our mouths and drink bottle after bottle of red wine, because in the end it'll be the same, anyway."

Caroline's lips were pursed. "Everything is pointless, right?"

On the trip back home, I kept fingering our tickets. Chicago/ O'Hare, they read, followed by a forty-minute second flight into Wisconsin. *Home*, Ike would call out sometimes when we were on vacation. *Home*, he'd call out from his car seat, from his low bed, from his high chair. Like a beaming device, a brooding horn: *Home. I want to go home.* On such flimsy pretexts as indecision, laziness, the offer of a good job, a fear of striking out into the world, the proximity to schools, a climate you liked, you created for your kids their first notion of what home was. A house, a lawn, a street, sounds, sights, smells coming from a kitchen. Lilacs, shrubbery, potholes, phone poles, music playing in the background. Or some scuffling uneventfulness—the clash of colanders drying on the sink rack, mud from the soles of shoes drying in the hallway, the limp, gallantly noosed figures of winter coats on hooks. "I don't see why we bother to own our house," I remarked to Caroline as we were preparing to board our second flight.

"Why?"

"Why do people buy houses anyway? So they can buy themselves an illusion of permanence. An illusion that they own land. That they're a permanent part of the world. That they're lashed to the earth. But that's all it is. A house can be liquidated just like *that*. Who are we? We're barely here. We're just brains and memories on stems they call backbones. We're all portable, we just don't know it. We're all flimsier than air."

With a week left in my vacation, I took Ike to the park almost every day. We brought along stale heels of bread to feed the ducks, but other similarly minded parents and children had come before us; the ducks had flown away, leaving behind ghostly, fluffed-out shapes of bread on the bottom of the lake.

That evening, when I informed Caroline of my intention to drive east to visit my sister, she seemed bewildered. "We've just gotten back."

"So?"

Her look was both tender and irritated. "I just don't think traveling will solve anything, John. You'll just take it along with you. It'll just end up postponing the inevitable."

"What's the inevitable?"

"I don't know. I just think you need to talk to somebody about all that's happened. I've been doing what I've been doing long enough to know that talking is a waste of time a lot of the time. But in your case, I don't think that's true." Caroline stood and went over to the sink, and when she turned back to look at me, her eyes seemed robbed of a familiar light. "We have our own family. Remember? Our little corporation? You and me both CEOs, and the kids our little business, our product? You barely look at the baby. Is Daddy mad at me, Ike keeps asking? All he wants to do is play dinosaurs with you—"

"You don't understand," I said after a moment.

"What don't I understand this time?"

"My relationship with him. It's implicit."

"Really? I see two more males not talking to each other."

"I wouldn't expect you to understand men," I replied, "or much of anything. In fact, this marriage is a joke."

I didn't mean any of this. The words fell out, unexpectedly, like clumps of hair, and they kept falling. But Caroline looked as though I'd smacked her in the face. "I'm sorry you feel like that," she said, and she walked hurriedly out of the room. I almost called her name, almost went to look for her, almost apologized, but in the end, I didn't.

the terns had left the island. Their absence, which had been predicted for a long time, was blamed on the new municipal dump at the end of the island, which had attracted packs of herring gulls. For years, they'd been a local nuisance, crowding the fishing villages, blinking in the still midday sunlight of downtown streets or else trailing behind the ferry, supernatural in flight, hoping a child would flip them a cracker or an onion ring. But after the dump opened, their population tripled. Now you saw them all over the place. Laughing gulls, black-backed gulls. They scavenged most of the terns' eggs and chicks, Tom told me during one of my visits. Consequently the terns had gotten smart. Infuriated and smart. They'd lifted up off the island, seeking safer, emptier, more protected climes farther north. Once in a while he still saw a roseate or a least tern, plunging gracefully into the water for sand eels or minnows, though it was a sight that was becoming rarer and rarer.

That wasn't the only change on the island. Everywhere you looked were new signs. STOP. YIELD. Where there'd once been a dangerous curve, and you knew it, and either touched your foot to the brake or took your chances, now there was a yellow sign: DANGEROUS CURVE. BLIND DRIVE. INTERSECTION AHEAD. New arrows, new flashing lights. What everybody knew had been spelled out. Celebrities were spotted at the airport or shopping for property, even though sections of the coast were still a mess. In January, a storm had pounded the southern beaches, pulling several houses into the water, sending tree limbs and branches toppling and splintering. Two Scotch pines on the front lawn of our house, trees that served the dual purpose of framing the view and concealing the blond boards of the new house being built next door—it flashed through the thinned trees like skin under a bathrobe—had fallen; and though Tom and I spent the better part of an afternoon sawing the branches and the trunk into footlong pieces, the overall impression I'd gotten was that the island seemed to be changing so rapidly that one couldn't keep up with it.

It wasn't only the trees but the water, which was ten degrees colder. Once there'd been a trick to telling if the tide was high; a sea bush, humble and scraggly, vanished from sight, and its four-to-five-hour disappearance provided an assurance that the bay bottom wouldn't be slimy or rocky, and that the swimming might be halfway decent. But in the aftermath of the storm, a precipice of land ten miles from the house was cut nearly in two, allowing ocean water to flood the inlets and bays with water two to three times colder than usual. Once the bay had been as warm as consommé; now, in midsummer, it felt autumnal. The sea bush had been washed away.

A few months after that, harbor seals made their first appearance. During my visit, Tom took Caroline and me out on his Whaler, and when we reached Hildreth's Point, fifty to a hundred black, doglike heads were sticking up out of the water, a sight I found vaguely disquieting, an impression shared by Tom. As the Whaler swiveled backward, its motor spitting and choking out bits of seaweed, he seemed melancholy. Later that evening, as he and I were cutting the last few legs of wood, he informed me that when the summer ended, he was quitting fishing.

I found this almost impossible to believe. For as long as I could remember, he'd fished, as a boy and later as a teenager, gunning his outboard out to the narrows and farther on to Masquinet Point. At age ten, he'd dropped green twine over the side of the boat, bringing home tubs of flounder and hake. In his teens, he'd graduated to rods, whittling the barbs off the hooks so the fish would be less likely to be cut. In the past few years—how long? I didn't know anymore—he'd owned his own dragger. And while I'd never defined my other brothers and my sister by the jobs they held, I associated Tom indelibly with his livelihood.

But the industry was in trouble. It wasn't the same industry it had been ten years ago, and even five years ago. There weren't any fish left, that was the problem. The Magnuson Act had helped (in response to my blank expression, Tom explained that that was the law forbidding foreign fishermen from coming to within two hundred miles off American shores), but over the past several years, the supply of groundfish had been decimated.

"It's overfishing," he said. "There's too many boats out there. Sophisticated boats, too. I can't compete with boats like that. They have navigational systems, satellite images. You can climb aboard, fall asleep and let technology do everything for you. I've been to the same places hundreds of times. I've made the same tows. And I started seeing all these little fish. Undersized ones. And you can't do anything with those."

At first, he'd thought it was merely a cycle. Cycles came and went in fishing; if you were smart, you paid attention to them. But most everybody agreed on one thing: there were too many people out there. "These days you can clean out whole schools of fish. The little ones used to be able to hide but now the radar's so sophisticated they can't hide anymore. Cod, haddock, flounder—their numbers are so low now it's not even worth talking about. And prices are getting ridiculous. I drag back two hundred, three hundred pounds a day now. In fact, that's all I'm *allowed* to bring back," and when I remarked that this sounded to me like a lot of fish, Tom looked exasperated.

"There's people who used to get fifteen hundred, two thousand pounds. A couple of weeks ago, cod was over two bucks a pound at the dock. You're talking six dollars by the time it makes it to market." He turned away from me. "And people wonder why fish are being raised in pens these days. That's why. Some of these guys use rockhoppers, too. Cables covered with tire rubber. They hold the net in place. And what they end up doing is beating the fish to death. Then the rubber breaks off into the ocean.'' Everything had become high-tech; the ocean was populated with modern-day cowboys. ''It's every man for himself. But not in a good way.''

His expenses were astronomical, too, and climbing. He had to pay for his boat and for gas. He had to pay when something broke or went wrong. And for insurance. He had to pay for a boy to come out with him. ''It comes to somewhere around fifty thousand bucks a year just to keep my boat in the water. I can barely make a living anymore.'' He was silent. ''You know what most of these guys will end up doing? Kids' birthday parties. Whale watches. Seal watches. Day charters. The whole thing is going to end up like a giant commercial. Like everything else in this world. It's all middlemen and paperwork and regulations and self-reference. I have to make a phone call the minute I leave the harbor and the minute I get back.'' There was talk, he went on, of turning the waterfront into a tourist attraction. ''As in boutiques. As in a *whaling* museum.''

We were working strenuously, the incoming fog creating a cool, itchy sheen on our skin, the boats offshore working against their ropes, back and forth. Fall had come early, like an embarrassment, and the leaves—cranberries, yellows, suedes, beets, liverish purples—lay on the ground in moist, scraggly clusters. A powerboat zipped across the dark blue water as gulls rose up crying over the marsh. Tom had brought up an old, unsturdy sawhorse from the basement, and he straddled one end while I sawed, and when my arm grew tired, we reversed our positions. Afterward, we loaded the scarred, sticky logs into the wheelbarrow and towed them into the cellar. Then Tom spoke suddenly. ''It's my own fault, too. I've overfished. Just like everybody else. I was greedy because I knew there were always lots of fish. But I've never cheated. I haven't done what some of these other guys have, like scraping the eggs off lobsters or dying the females in Clorox to change the color of their eggs, and so on, so you can trap them legally.''

He told me then he couldn't keep things away from himself anymore.

''What sorts of things?''

"Everything. The world. I came here to escape from myself. You know something? I've ended up *with* myself."

"So what's wrong with that?"

His response bewildered me: if you attached yourself to any life, he said, then that was still an attachment. "All I ever wanted here was quiet," he said. "And peace. And independence. And detachment. All I ever wanted was just to live my life the way I wanted to."

"Tom, you're asking yourself to be perfect," I said. "That's not human."

He gazed at me sorrowfully. "You have a fixation on this life." I don't think I'd ever heard his voice sound so tender. "I don't. I'm hardly here."

A chill went through me. "What do you mean, you're hardly here?"

"Just that. I told you once, it's like I'm locked outside a room. Pressed against the window. And I can see inside, see people and things, but I can't get into the room. It's locked to me. I don't know what to do."

"Well, that's good in some ways, isn't it? *Objective* and all? Isn't that what you always wanted?" I laughed uneasily. "That's what I've always wanted."

"Take it, then."

We stood there for a while longer, gazing out at the heightening water; earlier we could hear the slapping ruckus of the high tide against the half-moon of beach, but now, as evening came down, the water had become glass, an almost perfectly articulated oval mirror, minced green grass for its borders. The trees hugging the bend showed their reflections in the water's staring quiet.

"I love you, Tom." It was the first time I'd said those words to any man—a brother, a father, anybody. I had no idea why I said it then, and faintly ashamed, and seeing that his own eyes were damp, I took a recoiling step backward before excusing myself and going into the house. Thirty minutes later, when I gazed out of the kitchen window, Tom was standing where I'd left him, beside the wheelbarrow, facing the marsh and beyond it, at the mirror growing dark.

That was the last time I saw him. No, actually it wasn't: the next day, we had a hurried and unsatisfying good-bye in the driveway. Tom promised to visit the Midwest sometime soon, which I doubted; he'd been off-island only three times that I could remember. I wished him luck with the fishing industry and told him not to be so pessimistic. Empty, meaningless words. And so I've thought about that last image I had of him the night before. Did I know anything? Suspect anything? No—I'd never been talented, or tainted—with premonitions or inexplicable fears, and it was no different that time. And he was the last person I would ever expect to do such a thing.

And so I continued my life, assuming, given the laws of probability, that I'd see him in the near future, certainly talk to him before then. Back home, I busied myself with the warm, commercial maneuvers of domestic life. I tidied up the living room. Read the mail. Replaced a burned-out bulb in a dining room lamp. Hitched two breakdown trains together, at Ike's request. Snacked on a few stale-tasting Wheat Thins, Windexed the smudges off the side of the toaster, sprayed Fantastic on the sink counter tiles, wrapped leftover Brie in a pouch of Reynolds Wrap. Et cetera, et cetera.

*t*he fog floats into the bight like a mood. Not a good mood or a bad mood, just any softly galloping mood you can't keep away. It thins, it thickens, altering and overbearing; now and again you see the bright blink of sun, then all's vested and smoky again. A week or so after my visit, Tom set out—I discovered later—in a cool wet afternoon fog, one of those blanketings that had rolled in regularly off the water ever since I was a child. People saw the boat chugging out of the harbor. There were witnesses, up to a point. A few bystanders—boys playing one-on-one basketball at the town landing, retirees who in their ennui had appointed themselves watchdogs of public and nautical safety—complained that they'd seen, or heard, a dragger motoring out at twenty or thirty knots in an area where the legal speed limit was fifteen. They'd lost sight of the boat in the fog.

He must have been steering by memory. Memory and experience. He was familiar enough with the water, with the tides, the buoys, the channels, the position of every lobster and eel trap from Port Lucie Harbor to the outer flats. Once he'd reached the narrows, where the distance between the two shores is no more than five hundred yards, he slowed the boat down and cut the motor.

He'd always been the best of all of us at securing anchors to unlikely places—tufts of grass, ridges of sand, places that didn't seem necessarily adhesive but that would hold a boat tight, at least until the next tide came in. This time he simply let it drop, probably yanking it a few times to make sure it was in place. A coast guard cutter, patrolling the harbor and the outlying waters for fog-stranded boats, observed the trawler anchored and listing side to side. They radioed the harbormaster, but not surprisingly, he wasn't at his station. Though when they made their way alongside, signaling their approach over an onboard microphone, there were no signs of life. The net was down, which struck one of the officers as both relevant and bizarre; fog was still coming in, the visibility was almost nonexistent, and who went out in weather like that? One of the officers, new at his job, boarded, and after a search of the cabin, he came back empty-handed. With the help of his boatmate, he reeled in the net, though when it was back on board and its contents emptied, there was nothing in its stomach but trash fish. Thirty pounds worth. Fish, Tom had told me, that many fishermen had recently resorted to selling, something that would've been unheard of ten years earlier. A few minutes later one of them spotted a figure in the water, to the right of the stern, facedown, fully clothed, legs and arms outstretched. Tom had been dead—or so it was determined later—for less than twelve hours.

Over the next few weeks, I was able to piece information together, collate facts, other people's impressions. Months earlier, Tom had informed another day fisherman, a middle-aged Portuguese man with four children and another due soon, that he was giving him his boat. Not selling it, but giving it away. The man, who later showed up at Tom's memorial service, seemed baffled by the gesture. "He said—your brother—he was worried about how someone like me was able to get along with a house and a mortgage. He knew I was going to have to sell my own boat, if not this year then next year. So he told me he wanted to *give* me the thing. It's all paid up, too." The man looked uncertain. "I don't know if I want to take it."

"If he gave it to you," I said, "take it."

I was at home when the phone call came, and when I hung up the receiver, I recall not being surprised, though it wasn't until much later that I realized that I'd entered into a paralysis comparable to a snap frost.

*i*t had fallen upon me to make all the arrangements, and over the next two weeks, with a kind of fumbling, mole's blindness, I did—logging endless phone calls, arranging for a cremation, renting a church for a service, and when that was taken care of, going through Tom's belongings, though it was a burden that I would've insisted on carrying out even if the other members of my family hadn't expected me to. We were the last to file into the church, my mother on the arm of her new husband—she'd been remarried six months earlier—trailed by the rest of us. And afterward we repaired back to Saltair Road for a reception.

I couldn't stand to be inside the house for very long—rented out to strangers for the past two summers, it had taken on a postured, anonymous look—and during the reception a group of us managed to escape out onto the back porch. At one point my mother joined us, and for a long time she gazed out at the water and the sky, as though it could provide information, an essential message. Rose hip bushes, their diffident cling against the splitwood fence; sneakers draped like sausage links over the top. Two docks, one long and one short, like sticks tossed from a childhood bridge. The sky wet salt, the black passing geese pepper flakes. On the mainland the marsh and water had a Sunday-like fallowness, but farther out by the narrows I could make out choppier water, a suspicion of wild air.

Sam. Sam I might have expected to do himself in. A mix-up of white wine and affronted ambition and mixed-up sexuality; was it girls he liked? boys? I wouldn't have been surprised to find him hanging someday from a superficial rope, leaving behind in an obvious place a note full of divalike asperity and blame. Jay? No. His moodlessness, his sense of responsibility and fair play, as well as his team-player jocundity, would prevent him from ever doing such a thing. Sarah? Perhaps, though women were stronger in this department than men; an accident, yes (car, bike), deliberately, no. Me? I thought about my own death, speculatively, dreamily, almost every day.

Tom? Not Tom. It was Tom who'd seemed the happiest and the most secure of all of us, Tom who'd made choices based not on whim, or rote thoughtlessness, but on necessity. It was Tom who'd turned his back on most of what he'd been born with as an impediment to clarity, Tom who seemed to have made peace with his life. Humility. The word kept springing up like a puppet across my mind. *Humility.* Was it humility to kill yourself? Was it some supreme flexing of ego? Had Tom failed? Succeeded? Found himself in death? Lost himself in death? I was convinced of only one thing, that fishing had nothing to do with it, that it was a smokescreen.

If Tom had failed—if he thought he'd failed, that is—what did that say about the rest of us? How did a person like that give in to despair? Or did despair have anything to do with it? With no answers to anything, I sat back tensely on the porch steps as we all began casually misremembering my brother.

Was it Jay who remarked first that Tom loved days like this? Days like this? Like what? Gray skies? Water like a limp sheet? No one knew what he meant. "He'd be chopping wood," Sarah said from the swing, her voice idle, followed a moment later by a slightly pursed and prideful twist of her mouth, as though she'd proven to herself privately that she could contribute something the rest of us would recognize. "Tom always chopped wood," Sam echoed. "Boring." "He did not *always* chop wood," Sarah replied. "I didn't say he always chopped wood." "You just did." "Well, you make it sound like he didn't do anything else in his life but chop wood." "Well, I didn't mean to make it sound that way. He was my brother too." "Thank you, Sam, I noticed, you don't need—" "You know what I'll miss?" Jay this time, his valedictory ability to start things off. "He was so nice to our kids. Generous. Uncle Tom." "—'s Cabin," Sam added, as he always did. Then, "I wish all the guests would leave and go back home."

Gently, I could feel Caroline's hand on mine. "You look sick, John," she whispered. "Are you OK?" But how could I explain things to her without falling into the same trap as everybody else? That just as our father had, Tom was vanishing into memory, flawed memory, fallible memory, memory that would grow thin and in time disappear entirely. Tom was . . . kind, wise, tall. Big smile. T-shirt. Jeans. Flimsy words. We couldn't even agree on the right ones. Our words intersected, contradicted each other, only occasionally agreed.

I was reminded of the day in the playground Ike asked me what a slide was, and I'd pointed one out to him. "What'sat?" he asked next, indicating a swing, and when I told him, he pointed at a low shed. "What'sat?" A few minutes later, he stared at the swing. "Good-bye, slide." "Swing," I corrected. "It's a *slide*," he told me. "Swing," I repeated. "Slide," he insisted.

None of us could even agree on the facts of things, on what the same words meant.

My mother had moved closer to the foot of the porch, trailed by her new husband; he was a brisk, portly, sweet-natured man, a retired banker in a snappy bow tie, and all of us liked him enormously. "Do you know what I wish?" she said.

"What do you wish?" Jay said after a moment.

"I wish," she said, "that somebody—anybody—would kindly inform me what kind of a God allows a mother to outlive her own son."

• • •

When the kids in our family turned eighteen, we underwent a ceremony intended to commemorate our coming of age. It involved a thirty-minute car trip into the city with our father, and lunch on a high floor of a skyscraper in the financial district with him and his lawyer. I underwent this ritual several weeks after my eighteenth birthday, and when I was ushered into the corporate dining room, with its crystalline view of the waterfront, I felt the sudden, lurching and ambiguous weight of responsibility.

Every step of this meeting seemed designed to prod me toward adulthood. Did I want a drink? Bloody Mary? Screwdriver? Vodka and cranberry? Selections designed to steer me away from childhood juices and sodas. Both men peppered me with questions, asked for my advice and my opinions. Sports, politics, aspects of government, women. Over dessert, the lawyer removed from his pocket a check for eighteen dollars, which he unfolded on the table as gently as a blanket for two lovers. "Don't spend it all in one place," he said with a little laugh, but I could have recited the words along with him; four years earlier Jay reported hearing the same joking injunction.

A dollar for every year. I creased the check with militaristic precision (I was an adult now, orderly, clearheaded, a straight shooter) and placed it off-handedly in my pocket. But the check wasn't the point of the lunch; the check symbolized that for the first time I'd been handed control of my assets. It was money, my father would caution me again and again over the years, that I shouldn't spend. I would receive dividends, though, and with these I could do what I wanted, though he had advice on this score, as well. I'd plow it right back into your account, he said. And watch it grow.

It wasn't a lot of money, and yet I recall feeling speechless with gratitude and nervousness as I contemplated my portfolio at lunch—portfolio! portfolio! The gaily colored certificates like Oriental masks or props from a board game—though this was a lunch intended to communicate the idea that the season of masks and games and bright colors was over.

My brothers and sisters reacted to their newfound gains in different ways. Sam immediately started liquidating his stocks, pausing for breath only when he discovered the dismaying existence of capital gains taxes; the stocks had been bought so long ago, and had increased in value so much since then, that to sell them meant paying back nearly half their worth to the government. Jay began speculating in the somewhat uncertain schemes and businesses of college friends; before long, having had little success increasing the value of what he already had, he left his portfolio alone.

I was conservative; I used what little money I had as a padding throughout my twenties, and while I didn't live spectacularly well, I lived better than many people. Sarah was even more cautious. She hadn't touched her money since receiving it. "I'd feel too guilty," she told me. "It doesn't feel like *my* money. I didn't earn it. It feels like some kind of archival money. As though somebody might yell at me if I went near it."

The result, so far as I could tell, was that she was the best-off of all of us. Or so I thought up until the time Tom's will was probated. I met with his lawyer in his office on a side street in downtown St. James on a bright spring day two or three months after Tom's death. The lawyer began by offering his condolences; he'd always found my brother a pleasure to deal with. At his suggestion, he added, Tom had transferred all of his assets into a living will. Assets comprising his house—which was all paid for—his car, as well as various securities and money market funds.

"He took risks. Perhaps because he appeared to care so little about his assets he was able to. Risks I wouldn't necessarily have taken, and that didn't necessarily always have my approval. But they paid off well for him. And the value of his property has soared." Already, he said, there'd been offers from several interested buyers.

When the lawyer mentioned the figure, I wasn't even giving him my full attention. "I beg your pardon?" I said. It was a figure he seemed accustomed to dealing with, but I wasn't—I was stunned—though he repeated how much land on St. James had appreciated in recent years. I listened as he read off the various allotments. There were outright cash gifts to a number of people, as well as to our children; each child—this included Ike and Isabel—was to receive a hundred thousand dollars, to be placed in an irrevocable trust until he or she reached the age of eighteen. There were other minor disbursements. Ten thousand dollars to a local environmental concern, ten thousand dollars apiece to each of his two godsons, who lived in another state. The rest of it—the proceeds from the sale of his house and property, estimated, with beachfront, to net no less than four and a half million dollars, minus the estate taxes—was to be given to charity.

Six months or more might elapse in between the times I'd communicate with one or another of my siblings. It was nothing personal, nothing deliberate or vindictive, but more like a combination of forgetfulness and time. The others tended to fill in the news of those with whom I hadn't spoken, so that I rarely felt guilty or remiss. With an exception: Sarah. Over the past few years I'd made an effort to keep in regular contact with her, in large part since, with the exception of Sam, she was the only one of us who didn't have her own family.

But ever since the business with Tom, we, or rather I, had fallen out of touch. When I heard about her interest in buying the St. James house, I called her number, and when I didn't hear back, I became concerned. Later, when I tried her a second time, I got her answering machine and assumed she must be in the middle of her move. After several years working and living in the Northwest, she'd picked up stakes and trans-ferred her belongings to eastern New York State, where she'd gotten a job doing fund-raising work for a nature conservancy group. In the days fol-lowing the closing, I called to ask whether or not I might stop through, and though she'd sounded surprised and—was I imagining it?—not par-ticularly welcoming, she gave me her address and told me to stop by the house and let myself in; the key was under the mat.

If there were no such thing as locals—people who'd spent their lives in a single place, who had no desire to live elsewhere, who'd bought a house not far from where they'd grown up and who were now raising their kids in a way identical to the way they'd been brought up—I was convinced that some towns would be deserted. Such was the case with the tired-looking, red-brick-factory town where my sister was now living, which under a gray midday winter sky resembled nothing so much as an enormous graveyard. Snow was caked along the sidewalk when I pulled up in front of her house, and as I was getting out of the car, my foot plunged down into a puddle of brown-marbled water that rose up nearly to my knees. I hurriedly scrambled for the key she'd left for me, and after letting myself in, made a beeline for the shower.

Afterward, I made my way outside to the snowy backyard and took a seat on the stoop, where I sat drinking tea and gazing at the tall wet fence, and the snow, densely packed, but shiny, too, as though it had been rubbed with wax and a rag. Until a knock on the glass made me turn around, and there was Sarah, her car keys in one hand and a bag of groceries in the other.

She'd never been much of a kisser; instead, she offered me her cheek, stiffly and with an anxious smile, as a compromise, and as she was putting away her coat and her gloves, I took a seat at the kitchen table. "I bought you some ginger ale," she called over. "Isn't that what you like to drink?"

I was touched by her memory, and though I wasn't thirsty, I broke a can free from its muzzle, and after a few minutes of idle chatter, I heard myself commenting on the dinginess of the town.

"It's not that bad." Sarah's voice came in quickly, almost warningly. "I like it," but I couldn't help myself.

"These old mill towns have such a funny feeling to them. There's something so passed-by and beaten-down about them. Old brick, old businesses, old industry. I think if I lived here I'd end up having a Prozac drip installed in my left forearm."

Her response was immediate. "Well, that happens to be your taste, Jam. Just because we have different tastes doesn't mean I'm wrong and you're right."

"Sarah, I was joking—" I said, but she interrupted me. She'd had no time to buy stuff for lunch, and also, she didn't know whether or not I'd be hungry, or whether I'd stopped someplace along the way. I hadn't, and she suggested we walk into town. "We could drive," I said. Sarah shrugged, as if to say, Whatever pleases you, but as she was retying her shoes, she informed me suddenly that she wanted to walk.

The day, as I said, was cold and uninspiring, and the town was almost a mile away, though ten minutes later we were making our way along a snow-crusted sidewalk. During our walk into town, we made hesitant conversation, skipping from topic to topic: my drive there, the number of tollbooths in New York State, cross-country skiing, bad weather. At last I brought up the house. "I didn't know how attached you were to the place."

Her response was strangely cool. "I guess I thought it would be mean to sell it out from under Father. Actually, though, I'm—"

"So are you going to spend a part of every summer there or what, exactly?" I asked, but Sarah was noncommittal. It depended on her job, her vacations, her desire to drive three hours one way. I felt a vague apprehension; missing were her enthusiastic plans to turn the house into a modern-day base for our children, their children. "Maybe we can all come visit sometime," I said.

"Maybe, yes." Her voice was polite. "You all can."

At a certain point she steered me to a clearing between two houses, and we proceeded along a narrow path past a small pond. The branches of the trees were encased in ice, like flowers in a chill black vase, and half-way around I spotted a scattering of seeds on the ground. "Hey, what are those?" I called out.

"I have no idea."

"Oh, come on, give me a break, you know."

Sarah kept walking. She cleared her throat. "They're for bob-whites."

"How so?"

"How so what?"

"I mean, what are the seeds doing there, could you explain all that stuff—" and I paused, foolishly, on the path "—et cetera, to the layman, to somebody who doesn't know all that much about nature."

A moment later Sarah took a deep breath. "The snow covers up the seeds and the insects. A lot of things—birds, rabbits—don't have enough to eat in the wintertime. They get hungry. So people leave seeds out sometimes. So the animals don't go hungry."

"What about deer?" I interrupted. "Do you get deer here?"

"Um hmmm."

"What else?"

"I don't know. Raccoons. Rabbits. Big-eared rabbits."

"Yeah, but what's their *brand* name?"

"Jam, I have no idea what their *brand* name is."

Disregarding the testiness in her voice, I reminded her of the summer that Father had hired a local boy from down the road in Menemsha to kill the rabbits that were crawling under the garden fence and stripping his basil and lemongrass. His offer was straightforward—a beer per bunny, an exchange that the boy, who was only fifteen at the time, seemed to find fair, though at the end of the day, woozy and crooked from all he'd drunk, he'd shot a hole in the side of the house.

"Yeah, Father had an odd sense of humor sometimes," Sarah said, not looking at me.

"Maybe it's easier for boys when a father dies," I said. "I mean sons. I think sons start to turn into men when their fathers die. Some such rot like that. I read someplace they're free to become themselves, finally."

"Girls are different."

Again, the sharp, warning voice, signaling that this line of conversation was over. By then we'd reached town, a steep, narrow main street peppered with old businesses with names like Mullens (hardware) and Stieglitz (jewelers) and Gershen's (bikes). At the street's end, a steeple poked into the gray sky, puncturing the clouds. "I think I'd have to go into intensive therapy if I lived here," I remarked, and I was unprepared when Sarah whirled around sharply.

"Yes, John, you've already made that perfectly clear. You're not me, are you? This is where *I* live. *I* like it. Stop criticizing everything about my life."

"I'm not criticizing . . ."

The false innocence in my voice came across as high-pitched and artificial, even to me. "Yes, you are. Just because I have a life that's different from everybody else's. Oh, I forgot, I'm not supposed to have a life. I'm supposed to be this person you have this idea about. This nature person. Well, stop compartmentalizing me. There's more to me than that."

I was stunned. "I know there's more to you than that. I never said—"

"You just admitted that's the way you see me."

"I didn't admit—"

"Just please quit asking me these asinine *nature* questions, OK? Like I'm some goddamn Mother Nature person. Stop trying to *draw me out*, quote unquote. Just because you think the only time I come alive, quote unquote, is when I'm talking about the stupid fucking birds and the seeds and the trees and the saplings and the fucking squirrel prints in the snow. There's more to me than that."

"I know there's more to you than that," I said wearily, as we reached the restaurant and made our way toward an empty red-leather booth. The room was dark and grease-smelling, filled with old people; a lone elderly waitress stood behind the counter, taking short, brutal pulls on a cigarette, which she stubbed out before coming over to read us the specials. It was laborer food, mostly—meat loaf, mashed potatoes, chicken pot pie. To my surprise, Sarah ordered a beer, and I followed suit. "Cheers," I said, when they came. "Here's to you and your new town." I glanced around me. "Does this restaurant double as a day-treatment center for the local mental hospital?"

"I'm not even going to answer you."

Our food arrived with conspicuous quickness, as though it had been sitting for hours in the kitchen, waiting for the right people to come along, and consequently, despite my hunger, I only picked at my cheeseburger and fries. Sarah caught me up; her job was going well; no, she was not planning to go to Florida for Thanksgiving or for Christmas. "I think Mother thinks we're all so loaded," she said coolly. "She thinks we can just pick up stakes at her beck and call and fly down there. I don't *want* to fly down there. Florida gives me the creeps. All those hurricanes and serial killers." Sarah shook her head. "Honestly, this family—"

"This family what?" I said when she didn't finish.

"The level of dysfunction in this family is just absolutely overwhelming, that's all."

"Must you use that expression?"

"What expression?"

"Dysfunction. Dysfunctional."

"What's wrong with that expression?"

"In case you haven't noticed, it's slightly overused these days."

"Well, maybe it's overused because it's true."

"It's overused," I said sharply, "because people are looking to explain their own failures. These days everybody just wants to turn themselves into victims and poor little me's and whatever else they can invent, just so long as they don't have to take any responsibility for themselves."

Sarah's eyes were stubborn. "It isn't *overused*, Jam, as you say. All you have to do is look at us."

"I do look at us."

"And you don't see anything." There was a long silence. "Tom killed himself, remember? Sam's gay, and he's an alcoholic, too. Jay's this Republican bore. And Father, I don't even know what to think of Father."

Sam had had more than a year without a drink, I reminded her, and a promotion at work. "Jay's doing just fine," I went on tersely, "and so am I."

"Are you? I don't know if I believe that."

"Look, Sarah, we have our problems like everybody else does," I said after a moment. "Like most families do. But they're not things you can reduce to some expression you heard on some daytime talk show."

"It isn't a talk-show word. Our family *is* dysfunctional, Jam—"

For some reason, I was close to losing my temper. "That word is so completely meaningless. I can't even believe we're having this conversation. What the hell's a *functional* family? Something you saw on a TV show once?"

"I didn't bring up TV, you did."

"Something out of the movies? Something created by Russian Jewish immigrants running movie studios in the nineteen twenties and thirties? Some bogus, idealized idea of Main Street America they once had?"

"You're being anti-Semitic."

"I'm not being anti-Semitic, I'm being *truthful*. This isn't TV, Sarah. This isn't the movies. Has it ever occurred to you that families are a little bit more complex than that? That with five kids in one family, things are bound to go wrong now and again? I mean, what's normal to you? What does *functional* mean to you?"

"It's not us, whatever it is."

"Fine," I said. "You go join the Beaver Cleaver family in their house on the back lot of the Universal Studios in Southern California. And I have some news for you. You'll walk into that house, and you'll be hit by a flying two-by-four. You know why? Because it's not a house, it's the *front* of a house. And next door is where Marcus Welby, M.D., lived. With his nice hedge and his practice and his house calls. Walk into that house and you'll trip over a frigging generator. You'll trip over five electricians and a key grip and a makeup man. You know why? Because it's only the *front* of a house. There's no house there. There's no one living there. Those people are *actors*. They're acting out scripts written by writers who are writing things *people want to hear*."

"Are you done?" Sarah asked, her voice lightly slicked with sarcasm.

I wasn't. "Did you happen to catch a glance at that TV movie a couple of years back when all the Cleavers were reunited? Well, I have news for you. Beaver weighs close to three hundred pounds. He's divorced. He's depressed. He's turned into an obese and unhappy man. Did he grow up in a dysfunctional family, as you put it? No. So you know what must have happened? Very simple. He ate too much. Now what are you going to tell me in response? That Beaver's a victim of his own glands? That there's a bias against fat people in this country? That he hasn't gotten in touch with his inner pig?"

"This isn't what we were talking about."

"Well, it *is* what we're talking about if you'd only listen for a minute. As I was saying, when you have seven people crisscrossing and intersecting—"

"Five people. Father's dead, Tom's dead. Or haven't you noticed?"

I stared across the table at her nastily. "No, Sarah, I didn't notice. In fact, I was going to visit Tom and Father next week, but if you tell me they're dead, well, now you've saved me a trip. Will you let me finish? There's bound to be some problems—"

"—and there's bound to be some dysfunction, too. I don't know why that word makes you so crazy. You're the one who's not paying any attention to what it means."

I'd had enough. "Look, Sarah, do you want to know what dysfunction is? I'll tell you. Dysfunction is a father staggering drunkenly into his daughter's bedroom in the middle of the night and screwing her. And keeping it Daddy's little secret. Dysfunction is booze bottles shattering in the middle of the night, parents falling asleep on the living room couch with a cigarette smouldering in their hand. It's women being beaten up every night by their husbands, and the kids get to watch. It's parents shaking their babies so hard the babies end up brain damaged. It's scalding six-year-olds in bathtubs. It's incest and guns and violence and rape. *That's* dysfunctional. The rest—that's just . . ." but I didn't know how to finish. "We're a good family," I went on, my voice rising. "Better than most. At least we're speaking to each other. We're a good family," I said again, when she didn't answer.

"I don't really want to get into an argument about this," Sarah said at last. "Some people might say that you're not looking at some things."

"Some people might say you're full of crap," I replied nastily.

"You're pretending you're this official life expert, Jam. Like someone elected by the people. I happen to be older than you are."

"Well, I'm married and I have children, and you don't. And I happen to have had a different orientation than you've had."

"Well, so can you actually tell me that you're happy, Jam?"

"I don't know," I said. "I know that I have it a hell of a lot better than most people do. I know I have no interest in killing myself, and since that's the case, I'll go on. Pure and simple. That's the choice I've made. It's the choice I'll follow, because I've ruled out the other one."

Sarah was silent. "Life isn't perfect. Quote unquote. You didn't say that when Tom killed himself."

"That was different."

She shook her head, quickly, tremblingly. "It was not different at all."

We ate our meal in a charged silence; at one point, a truck backed up into the alleyway next to the restaurant, and so we were able to pretend that the racket it was making was too distracting to allow for conversation. When I ordered coffee, Sarah seemed annoyed; she wanted to cut the meal short. The afternoon passed. Sarah went back to work; I curled up in her living room with a book. By later that day, it had begun to snow, laggard, oversized flakes that covered the levels of ice on the roads and sidewalks. The next morning I woke up to learn that the highways were practically impassable, though I made preparations to resume my drive anyway. But before leaving, I turned to Sarah. "Don't take this the wrong way," I said, "but what in the world happened to you?"

She was making herself a cup of herbal tea; her back was to me. "How do you mean, what happened to me?"

"I just mean—" I was struggling to get the words out, my voice lame "—just what happened to you, that's all. You used to be this girl. This spirit." For reasons I couldn't quite fathom, I was close to tears. "It was like you weren't of this earth."

For the first time during my visit, Sarah's face softened, lapsed, less in memory, I think, than in pity for me. "Oh, Jam, Jam, Jam," she said, then, in a rush of gentle annoyance, "Give me a break, please."

I flashed back to a time when we were much younger. Sarah must have been eighteen. It was the end of the summer. In a few days she'd be leaving for college out West, and the rest of us would be returning to the city with our parents. She and Jay and I had gone down to the beach for a last late-afternoon swim. The sky was overcast; it was drizzling slightly, dazzlingly, the drops like pricks of a diamond. Sarah was stripping off her T-shirt to expose her bathing suit when the bra hooks got snagged, and the upward motion of removing the shirt took the bra along with it, and her naked breasts slapped back downward in reflex. Had I seen them before, even accidentally? Not ever, actually. They were larger, much darker and fuller than I'd expected. Without thinking, I stared at them before glancing away, embarrassed for her sake, though rather than crossing her arms or grabbing for her T-shirt, my sister had turned to face the water. "What are you both staring at?" she demanded. She sounded happy and impatient. "Haven't you ever seen tits before?" adding, "Don't worry, I'm not turned on by either of you, it's just cold."

Another memory, this one from when I was even younger. Coiled on the top of the stairs, I'd eavesdrop on her and her boyfriends. They stayed in the kitchen; that was as far as she liked to bring them into the house. Once I'd walked in on her and a boy by accident, in a clench. My sister was wearing my father's old brown bomber jacket, the one with the rooster head on the arm, and her cheeks were pink, not with embarrassment, but with the exertion that it took to kiss somebody. In the morning, I found evidence of the night before: plump stripes of candle wax across the mantle, chairs brought in close to a table, record albums in disarray. Sam was the only one of us who had the courage to ask, "So, did you all sleep together or what?" And she'd reply that it was none of his business, or else she might refer obliquely, tantalizingly, to having done "other things."

Sarah took a seat on the couch. "You romanticized me, Jam," she said simply, impatiently. "Everybody did. I'm sick of that. Here I thought you *liked* women."

"I *do* like women. I *love* women."

"No, you don't. Not if you romanticize us, you don't. You like the *idea* of us, that's different."

"I do not like the idea of you," I said angrily. "I like *you*. And I'm not a romantic."

"You are."

"I am not." We might have been ten years old again, quarreling before bedtime.

"Then, what are you? I'll tell you what *I* am. I'm tired." She reached down to pick up a scrap of something off the floor; when she rose up, her face was blood swollen. "I don't really think you know what it's like to be female. I get tired."

"So try a little tenderness, babe," but she didn't smile.

"It's tiring being single. It's tiring being *me*. I'm tired of telling different men the story of my life over and over again. Look at me, I'm getting old." She jabbed at the lines on either side of her mouth. "You see? These? They won't go away. They're *there*. I'm tired of starving myself, for God's sakes. All I want to do is meet some guy and settle down. Be able to eat a bowl of pasta and not sit around obsessing about food and worrying that I'll have to spend two hours at the gym the next morning. I look at myself in the mirror, and I've started to get this fucked look. God, Jam, look at your face, I've shocked you. Do you know what I mean? You don't, of course you don't, because you're a man. It's not equal. They say it is, but it's not. Men and women, it's just not."

"Well, is there anybody you're in love with?"

"I don't even know what love is anymore. I don't know if it's possible after a certain age. The whole thing is like musical chairs to me. The music stops, people take a seat, and the person who's sitting across from you at the time the music stops is the guy you end up marrying."

"That's the most depressing thing I've ever heard," I said.

"Well, tough shit, Jam, it happens to be true."

"Not in my case it wasn't true. Sarah," I went on, "what happened to you? I just don't *get* you anymore."

"You already said that. I told you, there's nothing to get." For a long time she was silent. "Just so you know? I'm not keeping the house."

"What house?"

"Our house."

I didn't understand. "You just bought it."

"I know. I made a mistake."

Speechless, my voice came out cold. "Well, what brought all this about?"

It turned out she'd visited the island recently. Brought along with her a few odds and ends of furniture and spent two nights on the couch. The house had spooked her, at night especially. There was a storm, rain and whitecaps on the bay, and in the wind the waving trees sounded as though they were cracking. "I had this paranoid idea that the trees would fall down onto the roof. And that then the house would slip into the marsh and into the water. I'd drown." She paused; there was a vague triumph in her eyes. "I think it's just that I've decided I don't want to live in the past."

"What else is there?" I heard myself saying.

Her gaze was scornful. "Well, let's see. There's the present and the future. What's the other one? Conditional. So . . ." She went on: the house was on the market again, in the hands of a new broker, and she hoped at least to make back what she'd paid for it. "Those were strange days back then. I'm not really sure if I want to be reminded of them."

"Go to hell," I said. The girl, the woman, whatever she was, in front of me, performing a series of cosmetic and dilatory kitchen tasks, infuriated me. She'd curled up, particularized; her life was small, routine and as numbing as my own. "Twist a knife into everybody else's backs, why don't you?"

"Jam, that house is the past. It's over."

"Sarah, the *lunch* we just had is over. *Yesterday* is over. This morning is over."

"I don't want—"

"This visit is over," I added, rising, collecting my bag and heading toward the door. "Now it's in the past. See, wasn't that easy to do?"

"Why are you so angry at me?" Sarah asked. There were tears in her eyes, and she kept asking the same question as I made my way outside to my car, though at a certain point she gave up, and the door to her house closed.

i'd eaten nothing all day—no appetite—and late Thanksgiving afternoon, after downing a barely hot mug of freeze-dried coffee, I left the house and went outside and began digging out my car, in the hope that the snow and the ice had eased its grip on the back wheels. The shovel was where I'd left it, indented on the ground beside the outside shower, and it came up in my hands like a revived corpse. Chipping away at the ice stuck under the wheels, I managed to dislodge most of the snow, and when I was satisfied that nothing stood between the wheels and the ground, I climbed inside, inserted the key and tried to start the car. But the engine wouldn't turn over, and I discovered to my dismay and embarrassment that I must have left the inside overhead light on. That in the confusion of that night, with the cops and the broken glass, I hadn't noticed.

I'm not a cryer, never have been one. Growing up, I embraced the idea that there was a certain superiority associated with an absence of emotion, and I rejected the argument that people who didn't cry, or who found it difficult to, were partial, somehow, or incomplete. In the same spirit, I've always recoiled from generosity or open displays of kindness, having found out more than a few times that other people's goodwill could reduce me with unexpected ease to tears. And yet despite the absence of any witnesses, any neighbors, anybody to watch or look on, I got out of the car and turned my head toward the bushes, because my tears were falling unchecked, and though I attempted to avert my face— from whom? nobody was there—I couldn't stop myself.

I have no idea how long I stood there like that, dumbly, on the lawn. A few minutes? Half an hour? An hour? There was a tedious, attractive softness to the air; the snow had begun to melt. At first it was only the icicles dripping onto the near borders of the lawn, leaving a series of orderly, colanderlike holes. The padding on either side of the front porch steps rose up in cloudy tufts, as if preening one last time before its descent back into the earth. Snow sat clumsily along the eaves of the roof; now and again there was a rumbling thunder as a burden of flakes slid down off the top of a tree and broke apart heavily on the ground. It wasn't only the lawn and the driveway, either: grainy patches of wet tar had reappeared on the sidewalk, and a little dirty, sandy stream of water flowed along the gutter. The air was filled with a strange, spectral fog, not the saltwater variety, but the kind that forms when well-laid ice meets warmer air. The breeze shook the hedge. The winter air tends to neutralize the smell of the water, yet there seemed in the wind the faintest reverberation of salt and lotion, a vague hint of warmer seasons.

I'd given up on the car and was making my way back up the porch steps to call Triple-A, or, failing that, a rental car agency, when I first heard, and then turned to see, a dark Volvo station wagon pulling into the driveway. It drew up beside my car, and a few moments later, Caroline got out. She stood there in the ankle-deep snow of the driveway, the door still ajar, her face—the part of it that wasn't obscured under her conventional winter uniform of a turtleneck shirt under a knitted poncho and a foot-long skater's scarf, that is—troubled and apprehensive.

After a moment, she raised her hand. "Hi," she called out.

I was so startled to see her—both in general and on the island—as well as so dependent after five years of marriage to allow the look on my face to speak louder than words, that at first I was speechless. All I could think to do was echo her. "Hi."

She came forward then, tentatively, her boots tromping through the softening snow, though she came to a stop a few feet away from the lattice that protects the outdoor shower. Sniffling once, not from any emotion but from the cold, she gazed up at the house. The occasional sun—a blurred circle that wandered tremblingly behind the northern clouds—touched the top windows, which bolted back light as if in a fellowship of madness. I followed Caroline's eyes as though the house were an opponent she were sizing up, before her gaze found me, and my own eyes had no place to go then but downward.

"How'd you know I was here?" I asked.

"I guessed. The date, the time of year and all." Caroline shrugged, an adolescent toughness to her shoulders, something stubborn and outcast.

"Where are the bambinos?"

"Why?"

"What do you mean, why?"

"I thought you were through with all of us." She'd left the kids with her mother in Rhode Island, she went on, where they'd spent Thanksgiving.

"Oh? And how is the old bird?"

"The turkey or my mother?"

"Both."

"OK, thank you."

"Kind of a long haul from here, isn't it?"

Another tough-girl shrug. "The roads were OK. Not too many crashes." Then, "I called up your office, when was it, a couple of days ago. The department secretary said she had no idea where you were. That you hadn't been to class for two weeks. They'd left about fifty messages at your apartment."

"I haven't called in for messages."

"Well, clearly you haven't. Nobody's heard a word from you."

"Well," I said slowly, "now everybody knows my whereabouts. Here I am, camping out. Since I never went to Outward Bound, this is my opportunity. I have a match, a flashlight, a chocolate bar and what's left of my wits."

"You look like shit," Caroline said after a minute.

"Why, thank you, darling."

"Why haven't you been to school?" she went on. "You can't just not show up in midsemester. Well, I mean, of course, you can do what you want—"

"I have tenure, I can throw grenades at students and they can't fire me." I shrugged, more wildly than I'd intended. I felt torn between inhibition and control, and was finding it hard for various reasons to control my movements. "I didn't see the point, that's all."

"The point? The point is it's your job. Your career. Not to mention our health insurance."

"The point of teaching, Caroline, I mean, do you see any point? Can you really tell me you think teaching does anybody any good?" She didn't answer. "People forget. Their memories aren't worth anything anymore. You don't have to have a business school degree to figure out that's kind of a bad investment, do you?"

"I called you a few times here, but there was no answer. I thought either I'd guessed wrong and you weren't here, or else you were on strike. Probably on strike."

The phone had rung the night before and early that morning, and both times I hadn't answered it. "There's no one to talk to. Plus, it's not like I know anybody here anymore. Everybody's either dead or they've moved along."

"Well, they're supposed to."

"Supposed to?"

"Yes, people are supposed to."

"Supposed to what?"

"Change."

"You mean die? Some people are, yes. Old people. Sick people."

"Just not a brother, right?"

The tears started up again, and this time I made no attempt to conceal them or turn away; Caroline had seen me cry before; what did it matter? I flashed back then to the five of us in the gazebo. Before. Back when Sam was going to be, what? An actor, a writer, a great success. Back when Jay and Tom couldn't miss either. Back when Sarah's beauty would take her wherever she wanted to go. Back when I—?

"You miss him so much, don't you?" Caroline asked.

Our potential—that's what I missed. Our heedlessness. Our youth. Our disregard for the rules that tied most people to their lives. In Jay's untucked white shirt end had once come a suggestion of confidence and offhandedness. In the breadth of a lawn had once come a promise of lastingness as graceful and assured as the future; in the freckles and valentine mouth of my sister was a forecast of romance so potent it had once made me believe that angels in disguise secretly roamed the earth.

The enemy was the specific. It took various forms. Getting older was one. Choosing a career. Moving to a town. Carving out something even, and day to day. Most people worked to extract themselves from the shapelessness of life; others, like me, gravitated toward it. I understood why Sam had chosen to live in New York City. It was a place for people who didn't want to live anywhere. Not anywhere else, but anywhere. A place for people wary of definition. It—immortality—was a myth that I'd chosen for us, because the other options I simply could not stomach. But those were what had happened.

I was furious at Sarah because she'd lived, and created another life for herself. She'd come unstuck; she was fumbling through like the rest of us. Hopelessly, I'd tried to stop time. I was furious at Sam for his weaknesses and failures. Furious at Tom and at my father, for dying. Furious that the past was gone, that it had been replaced by something minor, and onerous, and unexceptional.

Caroline came closer. I could have reached out then and touched her neck, but in the end I didn't, because some ancient animal reflex had already made me turn with a vengeance onto myself. I was crying still, and at the same time I couldn't stand the fact of my tears, the result being that my arms were crossing my body like two swords at odds, and I looked—and felt—deformed.

I heard Caroline's voice. "It's like you thought you were all immune to death, John."

I let out a harsh laugh. "No. Immune to life. Which is different."

"You romanticized your own family. I've been competing with them for the past however many years."

There it was again, that accusation. "You didn't want them to have lives," Caroline went on. "Or to move forward. It's as though you wanted them to sit there the way they were when you were a kid. Frozen. Before they turned into what they turned into."

"But that's who they *were*, back then. That's their essence."

"No. Their essence is who they are now. It's like you've carried around some romantic notion about them for the past twenty-five years, and you're suffering now because things didn't turn out the way you'd planned."

"I am not a romantic," I said after a moment. How many times had I said this over the years to various people? To my mother? To Tom? To Sarah? "I see things clearly."

"You don't see things clearly, John. You wouldn't be in the shape you're in now if you did."

"Well, then, Tom saw things clearly. But then look what happened to him."

"I don't think he saw anything clearly."

For a moment, I was shocked. "You didn't know him the same way I did. He was the only artist this family ever created."

"Wait, say that to me again?" but halfway through repeating myself, Caroline was shaking her head. "Give me a break, John. Tom wasn't any kind of artist."

"Yes, he was. He had the life it took for it. The isolation for it.

The quiet. No people. No dependents. He saw things clearly. Humility—''

"People who are really, truly humble don't end up the way he
ended up. Humble people don't have self-pity.''

"Self-pity?'' I repeated. "Tom? Forget it. Tom wasn't of this earth.''

"Tom *was* of this earth, for God's sakes.'' Caroline took a single step
backward. "Your brother saw things clearly? Like hell he did. You say
you're not a romantic, and now you're romanticizing what it takes for
someone to be an artist, quote unquote. People who kill themselves don't
see things clearly. They think they do, but they don't.''

"You didn't know him the same way I did,'' I repeated.

"I knew him enough to know that he wasn't any kind of artist, as
you seem to think.''

"OK, so he didn't sculpt anything or paint anything or—''

"John, I'm just saying to you that people who live their lives the
way he did, no matter who they are, can't be artists. They have no interest in life—''

"Tom was interested in life—''

"—that people who believe what Tom believes, they're as far away
from art and from creating anything as anybody can be and still be living.
They've lost interest. In people. And in things. In cause and effect. You
have to be *in* your life if you want to build something. You thought Tom
saw things clearly? None of you did, if you'll pardon my saying so.'' I
stared at her. "You're not alone in that either. Nobody sees clearly, and if
they do, they have to make concessions. They have to have some denial.
Because life would be unbearable otherwise. You're damn lucky you
don't see clearly, as you put it.''

I stared back at her stubbornly. "I do.''

"Do you? OK, then.'' Caroline seemed to be collecting her
thoughts. "OK, then, John, why don't you tell me what I'm like.''

I didn't understand. "How do you mean, tell you—''

"Just what I said. We've been married now for five years. You probably know me better than just about anybody. We live together, or at

least we did once upon a time. So now I want you to tell me what I'm like."

"Well, gee whiz, Caroline," I began.

"No, not gee whiz, Caroline, all I want is for you to tell me."

"This is ridiculous."

"It's only ridiculous if you can't think of anything to say."

"OK," I said after a moment, "you're dark-haired."

"Yes? That's very descriptive and insightful. And—?"

"And you're very pretty. Oh, you're on the so-called petite side. You have freckles on your shoulders. Which, by the way, are thin but at the same time pretty strong. Your shoulders, not your freckles. All the swimming you did when you were a kid."

Caroline was staring at me curiously. "I don't mean physical characteristics, John, I mean character characteristics."

"You're a very good mother to our kids," I said at last.

"*Character*, Jam. *Me*. Not me in terms of other people."

I thought of something else. "You go on car trips to these psych conferences sometimes. And whenever you come back home, your right arm is always just a little bit more tanned than your left. Because driving home the sun is on the right side of the car."

"What about *character*, John?"

"This is a dumb game," I said after a few moments. "It's a set-up, a no-win—"

"No. It's an interesting game. It's because I think you've romanticized me too. The way most men do to women. As though I'm not human. I don't think you have the slightest idea who I am after all these years. And that makes me really, truly sad. This is what I am," Caroline went on. "I'm somebody who's given up her career to raise our children," and when I held up my hand to interrupt, she said, "No, no, I'm going to finish. I'm someone who left the East Coast, where I always imagined myself living, to live with you in a God-awful icebox climate, where we don't know anybody and where I don't like it most of the time. I don't work anymore. There are times I think I'm going mad. I'm bored and I'm frustrated. It's a compromise, though. And that's *life*. You don't think sometimes I don't look around me and think, God, this isn't what I wanted? Or there haven't been times like this morning when I was all set to leave you?''

''Leave?''

''Oh, you can leave but I can't, is that the way it works?'' Caroline loosened her scarf. ''Do you know what a spirit is?''

''Of course I do, why do you ask?''

''Because you seem to want to destroy mine. I know you don't mean to, but that's the way it's been playing out. And I can't take it anymore. I'm not *that* much of a masochist.''

Where had I heard that before? On a boat, on water, a long time ago. On a night where teachers were on our lawn, and I claimed to have seen something I hadn't. My mother, Mr. Noerdlinger. A night I'd seen nothing but ghosts, and possibilities. Later on my mother had accused me of being a romantic. The wind that night like a warning.

''You know, John,'' Caroline went on, ''it's not as if people are always given tools to understand things that happen in life. But they can talk about it—''

''I don't want to talk about it,'' I interrupted. ''I don't want to talk about what I *remember*. It's just *words*. And not even words, but approximations. If I say to you somebody's thin, you build your own mental castle of what 'thin' is. You think Jack Sprat, I think Twiggy. We can't even agree on the goddamn definition.''

''John,'' there was scorn in Caroline's voice, ''let me tell you something. Words are *it*. Words are what we have *left*. Even if they're not good enough. Even if they're not the right ones. When everybody's dead and everything you know is gone, words are what's left. They're like hands. They keep things aloft. In the air.''

''Tom didn't need words—''

''You remember when we left the East Coast five years ago, or however long it was? And all our friends said to us, 'I hope you remember us.' And 'Please don't forget us.' And they'd look down at the kids and

they'd say, 'He won't remember me.' Or "A year from now you all will
have forgotten me." They'd all get this incredibly anguished look on their
faces." Recalling this, I nodded. "And that's basically all people have. In
the end that's what it comes down to. Memory. Remembering. Not forgetting." Caroline paused. "Now, I really have to pee, so if you wouldn't
mind—"

I followed her up the porch steps and into the house and took a seat
on the couch, and when she came back out into the living room a few
minutes later, Caroline's gaze first took in the piano and then me. "Have
you been playing at all?"

We had to begin again; whatever momentum we'd gained in the
past twenty minutes seemed to have stalled. "A little bit," I said. "Not a
whole lot else to do here."

"You haven't played in a long time."

"No piano in our house, that's why," and going up to the keyboard,
I placed my index finger on middle C.

"Why'd you stop?"

The question took me by surprise. "Stop what?"

"Playing."

"When, you mean today?"

"However long ago it was."

"Because," I said, not looking up, "I wasn't good enough, that's
why"

"So?"

"So I'm sure you might have done the same thing."

"It's one thing to stop if you thought you couldn't make a career
out of it, and it's another thing to stop something you loved and that gave
other people a lot of pleasure. Listening to you did, I mean."

"Did it give a lot of people a lot of pleasure? I really doubt that." I
was playing a few low chords now, followed by the first few bars of an old
Ellington tune. "Look, Caroline," I said, "I'm not an artist. I'm not a
natural. I always had to work too hard at it. Do you know what it's like to
be twenty-two years old, and the only thing you've ever wanted is to do

something in music, but then you realize that you haven't got what it takes?'' Words floated through my mind. ''Loose grip.''

''What does that mean?''

''It's something Tom used to say. That that's what I should strive for. In everything. When I played the piano. In all my friendships with people. In my work. I didn't ever understand what he was talking about.''

Caroline had removed her coat and taken a seat at the dining room table. ''Do you want to know my opinion why you never made it as a musician?'' I waited.

''The reason is because you're scared to death of yourself. You're scared of your own heart. Your own passion. You're too embarrassed.''

''I'm not embarrassed,'' and yet for some reason, I thought back on the memoirs my father had handed me that night in the spring three or four years earlier. I remembered the prose as lapidary, fearful, its tightness having less to do with literary style than with emotional constriction. It was a teacher's style, fearful of error and of wildness and of exposure, compact, sidelined, and yet lacking some quality I found it hard to put my finger on. And with a sinking acceptance, I knew what it was, suddenly, and how similar we were, despite all my efforts, he and I.

Caroline said quietly, ''The difference between you and somebody who plays for a living is heart. It's passion. It's emotions. It's not fear.''

I was stung. ''How the hell do you know that?''

''Because you used to play for me, remember? When we were first going out? It was like you were aware all the time that you were playing. It was squeezed out. There was something overpracticed about it. It's like there was a screw too tight in the side of the wall. You were technically perfect—I'm not saying you weren't that, or that it wasn't good, or that I didn't love hearing you—but afterwards you might as well have not played at all.''

My heart was pounding. ''You thought that?''

''As a matter of fact, I did. You were never *in* your music. You'd never allow yourself to make any mistakes. Or to screw up. Or to try a piece a new way. There wasn't any feeling.''

I saw my opening and seized it. "Do you know what the problem is in this country? There's too much emphasis put on feeling. Anybody who *thinks* these days is considered suspect. Or cunning, or untrustworthy."

Otherness. A loose grip. Heart. I gazed across the room at the dark fireplace, picturing my younger fingers arrayed on the keys of a phantom piano. Following music that was written out in front of me, playing melodies written by other people. Other people's songs, other people's music, my loafered feet pumping up and down on the pedals.

Heart. Was that what was missing when I played? *Heart.* It mattered. Perhaps it was all that mattered. And then it came to me, rushing, teeming, not just words but whole sentences, and answers. It wasn't control; it was relinquishing it. It was a grip, but a loose-fingered one. It was passion. This notion overcame me like a well-lit defeat, and for the next few minutes, I couldn't find my voice. If I'd ever had one.

"Look, John," Caroline said after a moment. "People don't die, really. Bodies die, but that's something else. People are always around us, dead or alive. We're all a mix of each other. We *are* each other."

"I'm never going to see Tom again, Caroline."

"Right. And I'm sorry. I'm so, so sorry. There's a lot of people I'll never see again. But you keep them alive by talking about them. Through what you *tell* about them. But not through silence. Silence *really* kills people. Tom won't ever be dead, not so long as you tell people about him, tell your kids, remind me, remind yourself. Your kids will tell their kids. Everybody's passed on. We're all of us custodians of one another. We're all members of one another. You *need* people, John."

"Tom said the same thing to me once," I said after a moment.

"OK. Now you turn around and tell it to someone else who's in trouble. Take what you know, take what you've learned from other people and you divide it. Send it right back out. Like a *teacher*," she added. "Which is what you are. Which happens to be what your father was. Which is what all of us are up to a point. Because all of us, even if we're not aware of it, teach other people. We divide up what we know and we give it back out. The littlest things get divided. The littlest thing you know can be turned around and taught to somebody else."

I opened my mouth to interrupt, but Caroline held up her hand. "Not to be queer, but think of it like an ocean. An ocean that gets fed by streams and creeks and little bits of water here and there. Like I told you, you know the best way to kill Tom? To have his dying mean nothing at all?"

I waited, both hands now on the keys.

"*Don't* talk about him. *Don't* mention him. *Don't* bring him up. Or anything he ever said. Or anything he ever taught you. Just do what you've been doing. Blank out his name in your mind. Walk around in silence like you're the dead one, not him. Change the subject. You idealized him, and everybody else in your family. Despite tons of evidence to the contrary. *That's* the problem here, *you* were the susceptible one. And then life happened. The way it happens to all of us. You've got to start forgiving people, John, for God's sakes, they're your witnesses, after all."

"My witnesses? What is this, a courtroom?"

"You talk and talk about the past being gone. But this is a minute in a dinosaur's age we're talking about. Someday nobody'll even remember you and I were in this room together. They certainly won't remember who was friends with who, or who belonged to what club, or who was invited here and excluded there. They'll remember who was alive at the same time we were, and who were the witnesses to our pasts."

*m*uch later that night, I awoke to a room black except for a fitful animation from the fireplace, two or three ragged lines of light wobbling above a practically extinguished log; Caroline must have lit the fire. A few confused moments later, I realized I was in the living room, that I'd fallen asleep—so it seemed—on the couch, with my neck at a crooked and slightly painful angle. An old Hudson Bay blanket covered my body, and after lying there in the dark for a few minutes, I made my way into my kitchen, where Caroline was sitting at the table, drinking a cup of coffee. She looked up. "The kids are fine. I called earlier. My mother hasn't killed them yet, and they haven't killed her yet, so . . ."

I sat down across from her, and for a long time bowed my head. When I reopened my eyes, she was gazing at me expectantly. "I was just saying Our Father," I said. "Tom used to be able to say Our Father backwards. When he was a kid. He'd go, Amen. Ever and forever glory the and power the kingdom the is Thine For. Et cetera. Once I timed him. He could do it in twelve seconds flat. Naturally, it lacked a certain elegance when you reeled it off backwards like that, but as a kid my only ambition in life was to beat those twelve seconds."

Caroline's eyes widened slightly, but she said nothing. "Did I tell you Tom taught me how to ride a bike?" I added. "It was at school. In a driveway near the hockey rink. A little red bike, I remember. It had a bell that sounded like the Avon Lady calling. I was wobbly at first, then I got it. Tom was running along me on the side, to make sure I didn't fall."

"And did you? Fall?"

"About a hundred thousand times. He was always incredibly patient with Sam. Tom was. Probably more so than the rest of us were."

"Was he?"

"Well, I think he understood Sam better than the rest of us did. Even though they were so unalike. When he, Sam, tried to break the *Guinness Book of Records* record—"

"Sam's in the *Guinness Book of Records*? Since when?"

"Didn't I ever tell you that story? Put it this way, he *tried*. Milk-bottle balancing. That was the category he chose. And I can't remember what the existing record was, but it was something like fifteen straight hours walking around with a milk bottle on your head. The Guinness committee was very humorless and strict. You were allowed to touch the bottle only once every twenty minutes. You couldn't use tape or glue or anything. Anyhow, when the big day came, Sam tripped on a rock and the bottle smashed into pieces; there was milk splashed everywhere. He was—as you can imagine—heartbroken. His moment of glory ripped away again. And then another time—"

"Another time what?"

I couldn't stop talking. Couldn't stop. For the next hour and a half, into the morning, I talked, the words coming forth in a flood. It was as though a coast had opened up inside me, a stretch of water and thin air and freedom. Whenever I protested that I was talking too much, Caroline looked impatient. "Keep going. It's good for you. It's *words*. Go on. What else did Tom do? What else do you remember?"

"I remember he taught me how to pitch a baseball. That sounds so stupid. That sounds so American—"

"Oh, quit censoring yourself for one minute."

"He oiled my glove for me. He put it under the mattress of the bed so it'd flatten the right way. And when I was first trying to play hockey, he taped up my stick for me so it wouldn't fray. Later he tried to get me to go to church, even though I found it so boring."

Two hours later, Caroline gazed up at the ceiling. "I'm starving," she said. "It's still Thanksgiving. Could we maybe go somewhere and get a bite to eat?"

I glanced over at the clock; it was 3:30 A.M. We hadn't stayed up this late, she and I, for years. "Sorry, honey," I said. "This is a little island, not New York. But I do have some crackers."

There was something I had to do, and the next morning, while Caroline was taking a shower, I called information. There were only two people with that name, with no addresses listed. I dialed the number, and when there was no answer, I briefly dismissed the idea. But an hour later, when I tried the number again, the phone was answered on the fifth ring, and though she sounded surprised to hear from me, I made arrangements to pay her a visit later that day.

Before leaving the island, Caroline and I drove to the beach and walked along the shore at Ames Point in an exultant wind that, before I knew it, had turned into two hours, then two and a half hours. The sand was moist, and walking was slow and sucking and enjoyable More and more, I was aware of the bright, hushed, warming air and of the birds, their high-up, scattered sounds as hopeful as church bells.

We'd decided to drive to Rhode Island after lunch, caravan style, and I was packed and ready to leave, when I remembered something. "You don't happen to have any jumper cables on you, by any chance?"

Despite herself, Caroline laughed. "Oh, for God's sakes, John, get it *together.''* A minute later, she pulled out a set from her back trunk. "You do it," and she handed over the tangle to me. "I'd probably end up blowing us both up."

Her car was already in position next to mine, and as she retook her seat behind the wheel and restarted her engine, I peeled back the rubber caps and placed the cable heads on the bolts, then climbed behind the wheel of my own car. A few moments later, the engine choked back to life, and the overhead light gleamed back on. I sat in the front seat for a few moments, relishing the surge of energy, the warmth roaring from the heater, the vague, chattering voices on the radio, and then, still keeping the engine on, I went around to the front of the car and unhooked the cables, before replacing them in Caroline's trunk.

The chain that guards the entrance to the ferry had just been lifted when we pulled into the town parking lot, and handing over our tickets, we proceeded inside the lower level, parking behind an old VW bug. The tide was going out; a few boats puttered out under the bridge past a row of lobster traps, toward the ocean; on the landing, men were hoisting boxes containing that day's news. It was hard to believe that just a few days earlier, the island had been under siege. For a long time, we stood there together, pressed up against the cold railing, and surveyed the land we were leaving.

In the Northeast, you can sometimes tell what state you're in by the side of the road, and the texture of the pavement. In the Midwest, spare trees hang back from the highway, and the roads are wide and pale. Rhode Island has its formal slate and stone gates and sidings, its precipitous drops toward the bay. Connecticut has its potholes and ragged roads. New York State has rock—huddled and brown and craggily definite, graffiti-strewn, often fronting cold, useless, shadowy woods.

As I drove, I kept thinking about my children. How at night they dragged out their good-byes, as if believing that was the last time they'd see us, and we them. How during the day, diving from the couch or jumping off the stoop and into the grass, they would exclaim, Look at me, Look at me. Watch. *Watch.* As though their dive or their jump lacked any meaning unless someone else witnessed it. Prove it, they seemed to be saying. Prove I was there, and that I did what I just did, and remember it.

Three hours later, Caroline and I pulled up across from the house, one after another, parked and got out.

The late afternoon sun was half-gold, half-shadow. It settled on the hedge and the fence, pinning them under its partial radiance. Above me, crows bawled; the smoke in the air nearly sent me spinning with its evocativeness; was it childhood? I couldn't remember anymore. What the past evoked was blurry, fragile, darkly lit. It lingered in gestures, in old trees, in the smell of burning wood, in birds crying out. It stuck to the ceiling, clung to the ground, adhered to old words given a lift or a lilt by a new speaker. It was alive in the way your kids walked, in the way they signaled with their hands, in their boldness or their timidity. Alive in people who'd take your place. Alive as breath, as rituals; and words, talking, as Caroline had pointed out, would help keep it aloft, away from the earth, like a kind of music, without beginning or end. Our lives were maybe not significant, but what we left behind was. The best and most we could do was to leave behind a distilled portion of something, anything, good.

Sarah was sweeping the sand off the bricks of her walkway, and as Caroline and I came forward, she glanced up quizzically. I don't know whether she recognized me at first. But I came forward anyway, unashamed, across the lawn, my feet ghost-light on the thawing-out ground, and a minute later I put out both my arms and gathered one of my witnesses to me.

about the author

Peter J. Smith is the author of *Highlights of the Off Season* and *Make-Believe Ballrooms*. His fiction has appeared in *The New Yorker* and his nonfiction has appeared in *The New York Times Magazine*. He lives in New York.